ONCE
NIGHT
FALLS

ONCE NIGHT FALLS

A NOVEL

ROLAND MERULLO

Text copyright © 2019 by Roland Merullo
All rights reserved.

Published by Lake Union Publishing, Seattle

www.apub.com

Amazon, the Amazon logo, and Lake Union Publishing are trademarks of Amazon.com, Inc., or its affiliates.

ISBN-13: 9781542007429
ISBN-10: 1542007429

Cover design by Faceout Studio, Derek Thornton

Printed in the United States of America

*For Amanda, Alexandra, and Juliana
with love*

Democracy is beautiful in theory;
in practice it is a fallacy.
You in America will see that some day.

—*Benito Mussolini*

Dictators ride to and fro
upon tigers which they dare not dismount.
And the tigers are getting hungry.

—*Winston Churchill*

SWITZERLAND GERMANY

A L P S

FRANCE

Gravedona
Lake Como (see inset)
Como
Milan
Salò
Lake Garda

AUSTRIA

Po River

SLOVENIA

A p e n n i n e s

LIGURIAN SEA

Livorno

CROATIA

SAN MARINO

A D R I A T I C   S E A

Grosseto

Tiber River

Gran Sasso & Monti della Laga National Park

La Maddalena Island

Lake Bracciano
Vatican City Rome

Campo Imperatore

Latina

ITALY

SARDINIA

TYRRHENIAN SEA

SICILY

SWITZ.

Gravedona

A L P S

Menaggio
Dubino
Mezzegra
Argegno

Lake Como

ITALY

Como

N
W   E
S

0   10   20 mi.
0   10   20 km.

N
W   E
S

0   50   100 mi.
0   50   100 km.

AUTHOR'S NOTE

In the summer of 2007, thanks to a generous book advance, my wife Amanda and I were able to take our two young daughters to Italy for six weeks. It was mainly a family vacation, but I was also doing the not-very-painful research for a travel memoir on golfing and eating that would be published the following spring. I had no idea that our time in Italy would lead, twelve years later, to the writing of a very different kind of book.

That summer, we rented half a duplex in a community of five houses that shared a swimming pool and a spectacular view down across the roofs of a small town on Lake Como's western shore. Amanda and the girls and I passed the sunny weeks swimming and eating, taking easy hikes, and making day trips to lakeside villages in search of restaurants and golf courses that would fit into the travel book. One afternoon, while the girls were playing with new friends, Amanda and I took a stroll along the unlined road that ran across the hillside in front of our house. We'd gone only a few hundred yards when we came upon an elegant stone residence, Villa Belmonte, that was set behind wrought iron gates and a copse of fruit trees. On a stone wall in front of the villa, we noticed a small plaque in the shape of a black cross:

BENITO MUSSOLINI
28 APRILE 1945

There was no information beyond the name and date, no mention of why the plaque had been set there. It didn't look like the kind of notice you sometimes see in the US: *George Washington slept in this house* or *Abraham Lincoln gave a speech in this auditorium*. I knew Mussolini had been born hundreds of miles away, so the plaque couldn't be marking his place of birth. And I knew—or thought I knew—that the dictator Italians once called *il Duce*, "the Leader," had been executed in a square in Milan, Piazzale Loreto. There's a famous photograph of his mutilated body and that of his mistress and three henchmen, hanging by their ankles above a gas station there.

But when I went back to our rented house and did some research I discovered that, although the photo was accurate, my assumptions were not: Mussolini and his associates had been executed, not in Piazzale Loreto but in front of Villa Belmonte in the hamlet of Mezzegra in the hills above Lake Como. Their bodies had been brought to Milan to avenge a particularly gruesome killing of Italian partisans on that spot some eight months earlier.

I had, of course, heard about the Italian partisans who'd helped defeat the Nazi occupiers in World War II, but only vaguely—so much more has been written about the French resistance. And I thought I'd known a fair amount about Mussolini's rise to power and twenty-three-year rule over the nation where my father's parents had been born. The plaque in front of Villa Belmonte piqued my interest, however. The more I read, the more fascinating the story seemed—especially the incredible events that followed Mussolini's removal from power in July 1943.

I grew up in an Italian-American enclave outside Boston, and I've been writing novels for forty years, so it was natural for my imagination to wrap itself around the struggle between good and evil in 1940s Italy. It seemed to me that the actual events offered the elements of a great story: heroism, treachery, secrecy, suffering, dignity, romance, and death—all set against the background of a country I'd come to love and the brutal war that tore it apart. Without Mussolini's grand delusions, war might never have come to the *bel paese* or would have come in a very different form. The lives of tens of millions of ordinary men, women, and children were ended, ruined, or damaged by his egotism and embrace of violence, and especially by his sycophantic relationship with Hitler. This novel, circling around the dark historical truth of Mussolini's fall from power, is intended to give a sense of the love, suffering, and courage of some of those ordinary people.

Once Night Falls was begun years later on another trip to Italy, but written mainly in Western Massachusetts, where we've lived for three decades. The story poured out of me quickly, as stories tend to do, but required extensive rewrites over a period of several years. I'm grateful for the helpful conversations and directions offered by Italian locals when we were staying at Lake Como, and I'm particularly indebted to five sources: Christopher Hibbert's brilliant biography, *Mussolini*; David Kertzer's Pulitzer Prize–winning account, *The Pope and Mussolini*; a historical compendium, *World War II: A Day-by-Day History*, edited by Peter Darman; another Pulitzer winner, Rick Atkinson's amazingly detailed *The Day of Battle*; and *Skorzeny's Special Missions*, a memoir by the incredibly courageous, diabolically skilled, and utterly loathsome German commando Otto Skorzeny.

Within the confines of the narrative requirements of storytelling, with some compression of time, and with plenty of license for imagined characters and conversations, I have tried to be faithful to actual events. I wanted to capture a tiny portion of the enormous suffering and incredible bravery of that place and time, the battle between violence and grace, hatred and tolerance—a battle that continues, in various ways, in various parts of the world, to this day.

One

As dawn broke warm and clear over the hills west of Lake Como, Sarah Zinsi summoned her battered reserve of courage, stepped out of the cabin where she'd been hiding for weeks, and hiked up through the hardwood forest to a natural spring. At the bubbling pool there, she stripped off her clothes and began to bathe, enjoying the water's cool shock and trying not to think about what would happen if a German patrol came upon her in that state. *Unlikely,* she thought. The ramshackle stone cabin had been unused for decades; the undergrowth this far up in the hills was dense and wild, what remained of the footpaths all but untraveled. Her lover, Luca Benedetto, had promised she'd be safe here, and he knew these hills better than anyone. Still, as she knelt beside the spring and washed herself, she couldn't help but feel as vulnerable as a tiny woodland creature hunted by hawks and owls. By then—summer of 1943—the Nazi occupiers had draped a shroud of fear across Italy from the Alps in the north to the beaches of Sicily in the south. *Bad enough,* she thought, *for men and Christians; so much worse for women and Jews.*

In the midst of her bath, she heard a rustle in the leaves, the snap of a twig, what sounded like footsteps. She went absolutely still, suddenly aware of every square centimeter of bare skin. She couldn't bring herself to turn and look. She waited, barely breathing, a minute, two minutes, frozen in place, until there was only the cloak of mountain silence again in the trees around her. *Un animale,* she told herself. *Un cinghiale.* A wild boar foraging for truffles.

She resumed her bath, cleaning the dirt and sweat from her feet, legs, and belly, using a scrap of yellow soap and one of the old towels Luca had brought her. She leaned over and splashed water on her breasts and face, washed her long chestnut hair as best she could. He would come see her today or tonight; she had that to look forward to. She had news for him. She wondered how he'd receive it.

Two

A hot day, even for Rome. In the Villa Torlonia, beside marble columns and beneath a sparkling chandelier, Benito Mussolini lunched on milk and fruit with his wife, Rachele. *Il Duce* frowned and fussed over the meal—bland foods were all his doctors allowed him these days—and did battle with an army of annoying thoughts, a series of regrets that assaulted him from every direction. He tried to concentrate on the food, to ignore the cramps and spasms in his intestines, but the regrets persisted, coming at him again and again, like attacking battalions, in waves. It seemed to him that he'd stayed married too long, stayed in power too long, that years ago he should have fled to Switzerland or Austria with Claretta Petacci, his young mistress, and lived a life of ease there, a life worthy of the sacrifices he'd made for Fascism and for his country. He should be riding horses, playing tennis, writing his memoirs, flying his plane across the Alps to one ski resort or another, an idol, a hero, a modern-day Roman god.

Instead, he was stuck in this government palace, in this marriage, and the nation he'd sewn together purely by the strength of his own will was unraveling. He blinked four times, quickly, and glared across the elegantly set table. Rachele's face—the straight nose and wide-set eyes, a face once attractive but now creased and worn by time—was pinched up into an anxious mask. During the course of their midday meal, she'd been saying the same thing over and over again: *"Non andare. Non andare. Non andare, Benito!" Don't go. Don't go. Don't go, Benito!* And now, as he watched, trying to will her to be silent, she practically wailed: "I don't trust this king, Benito. I've never trusted him. I never liked him. I had a dream last night that he took out a machine gun and shot you. Here." She pointed to her own chest. "Don't go, Benito. Please!"

But Vittorio Emanuele III—a pitifully small and hopelessly mild-mannered royal—inspired no fear in Mussolini. Not two weeks ago, the king had assured him of his loyalty and friendship, and at these regular Sunday meetings, he was unfailingly deferential, soft-spoken, and weak. Half a man.

Il Duce turned his eyes to the floor-to-ceiling windows and out at the white-hot afternoon. Fear was, to him, an alien emotion. For weeks, he'd been hearing warnings of a swelling dissatisfaction in parts of the Italian state. Regular as the sunrise, Rachele reported rumors of a coup d'état. His daughter, the countess Edda Ciano, said that her well-connected friends were talking revolution and that even her husband, Galeazzo, was complaining that Mussolini was driving the nation to ruin. Almost on a daily basis, aides claimed that this group or that—liberals, traitors, socialists, communists, his own supporters—were conspiring to replace him. Mussolini shrugged, stifled an urge to laugh. He'd survived combat in the trenches of World War I, decades of vicious political infighting, three assassination attempts. None of these people could touch him.

True, things had not gone well of late: there had been strikes in the factories of the north and rumors of partisan fighters in the mountains there; three nights ago, the Fascist Grand Council, full of doubters and betrayers (including his own son-in-law!), had met for the first time in years and, by a small majority, made a vote of no confidence in their leader. No confidence! Based on what? Yes, the Allies had staged a landing in southern Sicily and made modest advances there; yes, Hitler was sending more and more troops and armament to secure the peninsula, because the Italians, he believed, had no fight in them. For weeks now, the Führer had been pressing him to allow German control over all military actions in Italy, something Mussolini would never sanction.

No confidence! What none of them, not even Rachele, seemed to understand was that the leader of the Italian people still had an enormous amount of fight in him, could still charm or intimidate the king, and was still confident that the Allies—inferior soldiers led by madmen—would soon be chased back into the sea. His Claretta saw what Rachele did not: he was one of history's great men, the founder of Fascism, of a new way of life—and history had shown again and again that great men always faced great difficulties.

He swallowed a last sip of water, wiped the silk napkin across his lips, and abruptly stood up from the table. Rachele stood, too, and approached him. He signaled to the waiting Boratto to bring the car around; he let Rachele reach up and kiss him near the side of his mouth. He squared his shoulders, strode across the gleaming tile, out the door, past the impressive columns, down the wide front steps. Another few seconds, one last round of this "Don't go, Benito! Don't go, please!" sung from the doorway like a funeral dirge, and he was sitting in the back of his car, uncomfortable in a blue business suit (worn only so as not to intimidate the king!), instead of his customary military uniform. As the car began to move, he raised a hand to Rachele and then turned his face away and stared at the palm trees and lush gardens that lined the drive. He could feel drops of sweat at the back of his neck—merely the heat of the day. Everything would be fine. After this visit with the king—brief, a formality, nothing more than their regular exchange of views—life would return to normal. He'd have Boratto take him over to Palazzo Venezia; he'd sit behind his desk in the map room, make his decisions, give his orders, summon Claretta to visit for an hour or so, begin to repair the damage the Council had done. He had information on every one of its members—a secret mistress, an illicit Swiss bank account, an addiction, a bit of theft from the national coffers. A twisted arm, a threat, a word or two in a series of private meetings and the absurd no confidence vote would certainly be reversed.

Still, as they left the grounds of the Torlonia and glided along the nearly empty Via Salaria, past the broken columns of the Forum, past the Colosseum—monuments to the greatness of the empire—and then past the quiet facades of apartments and churches, the fusillade of regret and doubt erupted again. It seemed to him for a moment that he might be the most hated man in all of Italy. Not two years earlier, he'd stood on the balcony of the Palazzo with his chest thrust out, medals shimmering, and a hundred thousand of his countrymen had been screaming, cheering, raising the Roman salute. What had gone wrong in that short period of time? What demon of bad luck had taken hold of him? How could he shake it loose?

Three

For Federico Maniscalco, archbishop of Milan, there had always been something soothing about Vatican City. It was the home of his spiritual heart, the seat of his faith, an entire small nation devoted to prayer and good works.

Now, however, as he walked through its gardens and went past the Pontifical Academy of Sciences en route to a meeting that made sweat form on the palms of both hands, he realized that the war had complicated his feelings, even about this sacred place. Since Mussolini's alliance with Hitler, Pope Pius XII had clung stubbornly to a posture of strict neutrality. On the one hand, this policy made it politically more difficult for the Nazis—a strong and growing presence up and down the peninsula—to consider an occupation of Vatican City (a move that wouldn't help them much, militarily, and would enrage many Italian Catholics). On the other hand, the pope's stance had done nothing to aid the millions—Jews, mainly, but many Christians, too—who were being tormented, rounded up, and perhaps killed all across Europe. In his heart of hearts, Maniscalco found the pope's posture less than Christlike, a moral failure, though, of course, he could never say such a thing from the pulpit.

Still, within the Church's vast network of nuns, priests, and monks, there were many like himself who had decided that conciliation was not an acceptable option. This secret activity was a sin, perhaps, a breaking of his vow of obedience. And there was physical danger, too: outside these walls, the robes of the clergy offered no protection against Nazi atrocities and Fascist hatred.

At first, it had been the death of Giacomo Matteotti that had awakened him to the evil of Mussolini's mind. Matteotti, a brave, outspoken, and popular opponent of the regime, had been snatched from the streets of Rome and beaten to death by Mussolini's *squadristi*, and the thugs had dumped his body in a ditch on the city's outskirts.

Through subterranean channels, through small comments among friends, that outrage had connected Archbishop Maniscalco to the man he was about to see, a half-American who called himself Giovanni. As the months passed, as their friendship and mutual trust deepened, this so-called Giovanni had recruited him for a new cause, a secret battle against *il Duce* and his Nazi friends. Now, the trim, mild-mannered archbishop preached patriotism from the pulpit and ran a stable of underground resistance fighters. Through various couriers, Giovanni sent him money and supplies; he funneled them to the partisans. *I trust the man implicitly,* Maniscalco told himself as he stepped into the small trattoria where they'd agreed to meet. *I trust him more than anyone else in my life right now. I pray that will not turn out to be a mistake.*

After they'd greeted each other and taken their seats, Giovanni said, too loudly, "I've invited someone else to join us," and looked around as if he'd meant *join us for lunch.*

But the archbishop knew that was not what he'd meant at all.

Four

On that same hot July Sunday, in Milan, six hundred kilometers to the north, fifteen bodies—Italian partisans all of them—lay in grotesque poses on the hot cobblestones of an open square called Piazzale Loreto. To either side of this gruesome display—rotting flesh, broken bones, puddled blood—stood Nazi soldiers in their jackboots and lidded helmets, their spines straight, their gray eyes scanning the crowd. Not five meters in front of them, a distance enforced by swings of rifle stocks, huddled the families of the slain fighters. Mothers and wives, mostly, with a few old men and a number of weeping children. The bodies had been lying there for two hot days and two warm nights, and the assembled mourners could hardly bear the wretched smell. From time to time, one of the women would make a tearful entreaty, but the German occupiers had their orders: they would wait until the stink became overwhelming, until the bodies were crawling with flies, and only then allow the families to claim and bury their dead. It was an order that would come back to haunt them, a decision Italians would remember, along with the name of this humble square, for generations to come.

Safely behind the first rows of family members, smoking a cigarette with a nervous nonchalance and fingering a coded note in his jacket pocket, twenty-year-old Luca Benedetto stood and stared. With only one working eye and one strong arm, he'd been declared unfit for military service. A great relief, yes, but how he wanted to fight! He'd hated Mussolini from long before *il Duce*'s alliance with Hitler, and he hated the Germans—who'd sent his father to the Russian front—even more. People said there were already hundreds of thousands of Nazi soldiers in this country and more pouring over the northern border by the day. His only wish now, his only work, was to make their lives miserable.

He sensed he was being watched—a man in a felt hat standing to his left and slightly behind—but after the first glance, he didn't turn his head. In Milan for a clandestine meeting, he'd heard about the reprisal killings at Piazzale Loreto and decided to see the horror for himself. It was the kind of decision—spontaneous, risky—that sent his so-called superiors into fits of anger and vitriol, the reason, or one of the reasons, they hadn't given him bigger assignments. But the German treachery was more personal to him than it was to them. He stood to lose the three people he loved most on this earth—his beautiful Sarah, his mother, and his father—and so he waited there, fixing the horrific sight in his memory: disemboweled heroes missing teeth and covered with flies, smug *nazisti* with smirks showing at the corners of their mouths. Into the fabric of his brain he wanted to weave this vision tight. He wanted never to forget what he'd heard and seen in other places, too—the stories of raped Italian girls, the faces of terrified Jews as they were stripped of jobs and property and made to crawl in the streets like dogs. He pulled hard on the last of the cigarette, then turned to one side and spat. He swore a silent oath that Piazzale Loreto, this plain-faced square a kilometer northeast of Milan's *centro*, would one day be remembered in the history books. It would be remembered. *Sì, certo.* But not only for this.

Five

From her place at the deep, rust-stained sink in the kitchen of a hillside house above Lake Como, Luca's mother, Maria Osolla Benedetto, ran a knife through the hard crust of three-day-old bread, the last of their weekly supply. The windows were open on the warm morning, and a light breeze carried vulgar laughter from the house—a hundred meters away—where the Rosso family had once lived, a beautiful stone box of a house with a red tile roof and a magnificent view down over the lake and across to the eastern mountains. For the sin of refusing to turn it over to a group of SS officers, Rafaelo Rosso and his wife, Antonetta, had been beaten to death in the yard of that house, their bodies dumped there like slaughtered sheep. Now the bedrooms held SS officers with their women and drink. Late into the night, one could hear them.

Maria despised the Germans for taking her husband from her to fight their foolish war in Russia. She hated the harsh chords of their language, hated the way they fondled the local girls at will and convinced some of them—a few—to go into that house at night in exchange for food for themselves and their hungry children, or a sense of safety, or out of some twisted loyalty to *il Duce* and a way of life, a way of thinking, that, long before the Germans appeared, had seemed so alien to her, Sabatino, and Luca. She was old enough to have known Italy before Fascism. There had been problems, yes—social, economic, political—but there had also been a dignity and sanity to their lives. That was gone now.

When the hilarity ceased, she listened for any sound, any movement above her head. Her windowless attic hid Rebecca Zinsi, a Jewish woman, the mother of her son's lover and her closest friend since their second year of grade school. Maria knew that sometime after dark, she'd have to tap on the small hatch in the hallway ceiling, hand up a little food, and take Rebecca's slop pail. She was afraid, of course, every hour of every day, so she'd discovered it was better not to think about how hungry Rebecca must be, what kind of air she'd be breathing, hidden behind a wall of rough-hewn boards and plaster, sleeping there, crouching or standing stiffly during the long, burning days. Better not to think about Rebecca's daughter, Sarah, a local beauty who'd disappeared months ago and hadn't been heard from since. Luca promised he was taking care of her, but he wouldn't say where or how.

The war had made her son—always so happy and full of life—into a tight-lipped and intense young man. She suspected he was helping the partisans, the mountain fighters, small bands of men and some women, young and not so young, rumored of late to be sabotaging German troop movements and equipment. It made sense, because Luca knew the hills the way she knew her kitchen, the way she knew the touch of her husband's hands. But he never spoke of it. How sad she and Sabatino had been when Luca was born with one sightless eye and a weakened left arm. What a torment that had been for him as a boy. And now, it seemed, a blessing. The army would never take him. A blessing in disguise.

She heard a sound above her, a creak of boards as Rebecca shifted position—and she glanced quickly out the window at the Rosso house. No movement there. No laughter now.

Leaning wearily on the crutch of faith, she lifted a prayer to the Virgin Mother. That her husband and son might survive the war. That the bad times would soon pass. That the Germans would leave. That someone—the Americans, the British, even the Russians—might come and rescue them from Mussolini's insanity and the merciless SS. *How much worse can things get?* she wondered. How much longer would she be able to keep her guest alive on the meager amount of food she could buy in Mezzegra with the ration coupons, grow in the stony soil of her back yard, or accept from the local priest? She'd heard that there were house searches now in towns along the lake. How much longer before the men across the empty lot grew suspicious and came to check her attic?

Six

In the rectory of the church of Sant'Abbondio, a twenty-minute walk from Maria's house, Don Claudio DeMarco lifted himself with a grunt to a sitting position and swung his swollen legs over the side of the bed. As he did every morning upon rising, the priest sat for a moment and prayed for his relatives in the beleaguered south, for his neighbors and friends, for all those who were drowning in the terror of war. He prayed, too, for courage, something the Lord had never given him in abundance. He drew and expelled a breath and then, tapped by a finger of guilt, said a prayer that the twin demons—Hitler and Mussolini—would soon be killed. A sin, surely, to pray for someone's violent death, but he'd seen too much these past years, heard too much in the confessional. With the arrival of the German occupiers, some boundary fence of his faith had been trampled. Some sense of confidence in his own people had been undermined by their embrace of the violent cult of *il Duce*—his vicious gangs, the *squadristi*; his ludicrous military adventurism in Africa, Albania, Greece, and Yugoslavia; his friendship with Hitler, a living Satan; the murder of the heroic Matteotti.

Christ, he well knew, had dealt with evil people and had prayed for them. But that was Christ. He himself was Claudio DeMarco, round-faced and fat and, in better times, jolly. A man who loved to eat, who had sinned with one woman, and who had thought, many times, of sinning with others. To this day, the product of one of those sins walked the earth. In safety, he hoped. He said a special prayer for her every morning. He would, he hoped, be forgiven. And the Germans, he hoped, would never imagine what kind of work the fat local padre was actually doing.

With the ghost of fear wrapping its cold fingers around his thoughts, Don Claudio waddled into the washroom and cleaned himself, then shuffled into the rectory kitchen—abandoned by all the usual serving people now and by the one assistant priest—to make himself a weak cup of espresso and to prepare for morning Mass. Already he could feel perspiration gathering on his neck and under his arms. Beyond the window, the day seemed sunlit and hot, pure torment for a man of his dimensions. He would bear it as penance. He would trust in the Lord and ask that he be given strength to keep his secrets if the day ever came when he was caught and carried away to the torture cells.

Seven

When the car pulled through the gates of Villa Savoia, the king's summer residence, Mussolini noticed three carabinieri vehicles and a police ambulance parked there in patches of shade. Mildly unusual. It occurred to him that the Allied landing on Sicily—a fluke not a harbinger—had sent everyone into a panic for the past two weeks. The curse of his people was that so many of them were afraid of war. He was not. As the car rolled to a stop, he dropped one hand to his thigh and, through the fabric, absently fingered the raised scar from his battle wound. He'd nearly lost his life then, twenty-eight years ago, or, at least, he'd told people that story for so long now that he himself had come to believe it. Already in this conflict, his beloved son, Bruno, had perished in a bomber crash. People wanted a world without violence, but violence was as much a part of the human condition as was sexual intercourse: there was no life without it. Shying away from violence brought only destruction, humiliation, surrender. He knew that. Hitler knew it. He had tried to make his countrymen understand that fact, and for a while, it seemed they did. There had been successes: Albania, Libya, Ethiopia. But now a few battalions of American and British soldiers had come ashore in Sicily, a thousand kilometers to the south, and one saw panic in every face, and police vehicles at Villa Savoia.

Mussolini stood up out of the car, straightened the jacket of his suit with a downward tug and a flex of his powerful shoulders, then strode toward the steps of the grand stone building, where the king was standing in a pose of calm respect. Eyes at the level of Mussolini's shoulders, Vittorio Emanuele held out one soft hand in greeting.

"My king," *il Duce* said, trying not to let a note of sarcasm leak into the words. After all, it had been the king's weakness in the face of labor unrest that had opened the door to power for Benito Mussolini when he was just an ambitious member of the Chamber of Deputies; he tried always to remember that.

"My *Duce*. Come, sit with me inside. Today is insufferably hot."

They sat in an elegantly furnished parlor—velvet drapes, leather armchairs, walls hung with portraits of the king's ancestors and trimmed in dark mahogany—and were served small cups of espresso on porcelain plates by a manservant in a tight white uniform. Mussolini found the scene slightly disgusting: the tiny man they called king, with his high forehead and fluffy mustache; the servant with his effeminate ways; the flowers; the electric fans; the polished marble; the smells, already, of dinner being prepared in the kitchen. They might have been at an ambassador's reception in peacetime for all the sense of deprivation here. And outside, the police cars, the ambulance. For what? In case the king fell ill with a summer cold? It made his bowels ache.

"How are you, my *Duce*?"

"Determined, as always, Your Highness, but not well. The ulcers have me. Rachele is in a panic. Last night's Council vote, the Allied landing. I am the most hated man in Italy, it seems, after a lifetime of giving my blood and sweat to this land."

The king nodded solemnly. *A travesty, yes,* he seemed to be saying. He pursed his thin lips. "You have served your country well," he said after a long moment, but the first signal of trouble was his inability to meet Mussolini's eyes as he spoke. The king's direct gaze had been his one saving grace, his single manly aspect. Now that, too, was gone. Mussolini nearly snorted. "But as for the vote, *Duce*," the king went on, "I think it is a sign that your work is finished."

"Finished? How?"

A cough, a flicker of eye contact, a gaze into the middle distance. The king molded his face into an expression of sorrow. "We have arranged," he said quietly, "for you to be taken into custody. For your protection."

"Custody? Who will run the country? Who will lead the army?"

Another cough. "The generals and I. You have brought the war to our soil, *Duce. Il popolo non la voleva.*" *The people didn't want that.*

At this hideous comment, this siding with the masses against their leader, Mussolini felt as though the burning pain of the ulcer was expanding like an inflated balloon, swelling up through his midsection, squeezing the air from his lungs. It seemed to him that his chest was about to burst open, scattering the buttons of his shirt and pieces of bloody rib into the king's triangular face. A violent rage took hold of him; he had to set the clattering cup and saucer on the table. A few drops spilled on the oriental carpet. The king noticed. Mussolini felt the blood in the vessels around his eyes and wondered if he should strangle Vittorio Emanuele right there, then take the car home and face Rachele's righteousness. *Don't go! Don't go, Benito!* He could hear the words echoing in his ears. He swallowed. He said, in a voice shaking with anger, "What kind of custody?" and heard footsteps at the doorway behind him.

Eight

Silvio Merino spent three minutes in front of the mirror in his second-floor apartment on Rome's most fashionable street, Via Veneto. He made a slight adjustment to the knot of his silk tie, brushed an eyelash from the lapel of his sport coat, flashed his smile at himself. He tucked one errant hair back in place above his forehead. Already a touch of gray there, he noticed. Perfect.

He had an important meeting that afternoon, so it was essential to make a good impression. The meeting involved a military man. Or perhaps a political man. Or perhaps a man who combined both. His contact had been a bit vague, saying only that there was intrigue involved, possibly real danger, but assuring him there could be a substantial profit. And that, of course, was the part that mattered: money whispered to him like a lover.

Silvio thought of himself, to use a word popular in his Sicilian dialect, as a *facciatu*. A *maker*. Someone who made things happen by any means available. A more proper word might be the Italian *facilitatore*—facilitator, but Silvio preferred the sound of the rougher title. *Facciatu*. Fa-chia-TOO. On the island of his birth, it was sometimes considered a compliment. As, he thought, in his case at least, it should be.

He closed and locked the door of the apartment with a satisfying *click* and made his way down two long flights of marble steps. From centuries of human traffic, the stair treads were worn in the center, a detail he loved. It spoke to him of the perspective of time and, as he descended them and then went out onto the winding downhill street he also loved—where else in Rome would one want to live?—he set aside a moment of nervousness by recalling his heroic triumph . . . over the circumstances of his birth.

He'd come, as the expression had it, from nothing. The last of eleven Merino children reared on a patch of dusty farmland in central Sicily, he'd been the only one to understand, at a very young age, that the world was there to be manipulated. Played, in the same way an instrument was played by a master musician. Girlfriends, teachers, older relatives, even the midlevel mafiosi who ran that part of the island—he'd always been able to shine a smile on them, make a remark, a joke, tease, grin, empathize. Charmed and flattered, they'd do whatever it was he wanted them to do. Surrender their honor, give him a passing grade for substandard schoolwork, yank him from a nasty fistfight and make sure his opponent never bothered him again, slip him a coin and tell him he should enjoy life.

Enjoy life. He always had. At sixteen, he'd moved away from the arid poverty of his home island and gone first to Naples, then to Rome, in pursuit of the reward that made the earth spin: money. As if he'd been born to the trade, he became a master at doing favors, at providing goods that were in need, at recommending and advising. If a Mafia friend required a contact in the Rome construction business, Silvio Merino made the introduction. For a fee, of course. If he heard about a shortage of artichokes on the mainland, he notified a Sicilian grower he knew; found trucks to carry the produce, a strongman to make sure not too much of it disappeared en route; hired a pretty young woman to sell them at market. And, naturally, took a percentage.

He considered himself a patriot, a Christian, a moral man—though morality had always seemed to him a tricky business. Yes, of course, the American cigarettes he helped his Mafia friend sell in Rome had been pilfered. A shame for the company that made them. Then again, a bonus for his friend's not very bright and otherwise unemployable nephew, who sold them, and for the store owners who bought them at a bargain price. Even the smokers benefited. Where was the sin in that? It was the way the world worked. Yes, two or three of the women he'd slept with had been promised to other men. But if the husband, fiancé, or boyfriend had been making them happy, why would they stray? He liked to think that by temporarily satisfying certain women, he'd kept intact many more relationships than he'd ruined.

When the hard times came, Mussolini's Thirties, rather than weeping and complaining as so many others did, Silvio found ways to turn events to his advantage. It proved easy enough to come by a certificate claiming he suffered from heart trouble and was therefore unfit for *il Duce's* army. So, together with a printer friend, he formed a small enterprise and offered that same service, quietly, to a limited number of others. Soon he and his friend were providing various kinds of fake permits, ration cards, certificates of residence in Vatican City, and employment in homes and offices that did not actually exist. The tighter *il Duce's* grip, the stricter the regulations, the more Silvio Merino flourished.

Much as he hated the war and despised the Germans (how could you respect a people who valued efficiency over warmth?), their increased presence in the early 1940s created fresh opportunities. He gave assistance to members of the clergy and to the few resistance fighters who trusted him enough to reach out. He and his Mafia contacts had even played a small but important role in the recent Allied landing on Sicily. He made connections among people on this earth; that was his job.

On that fine, hot afternoon, comforted by his musings, Silvio strolled along the Via Veneto, nodding to neighbors, smiling, tossing off a remark to brighten their dark days, slapping a shoulder, pinching a cheek, tucking in a loose bit of someone else's shirttail. *"This meeting involves intrigue,"* his source had said. Perhaps real danger. He found the idea mildly titillating: he could make another contribution to the liberation effort, and without ever having to wear a uniform! Afterward, if the Allies triumphed, he might be seen as a minor hero; it would be good for business, good for his love life.

Fashionably late, he arrived at the Café Dello Sport for his encounter, and, after studying the seated patrons for a moment, decided that the person he was supposed to meet must be the solitary, bespectacled gentleman in the back left corner. Silvio glided over, introduced himself, and shook the man's hand as if they'd been friends since the first war. Giovanni was the name, no family name offered. *"Facciamo una passeggiata?"* Giovanni suggested quietly, in elegant Italian. *Take a walk?*

"Sure, of course, naturally," Silvio told the bespectacled stranger, but there was a whisper of concern in both ears now: Who knew which side this Giovanni worked for?

As they stepped back out into the heat and set off at a leisurely pace, Silvio reminded himself to stay alert. Maybe his small gestures of assistance to the partisans had not gone unnoticed in Fascist circles, and he would now pay a price. These days, even on the streets, even in broad daylight, anything might happen.

Nine

Luca stood in the death stink of Piazzale Loreto for another hour, fixing the scene in his memory, watching the mothers and wives spill their grief into the hot afternoon as if it came from bottomless wells in the center of their bodies. *The famous* Duce *has brought you this,* Luca wanted to tell them. *The famous Mussolini bears the guilt for the murder of your sons.*

He breathed in the smell without flinching, refused to look away. His eyes kept returning to one partisan in particular, a boy of fourteen with whom he'd done a small bit of work—two quick conversations—less than a month earlier. Alonso, the boy had called himself, another friend of the archbishop. Handsome in the first blush of his maturity, Alonso had been beaten so badly as to be almost unrecognizable. A woman who appeared to be his mother was there in the front row, on her knees, rosary beads wrapped around her clasped hands, pearls of sweat on her forehead, wailing and keening. What she wanted, all she wanted, was to be allowed to bury her mutilated child. But no. One of the soldiers rested his eyes on her for ten seconds, and Luca searched those eyes for the smallest trace of sympathy.

Nothing. Ice. Metal.

At last, Luca turned his back, tossed his cigarette butt onto the cobblestones, and walked away, trying to make himself as inconspicuous as possible, someone who did not know the archbishop, who wasn't carrying an important message, who wasn't seething; just another one-eyed mushroom gatherer and unemployed stonemason heading to work in the forest so there would be food for the sadistic armed forces of the Reich and their half-starved Italian servants.

He walked past a row of shops that showed colorful awnings and half-empty windows beneath the balconies of stucco-walled apartments. He crossed the northwestern corner of the square, angled down a brick alley between two warehouse buildings, and, without a backward glance, moved toward the Maggiolina neighborhood and the train station there.

He could sense—and sometimes hear—that someone was follow-ing him. If the Nazis had chosen to slaughter the young Alonso by chance, that would be bad enough—for every German soldier killed away from the battlefront, they took the lives of ten Italians. It was pos-sible they'd just grabbed the first ten men they came across, tied their hands, clubbed them to death one by one as the others watched, then dumped the bodies in the square.

But if, in one of the city's secret interrogation rooms, someone had given up the boy's name, and if others in the archbishop's circle had been betrayed as well, then he and Don Claudio were in trouble. Which meant that his mother and Sarah and Rebecca were in danger, too. Which meant it had been tremendously foolish to let his curiosity draw him to Piazzale Loreto.

He reached the Maggiolina train station and stood on the platform in a loose crowd of other wartime travelers, forcing himself to keep his eyes straight ahead. He smoked his last cigarette, doing everything he could to seem completely relaxed. It was possible that this man tailing him was just another person heading north. But it seemed more likely that he'd noticed Luca on the Piazzale—the only other man of military age there—and was one of *il Duce*'s Blackshirts with nothing better to do than spend his days tracking down so-called enemies of the State.

To the south, the train whistle sounded its loud wail. Luca tossed the cigarette butt onto the tracks and stared down at his two bare forearms.

The skinny left one—functional enough—might have belonged to a young boy who'd never known physical work. But the right arm, after almost twenty years of compensating for its weaker partner, was a thick cylinder of muscle, the hand calloused and powerful, a weapon.

He hoped he was wrong. He hoped the man was simply on the same route by coincidence, because the gruesome scene at Piazzale Loreto, the vision of Alonso's ruined face, had caused angry music to erupt in his inner ear, a violent symphony. He didn't know where it might lead. As the train came to a stop a meter in front of him, he listened to the new sound and felt a fine coating of perspiration form on his neck and face. It had nothing to do with the heat of the day.

Ten

By the time she finished bathing, Sarah could feel that the sun had climbed over the mountains beyond Lake Como's eastern shore. She pulled on her clothes and started back down the narrow, broken path that led to the cabin, but the usual post-bath comfort had already abandoned her. From the time she'd been a small girl, she'd had a sharp intuition—almost a mystical sense—not so much for specific events (she couldn't predict the future) but for what she'd told her mother felt like "bad air." It was as if news, especially news of trouble or danger, reached her first via this cloudy sense of concern, and then was delivered in its specifics.

She wondered now what it could be, because, making her way down the stony path, with leaves and branches brushing her shoulders and hips, she could feel a premonition as clearly as she could feel the warmth of the day rising in the air around her. Not Luca, she hoped. Not her mother or Maria. She tried to tell herself it was only an echo of the momentary terror she'd felt at the spring. Then she tried to convince herself, again, that they'd been animal noises, that, if it had been a person—a German soldier or Blackshirt—something more would have happened.

But the bad air followed her until the cabin's damaged roof came into view. Instead of going inside to eat her simple breakfast and then take up her notebook of poems, she sat in the trees, well hidden there, and waited. Luca had promised to come to her today, but he hadn't said exactly when, or how far away he'd gone, or on what kind of mission.

It was beginning to seem to her that she'd have to move again, that her days in the cabin were numbered. Maybe this bad air, this feeling, this premonition, was only that: time to leave.

Eleven

After midnight, when the laughter from the Rossos' house had been replaced for a short while by worse noises, audible even at this distance, Maria went to one of the front windows and peered out. From this vantage point, she had a view of a slice of the lake, ink black in the darkness, and of the lacy jewelry of stars above the mountains on the eastern shore. As was almost always the case, the road in front of her house was empty of people. She wondered if her husband was still alive and where he might be sleeping on this night. She and Sabatino had moved here for the view and the quiet of the hills, the sense of peace. That word, that memory, carried such a bitter taste now. They had wanted to raise a brood of children, but she'd been able to bear only one: the crippled star around which she and her husband had orbited these past twenty years.

Barefoot, she went back along the hallway, took the broom, and tapped the end of the handle twice, gently, on the hatch above. She could barely hear it open. Rebecca's face—a face she'd known for forty years—appeared there, little more than two large eyes, angles, and shadow. Mumbling an apology as she always did, Rebecca moved the slop bucket over the opening and carefully lowered it. Maria took it in both hands and carried it to the toilet, dumped it quietly there, washed her hands in the sink, then handed up two boiled eggs, a small tomato, and a clean washcloth. Rebecca reached down and clutched them in her fingers. There was no more speech between them on that night. The need for thank-yous and warnings had left them weeks before. Maria could hear lips sucking greedily at the tomato. Rebecca dragged the hatch closed, and Maria went out into the back yard to wash the bucket clean at the outdoor faucet and to look at the stars and pray. Just as she'd started an Ave Maria, she heard a voice behind her in the darkness. A voice with a German accent. *"Che fai, donna?"*

What are you doing, woman?

Drunk to the point of imbalance, the man must have wandered, shirtless, from the Rosso house across the weedy, now unused field, through her small grove of olive trees, and as far as the gate in the fence that bordered her property. The moonlight shone from his completely bald head. She couldn't speak.

"What are you doing?"

"I-I-I," she began, and he let out a drunken chortle. "Toilet broken."

"Ah, Italian shit. And so late."

"My stomach. Illness. I-I . . . Diarrhea." She was sure he didn't know the word, but even in the half darkness, she could see a terrible smile pasted on his face, and she wondered now if she'd be marched back into the house and made to show him where Rebecca was hiding, or if her exhausted guest would make a noise inside, drop the small door down into the hallway, sneeze, burp, call out.

"I won't keep you from your shit work. We want you to cook for us. Our other cook disappeared . . . a mystery, where she went. You have these chickens. We want you to make us a dish with them."

"I'll lose the eggs."

"Keep all but one, then. Make the sacrifice of one chicken for the Reich! Ha! Every night now, we want a nice Italian dinner. We have the food. There are five officers and sometimes . . . guests. Every night starting this next one."

He stared down at her, and Maria realized she was trembling. Fear, bitterness, loathing, an enormous wave of stifled emotion. If she'd had a gun in the pocket of her dress, she would have pointed it at his bare chest and fired.

"I'm very weak. I'm old."

"Nonsense," the man said. "You're a woman in the prime of life!" With that strange comment, he turned away and stumbled back across the empty lot toward the Rossos' house. Over his shoulder he said, "Dinner for us tomorrow, and make certain to wash your hands before you come work!"

Twelve

Captain Otto Skorzeny, thirty-five, battle-scarred from fighting on the Russian front, his body as trained and taut as an Olympic athlete's, had been called back from the outskirts of Moscow some months earlier for, of all things, colic. A child's illness! It embarrassed him to speak of it, and it made him slightly uncomfortable to have been pulled away from the fighting. Still, looked at a certain way, the illness was consistent with the perfect good luck that seemed always to follow him: it wasn't the worst time to leave Russia and Stalin's T-34 tanks. German forces had passed two winters on the steppes; things were no longer going so well there.

Besides, the return to Germany had brought him a promotion and a new opportunity: always fond of strategy, he'd been moved from anti-tank artillery to a commando unit and trained in the subtler arts of war—espionage, sabotage, trickery, interrogation. Thanks to that work, he'd made the acquaintance of some of the Reich's best field officers and most important higher-ups. In the process, he'd been awarded the Iron Cross, second class, and had made something of a name for himself, just as his father had long ago predicted.

When his phone rang on this July morning, he was back in Berlin on a short leave, relaxing in a hotel bed with a woman he'd met the night before. With the tip of one finger, the woman was tracing the looping scar on Skorzeny's left cheek, reminder of a piece of Soviet shrapnel. He rolled over, lifted the receiver, and heard the voice of Second Lieutenant Goss, one of his assistants. There was a nervous excitement in his words. "You've been summoned," Goss said. "They'll pick you up in twenty minutes and take you to the airport."

Nothing more was said, nor should there have been. Skorzeny washed and shaved, dressed in his uniform, nodded once to the woman—still naked, last name forgotten, bedroom tricks and phone number filed away for future visits—and, just before stepping out the door, was surprised by a possibility he hadn't considered. He turned back to look at her, a dark-haired vision in the sheets. He studied her face. "You're not by any chance Jewish, are you?" he asked.

Her laughter followed him out into the hallway.

Skorzeny stepped from the building just in time to see a black staff car with swastika flags on its fenders turning onto his street. The car pulled to the curb. A uniformed lieutenant jumped out, saluted, opened the door. Skorzeny took a seat in back and lit a cigarette. No information was offered and none asked for. He ran two fingers over his combat decorations—a superstitious gesture—and wondered what this next assignment would be. Who could say? Something wild and adventurous, he hoped. Unorthodox. A job rife with thrill and danger.

At Tempelhofer, a Heinkel was waiting, propellers turning. German cross on the fuselage, swastika on the tail, an elegant machine. He climbed aboard—strangely enough, the only passenger—and they made a rough flight to Munich and landed at Neubiberg without incident. From there, he was put on a smaller plane, a Storch, and flown—toward East Prussia, he guessed from the landmarks below—by another peculiarly silent pilot who landed them on a tarmac airstrip with admirable skill.

Another staff car, two colonels in front this time, red and silver braids on their epaulets, more silence. By now—colonels as chaperones, no less!—Skorzeny was beginning to suspect that what awaited him was more than a meeting with an ordinary field commander. He felt a twist of excitement in his belly. The car raced out of the city—he saw a sign, RASTENBURG—and then sped along an empty highway, heading northeast. After half an hour, they turned off the main road and soon encountered a checkpoint. Rifles, salutes, the usual treatment. But there was only a five-second delay—who were these colonels?—and they raced on, into deeper country now.

Another quarter of an hour, another checkpoint. More thorough this time. The men looked under the car, in the trunk, studied the colonels' papers for a full minute, asked Skorzeny for his name three times, checked his paybook. Then more salutes. More *Heil Hitler!*

As twilight settled, he stared out the side window. This particular summons—the mysterious flight, the colonels and checkpoints, the silence—had a sense of destiny to it, a kind of grandeur. It suited him perfectly.

Soon they passed through a gate in a guarded barbed-wire fence, then beneath overhead camouflage—branches across netting—and pulled up in front of a drab concrete building so perfectly set into the forest that it was barely visible even from two car lengths away. When Skorzeny stood up, he saw that there were trees placed on the roof so nothing could be seen from above. He was escorted into a large room with a long wooden table half-covered with maps. Four other officers stood at attention there. He joined them in line. The colonels had disappeared. Now he could feel his heart thumping: in this kind of a place, with this kind of security, they could be waiting for only one man.

The door was opened, and that man strode into the room. He was smaller and thinner than Skorzeny remembered—he'd seen him only at a distance before this—but there was an electric charge emanating from his body. His eyes, especially, seemed to be thrumming with energy, with certainty. Skorzeny and the other officers saluted, and he told them to stand at ease.

For a full minute, he paced back and forth in front of them, staring at the floor, hands clasped behind his back, his body rigid with tension, rippling with energy. *I would gladly die for you,* Skorzeny found himself thinking. They were each asked to give their name and rank.

At last, the Führer stopped and faced them. "Who knows Italy?" he asked.

Skorzeny was the only one to raise his hand.

Hitler nodded curtly and resumed his pacing.

"Assignment," he said in a clipped tone. That single word, *Zuordnung,* echoed against the walls. And then, "News reached us last night that Mussolini has been taken prisoner by his own government, a disaster for our forces in Italy." He made a fist and slashed at the air with it. "No doubt the Italians are now on the verge of surrender. No doubt the spirit of the fight is completely gone from them. We need to learn his whereabouts, design a rescue plan, find him, and restore him to power or else our southern flank will be . . ."

Hitler stopped speaking. A terrible pause seemed to swell out against the windows as the officers waited for details, for instruction, to be given their commands. And then Skorzeny felt his intuition click into gear: something in the Führer's tone, eye movement, or body language made him sense that Hitler wanted one man, not all of them. One man would be chosen to develop a plan and find and rescue the Führer's good friend. Exactly the kind of assignment he'd been hoping for.

"Herr Führer, I am Austrian!" The words had burst from Skorzeny's lips, unintended, but the meaning behind them was clear: Austria had been forced to cede South Tyrol to the Italians after the World War; in the mind of a true Austrian, there was no love lost for the Italian military, and there would be no mercy shown to Mussolini's captors. Hitler's eyes bored into him like sabers. Skorzeny thought, for a moment, that his disrespect would be rewarded with demotion or even court-martial.

But there was something else in the eyes. Recognition. A flicker of admiration perhaps.

"From where, exactly?" Hitler asked him.

"Vienna, *mein* Führer."

Hitler stood in front of the captain with the deep circular scar on his left cheek and skewered him with his eyes. The Austrian führer, it turned out, wanted an Austrian for the job. "The others are dismissed," he said. "Captain Skorzeny remain."

Thirteen

During the seventy-minute ride north from Milan to the station at the southern tip of Lake Como, Luca stared out the window and clenched and unclenched his fists. Stepping up onto the train, he'd slid his eyes right for one second and seen the man in the felt hat board the car behind his. There seemed to him little chance now that the man was there by coincidence. You didn't stare at someone instead of looking at dead bodies and then just happen to follow that person for two kilometers on a crooked route to a train station and then just happen to get into the car behind him. If the man had hard evidence from Alonso's interrogation, Luca would have been in German hands by now—he knew that. If the man were working with the archbishop, or with someone else among the partisans, there were better, safer ways to make contact. *No*, Luca thought, *he has to be one of Mussolini's men.* A Fascist bully, perhaps working for pay, perhaps only for the cause, acting on a hunch, hoping Luca would lead him to a secret meeting, a hidden Jew, a cache of weapons, hoping to make a name for himself among his fellow thugs.

The woman sitting to Luca's right held a loop of rosary beads in her gnarled old hands. Short, wizened, dressed all in black, she whispered her prayers just loudly enough for him to hear. He'd been raised Catholic, was close with his devout parents, and was now working with a brave priest and an even braver archbishop, but Luca had little feeling for their faith. He'd left this woman's God behind with his adolescence. To his mind, the Church offered no proper explanation for the world's inequities, for why some were born whole and others not, why some tortured and killed and others made peace. Christian or not meant little to him: the love of his life was Jewish. Religion was all superstition, all wishful thinking. How, after a horror like what he'd just witnessed, could any just God ask you not to kill?

The train left its passengers at the Como station and reversed direction toward Milan. Luca helped the old woman down onto the platform and, trying to seem casual about it, headed off toward the hills. He'd left his knapsack there, hidden in a favorite place, because he hadn't wanted to be stopped on the streets of Milan with a hunting knife and wire cutters in his possession. Now that seemed like a mistake. Across the outskirts of the small city he went, up a cobblestone road through the streets of Santa Eligia, an hour's walk still from the cabin where Sarah was waiting. If the felt-hatted stranger followed him only a bit farther, the man would discover something very different from a cache of arms or a hidden Jewess.

The road turned to dirt, passed a handful of close-set houses—not a creature to be seen here, except for one small, fenced-in mongrel that barked at him as he passed. Luca did not turn around. The road curled to the right, narrowed, passed an old farmhouse and its fields, two scrawny goats chewing on a leather strap and eyeing him without affection. Well behind him, he heard the small dog again. No question now: he was being tailed. He walked faster.

Beyond the end of the last cleared field, the road narrowed to a path through thick woods. He was strangely calm—this was his territory—his mind eerily still, as if he'd been anticipating this kind of encounter for a decade. When he reached the tall stone behind which he'd left his backpack, he veered off the path, making no sound. He bent over the small pack only long enough to take out his father's hunting knife, then crouched there, quieting his breath, listening, waiting.

Another two minutes and Luca heard the man approaching. No chance now that he was an ally in the cause. No, an ally, a fellow fighter, would have called out to him. The man's steps were quick and quiet, small rhythmic touches of shoe leather to dirt. He would be armed. A pistol, a switchblade, brass knuckles. He'd also be carrying a fanatical allegiance to his *Duce*. A fire of hatred in his brain. An urge to help remake humanity according to his idol's twisted ideas, any and all means justifying that end.

As the sound of footsteps came closer, Luca felt his mind pull tight into a single point of focus. His heartbeat seemed to slow; he drew a long breath. The man went past the stone at a steady pace. Luca saw the felt hat, saw something in the man's left hand. He leaped out from behind the stone, and the man heard him and turned, but Luca was upon him, thrusting the knife up just below the bottom of the breastbone. Their faces were very close; the man's eyes were opened wide; a hideous gasp escaped between his teeth. Luca drove the knife in as far as it would go, lifting the Fascist off the ground with the force of his one strong arm. The hat fell off. Something—a knife—clattered on the gravel path. Luca tumbled forward, pinning the man beneath him, his left forearm across the stranger's throat. He heard a choked last breath, then ripped out the knife and felt the Blackshirt shudder beneath him once and go still.

Fourteen

As Don Claudio expected, there were exactly four attendees at morning Mass, all of them women of a certain age. It didn't matter; the point was that the daily Mass was being said. So far, at least, the Germans, while occupying the town and committing every manner of atrocity and indecency, had left the services alone and left him alone for the most part. Foolish of them, of course. In their eyes, no doubt, he was nothing more than a fat priest, a fool for loving his invisible God. Let them always think so.

Thanks to his heroic friend, the archbishop of Milan, the same man who'd gotten him involved in the secret work, he had enough wafers and wine for another three months of services. Sometimes, knowing what he knew of the hunger in the towns along the lake, Don Claudio wondered if it would be more Christian to hand them out as food and drink rather than saving them to be turned into the body and blood of Christ. But a gesture like that would only draw attention to him, and the good it might do wouldn't last long in any case.

So, in front of his meager congregation, in the nave of dark marble and candle smoke, he went through the ancient ritual, its stately liturgy, its slow dance of familiar gestures. When Maria came up to receive the Eucharist, he met her eyes for a few seconds. A husband on the Russian steppe. A son in the hills. A Jew in the attic. If the Germans found out either of those last two facts, she would suffer horrifically, as they'd both seen others suffer: the Rossos had been beaten to death with boots and clubs, slowly, brutally, in front of an audience. The memories of those scenes played before his eyes at night like visions of hell. He did what he could now to banish them. He offered Maria a smile of encouragement, a tiny testament of faith in something beyond this awful world, and placed the host gently on her tongue.

Don Claudio found himself wondering if this was, in fact, not earthly life but purgatory, if they were all locked in a dream. Could it be that their souls were being purified in preparation for some great celestial joy? He sighed at the thought, let his hand rest briefly on Maria's shoulder, let her brave "Amen" cleanse his thoughts of fear. Here was a woman of substance, of holiness, of a remarkable courage that cast his own timidity into harsh relief. If Rebecca had sought shelter in his church instead of Maria's attic, would he have welcomed her?

He returned to the altar and wiped the chalice clean, drank down the last few sips of consecrated wine, recited the closing prayers.

Afterward, Maria came to him as he moved toward the cloakroom, anxious to shed his hot robe. As he knew she would, she asked if he could hear her confession. In all the town of Mezzegra, this was no doubt the place safest from Germans. They seemed to have a superstition about it. When the stocky redheaded officer with the thick neck and big thighs had come, on that first day, to inspect the building, wondering if it might serve as a place for his men to live (not enough beds in the rectory, he'd decided; they wanted their comforts), he'd barely glanced at the confessional, had even seemed to shudder as he walked past it. Don Claudio had, of course, noticed. Now he went and sat in the central chair in darkness, the stole worn during the sacrament draped around his neck. Maria knelt to one side behind a curtain, leaned forward, whispered, "They are making me cook for them now."

"Cook how?" he whispered back. "What do you mean? With what food?"

"The new SS officers who've come to the Rosso house. They have the food. A tall one came to my fence last night, drunk. Ordered me to kill one of my chickens and to cook for them . . . every night."

Don Claudio looked down at his clasped hands, stared at the ends of the purple stole beside them, pressed his eyelids tight. "You can't refuse," he said after a time.

"I know."

"Perhaps it will lead to something good."

Silence. Maria, like the others, had grown tired of his optimism, forced as it was these days.

"Maybe," she said at last, a note of bitterness in her quiet voice. *Forse.* "Or maybe I will confess something else here one day. Something worse."

Don Claudio let the words, the idea, settle around him. "We cannot let hatred overtake us," he said.

Silence.

For a time, they were quiet with each other, surrounded by darkness and stone, one kneeling, one sitting, their faces separated by a thin screen. *How quickly life has changed,* he thought. How far they had come from the people they used to be. "Is Rebecca all right?"

"Alive."

"Any word from . . . your son?"

"Not lately. You?"

"Yes. He said he was going to Milan."

"Can you tell me who he meets with in Milan?"

"I shouldn't . . . Any word from your husband?"

In the dim light from the nave, he could see Maria shaking her head. He heard one muffled sob. He wanted to reach through the screen and take hold of her. "Sarah?" he asked very quietly.

"Alive, also. Beyond that, Luca tells me nothing about her, like you, in case . . ." Her voice trailed off into a chamber of sordid possibilities.

"Hold to a vision of heaven," Don Claudio counseled. "Hard as it may be, Maria. Hold to that vision. God will bless you for what you are doing now. Your sins, if you have any sins, are forgiven."

She listened to the lengthy Latin absolution, thanked him, stood. He heard the curtain being pushed aside and then the tap of her footsteps on the marble floor. She was kneeling at the altar rail, saying her penance. Then more footsteps, the squeak of door hinges. When all was silent again, Don Claudio sat in the confessional for a long time, fingering the ends of the stole. She was being made to cook for them now. The Nazis would be closer to her, would visit her home, bringing food to prepare. One slip, one sound from the attic, one careless word on her part or his, and their secret work—probably their lives—would be finished.

Fifteen

Mussolini hadn't been able to sleep—his captors left a light on in the corridor—and he was sitting on the edge of the cot with his face in his hands. They'd taken him in the back of a police ambulance, accompanied by uniformed men with automatic weapons, all of them sweating in the metal box. *"For your protection,"* the king had said, placing a tiny, womanly hand on his back as he was escorted away. Why the ambulance, then, and not his own car with a bodyguard? And why hadn't the captain in charge offered an explanation—instead of a tepid salute, the same words, *"for your protection,"* then silence? And why now was there a soldier outside the door of this room—a police cadet station it was; he knew that—peering in through the glass every half hour in just the way a guard might check on a prisoner?

His stomach hurt more than usual. He missed Claretta. Ordinarily he would have called her to Palazzo Venezia or stopped by to visit with her on his way home, and even in pain, even after a day of terrible news, his body would function as it had always functioned, and she would cry out in his arms and squeeze him against her large, beautiful breasts so tightly that, for a minute, the weight of his worries would lift away. Sometimes, afterward, he'd serenade her on the violin, and that would send her into a different sort of ecstasy. She'd close her eyes, tilt her head to one side, and smile as peacefully as any of Bellini's Madonnas.

By the time he returned to Villa Torlonia, Rachele would be sleeping, or pretending to sleep, and he'd lie awake for an hour beside her, going over the events of the day, searching the words of the great philosophers for a line or phrase that might make sense of his life.

Now, the steel springs of a cot and a prisoner's meal, most of which he couldn't eat; dark army trucks standing like gravestones in the walled courtyard; and a circle of betrayers around him like hungry wolves circling a deer. Who could make sense of that?

If this were, in fact, what he was beginning to suspect it was, an imprisonment that had nothing to do with his protection, then Hitler would surely find out. There were German spies everywhere—in his own office, perhaps among the servants in Villa Torlonia, among the secretaries of the Council and lackeys of the king. Hitler needed Benito Mussolini to lead the Italian forces against the Allies; they'd never fight for anyone else. It was obvious then: the Führer would find out what had occurred and send a team to rescue and reinstall him. If there were not that certainty in this world, that friendship and mutual esteem, then there was nothing.

He lay down again and slept fitfully, dreaming of his father's blacksmith hands and harsh words about the Church, his mother at the stove, cringing, cooking. From the brown stucco two-story house in Forlì, the scene suddenly shifted, and the face of Giacomo Matteotti flashed before him. Those dark eyes, that downturned mouth. Haunting him in his dreams. Mussolini awoke in a sweat. This was how you paid for your sins: you were assaulted by your own memories, tormented by them in the night. But had it been a sin to rid the country of such a force for disruption? Such a traitor? A disrespectful socialist opponent, however popular? Had it truly been a sin? Hadn't it been done for the good of the nation?

He turned and turned, got up, paced, lay down again on the sagging cot. Eventually he fell back into a shallow sleep, a few bad hours torn by images, snatches of dream, voices echoing in church naves.

In the deepest part of the night, he was awakened by the screech of the metal door. He opened his eyes and saw three unfamiliar men in uniform, one a lieutenant colonel. *"Duce,"* the colonel said in a sly tone, an order ribboned with fake respect, "you must now please come with us."

Sixteen

Seconds after the felt-hatted Fascist expelled his last blood-choked breath, Luca heard the small dog start barking again. In the time it took for him to get to his feet, the eerie sense of calm deserted him. There was blood halfway up his right arm and on the front of his shirt and pants, and the man lay on his left side with his knees drawn up and his right arm flung out as if he were about to burst into song. The face was contorted, frozen in agony, the eyes open and dull. A switchblade knife, unsprung, lay on the path not far from the felt hat. For one long moment, Luca stood over the body, breathing hard, his mind whirling, then he kicked the knife into the underbrush, lifted his backpack from behind the stone, and angled off into the trees. Moving blindly, with hurried steps, he crashed down through a shallow ravine, then climbed the other side. Brambles and tree branches scraped at his face and arms, and a voice—overridden by an urge to put as much distance as possible between him and what he had done—kept counseling him to go back, go back now, take the switchblade, hide the body. He could no longer hear the barking dog.

After pushing himself hard for an hour through the dense undergrowth, he came, at last, upon a stone ridge that ran parallel to the slope. A familiar place. He and his father had spent a night here on one of their many expeditions, six or eight years ago it must have been. He sat on a ledge, back against a wall of rock, and stared out into the trees. A gruesome satisfaction had taken hold of him, grim, dark, coated in what felt like evil. This was what he'd wanted, to be a fighter. But there was something else behind that vague dream now, a sense that he'd crossed into new territory and, in doing so, left part of himself behind. He lowered his eyes to the dried blood on his skin and clothes. He couldn't be sure, couldn't grasp the truth behind the feeling, but he worried that the Luca he'd left behind was the person Sarah loved.

He worried, too, about the body on the path and cursed himself for his moment of panic. It would have taken only a minute to drag it into the woods, cover the blood, hide the hat, take the knife, rifle through the man's pockets for the Fascist Party card he knew would be there and for whatever money he might have been carrying. Luca ran his mind back over the past hour, wondering who could have seen him starting up the road by the farmhouse. Two goats, a dog, maybe whoever it was who had caused the dog to bark a third time.

There was a little food and a bottle of water in the backpack, along with wire cutters, a small flashlight, extra batteries, a balled-up mesh bag. The tools of his trade. But he couldn't eat now. The thought of it made him nauseous. He'd finish the long climb to the cabin, wash off the blood, tell Sarah what had happened, and hope he hadn't left behind all his tenderness, all his youth, all the parts of himself she seemed to admire.

After a while, he stood up and began to walk, more slowly and carefully now, making little sound, going along according to a mental compass it seemed had always been built into his bones. Flashes of guilt lit the dark sky of his thoughts: he could just as easily have ducked into the trees and let the man go on his way, but it was almost as if he'd had to prove something to himself, as if the scene on Piazzale Loreto had terrified him, and, in response to that terror, he'd had to become a killer, brutal, fearless, immune to what Don Claudio always called "the sanctity of human life."

Battered by these thoughts, he'd gone only a short distance, making his own path through the trees, when he came upon a cluster of *Galerina marginata* growing from a rotting log. The mushrooms looked like nothing so much as keyboard notes of the song of death itself. *Lepiota* was the slang term for them. Normally he would have passed on by, but something—the persistent echoes of Piazzale Loreto, maybe, the evil skin that covered him now, the guilt—made him stop and crouch beside them. He remembered his father pointing them out to him so many years ago, explaining how poisonous they were and what a horrible death would be experienced by anyone who ate them. "The only saving grace," his father had said, "is that you die quickly." Luca remembered thinking, even then, that there was a certain vicious beauty to these *funghi*, the toasted brown heads and elegant white stems, the way they lifted up from the log in a gentle curl. It was easy to understand how, over the centuries, people had been fooled by the shapeliness, had picked and eaten the *lepiota*, thinking them a gift from God. He could understand, too, suddenly, how it was that a person could decide to take his own life.

He stared at the mushrooms for a while, counted eleven separate heads, and then, in an odd gesture—this was the new Luca acting, a different man now, a killer—cut them off at the base with his knife, one by one, and, using a large leaf to protect his fingers, loaded them into the mesh bag. He put the bag carefully into his backpack, cleaned the knife blade in the dirt, and walked on.

He traveled on legs accustomed to twenty or more hard kilometers a day, feeling the sun make its slow arc across the afternoon and dealing with a new urge—alien to him—to ask forgiveness. He could almost sense the earth's silent spin, almost feel a lost kinship with the lake and the hills, almost believe that he had now set himself outside the natural order by taking a life he could have spared. In time, as he knew he would, he came upon a rough dirt road, long unused. The road turned into an old donkey path, then a trickle of trail heading deeper into the high hills, then a line of eroded stones that would mean nothing to a person who didn't know this forest. From the end of the trail of stones, he was able to see just the roof of a cabin where shepherds had once taken shelter in storms. The cabin—little more than a shack, really—hadn't been used since long before Mussolini came to power, fifty or even a hundred years. Overgrown with vines and surrounded by trees and bushes, it blended into the landscape so perfectly that you could be standing thirty meters away and not see it. The small fields around it were overgrown, the sheep only a memory. The cabin itself had a leaky roof, vipers in the foundation, no glass in the two small windows, a door made of three planks and a rusty handle. He looked down at his bloody clothes, stepped forward, and tapped twice on the wood. No one answered. For a moment, he felt a surge of panic, but then he heard steps and saw Sarah coming out of the trees, her hair freshly washed and her beautiful face touched only lightly by the fear of what she was seeing.

Seventeen

The German officers treated Maria as a servant—something she expected. But on that first night, at least, they didn't touch her, or say crude things in front of her, or invite their women to the table. In a pantry next to the Rossos' kitchen, they kept a larder of vegetables that would have fed all of Mezzegra for a week. Maria had no idea where the food had come from, deliveries from Vienna or Berlin, or maybe they simply took what they wanted from the local markets. Who was going to complain or stop them?

Though there was meat, too, in the refrigerator, she did as she was told and cooked the chicken she'd killed and made a sauce with the tomatoes, onions, and peppers, a kind of cacciatore, a simple hunter's dish but one that her husband, Sabatino, had favored. She'd loved his passion for food and, in the early years, for her. He was a rough man, unshaven half the time, with calloused hands and a blunt way of speaking. Her parents, educated people, had wanted more for her, better, richer, more refined. But Sabatino had always been amazingly tender, always a gentleman in his own rough way, always a man who cared about his house and made their family the heart of his days. Instead of going down to the bars in town to drink coffee and play cards with the other men, he'd take their one-eyed Luca up into the mountains on camping and hiking trips, even when the boy was very small. He taught their son which snakes to avoid and which plants were edible—almost as if he could see into the future and had been preparing him for the deprivations of the war years. She remembered so well the way her men had said goodbye to each other when Sabatino had been sent off to war, the two of them, one stocky, one slim, standing in the road in front of the house and looking down at the lake. Before dawn on the day Sabatino left, they'd stood that way for the better part of an hour and then turned as if on some shared instinct, held each other close, and quickly walked off in separate directions.

Luca told her later that his father had given him his prized hunting knife.

She wondered, at times, if Sabatino had seen into the future another way, had known he would never return, and so the parting had been that much more difficult for him. She wondered if Luca and his father were both killers now, a thing she could not imagine.

Thinking about that possibility, she cut her hand with the Germans' sharp knife. A superficial wound, a scratch. She sucked the blood from her finger and brought her thoughts back to the meal. They even had salt, the *bastardi*. She spent two hours over the preparations—she did not know how to cook other than the slow way her mother had cooked—and the men, eating in their undershirts (something Sabatino had never done) seemed to appreciate it. They didn't offer her any food, however, or speak a single compliment, and they drank more than she expected SS officers to drink.

But when the meal was finished, one of them, a boyish-looking redhead with a weightlifter's thick neck, actually thanked her—a single, quiet, heavily accented *grazie*—and as his comrades went off to their rooms, as women slipped in the door so that all Maria could see of them was their backs and shining, just-washed hair, he said he'd eaten his fill and left her a bowl with a third of a meal in it. When he walked away, she ate it with a fresh spoon, quickly, quietly; cleaned the dishes; and left.

On that first night, she did not dare steal so much as half a carrot, but she carried away an idea. It was the kind of vulgar idea she never would have entertained for so much as a second before the war; it was spawned by hatred, by hunger, by the awful things she'd seen with her own eyes and heard about from friends. She'd used the last of their oil, and the man who seemed to be in charge, the tall drunk with the bald head, the one who'd sneaked up behind her in her yard, told her she should bring her own oil next time, because "You Italians can't cook anything without it, and surely you must have some from your trees." She said that she did, which was true, and, leaving in the summer darkness, with a few drops of light rain pattering on the leaves and a furious hatred boiling inside her, she carried away an idea.

That night, with great care, almost as if it were a religious ceremony, she took a spoonful of urine from Rebecca's slop bucket, mixed it into a large bottle of olive oil, and set it on the counter for use at the Germans' table.

Every time she cooked for them now, they would be consuming some of a Jewish woman's piss.

Eighteen

As the two of them strolled away from the Café Dello Sport, Silvio decided he liked this "Giovanni." The man had style, flair. The lenses of his eyeglasses sparkled; his cheeks and strong chin were perfectly shaved. But, in contrast with the elegant grooming and the clean lines of his jaw, Giovanni's nose was bent sideways, as if he'd been a boxer in his youth. His hair—just enough gray to add a distinguished touch—was swept back from his forehead, his shoulders wide, his walk . . . what was the word? *Disinvolto. Jaunty.* Probably in his late forties, the man cut a *bella figura*. And what mattered more than that?

They meandered past the American Embassy—closed, of course; Americans were an extinct species now, in *Italia*—the two of them attracting the stares, it seemed to Silvio, of every woman they passed. They turned onto Via Ciambotta, one of the nicest side streets of the Ludovisi neighborhood, flowers gone from the grand entranceways of the three-story houses here but the same sense of amorous intrigue hiding behind the curtained windows and leonine gargoyles.

"So," Silvio said after they'd passed several blocks with no conversation, "I understand you are a military man, an officer."

"Something like that," Giovanni answered. As they walked, he looked around them with subtle glances, as if expecting to be spied upon, listened to by operatives of one side or another. Not working for the Germans, Silvio hoped, but he couldn't quite bring himself to raise the question.

"Born where?"

Giovanni glanced at him out of the corner of his eye, smirked, sauntered on. "Chicago," he said at last. Barely moving his lips.

"You're an American?"

"Not so loud with that word, please."

"But your Italian is impeccable. Better than mine. I have the Sicilian accent, the *U* sound where the Florentines and Tuscans say *oh*. And your look, your walk. Everything sings 'Roman nobility'!"

"Yes, and I was told you specialized in flattery."

Silvio laughed. "Only for those who deserve praise. Truly, I never would have guessed."

"Italian father. American mother. I moved back here for love years ago. Was drafted, against my will. Completed my service in peacetime and went into intelligence work. I tolerated it, endured it . . . until the racial laws, until Hitler."

"Amazing. And now?"

"Now I'm a midlevel functionary. Military intelligence. I have an office in Palazzo Venezia."

"Mussolini's White House. Perfect. You've seen many things."

"Too many."

"You no doubt have access to sensitive information."

"No doubt."

"And you're using it how?" Silvio was finally able to say. "For which cause, which side?"

"You don't need to ask that question," Giovanni replied quietly. "We know your sympathies. I never would have contacted you otherwise."

"And this knowledge of me comes from where, exactly?"

"A long period of surveillance."

"Which means the other side knows my sympathies, as well."

Giovanni shrugged, appeared to smile. "I would advise you to be careful, that's all. To work with professionals not amateurs. It's one thing to help would-be resistance fighters steal a truckload of cigarettes. Something else entirely to be seen helping the actual enemies of the Reich."

"But isn't that what you're about to ask me to do?"

"Yes."

"And the difference is?"

"The difference is you've been helping amateurs who were playing with dynamite. We package our dynamite better and use it more carefully."

"Literal dynamite?"

Again the partial smile, a shake of the head. A pause, as if Giovanni were deciding how much to reveal. "Money, messages, sometimes weapons. You were vouched for, among others, by someone at the Irish embassy."

"Where my blessed father is employed."

Giovanni grunted as if he knew. "And someone else I won't mention."

"I have many friends."

"I'm sure they want you to remain alive."

"Yes, of course," Silvio said, but the remark had seemed vaguely like a threat. He wasn't sure now how much he liked this Giovanni, and he suddenly wondered if his dabbling in the partisan movement—tiny favors, really, and the movement itself was in its infancy—had been worth the small sums it had earned him.

"Still interested?"

"Most likely, yes," Silvio said after the smallest hesitation. His own words surprised him, but he could not seem to stop himself. He felt he was being seduced but, for once, not by money. "Tell me how, exactly, I can be of service to Uncle Sam." Silvio put a hand over his heart and made a solemn face. "I have great feelings for America, great feelings."

"Two things," Giovanni told him. "First"—he paused, looked around—"we need someone to carry a sum of gold from a priest at the Vatican—"

"Father Hugh O'Neil."

"How did you know?"

Silvio shrugged, smiled. "The famous Irishman. Even the Germans have heard of him."

"From the Vatican to the archbishop of Milan."

"Federico Maniscalco."

"Another friend?"

"I don't know him. But I've heard—this is perhaps inaccurate—that he has the most impeccably pro-Fascist sympathies."

"Utterly inaccurate, as it turns out."

"The second favor?"

"The second favor is simple. Mussolini was deposed. We—"

"My God! Is this true? When?"

"Two days ago. We would very much like to know where he's being held."

"Ah, but there's been no announcement, so that must simply be a rumor. We Italians are, as you know, famous for exaggeration." They were passing the apartment of one of his former lovers. Silvio glanced up at the concrete balcony. No flowers there now, no sign of her, but the memories were so sweet! He was sure she still kept a photo of him in the drawer of her bedside table.

"Well, the whole world will know soon enough."

"Amazing," Silvio said. He still didn't believe the report, but it piqued his interest. "I have two questions for you, then, Giovanni, one for each favor. First, I have a courier in mind, someone whose credentials are beyond doubt, a man who, even under torture, would not reveal his sources. However, he is said—more rumor, perhaps—to be associated with certain men in Sicily, a certain organization there, if you understand my meaning. An organization that, for business reasons more than anything else, does not welcome the German presence. I'm assuming that would be fine with you?"

"No good."

"But I vouch for this man with—"

"We want you to carry the money yourself. I'm sure you see why. The fewer people involved, the better."

"Possible, but difficult."

"Go on."

"Expensive."

"Not a problem."

Silvio stifled a smile. "As for *il Duce*, if it is, in fact, true that he's gone—"

"It's true."

"Then such a man would be difficult to hide for any length of time. I'd be happy to put out the word to my friends. But again, payment would have to be made. A reward, perhaps. An . . . incentive."

"Money's not an object here," Giovanni said curtly.

Silvio thought: *Words that are the anthem of my soul,* but he kept an earnest expression on his face, lips pursed, eyes forward. Politics, he'd long ago learned, was a serious business. Power was involved, not simply money, and the lust for power was much more dangerous than greed. Especially now, especially here, there could be all sorts of complications. "Dangerous," his contacts had said. Strangely enough, he found the idea appealing.

A friend passed, going in the opposite direction. They greeted each other with slaps on the shoulder and a promise of a meal together, later, soon, perhaps even that same evening. "What's fascinating to me," Silvio said when the friend had passed on and they'd circled back to Via Veneto, "is the way information travels in wartime. There are spies everywhere, secrets in every office, every household, every brain. And the trust that must be established in order for things to work out well, that trust is more delicate, even, than the trust required for a marriage to be nourished, the trust between husband and wife."

"Agreed."

"Not to be blunt, of course, but . . . how will you pay me?"

"We just walked by your apartment building," Giovanni told him.

"True."

"I nodded to the man standing near the eucalyptus tree in front. There will be a package delivered to you now. You should delay for ten minutes, take a short walk, have a coffee. The payment is in gold. I think you'll find it satisfactory."

"Second floor, left side," Silvio said. "The landlady loves me, and I trust her completely, so your courier can leave the package in the tiny alcove next to my door with no worry."

Giovanni stopped, extended his hand, let the tiny smile play at the corners of his lips. There did seem something American about the man now, Silvio thought, something not quite cold but *businesslike*. "When you get back to the apartment, your payment will be in the top drawer of your bureau. Beneath the mirror you like to look in so much."

Silvio kept all reaction from his face. "Who, exactly, are you?" he asked very quietly.

Giovanni had not let go of his hand. He seemed, now, less like a *bella figura*, less like a businessman, and more like the *capi* mafiosi Silvio knew so well: killers in silk suits, men who let underlings do the danger-ous work for them but who, if called upon, could take a life as easily as others would dip a piece of bread into a dish of olive oil. "For the time being, I'm Giovanni," the stranger said. "After we've done some work together, if we both survive, maybe I'll tell you more."

Nineteen

Mussolini was put into the back of a car with a young soldier beside him and the older man, the lieutenant colonel, in the front passenger seat. On their way out of the city, they passed German and Italian military vehicles, one or two ordinary cars, a stalled bus, and an ancient church, the front wall of which showed damage from a recent air raid. Mussolini knew that, once or twice a week, a few Allied bombers were getting through the air defenses, and as he stared at the church, another wave of doubt washed over him. If he couldn't protect the capital . . .

The driver was someone he thought he recognized, a tiny nut-brown man with a face as cracked and lined as the stone of a mountainside. He'd seen him somewhere, perhaps even during the March on Rome, the glorious night that had lifted him and his Fascist brethren to power. More than two decades ago, it was; the man would have been in the prime of middle age, small but brave, devoted, willing to sacrifice his life in order to create, out of the mess that was Italy then, a great empire worthy of their Roman ancestors. Mussolini stared at him in the mirror as the man piloted the car through the dark streets. A person, he thought, who could be trusted; a rare creature these days. *Il Duce* willed the man to look at him and, once they were out of the city, heading south and east, the driver glanced once, looked away, glanced again. Mussolini saw recognition there, penitence perhaps. Apology for the disrespect being shown to the great *Duce*. Mussolini made a small nod of forgiveness, the way a king—a real king—might forgive, and the driver moved his eyes back to the road and kept them there.

No one spoke. They went slowly through the dark streets and then, with greater speed, along an even darker highway. Just last week, because of the air raids, he'd ordered most of the streetlamps to be kept off. Now he tried to read the road signs in the dim sweep of the car's running lights, tried to guess where they were taking him. South, it appeared. For one bad moment, he thought he might be in the hands of the plotters of some kind of coup within a coup, and these renegades had captured him—no doubt without the king knowing—and were taking him to meet the Americans in Sicily. He'd be handed over to a smug, pale-skinned general in a tent or in a Palermo palace, interrogated, mocked. The Americans would put him on trial before the world, torment him with questions, try to make him implicate his associates, which, of course, would never happen. He'd starve himself to death first.

For an hour and a half, the wizened old man carried them along the dark highway. *Il Duce* stared out the side window, catching a few of the signs. Pozzi, Anello, Nettuno. They were heading toward the sea.

They slowed again, exited the highway, then pulled off the road and into a parking lot beside a small harbor. He saw a few fishing boats at anchor and a military ship, a cruiser, waiting there beside a lit section of dock, the name *Persefone* painted on its hull. That was it, then: they were sailing by night to Sicily to arrange a surrender. International disgrace. The only way they'd get through the fleet of American warships assembled there was by betraying their own *Duce*, their own homeland. The pain in his stomach was like fire. He wanted to cut himself open and rip out his entrails.

But then the colonel in the passenger seat turned and looked Mussolini in the face. *"Duce,"* he said somberly, "everyone is after you now. The Allies, the Germans, the partisans. We're taking you someplace for your own protection. Kindly cooperate with us."

"Where?" Mussolini asked. The colonel stepped out of the car without answering. *Il Duce* followed. The soldiers formed a loose circle around him, as if, he thought, he might be able to outrun twenty-year-olds. Or as if some partisan in the hills was training a riflescope on the back of his head.

"Where?" he asked again.

The colonel pretended not to hear.

"Where?" he said a third time, in a certain tone of voice that had served him all his life.

"La Maddalena, if it's safe," the colonel said at last, and then, "Please go aboard."

Mussolini followed one of the soldiers up the gangplank. He could feel the others behind him. In the garish light from the captain's bridge, he saw two faces staring at him in awe. Awe and pity. He threw back his shoulders, lifted his chin, strode onto the ship as if it belonged to him. Which, in a certain sense, it did.

La Maddalena. An island a short distance off the north coast of Sardinia. It made sense only if they were going to hand him over to Hitler there. Yes, it made sense. Hitler had been notified—by spies or through official channels, it didn't matter. Italy still controlled the waters of the Tyrrhenian Sea. The Führer would send a small flotilla to carry his friend back to Corsica or France and then to Germany. Perhaps Rachele and the children were being rescued now, as well. Perhaps Hitler would send someone for Claretta, too. He could sit with the Führer in Berlin and direct the war from there. They'd engineer a twin empire, preside over Europe, chase the Americans all the way back to New York . . .

He thought he heard a small explosion behind them, up in the hills to the east. The sailors on deck turned their faces in that direction, then away, and spoke quietly to each other.

"*Duce*, please," the colonel said, "let me show you to your cabin."

Twenty

From long before the day when Luca had convinced her to go into hiding, Sarah had been working to harden herself—against fear, against discomfort, against pain. So when she stepped out of the trees and saw the bloodstains on the front of Luca's clothes and the blood on his arms and hands, she did what she could to mute her reaction. She didn't scream or burst into tears or batter him with questions, as the prewar Sarah would have done. She reacted, of course—how could you not react to the sight of that much blood on a loved one's body? She let out a half-stifled shout, ran across the last few meters, and tried to embrace him—he motioned her back—but she was conscious of holding inside her a flood of emotion, of keeping panic at bay, of showing him how strong she could be.

Without asking a single question, she went into the cabin for his clothes, then led him up to the spring. While he bathed in the small clearing, backpack kept within reach, she wrapped his bloody shirt and trousers into a tight bundle, carried them into the trees, and buried them under a pile of dirt and leaves. They hadn't said four words to each other. She went most of the way back but paused at the edge of the clearing and watched him without letting him see her. His black hair had grown long now and rested in curls on the back of his neck. His legs and right arm were packed tight with muscles that flexed beautifully as he moved, but his left arm looked as if it had been transplanted from another person. A boy's arm attached to a man's body.

Because she was standing to his left side—the side of his blind eye—she knew he couldn't see her. She was able to watch him bathe, and there was a strange intimacy to that, his hands moving over his own naked body, his vulnerability when he bent forward and splashed water on his face and combed fingers through his wet hair. She was suddenly aware of the heat of the day. She pulled her dress up over her head, smelling her own sweat—sweet, he said it was—feeling the material brush lightly over her skin. She didn't try to be quiet and, as she knew it would, the sound made him turn and look. His beautiful smile bloomed—quick, cut off before it had fully formed, almost a prewar smile—and then he stood and came over to her.

They went a little way farther into the trees and made love on a patch of mossy ground, Luca on his back. "You'll have to wash again," she said, but he seemed unable to speak.

From the moment he brushed his palms across her breasts and nipples, Sarah felt a kind of electric current surge through her. Physical, yes, but something beyond physical, too, as if he were carrying her into another world, a place of light and warmth and the complete absence of fear. In its place, another feeling—*love* did not do the feeling justice—that she'd tried so often to describe in her poems. A shimmering comfort was the closest she'd been able to come, *un conforto scintillante*, as if the cells of her body were humming joyous background music to something beyond the bodily world, a bird singing out in darkness.

It had been this way from their first kiss—fourteen months ago on the bus as they approached the lakeside park in Tremezzo. Luca's left hand had half the strength of his right, but this wasn't about strength. He ran his fingertips up and down her sides, breasts to hip bones, touching her so lightly, it was as if a handful of feathers were being brushed across her body, and when he held her against him, bare skin to bare skin, everything else simply disappeared. There was no war, no

German soldiers looking for her, no Judaism or Catholicism, nothing but her thumping heart and the electricity.

She weighed so little on top of him. She could feel his fingers on the ribs of her back now, tracing, stroking. She moved gently, in almost complete silence, her hair swinging back and forth against the sides of her face as she rocked over him, the electricity evolving into heat, as if her insides had turned molten. She was making noises now, rhythmic but quiet, then falling on top of him, chest to chest again, both of them breathing hard, the war, the world, slowly coming back into focus around them.

She lay against him, letting her breath slowly settle. There was a dimension to the lovemaking that had been missing in the glorious days before the Germans arrived, when they'd used a friend's apartment on the lakeside road—the *statale*—and made love to a chorus of *motorini* and bus engines, their flesh firm, their bellies full. In those times, she'd had lucrative work translating English articles for scientific journals, and once a month, she was required to travel to Genoa. Luca would take leave of his stonemason job and his mountain excursions and meet her there, and they'd sink into the luxurious hotel bed with sheets that were soft and cool and so finely woven they seemed like a human embrace. He'd caress her gently, and they'd tease each other for as long as they could bear it, Luca running the backs of his fingers up the insides of her thighs, painting her neck and ears with small kisses. Afterward, she'd fall into the deepest sleep and dream so often of having children that she wondered if she might, in fact, be pregnant.

In the morning, there would be an elaborate hotel breakfast—eggs, cheese, pastries, cold cuts, coffee, fruit—and they'd talk freely about their work, their plans for the day, their future.

This new dimension was more love than lust, a tender compensation for the harshness of wartime. She was anxious to ask about the blood and afraid to at the same time. Anxious to tell him her news but wanting to wait a bit, to savor the feeling of his flesh against hers, the smell of the forest on his skin, to try, again, even for a few minutes, to forget the outside world. When they'd been quiet for a while, lying against each other, lightly coated in sweat, a gentle rain started to tap on the leaves above them. Luca was flat on his back, she on her side against him, and she said, "Do you want to tell me?" and felt him flinch, as if she'd jerked him back into a harsher orbit.

It took him almost a full minute to speak, and then it came pouring out—the scene at Piazzale Loreto, the train, the man, the knife, the *lepiota*. By the time he was finished, tears were streaming down her face. On the heels of a story like this, she couldn't bear to speak the words, to present him with her great secret gift.

"I feel," he said, then fell silent. "I feel like an angry beast has come to live inside me. When I was standing over him, I wanted to just keep stabbing and stabbing, to cut him into pieces. When I was at Loreto and seeing all that, I wanted to get a gun and shoot all of them. I wanted to go to Rome and go into Mussolini's office and shoot him in the face and—"

She put her fingers over his mouth and then on his chest. "You're twenty" was all she could think to say. "We're only twenty."

"I feel like I'm a hundred and twenty."

Just then, Sarah heard something like what she'd heard that morning. A rustling in the trees on the far side of the clearing. A pause. What sounded like footsteps. Luca heard it, too, and reached quietly for his backpack and drew out his knife. He turned his head all the way around so he could see the spring. Another few seconds and out of the trees stepped a wild boar, only the second one she'd ever seen. It was a hideous creature, brown-black and covered in coarse hair, all snout and ears and humped back and short, ugly legs. She felt Luca relax beside her. "The blood," he whispered.

The boar went straight to the pool, sniffed, lowered his snout to the red-tinted water, then began to lap at it greedily, grunting with pleasure, twitching its small rough tail.

Twenty-One

Since the start of the war, one of the things Don Claudio had always found most difficult was the long, empty stretch of daylight after the conclusion of Mass. His counseling duties had shrunk almost to zero. His invitations to meals at the homes of parishioners had abruptly ceased. The rectory staff—a cook, a maid, a junior priest—had fled Sant'Abbondio for parts unknown, so, unless he made the difficult walk back and forth into town, there was no one to sit with and discuss life, no one with whom to play cards or talk theology or even to watch as she prepared a meal. What did that leave him? The secret duties were few at this point, new and coated in terror: the monthly trip to Milan, the passing on of an occasional message. The rest of his days were empty. There was only so much time an ordinary man could devote to prayer. There was little now with which to fashion a lunch, just odds and ends of food brought to him by parishioners. One old tomato. A heel of bread. Thanks to Maria's trees, he had oil, but no salt. Thanks to Luca, a bottle of wine that, he suspected guiltily, might have been stolen.

He sat in the rectory kitchen and cut a slice from the tomato, soaked it in a dish of oil, broke the bread and dipped it into the oil, took a small bite, sliced off another piece no larger than a communion wafer, had a sip of the wine. Wartime wine. He grimaced at the taste of it. He took as much time over the meal as he could, then sat beneath the stone outcropping of the roof and said a leisurely rosary while looking down over the lake. That done, he went up to his room and lay in bed, hoping to sleep for an hour. But despite the bad night, he couldn't seem to sink into the world of dreams. His mind brought him back to his sins—he supposed that was, in fact, the earthly part of his punishment. He recalled his hours with Rebecca Zinsi, the one lover of his life, their great, illicit passion. A sin, clearly, a breaking of his sacred vows, a surrender to passion, to the flesh.

Still, he had never quite been able to make himself feel completely guilty about it. What was it? A handful of weeks twenty years ago. Perhaps this lack of regret came from the fact that a child had been the product of their secret union, a beautiful young woman now. Rebecca had been stoic in her disgrace, carrying her large belly through the town and, he suspected, never, not to any soul, admitting the true paternity. No, she'd told no one—he was sure of it. But how many times she must have been asked! Mocked. Tormented. And not once had she spoken the words that would have ruined him. For a time, he'd wanted to leave the priesthood and marry her. They'd had a number of whispered conversations about it; he'd offered, sincerely, on multiple occasions, but she wouldn't hear of it. The guilt was too heavy on her even without that, she said.

He'd revealed his secret only to the man who was now the archbishop of Milan, and only in the confidence of the confessional. A secret that would never be shared.

The daily Mass was finished, his rosary, his lunch, his musings on the past . . . and there remained hours and hours of daylight to get through.

He washed himself and made the long, steep downhill walk into the center of Mezzegra in a light summer rain. At the Bar Lake Como, he found his coterie of old friends, men he'd known since grammar school. Among them in these times, no one had much money, but Orlando the owner let them run an endless tab. "When the troubles finish," he liked to say, "you will pay me triple price!" They joked and bantered in the local dialect, Comasco, as different from Italian as English from Russian, and they knew their priest well enough, and had known him long enough, that when Don Claudio appeared and took a seat with them, the jokes became, if anything, more ribald not less. And yet not one of them seemed to suspect the province of his secret sin.

"Heard the news?" Mario asked quietly—the way they all spoke now—but in a tone of muted excitement.

Don Claudio sipped his espresso—weak but passable—and shook his head. Isolated in his church at the top of the hill for days at a time, saying Mass to his four elderly women, reading no newspapers, hearing no radio, he sometimes felt completely cut off from the outside world. It was not an unpleasant feeling.

Mario ran his eyes in a loop around their dark corner of the bar— one other group of customers, two couples, unfamiliar—then out at the street windows, suddenly ablaze in sun as the rain clouds parted. "*Il Duce* . . . gone."

"Gone? How, gone? To Berlin?"

More headshaking. The others joined in, barely above a whisper. "People are saying the king deposed him. Three days ago."

"Deposed? How deposed?"

Mario looked around the circle of friends, held on to the information as if keeping the last glass of a fine bottle of wine for a late-arriving relative, and then, in a low voice, "Gone. No one knows where."

Don Claudio hid his mouth behind the rim of the espresso cup. Perhaps, through the love affair and the years of pretending that had followed it, God had been training him for the work he now did. The ability to keep secrets, to deceive. The chance to overcome an old cowardice it seemed he'd been born with and had carried like a hideous birthmark all his days. This time, though, there was no deception, except perhaps to hide a measure of his joy: he'd heard nothing of this and still only half believed it.

Mario and the others were happy about the news—they were, of course, all of the same politics—but, even there, even among friends, it was best to bury one's true feelings. The Germans had ears in the soffits, eyes in the window mullions. And it wasn't just the Germans or the OVRA or the Blackshirts. Even after all that had happened, Mussolini still had his defenders among ordinary Italians. They remembered the days before he'd taken power, the violence, the chaos, the strikes, the marauding gangs, the sense that anything could happen. Full of doubt themselves, they'd been seduced by his exaggerated self-certainty. And their egos weren't immune to his promises to bring Italy back to greatness.

Orlando came and served them a dish of stale croissants. "The best I can do," he said. Kind as the bar owner was, he had a quiet, almost secretive demeanor, and the men did not speak openly in front of him. No one knew his politics, not exactly, not with enough confidence to bring him into their circle when certain subjects arose. When he'd returned to his kitchen, Mario said, "Now the war is over."

But Don Claudio was already wandering the dark avenues of a different calculation. He didn't think the war was over, couldn't let his hopes stretch that far. The men sat and chewed the stale pastries, sipped at their coffees as if they'd been brewed with the last available water and beans on earth. Their priest tried to puzzle out what the news could mean. The majority of Italians had never been fond of Italy's entrance into the war. Of late, with the losses in North Africa, especially the defeat at El Alamein, that sentiment had only grown stronger. Naturally enough, they blamed Mussolini. His little-boy admiration of Hitler, his alliance with the Devil. During the previous week's card game, Mario had told him there were massive strikes in the factories in Milan and that the Alpini—Italy's best fighters—were rumored to be singing songs about *il Duce*'s demise. If Italy had ever been a solid pillar in the Nazi house of terror, it was clear to everyone Don Claudio knew that the pillar was badly cracked now, shaking, perhaps about to collapse, leaving Hitler's house tilting sideways. It only made sense—again, as the rumors had it—that the Führer was pressing Mussolini to cede all military control, to let Field Marshal Kesselring and the other savages give orders to Italian troops. Now, if it were true Mussolini was gone, that would certainly happen. Any Italian soldiers left in the fight would have Germans at their backs, machine guns pointed. Or they'd mutiny and force a civil conflict, brother against brother. *No, he thought, no, the war is far from over.* But he couldn't bring himself to say those words aloud.

When they'd sat there for several hours, his friends—too old for military conscription, thank God—collected their cards and tallied up small victories and losses, sums that would never be paid. One by one they sighed, stood, thanked their host, shook hands or embraced, and took their leave.

Don Claudio felt light-headed. Lack of food, he told himself. He stepped into the sunlight and stood on the sidewalk in front of Orlando's bar and tried, again, to make sense of it all. *Il Duce* gone. *Il Duce* gone! For a long time, he didn't move, returning the greetings of neighbors and friends by reflex, running various scenarios through his brain, trying to see into the future.

Hitler would never allow Italy to be lost. If Italian soldiers mutinied—and surely now many of them would—they'd be replaced by better-trained Germans with no sentimental feelings whatsoever toward Italian life, Italian women. Mussolini's laws—a violent assertion of Italian manhood—would be replaced by those of an even more vicious and insecure devil.

As he was standing there, an SS officer he'd never before seen came walking along the sidewalk toward him. The man was short and barrel shaped with jowls, a long nose, and large ears, and he was carrying a riding crop in his right hand. What a strange race of men they were!

"Buongiorno, Padre," the German said with a thick accent, stopping beside Don Claudio and running his eyes from the priest's hairline to his plain brown shoes and back again.

"*Buongiorno.*"

"I wonder if you could help me. My colleagues and I have noticed an increase in 'accidents' in this area. Broken telephone wires, damaged roadways. Sabotage, we suspect. I wonder if you might know of the person or people behind such criminal acts."

"I haven't heard any of this," Don Claudio said.

The man was pursing his lips and staring hard into Don Claudio's eyes. "No?"

The priest shook his head, even dizzier now.

"We have food."

"I'm glad you have food. You should share it with the people of this town. That's what Christ would want of you."

The officer laughed. "Food for you, I meant, in exchange for information."

"I'm a priest, Officer. I have no information except that which pertains to eternal judgment."

"No local secrets? From your confessional, perhaps?"

"None."

The German stared at him without blinking. "We are not unlike your Christ," he said at last. "A kind people, if you obey us. If not, we exact a punishment like the burning in hell."

It was everything Don Claudio could do not to look away. The man was surrounded by a vapor of the purest evil. He could feel the soles of his feet trembling. "I know nothing of these accidents, Officer. No one speaks of them. I haven't seen them with my own eyes. The first I heard was—"

"Fine, *Padre*. But if I discover you are lying, I'll have my men tie you to a chair, and I will pull out your teeth, one by one, with a pliers."

The shaking had moved up into Don Claudio's legs. He looked away, then back. "I am not a brave man, Officer. A priest not a soldier. Faced with such a threat, I would surely tell you if I knew anything."

The officer turned and spat, then slapped the riding crop against his own leg once and walked away.

Don Claudio turned to watch him go—the ridiculous jodhpurs, the riding crop—he was a short, ugly caricature of a man who, by virtue of his führer's insanity, had been given a terrible power over other men and women. The power had ruined him spiritually. Don Claudio believed that without any doubt. Still, his whole body was shaking, and he could not take his eyes from the man's back.

If Mussolini was, in fact, finished, then these were the new masters.

Twenty-Two

By the evening on which Maria made her grim hundred-meter walk to the Rossos' back door for the fifth time, everyone in Mezzegra had heard the news. Mussolini was gone—no one knew where. Rumors whirled around the lakeside towns like flocks of frightened birds: that *il Duce* had been flown to Berlin to plan the cessation of northern Italy and to form, with Austria, a massive German state; that the German language would soon be taught in schools as far south as Naples; that Catholicism would be outlawed; that the Americans were already in Rome and marching up the peninsula unhindered; that Hitler was dead in a suicide pact with *il Duce*. The Italian imagination took them on endless voyages, she thought, but the only reality was this walk past her olive trees and across the empty weed-strewn lot where the Rossos had once raised goats in a fenced-in corner and planted cabbages and tomatoes and fennel and eggplant, this bottle of oil in her hand, the growling hunger in her belly, a friend in the attic, and the song of terror that played in their ears night and day.

Familiar with the ritual now, Maria stepped through the back door without bothering to knock and began her preparations. As she worked, she could hear the men carousing in the dining room, but the redhead came and stood not far from her in the kitchen. He had a glass in his hand, the sour-smelling beer they seemed to prefer, and as she cut up one of their fine, firm onions and set the slices in a pan, he watched her carefully. "You brought your own oil," he said in a friendly way, in his understandable but mangled Italian. "A new bottle." *You brung you the oil,* was the way it sounded in her ear. She thought: *They rape our women; they mutilate our language.*

She nodded, half turning her head but not looking at him.

"Drink some," he said after a pause. Not so friendly now.

She turned her head farther and met his eyes. *"Scusa?"*

"Drink some. Just a swallow. I have orders; I have to make sure you aren't poisoning us."

She couldn't show the slightest hesitation. She turned away from the stove and, keeping her eyes fixed on the redhead's wide face, put the bottle to her lips and drank.

He watched, as if expecting her to fall over dead, but after a minute, he gave her a rueful smile, almost an apology, and nodded.

The redhead went back to his coarse friends. Maria went on with her cooking, but now, even if she had to consume it herself, she wished she'd mixed some of Rebecca's shit in with the piss and oil. How she hated these men. Prices of pasta had tripled for Italians; the Germans had boxes of it. Decent vegetables were as rare as gold; they had a pantry full. She purposely overcooked the spaghetti, bringing to their loud table pasta so soft and lacking in flavor that even her kindly Sabatino would have refused to eat a second bite. Spaghetti, tomatoes, onions, oil. Their fresh bread, butter—something Italians never put on bread. They even had Parmesan cheese, the bastards, and grated it carelessly over their plates with their military knives, spilling some on the table. The tall bald one—their leader, it seemed—caught her looking and pressed his finger down into the yellow crumbs, then held the finger up to her. "Lick," he said.

She pretended not to understand and was about to turn away when another of the men grabbed her roughly by the arm. She sensed the redhead was about to say something in her defense, but he pressed his lips together.

"Lick," the tall one said again. *"Lecca!"*

Maria hesitated, felt her forearm squeezed in a vise grip. The man let go; she went over and licked the cheese from the tall one's finger.

"Say thank you."

"Thank you."

He nodded drunkenly, said, "Next time I make you suck," and waved her out the door. Walking across the lot, she spat eleven times. The flame of anger in her empty belly had turned to a furnace. But were they stupid, these men? Hateful, evil, vulgar, yes, but also stupid? Did they imagine the Italians would love them for this? Respect them? Obey them? Keep from killing them if they had the chance?

She thought of her Sabatino, forced to fight for them in Russia, and she spat again and brushed at her eyes.

Twenty-Three

Luca rose before dawn and was putting on his clothes when he heard Sarah stir. He saw her sit up in the shadows. Gaunt face, tired eyes, chestnut hair, still miraculously beautiful to him, even with the loss of so much of her strength and with small welts of mosquito bites freckling the skin of her neck. The vision of her in the sheets, one bare leg showing, made him think of the time he'd first seen her, walking along a corridor in middle school. Braids swinging, a smile like the sun. Their mothers had been friends forever, and they'd seen each other occasionally in town, but that was the first time he'd thought of her in a different way. It took him six years to find the courage to ask her out. Six years.

"Luca," she said quietly, and something in her voice made him look at her more closely.

He knew what was coming. They'd had this conversation before. "I'll find you another place to live now, a house," he said. Keeping her here was selfish of him; he knew that. He risked so much, was willing to sacrifice so much, but he wanted this woman for himself. In a safe house, there would be fewer chances to sleep together—their only pleasure in life now—and he'd have to put his trust in the other people who lived there. Here, secure in the belief that no German would hike up through the brambles to such a remote place, all he needed to trust were the trees and stones and Sarah's incredible force of will.

"It's not that," she said. Her face was composed, even more beautiful now. "I'm . . . with child."

He studied her for the time it took to draw and release a breath, and then he went over to the makeshift bed and sat down beside her and held her. "The best thing in life," he said into the hair above her ear, "the thing I want most in life . . . at the worst time."

He could feel her shaking her head against his neck. She pushed him to arm's length and met his eyes. "The best time," she said. "They won't bother a pregnant woman. I'll start to show soon. I can be a courier and help with the work you do. We can use doctors and hospitals. I can visit there with no suspicion."

He didn't answer.

"Other women do it. You said that yourself."

"Other women aren't Jewish."

"Some of them are. You could get me false documents; I know you could. And I'm withering away here. Look at me!"

He wanted to lie to her. It was true that he could get the documents; he knew exactly where he could get them. But as a grayish light seeped through the window, he understood that there was another truth: he'd been clinging to a vision, a fantasy. Even with everything he'd lived through in the past three years—Mussolini's madness, the appearance of German troops, the friends and relatives sent to die in Ethiopia, Greece, Libya, his own father on the Russian steppes—he'd still clung to a vision of this beautiful woman as his wife and the two of them raising children in a small, lovely house on the slopes west of the lake, growing food in their yard, taking the kids on outings to the mountains and the sea, making love in a soft bed on winter mornings.

There was nothing wrong with the vision. Except that he'd never actually shared it with Sarah. He had no idea if it matched her fantasies. He'd been perfectly content to play the role of partisan hero, making trouble for the Germans in the mountains he knew as well as he knew the planes of her face, and keep her here like some kind of flower in the pages of a book. He'd seen other partisan women, yes. Two to be exact. The war had only recently come to Italian soil, and the movement was in its earliest stages. They were strong and brave and as willing to die for a free Italy as he was. Yet he'd never been able to put Sarah into that picture, and her pregnancy would make doing so even more difficult. Inside him now, as he watched the light change on her face and saw the hope and courage in her eyes, two halves of him did battle. "We've talked about this, Sarah. We—"

"I can't stay here indefinitely."

"I know. You're right. I . . . But now . . . the child . . ."

"I can't just sit here all day, Luca, writing poems while people are being slaughtered!"

"Yes, I know. I agree. But . . . can we talk later?"

She nodded. "Tonight?"

"Tomorrow or the day after. I have to go. Do you have enough food?"

She nodded, watched him. "Can you get me the documents?"

"I'll try. I think so. It might take a little time."

"You'll promise?"

"Yes."

"You don't think they're following you now, that they know what you're doing?"

He shook his head. "It was one man. A Blackshirt. I shouldn't have gone to Loreto."

"You'll see your mother? You'll ask her about my mother?"

"If I can, yes, of course, always. Please be careful. Now especially. With . . . our child."

"Yes, and you." She studied his face, as if, he thought, she was looking for the killer there, the killer who would soon be a father. "I'm at the bottom of my patience, staying here," she said, "really." She lifted her face to his, and he thought there was something new in the feeling of her lips against his, a new hope or a different kind of fear.

Twenty-Four

Mussolini had always enjoyed being out on the sea at night. Even in a boat like this one—*Persefone* was a grumbling rusted wreck bumping along in a vapor of diesel exhaust—even with the uniformed soldiers lurking at either end, watching him while pretending not to, as if they thought he might leap overboard and swim for the coast of Sardinia, even with all that, he enjoyed the sight of the stars and the smell of the sea and the unpredictable movement of the steel deck beneath his feet. It felt like flying, like freedom, and, he thought, he hadn't really known freedom in twenty-three years. Those years had been about service, sacrifice. Every ounce of his strength and energy had gone to his country . . . and the people had responded. They'd adored him, stood in line to catch a glimpse of him, named their sons—and even some cities—after him. He felt, now, that he was owed something for all those years of work, worry, and sacrifice. His freedom, if nothing else.

The moon had not yet risen, and once they were far enough from the lights of the shore, he began to see stars in great numbers. A pleasant thought swept in across the bitter interior landscape on which he'd been traveling for the past twelve hours: the stars were always there, always. The same must be true, no matter what happened now, for the core of his reputation. Few men, a handful of men, really, had made history. In every case he could think of, there had been times in the lives of those men when their greatness was obscured—just as stars were not seen in the day. Napoleon had been imprisoned. Jesus Christ had been arrested, mocked, dragged through the streets. Caesar had been stabbed by a mob of supposed friends.

But their legacy lived on. And he was in a league with them, a piece of history. No one could ever take that away. No matter what they did to him now, these conspirators, no matter what the Allies had in mind, the name Mussolini would survive.

Lost in his musing, he didn't realize that the captain had come up and was standing beside him at the rail, hovering at a respectful distance like a waiter anticipating a dinner order. "Are you hungry, *Duce*?"

He glanced at the man, then away.

"Please do not be angry with me. I am following orders."

"Given by whom?"

"Badoglio . . . and the king."

Mussolini spat over the side of the boat. "Badoglio is a nobody, a former patriot, a bad general. I made him who he is."

"Head of government now."

"Don't joke with me in such a way."

"Not joking, *Duce*. On his orders, we are taking you away . . . for your safety."

"Safety from whom?" Mussolini barked. "From what? My own people? My German friends? The Allies, who are a thousand kilometers away? Badoglio himself?"

"I'm not a man of politics, *Duce*. But forgive me if I speak the truth . . . I think there are many people now who would want you captured or harmed."

"People have always wanted to harm me! I survived three assassination attempts! Three!"

"I know, *Duce*, but this time—"

"And so you are taking me where? A place where there are no people? Outer space? To live on the moon? On Saturn? Or are you taking me to be drowned, to be thrown off the boat at sea and never heard from again?"

"I would never allow it."

"Then turn the boat around and bring me back to Rome. I want to speak to the king personally. I want to take a shovel and smash Badoglio's head into pulp. I have been duped."

A stubborn silence. Mussolini turned and looked at the man again. Black hair that stood up straight from the top of his head, like a boy's. Two or three days' growth of dark stubble. A chin that went sideways below his mouth, as if he'd come out of his mother's womb whispering a secret to someone beside him. The man seemed sincere, a good man. Still, he was slim and not muscular, and Mussolini had an all but insuppressible urge to pick him up by the knees and topple him over the rail.

"We are taking you to La Maddalena, as I said," the man told him earnestly, apologetically. "If we determine that it's safe, we will have you stay in a private home for a time. The helpers there, a man and a woman, have been preparing for your arrival."

"And then?"

"And then I don't know, *Duce*. I have orders to leave you there if it seems safe and then return to the mainland."

Mussolini grunted and looked away, a dismissal. The captain waited at the rail for another minute, then mumbled an apology and went back to his bridge.

Mussolini heard the growl of an airplane propeller, not far to their north, angry dog in another universe. *A British bomber,* he thought. *Or Hitler looking for me.* Another man whose reputation, whose greatness, would live on, no matter what the cowards and fools did to him. He looked up and saw that the plane, a bit closer now, was flying at low altitude and with a minimum of running lights.

So perhaps it was an Allied spy plane and he was, as the captain suggested, being hunted. A helpless rabbit being moved from place to place as the hunters closed in with their rifles and dogs. A bird. A wild boar. If they did leave him on La Maddalena, a place that, despite its beauty, had always made him vaguely uneasy, he would ask for a pistol. If the Allies came to take him, they'd find a dead man.

Twenty-Five

From Hitler's secret bunker in East Prussia, Captain Otto Skorzeny was flown back to Munich and then to Rome. There, he was given a room and an office in the German headquarters in Frascati, at the city's southernmost edge. The building—four stories, stucco, gray as rain—included a windowless room in which prisoners were interrogated, but that room was on the far side of the building and one floor belowground, and the only time he heard the screams was on the first morning, when he went to introduce himself to General Kurt Student—who had an office nearby and who seemed, judging by the look on his face, to take pleasure from the sounds.

Immediately after reporting to the general, Skorzeny began assembling his team: Radl, his right-hand man; Goss, his secretary; the half dozen available commandos who'd worked on the invasions of France and Belgium. After lunch, he sat down with SS *Obersturmführer* Selenzen, interim assistant head of intelligence for the Italian front. Selenzen was a short, fat, crafty man with jowls and large ears, steel-rimmed spectacles pinched into place by round cheeks, a Bavarian accent, and a passion for chess, sweet Mosel wines, and young boys. The last interest made Skorzeny squeamish, but Selenzen was said to be a master at raking his fingers through the moldy undergrowth of Italian society and coming up with nuggets of information. Radl told him Selenzen would hold these nuggets in his fist until just the right moment—a key meeting, usually one attended by General Student or Field Marshal Kesselring—and then open his hand and display them with a toothy smile. The information he gathered was more than enough to encourage his superiors to leave him to his tawdry pleasures.

The smile, however, was not in evidence on that rainy Roman morning. Selenzen sat in a leather chair with his fat thighs spread and his lips pursed. "I've just come from the Lake Como area," he said slowly, flicking a piece of fried egg from his uniform and onto the floor, "and I've reached the conclusion that the Italians are not warriors. You know this, Captain, I'm sure. Not brave, not warriors, not worthy of us. However, they are masters at deception, at secret-keeping, at making feints and false moves."

"In other words, you have no idea where Mussolini is."

"In other words, yes, for the time being. It's been only a few days, Captain, and I've been focusing on other matters. I have my pawns out in the streets. One makes the assault on the king gradually. First the pawns, then the knights are moved into place. The bishops. A period of attrition, and then perhaps the queen and the castles come into play. When do you want him by?"

"Now. Today. This instant," Skorzeny said.

Selenzen let out a low chuckle, a few notes of sarcastic mirth. He squeezed the bottom of his nose between thumb and forefinger. "We know he had a meeting with the king, but we're not exactly on good terms with the king, as you must be aware."

"You have no one inside the king's circle?"

Selenzen shook his head, making the big cheeks wobble like the hindquarters of a beast.

"No one in the police? The military?"

"We have people there, yes, but from the looks of things, there are, outside the king's inner circle, possibly five men who know where Mussolini has been taken. We're squeezing every source, though. Every source."

"Squeeze harder," Skorzeny told him.

Twenty-Six

Don Claudio found four decent plums at the market near the Bar
Lake Como, paid for them with small coins, and started back home.
The route to the Church of Sant'Abbondio took him along a painfully
steep hill, one kilometer in length. He considered the walk peniten-
tial. Difficult as it was for a man of his age and corpulence, the priest
accepted the penance willingly, as he accepted all life's difficulties. At
the base of this acceptance was the belief that the world had been made
with a divine logic and fairness at its heart, even though that logic
and certainly that fairness was, from time to time at various points in
history, invisible to the human eye. Why did pain exist? Why did evil
exist? Why had God allowed men like Hitler and Mussolini to come
to power? These questions were, to his mind, simply beyond the realm
of human understanding. Answers, he believed, would come only after
death. The Merciful One would judge all souls then, would separate
the good from the evil. He'd given his adult life to the Church, to his
parishioners. He'd sinned a few times, yes. But he'd been a devoted
priest. That devotion, he hoped, would save him.

Still, the walk back to his church caused him a fair amount of physical distress. Since the start of the war in Europe, and especially since the
first day they'd seen the soldiers of the Reich on Italian soil, and most
especially when he made this walk, Don Claudio had had occasion to
wonder how he'd behave under torture. The recent conversation with

the short German officer had done nothing to soften such thoughts. How would he behave? Not well, he supposed. He was not a stoic, not known for his courage nor brave with pain; even the small Lenten sacrifices he made—giving up wine for six weeks, rising early for prayer—seemed to him to exact a price out of all proportion to his willpower, as if the cells of his lungs were being consumed by tiny fires, as if, now, the enormous suffering of hell was reflected in miniature in the beads of sweat on his arms and face as he climbed. It wasn't his fault, not really. Even on the war diet—consuming a third of what he used to consume—he'd shed only ten kilos, less than half of what he needed to lose. Not his fault.

A dozen times on the way up the hill, he had to stop and catch his breath. During each of those pauses, he said a quiet Ave Maria—even once nodding to a passing German staff car as he recited the prayer. An officer in the back seat stared at him and seemed to be making mental notes: *check on the fat priest; who knows what goes on in his church?*

At last, Don Claudio reached the soccer field just below Sant'Abbondio: fifty or sixty more steps and he could rest. The grass on the field was baking in the afternoon sun, but the church itself, all dark marble, dark wood, and walls thick enough to keep out the winter chill, would be cool and still, a refuge of body and spirit.

Once he'd wiped the sweat from his neck and forehead and set down on the pew nearest the door the paper bag that contained the four plums, he made his way to the vestry and the metal offering box. He found the key on his key ring, turned it in the lock, lifted the oblong door, and saw there what he had hoped and dreaded to see: a slip of paper next to a lira note and a few coins. Hoped, because the note meant Luca was still alive. Dreaded, because the message—delivered while he was at Bar Lake Como with his friends, no doubt, the young man slipping into and out of the church like a breath of wind—would contain his instructions. Those instructions might lead him anywhere, including the German torture cells. Even in the cool of the nave, he felt sweat form instantly on his palms. He was, he thought, no hero.

He pinched the bill and brushed the coins into one hand with the fingertips of the other. Before taking out the note, he surveyed the interior of his church. It was not beyond the realm of possibility that a spy might be hiding in the shadows, a German soldier come to torment him or even, perhaps, to make a confession. There were, Luca had told him, safe houses up in the hills, but no place, not even a church, was completely safe in these times.

Sure that he was alone, Don Claudio grasped the slip of paper between the top knuckles of his second and third fingers, drew it out, and unfolded it. Printed there in pencil was a capital letter *M*, what might have been either an upside-down *U* or an arch, and a small arrow with the numeral two. After studying the marks for a moment, he understood. He closed and locked the offering box, carried the note over to the bank of votive candles, held it there until it burned almost to his skin, then dropped the ash on the marble floor at his feet and the last bit of paper into the red glass that held the nearest candle. He scuffed the ashes and went to his room to make a late lunch of two fresh plums and half a glass of wine. The other plums would go to Maria and Rebecca.

M was for Milan, the arch for the archbishop, and the arrow and two meant two more days. He had his assignment, then: travel to Milan on Friday to pay a visit to Archbishop Maniscalco, surely the bravest and best of men. He sighed, raised up a prayer for courage, ate his meager lunch, then repaired to his bedroom—visions of pliers and bloody teeth running through his mind's eye—for a late-afternoon rest.

This was the power of evil, he thought before drifting into a light sleep. Nothing need be actually done to you, just the idea of it, the rumor of it, the sense of the possibility of it. That was enough.

Twenty-Seven

From the cabin, Luca hiked down slowly toward the town, a walk of nearly two hours, keeping in the trees. He stood behind the church for a long time, watching to make sure no one would notice him. He saw Don Claudio leave the rectory and make his way toward the town and his weekly rendezvous with friends. The back door was unlocked, as he knew it would be. He slipped inside, made his quick delivery, then ducked into the woods again and began to climb a steep, serpentine path, northwest toward the Swiss border.

He wouldn't cross the border, of course—it would take three hours or more to hike that far, and the chances of encountering a German guard were too high. Instead, he followed the path for an hour, sweating but not really breathing hard, until it disappeared into a delta of small stones. At that point, any curious hiker or soldier on patrol who didn't know the terrain would surely give up. Beyond the delta of stones lay an even steeper terrain of dense underbrush and five-meter cliff faces, vipers in the shadows, wild boar in the trees. Impassable, it seemed. But his father had taken him here, too, as a boy, so he knew it was possible to go on. This section of hills was too high and too dry and not shaded enough for mushroom hunting, but his father had loved the high terrain, and they would sometimes come up here on a summer night, provisioned with food his mother had packed. They'd climb rock faces using hands and feet (a challenge for Luca with his one weak arm—his father encouraged but never helped him), crawl beneath brambles, search for berries and walnuts. Often as not, they'd go as far as the border—fences and signs even then, but no guards—and have a meal there. When darkness fell, they'd wrap themselves in blankets, study the stars for a while, and then sleep. His father's passion had led him to the Alpine Corps and so, most likely, to his death—they'd heard nothing from him in many months. But perhaps it had also led his son to the work he was doing now. Maybe, Luca thought, all the world turned according to some great design like that, with good and evil locked eternally in a fierce war, the battleground moving across the globe and through time, individual soldiers guided by mysterious forces they could never discern. Maybe, instead of some man-in-the-sky God, there was a system of firing brain cells, elaborate beyond imagining. Maybe even his killing of the felt-hatted man was part of that grand design. He did not pretend to know.

From the stony delta, he turned parallel to the slope, worked his way painstakingly through hundreds of meters of brush, using his knife and wire cutters in places but trying not to leave too obvious a trail of broken and cut branches. He came out on a narrow path he remembered well. His father had told him once that the path might have been used by the people who'd inhabited this area thousands of years before it was called Italy. Every twenty or thirty steps, the footpath was broken by brambles or small rockslides, but Luca was certain no one else knew about it and even more certain the Germans would be too lazy to find it or, if they happened to find it, too lazy to follow it. He went along for two hours, stopping once to drink from the water bottle and once when he came upon the pleasant surprise of a bush of ripe elderberries—bitter but nourishing.

In late afternoon, he crossed a small grassy ridge, then a stream where he filled his stoppered bottle and splashed his face, and then, finally, a rock overhang similar to the one where he'd rested the day before—one wall and a stony, slanted ceiling. He sat there and chewed on bread and his last piece of cheese, thought about Sarah and their child and the things she had said, and waited for darkness.

Whenever the wind puffed a light gust in his direction, he could hear engines downshifting. German cars and troop transports they would be, making their descent along the hairpin turns at the pace a man could run. They came into Italy through the pass from Austria, moved between the western side of the lake and the Swiss border and then along the crooked roads that led to the *statale* and, eventually, to Milan and points south. The Nazis were filling the country with armament now—tanks and artillery and troop transports and motorcycles—pouring their hatred and violence into Italy. And the Blackshirts were welcoming them.

Great care had to be used in fighting them. Great care, skill, courage, and a large measure of luck.

Sabotage was his main work, his piece on the chessboard of the grand strategy of resistance. The archbishop had connected him to a local farmer named Gennaro Masso and, through Masso, to three men who worked the hills north of Gravedona. Though it frustrated him not to be asked to do something larger, and though he didn't like the men, he had so far obeyed them without question. Small acts of . . . *disturbance*, that was what they expected from him—the placing of the occasional pebble in the jackboot of the German giant. He liked to think a better man for the job could not have been chosen because the sabotage had to be made to look like merely the quirks of nature—a thick tree branch falling across a road with no saw marks on it, as if blown there in a storm; bits of glass or a few nails sprinkled on the asphalt as if spilled by accident from the back of a passing truck; a slick of oil, all but invisible in darkness, left—so it seemed—by a faulty engine just at a turn in the road and just wide enough to send a troop transport careering into the ditch; one telephone line, torn from its mooring as if by strong winds or cut by a falling branch. His instructions were to space out these events no closer in time than one a week and no closer to each other than ten kilometers. Much as he enjoyed the work, it made him impatient. People were being killed, tortured, raped, starved to death, forced to hide in attics and mountain cabins, and he was delaying a single convoy for a few hours, ruining one or two engines, disrupting a handful of phone calls. If he'd been older, or a man with two working eyes and two strong arms, they would have treated him differently. He reminded himself to speak to Masso about it.

In the days between these acts, he visited Sarah in the cabin, left notes and money at the church, checked the ceramic jar in Masso's back field for messages, stopped for a quick visit with his mother, made trips like the one he had made to Milan—just to see things for himself and pass on any messages that had been sent from Archbishop Maniscalco, through the mustachioed priest at the Duomo. He gathered mushrooms, herbs, berries, made weekly trips to the towns north of Gravedona in Masso's cart, caught a few fish in the lake or trapped a pheasant, and sold them in the town to keep up his disguise and to feed himself and Sarah. But the urge to do more gnawed at him like a cancer. Today it was even worse. He was going to be a father now—father to a son, he was sure of it. He wanted, years down the road, to be able to tell his son that his one-eyed, weak-armed father had made a difference in the war, had played a role in bringing peace and freedom to Italy, something grander than stabbing a lone Fascist on a mountain path or cutting a few telephone wires.

When darkness fell, he waited another hour until the moon rose and then, using his flashlight sparingly, going step by precarious step, made his way back to a point he'd scouted out earlier. There, he lifted the largest rock he could lift and placed it strategically above an alluvium of stones and gravel. He listened. No sound. No lights on the roads above. He released the boulder and heard it clatter down the slope and veer off into the trees. And then silence. Working awkwardly with his mismatched arms, he lifted another large stone, set it in place, pushed it forward at a slightly different angle. Same result. Frustrated, he tried four more times before he heard the released stone banging its way down along the slope, disturbing the gravel as it went, gathering smaller stones behind it, like a partisan leader gathering recruits, that had been lying in wait for centuries. He held his breath and listened: this one would work. By the time it reached the guardrail at a particularly precarious turn, two hundred meters below, it would be leading a small battalion of granite and quartz. Some of the rockslide would be stopped by a partial guardrail, but most of it would spill out onto the pavement in what he hoped would be the most natural-looking display of nature's caprice.

He waited until the sound slowed and gradually stopped, until the last trickle of moving gravel had ceased, and then, wrapped in a moonlit silence, he waited another hour, trying to stay awake, nurturing a seed of hope. At last he heard the engines of what he assumed to be the regular nightly troop transport making its slow descent. Loud gears sounded on the straightaways, then they were muted as the vehicles turned behind a hill. Then loud again. And then, precisely what he'd been hoping for: the squeal of brakes, the sluicing sound of locked tires on pavement, a resounding crash as something—a truck filled with men and weapons?—skidded off the road and into the rock face. Perfect. The accident would delay one load of supplies for an hour or two. That would have to be his contribution for this day.

Twenty-Eight

Late at night, not five minutes before Maria was going to tap the broom-stick twice against the attic entrance, she heard a scuffing of feet at her front door and then two light knocks. *"Signora?"* A man's voice. German accent. Familiar. She barely had the strength of will to walk down the hallway and pull open the door. There, on stone steps her husband had laid in their first days in this home, stood the redheaded officer.

"Did I wake you?" he asked politely in his broken Italian. *I you wake up?*

She managed a shake of her head.

"I came to say I am sorry for the actions of my friend. May I come in?"

She hesitated a second but, deciding that she had no choice, led him down the hallway, directly beneath the trapdoor, and into her kitchen. Without asking, he took a seat at the table and gestured for her to join him there. She was at the point of asking if he wanted something to drink, but it was nothing more than a hospitality reflex, born of thirty Italian generations. She held it in her heart and sat stiffly.

"Again, I apologize."

She nodded, struggled to swallow, to speak.

"Have I disturbed you?"

Maria shook her head, clasped her hands, willed the words out of her mouth. "It's very late," she said. "Usually I'm in bed."

"The dinners are delicious."

"Thank you."

"We won't ask for any more of your chickens. You can keep them for eggs."

"Thank you."

"But the actions of my friend . . ." The officer shook his head sadly and left the sentence unfinished. "I realized you don't even know our names. My name is Rolf." He reached his hand across and shook hers, but too forcefully. It almost hurt.

Her cheeks were twitching. She made herself speak. "Why did you come here?"

He hesitated, perfectly sober it seemed, looked from her face to her breasts and back again. He smiled just by pinching the muscles of one cheek, but there was something wrong with the smile, a note of superiority, of evil. She thought she heard a tiny noise above her head and willed herself not to move or change expression. Rebecca was waiting for her food.

"You are not in danger from me," he said in a sly tone she didn't trust. "In any way you can imagine."

She nodded again. He was mocking her, glancing at her large, sagging breasts, her fat thighs, stifling a grin. The Germans wanted their women young and lithe and without morals.

"I'd like to help you if I can," Rolf went on. "I could see that you are hungry, so I would like to help you."

"I have enough," she said. "But I don't want to be treated like that again. Here in Italy, men don't treat women that way. Good women."

He gave her a false nod, seemed to be forcing himself not to burst out laughing. "I'll be happy to speak to my friend on your behalf, Maria."

"Thank you."

"You are quite welcome." Rolf put the fingertips of one hand on the table, palm lifted, and arranged them there as if on piano keys. His nails were perfectly clean, expertly trimmed. He relaxed the hand and raised his eyes to her. "In return for one small favor."

She waited, blinked, felt a prayer begin inside her.

"I would like you," he said, "to bring me one Jew. Only one. If you can point out to me one person in the town who is Jewish, or half-Jewish, or even someone you think has sympathy for Jews and is helping them in some way, then I can guarantee that you will not be hurt or insulted, and we'll even give you a healthy ration of our food to take home with you on a regular basis. As a reward."

"There are none," she said quickly. "No Jews left here."

"Ah. I have heard that. But I don't quite believe it."

"I'm not lying to you. There were two Jewish families in Mezzegra, but when the . . . when the war started, they ran off. Maybe to Switzerland."

"The Swiss won't take them. No one will take them. Only us. We'll put them to work, that's all. Nothing worse than that. They'll be kept away from the war. In a way, we're saving them."

Maria shrugged. "I have no idea where they went. They didn't leave any word. Two families."

Rolf stared at her for a moment, then removed his hand from the table, pushed his chair back, and made as if to stand. She saw his big thigh muscles flex beneath the cloth of his gray trousers and noticed again his powerful shoulders and neck. "But if there were Jews here in this town, you would tell me, yes?"

"Of course," she said immediately. "We know the laws. We've known them since long before . . ."

His pinched smile stopped her. "Long before we arrived in your beautiful land, yes?"

She couldn't speak.

"That's fine," he said, standing. "We know you don't want us here. That's perfectly natural. But we deal in facts, in logic, not feelings, and the fact is that we *are* here, probably for many years. Generations, perhaps. And another fact is that we enforce the laws a bit more strictly than what you have been accustomed to with your *Duce*. He's gone now, as you no doubt know."

"I'd heard. Yes. At the market. I thought it was a rumor."

"No rumor," Rolf said wearily, standing now. "Gone. Disappeared. Perhaps he fled to Switzerland . . . with his girlfriend."

She stood, too, watching his crooked, malevolent grin. She was trembling in a way she hoped he couldn't see, her ears alert to the smallest sound above them.

"But for those who obey the laws, we have nothing but respect. So thank you for your promise. I shall hold you to it, and you shall hold me to mine. You won't be treated that way again as long as you help us, and I will not make any more late-night visits. Please act as quickly as you can, however, because some of my colleagues are not as . . . understanding . . . as I am. Nor as patient."

She saw him to the door and made no response when he bade her good night, and she watched him as he crossed the lot in the moonlight, not looking back.

Twenty-Nine

The size of the advance payment from the mysterious half-American, found in the top drawer of his bureau exactly as promised, pleased Silvio Merino greatly. So greatly, in fact, that he decided to turn the trip to Milan—not without risk, of course; it would have been safer to send a surrogate—into a weekend vacation. Lisiella Aiello lived there and would no doubt welcome a visit. If her bed happened to be otherwise occupied, there were always other pleasures: the Grand Hotel de Milan with his manager friend Bella and its American bar and exquisite food.

That same night, he made the short walk to Via Sistina, to the garage where he stored both his vehicles: a simple yellow Fiat Cinquecento, which he used for his more mundane outings, and a lime-green 1942 Oldsmobile Custom Cruiser convertible. Five-speed. White-walled tires, white canvas top, lime-green leather seats. His excursion car. The vehicle that seemed to him like an extension of the truest part of his personality.

For a little while, Silvio paced in circles around the two vehicles, studying them, letting his intuition settle the matter. Which would be better for the trip to Milano? The Fiat would attract less attention. Then again, the truth was that, these days, any private vehicle attracted a certain amount of attention. Logic counseled the more modest choice.

After he'd pondered for a while, however, it began to seem to him that the Oldsmobile was the wiser option. Yes, it would be slightly suspicious to be seen driving an American car, but the more successful members of society were often seen in American cars. He'd look more important, less like someone the Germans or police could intimidate. His intuition, always trustworthy, nudged him in the direction of the Oldsmobile. He didn't resist.

He left at dawn the next day and took the coastal route, E40, heading north and west from the capital. He passed through Argentario and Grosseto, then a series of small villages with clusters of stone houses on the hilltops and fields spreading out below. He went as far as Livorno before turning inland. All was well to that point—he loved the feeling of piloting the magnificent vehicle and kept the top down in the warm day—though here and there, he saw evidence of Allied bombing raids. Except for assaults on a few factories and rail yards, the raids were relatively infrequent this far north, at least for now; still, people were suffering, and he felt the smallest twinge of guilt as he glided through the streets in the coupe with a thousand lire in gold packed into a ceramic statuette of Saint Jude—Giovanni's "package"—in the glove compartment.

All was well. But then, just at the southern border of the city of Milan, he came upon a checkpoint. Nazi soldiers, six of them, strutting about like show dogs in their shining leather boots and matching black holsters. One of them waved him to the side of the road. Silvio pulled over.

The officer took his time about approaching, seemed almost to be ogling the car. He walked behind and checked the plate, circled around front and fingered the grill, actually kicked the tires, and only then came up to the driver's door and looked sternly down at the man behind the wheel.

"Papers," he demanded, pronouncing the word in more or less understandable Italian.

"Of course, sir." When Silvio reached into the glove compartment, the loaded Saint Jude tumbled out. He laughed, mumbled something about good luck, returned the statue to its place, and calmly produced his papers. Impeccable, they were. Beyond question. He'd designed and printed them himself.

"From Rome?"

"Sì. Roma."

"Purpose of the trip?"

"A girlfriend in Milano and a bit of business there."

"What kind of business?"

"It says on the papers," Silvio said, pointing. "Restaurant consultant. We have the Grand Hotel de Milan. Business is poor. They're thinking of closing, and I'm going to try to talk them out of it."

The officer smirked, studied the papers, lifted his face to Silvio, and engaged in some kind of eye-contact battle. Silvio smiled, allowed the man to win. It meant nothing. At last, the officer handed back his papers. And then, just when Silvio thought he'd be free to travel on, the man said, "What about taking a German friend for a ride?"

"When, now?"

"Exactly. I'm a car lover. This is a classic. If you're not in too much of a hurry, take me for a short excursion."

The man's face did not show the slightest evidence of a smile.

"You're serious," Silvio said.

"Absolutely."

On the two-lane highway, with the officer sitting at his ease in the passenger seat—an arm's length from the gold-filled Saint Jude—Silvio focused on the road and kept a pleasant expression on his face. A spider of nervousness had taken up residence in his lower abdomen, but he tried his best to give off an aura of satisfaction, hospitality, Italian good-heartedness. The German appreciated his beautiful car; he was happy to oblige.

But as they passed through the small town of Caverna del Valle, the officer said, in a tone that might have been casual and might not have been, "Why aren't you in the military, fighting for your country?"

"A bit old," Silvio said.

"The documents said thirty-four. I, myself, am thirty-eight."

"And heart issues. Inherited."

"Truly?"

Silvio nodded in a sad way, as if nothing would have pleased him more than to be able to fight for the Axis powers, to be sent by the idiot *Duce* to bake in Libya or freeze on the road to Moscow, to give up good food, wine, women, the company of friends and the comfort of his apartment—all for the great cause of bringing the disaster that was Fascism to the rest of Europe.

For a little while, the German said nothing. And then, "Take me on a winding road. Let me see some of the famous Italian driving skill."

North and west of the city, winding roads weren't difficult to find. Silvio turned toward the hills near Lake Como and pushed the Oldsmobile into a fast climb. Soon, they were making switchback turns and, engaged in the steering and shifting, he'd half forgotten the man beside him and all concerns about his military eligibility. The wind rushed over him, twirling strands of hair at his temples and rustling the open collar of his shirt. Stunted pine trees flashed past. He loved the song of the gears, the hum of the tires, the way the weight of the Oldsmobile shifted left and right on the turns. They crested a rise and began to descend, still at a high rate of speed. Soon the road flattened. Silvio found himself behind a farmer's delivery truck, running alongside a set of railroad tracks two kilometers north of the city center.

"Pass him," the German said, just as the road made a gradual turn to the right.

"But—"

The officer unbuckled his holster and held his pistol up to Silvio's right temple. "Pass him. Let's see if your bad heart comes into play."

You people enjoy playing the bully, Silvio thought. It's what you have instead of good food. But he had long ago mastered the art of the falsely confident laugh. He let the laugh settle into a wide grin, shifted, pressed his foot down on the pedal. He could feel the tip of the pistol hovering a few centimeters from his right temple, but he didn't flinch in the slightest. He slipped smoothly into the opposite lane; the driver of the truck had nowhere to move over, the road in front of them blocked by the hillside; he could see only a hundred meters ahead.

The nervousness was gone now. He could feel the fear trying to take hold of him as he focused on the road, but something much stronger than fear was upon him, his pride rising up like a wounded prince on the field of battle. If the German wanted to die, that was no problem. He himself had been ready to die from the time he'd been fifteen years old—that was the key to enjoying life! One had to die. One didn't want to spend ninety-five years avoiding death at all costs only to waste away in a *casa di riposo*, fed by nuns and shitting in a diaper. He kept the grin in place, felt the wind battering his face, felt the weight of the big car shifting left, the pressure on the wheels there, the tires singing.

And then, from behind the hillside, he saw the front of an intercity bus appear, coming directly at them like the face of a joking devil. Perfect. He pressed down even harder on the pedal. The German lowered the pistol, pushed the soles of his boots nervously against the floor. Without changing expression or making a sound, Silvio kept the coupe at top speed, raced up to within twenty meters of the bus, then slid deftly to his right, past the delivery truck and into the other lane just in time. An angry horn wailed and faded behind him. He laughed again, downshifted into the turn. The German wiped his free palm on his trousers, and when Silvio glanced sideways, he saw a small dark sweat stain there. The pistol had gone back into its holster.

They were returning to the roadblock now; he could see it there, three hundred meters ahead. Instead of slowing down, he pressed hard on the accelerator, shifted back into fifth gear, sped up. Two hundred meters now. One hundred. With eighty meters to go, he felt the German start to squirm. *"Attento,"* the man said between his teeth—*careful*—and after waiting two more seconds, Silvio slammed his foot down on the brakes. The coupe went into a long, screaming skid, two thousand kilos of chrome and steel heading straight for the barrier. He saw the other officers at the roadblock scurry aside. A few car lengths from them, he turned the wheel sharply left, swinging the rear of the coupe around and bringing it to a stop parallel to the barrier, less than two meters from the terrified soldiers. He turned to look at his passenger. A bit of green there above the gray collar. Hands still clutching the sides of the seat.

"Basta?" he asked. *Enough?*

The officer nodded, made a strained smile, and, trying for the tone of authority and badly failing, said, "You are now free to go."

Yes, Silvio thought, and you are now free to clean the shit from your underpants.

Thirty

The train to Milan left from the Como station six times a day, exactly on the hour: 6:00, 9:00, 11:00, 2:00, 5:00, and 8:00. To save himself the uncertainty and expense of a bus trip, Don Claudio asked a farmer friend, Gennaro Masso, to take him there in his truck. It was a substantial favor—gas was as precious as silver then, and it was a ride of over an hour—but Masso was a friend of many years and quite well off, too. More important, besides Luca and the archbishop, Masso was the only person Don Claudio knew to be involved in the secret work. In a very quiet conversation on a Milan park bench, Archbishop Maniscalco had explained to him that the cells were designed that way: each partisan knew only two or three others, so that, even if he were caught and interrogated, the Germans would get, at best, a small number of names. It was, the archbishop had told him, "a web of trust."

On the day of his trip to Milan, Don Claudio rose earlier than usual, walked down the long hill into town, and arrived at Masso's farmhouse on the southern edge of Mezzegra before the sun had risen very far above the mountains on the eastern shore. Masso was already waiting for him, sitting on the back edge of the open truck bed, chewing a stalk of celery. He offered a second stalk in greeting. They climbed into the front, set off along the *statale*, and soon found themselves behind a slow-moving line of German military vehicles. Masso kept his distance.

"This is a great favor, Gennaro. I was sorry to ask." Don Claudio turned to look at his friend: bald head, cleft chin, short, thick arms. Masso was one of the few people he knew who had retained the ability to laugh the way he'd laughed before the war, who somehow managed to stay optimistic, even happy, in the face of fear and deprivation. A truly spiritual man, he thought. A man who has faith in another world. And yet he was never seen at Sunday Mass.

"For my priest and spiritual adviser," Masso said happily, "no favor is too great."

They went on a short distance without speaking, the engine of the old truck grumbling and spitting, Masso shifting gears. To their left, sunlight sparkled on the surface of the lake. To their right, the forested hills folded in behind one another, up and up, toward the border with Switzerland. There were times, Don Claudio mused, when he forgot to appreciate the fact that he lived in one of the most beautiful places on earth.

As they passed through the small village of Argegno, the vehicles in the German convoy pulled to the roadside, and Masso was able to pass. With luck, Don Claudio thought, he could make the nine o'clock train. Eleven was his usual meeting time with the archbishop; that shouldn't be a problem.

"Strange goings-on lately," Masso said when they were on the open highway again.

"Our beloved *Duce*, you mean."

Masso grunted. "That and other things . . . A few days ago, none other than an assistant chief of German intelligence for Italy made a trip up here to the lake and was sniffing around."

"Who told you that?"

"Friends."

Don Claudio waited. This, too, was typical of the man. On the surface, a simple farmer, his face worn from years in the sun and his hands large and coarse, Gennaro Masso seemed, of late, to have mysterious sources of information, hidden "friends," secret duties. Don Claudio wondered if he might be not simply a collaborator but one of the partisan organizers, the archbishop's main contact, perhaps. Or if he was just a man who made it his business to catch every scrap of news that floated along the lakeshore. A tiny note of suspicion sounded in the priest's thoughts. What if Masso . . . ? But that was another sin. One had to have faith, to trust.

"What does he look like?"

"Short, like me," Masso said. "Fat, like me. Only uglier." He put one hand up near the side of his head. "Huge ears."

"I saw him."

"Where?"

"In front of Orlando's. He stopped and asked me if I knew any saboteurs. Told me he'd pull out my teeth with pliers if he found I was lying."

"Your first interrogation."

"It was just one question, out on the sidewalk, in public. My legs were shaking."

"Natural enough, Claudio. Anyone would be afraid."

"Why would someone like that come here?"

"Because right now, there's more partisan activity here than anywhere in Italy. We're on one of their main supply lines . . . You saw the convoy just now." Masso focused on the road for a moment. Don Claudio could see that he had more to say. "Plus, two days ago, someone stabbed a Fascist Party member to death on a path in the hills outside Santa Eligia. Another friend of mine was hiking up there, looking for food, and came upon the body. He dragged it into the trees and found the Party ID in the man's pocket."

"And told people this?!"

"Told me. I'm telling you. You, I hope, tell nobody."

"Of course. I have a long history of secret-keeping."

"In the confessional, you mean."

"Yes," Don Claudio said, and then he almost said something else. There were days when what he thought of as his "life's secret" felt like a wasp in his mouth, stinging and stinging, desperate to get out.

Masso glanced at him and then turned his eyes back to the road. "It's a dangerous moment, Claudio. They're all in a panic now, the Germans, trying to find *il Duce* before the king makes a deal with the Allies and they're left to fight on their own. Our troops in Sicily are surrendering by the thousands. They didn't want to fight, even while Mussolini was around. Now that he's gone and the Americans have arrived . . ."

Masso left the thought unfinished. Near the southernmost point of the lake, he took an exit for the city of Como and followed side streets to the station. He pulled up near the platform and turned to fix Don Claudio with his kind eyes. "Back tonight?"

"Tomorrow, I think. I'll take the bus, though. I'll stop in if I have anything to deliver. Thank you for doing this, my friend."

Masso waved the gratitude away, and they shook hands. "Be careful now," he said across the front seat, in a voice that made his passenger shiver.

Don Claudio stepped out of the truck and watched Masso drive away. *A web of trust,* he thought. Masso, Luca, the archbishop, Maria, Rebecca, no doubt Sarah, too. All the good lives in danger now, and all of them linked to each other. One betrayal, and a trapdoor would open beneath their feet, sending all but one of them hurtling toward an agonizing death.

But he sensed the tiniest sparkle of hope in the latest news: *Duce* gone, Fascists being murdered in the hills, the Allies in Sicily, Nazis in a panic.

He wondered if there was actually a chance that good might eventually prevail.

As he boarded the train, Don Claudio knew what to expect. The trip by rail to Milan took an hour and twenty minutes and passed through low hills at first and then flat, featureless territory that was a great disappointment after the scenery around the lake. In peacetime, whenever he'd had reason to travel to Milan, he preferred to say a rosary on that section and then sleep. He would awaken in Milano Centrale, in the massive station that seemed to have been built as a temple to the gods of steel and machinery, with people boarding and disembarking and visitors from all over Europe, indeed all over the world, crowding the platforms, ordering beer and panini in the cafés, hurrying off to visit the Duomo or the city's many parks and high-class clothing shops, or making connections to Florence, Venice, Bologna, and points south.

The doors closed, the first announcements were made. Tired as he was from rising so early, Don Claudio had the sense that the peace of sleep would elude him on this day. He began to run the beads through his fingers, mouthing the first few Hail Marys, nervous at his errand and working hard not to admit it to himself. "Be careful now," Masso had said, and Masso clearly knew things that others did not.

Just as the train left the station—exactly on time: they had Mussolini to thank for that, at least—the empty seat beside him was taken by a man whose accented greeting marked him as Austrian. He wasn't wearing a uniform but had a military bearing, square shoulders, short hair. The man glanced at the rosary beads and frowned too obviously. Don Claudio turned to look out the window. For some reason, he felt instantly uncomfortable in the man's presence and was at the point of feigning sleep when the stranger tapped him on top of his thigh. "A priest, yes?"

Don Claudio turned to him and nodded.

"Catholic?"

No, he thought, *Hindu. "Si, si."*

"And you are traveling why?"

The man, it turned out, spoke capable Italian, though with the thick accent.

"Church business."

"Ah. May I inquire as to the nature of your church business?"

Don Claudio wanted to say, *No, you may not inquire.* Or, *In Italy we often introduce ourselves first, before we begin asking such questions.* But this was another aspect of the war and the foreign presence, though it had begun, in fact, in Mussolini's early years, before the Germans came: the rules of decent behavior had been suspended and new rules put in place. Behind the new rules stood the fist.

"Of course. And I'm Don Claudio." The men shook hands, but the Austrian didn't offer his name. "In my order, the Dominicans, we're required to make regular visits to our superiors. We confess our sins and receive absolution. We're given direction as to the spiritual guidance of our flock. And so on."

"Ah. And is the guidance political?"

"Not often, no."

"And have you heard the political news?"

"Which news is that?"

"Your Mussolini and so on."

"Yes, I did hear it."

"And do you have an opinion?"

"Honestly, no. My work concerns the spiritual well-being of my parishioners. My interest is in the news of Our Lord not of our king or—" *Dictator,* he almost said. But he hesitated a fraction of a second and added, "Other leaders."

The man's face showed no expression whatsoever. It was thin and sharp boned, plain as a warehouse wall, cold as concrete on a December morning. "But you thought Mussolini was a good man, didn't you?"

"He did some good things for the country."

"Brought order."

"Yes," Don Claudio said. By torturing opponents and having his thugs beat or kill them, by controlling the press, by eliminating his enemies, by manipulating the people with his gift for speechmaking, by pitting Italians one against the other. "Sanatoriums, clean water, efficient trains. Many things."

"And now?"

"As I said, sir, I have no idea and frankly, though I dislike war as much as anyone else, the focus of my thoughts and prayers is on bringing the peace of Christ to earth."

"So you approve of the so-called armistice your king is reported to be considering? In the name of this 'peace'?"

"I wasn't even aware of it, *signore*. The king is a friend of Mussolini's. I doubt very much that he'd do such a thing, since Mussolini would not be in favor of ending Italy's involvement in the war."

"Do you approve of the recent attacks on German soldiers, the sabotage, the murder?"

Don Claudio wondered if a trio of passengers on the other side of the aisle could hear these questions. He felt the muscles of his neck stiffen and a familiar shaking creep into his lower legs. It occurred to him that the Austrian might not have sat down beside him by accident, that the intelligence officer in front of Orlando's might have been more suspicious than he'd seemed, might be having him followed. He had never been a very good liar. *Be very careful,* he thought.

"*Signore,*" he said in as firm a voice as he could summon. "You are speaking with a Catholic priest. Harming others, killing others, destroying property, these things run absolutely counter to our faith. I'm surprised you would even ask such a question. And now, if you don't mind, I'd like to continue with my prayers."

The man ran his eyes over Don Claudio's face, then turned forward. He exuded tension, Don Claudio thought, as if he were clenching every muscle in his trim body, from toes to forehead. It was part and parcel of their philosophy: muscular strength, discipline, an absence of forgiveness. They cherished this idea of a master race, an idea that must, at all costs, be upheld by its practitioners . . . and then they'd devolve into nights of the most hideous debauchery. A strange thing, he thought, the way the human mind could form false systems of belief and cling to them in the face of the laws of love and the certainty of death. A whole nation could go suddenly insane. Two whole nations. He wondered how God could allow it.

For a while, he was left to work his beads in peace. When he put them away in anticipation of their arrival in Milan, he looked out the window again, and his eyes were drawn to a beautiful green-and-white car, a convertible, racing along the road there at much too high a speed, cutting in front of a farmer's truck just in time to avoid crashing head-on into a bus. Reckless, yes, but there was something beautiful about it, too, an absence of fear, a trust in one's fate and the protection of the Lord. Don Claudio found himself envying a man who could drive like that, who could live like that. Beside him, the Austrian, emboldened or perhaps frustrated by his neighbor's contemplation, said, "Do you know what my God is?"

"I have no idea, *signore*."

The man suddenly took hold of Don Claudio's left hand, grabbed his fifth finger, and squeezed the nail between two knuckles as if in a vise. Don Claudio let out a cry and managed, after a moment of struggle, to pull his hand away. The Austrian was grinning. He stood up to be first at the door but leaned his face down almost in the priest's and hissed, "The ability to endure pain!" And he was gone.

Gathering their belongings and standing up out of their seats, the passengers on the other side of the aisle kept their eyes turned away.

Thirty-One

On the overnight boat from the Italian mainland to La Maddalena, Mussolini held to a glum silence. He was used to action, decisions, work, and now he was being moved, against his will, into a new stage of life, almost like a man in his nineties whose family members had stopped caring about him and were placing him in a rest home watched over by nuns. Instead of nuns, he had his keepers on the *Persefone*. They were young and fit and looked good in their uniforms, but not one of them came anywhere near him. If he caught them looking in his direction, they immediately turned away.

At daybreak, the ship slowed and angled into a narrow channel, cleared of mines, he hoped, with the island of Sardinia to his left and the much smaller La Maddalena Island to his right. The water was translucent, tropical greens and blues dancing in the early-morning sunlight. The sight of it, and the view of Sardinia's low, stony hills, gave him a few seconds of pleasure.

People talked about the draining of the Pontine Marshes south of Rome as being his major land-reclamation project, and that was true enough. But the idea had begun with the Sardinians—a strange and mysterious people, renegades after his own heart—years before he came to power. The first marshes he himself had ordered reclaimed weren't the Pontine but the swamps on the Terralba plains, not far from Oristano in Sardinia. He'd had three new cities built there, too, the first, Mussolinia, named in his honor. He'd drained the swamps, called in the best architects to plan the towns and construct beautiful public buildings that would remain monuments to his vision for hundreds of years. He'd provided hydroelectric power using the same water that had once been only a breeding place for malarial mosquitoes.

Those were the kinds of marks he'd made on the Italian nation, and this was his reward: captivity, boredom, the captain's "following orders" nonsense. The ship slowed again into the harbor and nudged up alongside a dock. The soldiers assembled, and their captive, the former *Duce*, was marched down the gangplank and along the stone pier like a murderer.

Mussolini was wearing the same blue suit, crumpled now, in which he'd gone to visit the king. He kept his hat pulled down almost to his eyebrows. The captain had told him there had been air raids on some of the smaller islands off the western coast of the mainland. Evacuations, too. Perhaps that was why he saw so few people at that hour—two women washing clothes in the fountain, an old drunk sitting on his haunches in a doorway. They watched curiously, not recognizing him, it seemed, wondering who the stranger might be, unsure why he was being imprisoned, or protected, or at least held in a phalanx of soldiers on their quiet piece of sand and stone. Mussolini felt their eyes on him. In his inner ear, he heard Rachele's *Don't go!*

He didn't believe in introspection—a waste of energy—but as he walked along the dock and was led across a road and up a gravel path, he could feel the snake of regret slithering through his thoughts again. He hadn't taken Grandi's resolution at the Council meeting seriously, hadn't worried about the warnings of his aides and family members, hadn't felt the slightest concern about the intentions of the king. How could someone like him have made such a tactical error?

He tried to leave those thoughts behind, but they followed him along the path like the notes of Rachele's nasal whine. Here was the house—Casa Weber, he was told, as the captain and his guard left him at the door and began setting up positions in the yard. He heard one of the soldiers say the house had once belonged to an Englishman! Gray stone, turrets, it had the look of a small castle. A peasant woman, hair wrapped in a red kerchief, greeted him with respect and led him through the front entrance and to an upstairs bedroom furnished with a bed and bureau. The walls were whitewashed as if it were a room in an asylum. There were two windows looking out on a view of La Maddalena's low-lying landscape of wind-carved gray stone and lively green sea, but there was no mattress on the bed.

"The mattress we will get tomorrow, Excellency," the woman said apologetically. "We had barely any notice from the authorities. Only last night, we were told—"

"Fine, fine, what is your name?"

"Nicolina, Excellency. We are glad to have you here. There is a woman next door to do your laundry, and I will cook for you. And the soldiers will guard the house. The fish is fresh nearly every day, and, though they told me you can't have radio or newspapers, you can walk and swim. And there is a man here, Vittorio, to play cards with."

"Bene, grazie," he said. "Vittorio is also the name of my first son."

Nicolina stood there for a moment, her hands clasped in front of her apron, then eventually seemed to understand that her new guest wanted to be left alone. She excused herself and closed the door quietly behind her. Mussolini took off his jacket and rolled it into a makeshift pillow, then lay down on the steel coils. He had always been proud of his ability to endure discomfort. He'd skied bare-chested on the Abruzzan slopes; he rose early, usually on a few hours' sleep; he ate little, even in the days when his stomach could have endured a larger meal. Usually these disciplines gave him a strange kind of peace.

But peace was the last thing he was experiencing at that moment. An impenetrable darkness had fallen over him, a sense of hopelessness, of the future being emptied of anything worthwhile. He lay on his metal bed, listening for the sound of planes. But there was only silence now. Maybe later, he'd get up and write Claretta . . . if they would even allow him pen and paper. But what would he say? And what were the chances he would ever touch her flesh again?

He rolled onto his other side. All those years, all that effort, and here he was, sleeping on metal coils with a wrinkled suit coat for a pillow.

Nicolina had called him *Excellency*. At least they'd arranged for him to be taken care of by kind people while awaiting his destiny.

There was a knock on the door. A man appeared there with a change of clothing and to ask what *il Duce* wanted for his midday meal. This man, too, referred to him as *Excellency*, was deferential, respectful. Perhaps he understood, as others in this country seemed not to, what this *Excellency* had done for people like him, what Italy would have looked like had this *Duce* not been in power the past twenty-three years. Perhaps he remembered the violent trade union demonstrations, the strikes that had crippled whole industries, the street crime and ruinous inflation, the way Italy's reputation—even as one of the victors of World War I—had been turned to shit.

When the man left, Mussolini got up and washed in the basin, changed into the brown trousers and white shirt, threw open the shutters, and stood there, looking out. Soldiers around the house, even a machine-gun emplacement! Beyond them, a road, a few plain homes, a stretch of stony beach, and two fishing boats in the small harbor. He could see the *Persefone* steaming away across the wind-whipped bay. A plane growled and crossed the airspace above the island. He squinted, trying to read the insignia, and could not.

Thirty-Two

In the early-morning hours, having awakened on his mossy bed before first light showed over the mountains of the Valtellina, Luca made the long trek down the hillside behind his mother's house and waited, silent as a fox, in the trees behind her yard. *Your son has come home, a killer,* he thought as he watched the back door and ran his eyes across the roofline. The woman hiding in the attic was the same woman who'd welcomed him into her poor little house—moldy walls, crooked floors—a block from the lakeshore when he arrived to take her daughter out for the first time. That date, unforgettable, was for a musical evening at a villa in the hills, and it had cost him a week's pay. Dressed in their finest clothes, he and Sarah had sat on wooden folding chairs on an expansive lawn. A uniformed server moved through the crowd, offering glasses of wine and small plates of various delicacies. They'd sat close to each other without touching, then kissed for the first time on the bus ride home.

It was painful to remember those days, that luxury, hard to believe it was anything more than a dream. Harder still to think about Sarah alone in the cabin and her mother suffering in the attic heat. As a boy, he had sometimes asked his parents to let him climb up there, and on those days, he'd concoct imaginary worlds with a few old boxes and the extra set of pots and dishes his mother had inherited and which the family never used. One of his grandfathers, long dead now and a veteran of the Great War, had made him a gift of a set of painted wooden soldiers, tanks, artillery guns, airplanes. On cool fall Saturdays, he'd set up imaginary battles on the boards of the attic floor, make heroic assaults, fly the miniature wooden plane over the front, machine-gunning the enemy.

He remembered it now with an odd mixture of nostalgia and shame. War had seemed so simple then, his own heroism inevitable. Now he understood all too well that war was the most purely evil aspect of life. Sin in the flesh, not thrilling or romantic in the least. And heroism, he suspected, was always, always, peppered with terror.

Even before the Germans arrived, he'd witnessed that evil and that terror: the Blackshirts and Fascist *squadristi* marauding through the streets looking for victims to beat and torture. One of their favorite entertainments, in the name of *il Duce*, of course, was to find someone who displeased them—a union member, a liberal journalist, a socialist, an academic—hold the man down, and pour castor oil into him by force, filling his belly with it until the man begged them to stop, and then, when they stopped, he'd shit his pants and vomit and often enough end up dead of dehydration. Tormented, humiliated, tortured, and killed. And these were Italians murdering Italians.

He remembered that his father had kept a photo of Giacomo Matteotti up in that same attic, between the pages of a family scrapbook. He wondered if it might still be there. Matteotti had been a socialist, his father told him, and had stood up to Mussolini—perhaps the only politician in all of Italy with the courage to do so. One day he'd been snatched from the streets of Rome by a carful of these *squadristi*. Pulled into the back seat as he walked home from his office. A few days later, his body, brutally beaten, was found in a ditch in the hills east of the capital. Matteotti was a popular figure, a hero to many, and his death, and the obvious connection to Mussolini, had come within a whisker of toppling *il Duce*.

As he waited, Luca tried to understand Mussolini, tried to probe the man's mind. It all came from the urge for power, he supposed. But, having so little urge for that kind of power himself—the power to injure others—it was a difficult concept to grasp, a puzzle. It was like the situation with the Jews, another puzzle. In the early years, Mussolini had said nothing about Jews. He'd even had a Jewish mistress for a time, and the woman, Margherita Sarfatti, had remained his friend and adviser until she fled to South America in 1938 when, under Hitler's influence, Mussolini instituted the "racial laws." Everyone knew this. Until that year, even Fascist Party membership had been open to Jews. And then, by some evil magic, Mussolini had fallen under Hitler's spell, and his urge for power had been twisted even further. Now it wasn't just labor organizers and socialists who were the enemies but Jews, all of them, even completely powerless ones like Sarah and Rebecca, people who would cause no trouble at all to anyone, ever.

As time went on—1939, 1940, 1941—Italian Jews were tormented, stripped of their jobs and titles, as if Mussolini were a little boy trying to please his violent older brother. One could imagine him signing the new decrees and looking north and west, catching the brother's eye, hoping for a nod of approval.

But Mussolini himself had never sent Jews to the work camps. That was a new development, Hitler's idea, and the rumors flew. That they weren't really work camps at all but death camps. That there was a fleet of trains bringing them to these camps, like cattle, by the hundreds of thousands. Luca had heard of these things but never witnessed them with his own eyes. Still, from the stories about the *squadristi* and Matteotti, he understood that violence fed on itself, achieved a kind of mob momentum, and that it wouldn't stop until it was met by violence from the other side.

At that point—just when news reached him that the Germans had begun rounding up Jews in France and sending them away—he'd told Sarah that similar arrests would soon happen in Italy, and he'd convinced her, against her will, to leave her home and move to various safe places and then up to the cabin. He'd told his mother to warn Rebecca and, as it turned out, not a second too soon. Two days later, the Gestapo came to their house on Quercia Street in the flats down by the water. They'd smashed windows and taken what little of value they could find. But Sarah and Rebecca were gone.

Now he hid in his own back yard, waiting to see his mother.

Shortly after first light, she emerged, as he knew she would, and brought out food for her hens, collected the eggs, filled a bowl of water for them. Luca counted eight now instead of nine. He wondered if a fox or one of the local dogs had gotten a free meal. It would mean fewer eggs.

He watched his mother move on her heavy legs and aching hips, and tried to imagine guiding her and Sarah and Sarah's mother over the mountains into Switzerland. Six kilometers it would be, no more. But in places, the terrain was all but impassable, steep as a ladder leaning against the second story of a building. And the border was heavily guarded by soldiers who set their dogs on you first and asked for identification later.

When his mother finished her chores, Luca made his low two-note whistle, then the *coo* of a dove. He watched the joy bloom on her face; saw her look around, as if casually, glancing twice at the Rosso house; and then saw her step into the woods as if searching for some lost item there or hunting for berries or ferns to stanch her hunger. Without much difficulty, she was able to climb up as far as the stone behind which he hid. She looked around again, then reached down and put her hand on the side of his face as she'd always done. He held the hand there briefly and asked how she was.

"Fine, Luca," she said. "Everything the same."

"I know when you're lying," he told her, and she looked back again, then crouched down and told him about her new duties—cooking for the Germans!—and then, after more hesitation, about the way she had been treated and the visit from the redhead.

Listening to her voice, watching the face he knew so well twitch with humiliation, Luca felt a familiar tightening in his chest. He was breathing through his nose, lips pressed together; he was remembering the fury—almost a satanic spirit—that had come over him when he'd stabbed the Fascist. He was remembering the scene at Piazzale Loreto. He pictured the SS man making his mother suck crumbs of cheese from his finger, and he suddenly knew that he would kill again. He understood perfectly now, from inside his bones. He let the fire build. By the time his mother finished speaking, he already knew what he would do. "I've brought you some mushrooms," he told her, squeezing the words out between his teeth.

"I know. You always do."

"No, Mother. I've brought you some *lepiota*." He took the small mesh bag from his backpack and handed it to her. "Please be careful with them. Don't use them unless it's an emergency. But if you have to, one day, when you feel the time is right, when we decide you're ready to escape, mix them into a cacciatore and let your new friends have a fine last meal."

His mother hesitated, fixed him with a look. Not judgment, not even surprise, just a kind of curiosity, as if she were wondering what had become of her gentle son. Instead of resisting, as he expected, she said only, "How long will it take? For them?"

"An hour at most. One very bad hour. By then, you and Rebecca will be gone."

"How?"

"Up, over the mountains."

"And then how?"

"I'll find a way."

She nodded, glanced down at the mesh bag and then at him, almost as if it gave her a physical pain to see his face so infrequently. He thought she might change her mind then, refuse to take the *lepiota*, and part of him wished she would. But she held on to the bag and stood up. Her legs were strong, he thought; she'd be able to make the climb.

"How is Rebecca?"

"Alive."

"Sarah's alive, too. Tell her mother she's—" He'd started to say the beautiful word *incinta*, *pregnant*, but then, for some reason, he felt a spasm of superstition and held it back. "She's well, Mother. Tell Rebecca she's well."

A weak smile. His mother made the sign of the cross over him and then, before leaving, said, "Don't take them yourself, Luca. The *lepiota*. Please don't ever do that to me."

"I never would," he said. "You don't take them, either." She nodded, touched the top of his head with two fingers, and made her way back to the house.

Thirty-Three

For Don Claudio, it was a walk of almost thirty minutes from Milano Centrale station to the curia where Archbishop Federico Maniscalco had his offices. Women nodded to him and made the sign of the cross as he walked from the station—at the pace of an elderly dog, he thought. German soldiers and two smiling carabinieri eyed him with scorn. He was used to that now. At one point, he stopped and, pretending to scrape something from the bottom of his shoe, peeked down the sidewalk behind him. No one following.

He went on, passing in front of the magnificent Duomo with its concrete turrets reaching into the sky and its massive stained glass windows. He found himself wondering if the Allies would bomb that, too, in the name of victory, if all of his country's great storehouse of beauty would be sacrificed on the altar of war.

At the curia, not much had changed since the Germans appeared, at least not on the surface. The same red door with the crucifix above, the same sleepy guard outside, spilling over the edges of his metal chair and making a desultory perusal of *La Gazzetta dello Sport*. Don Claudio sometimes passed the time wondering if there was a way to measure how much of life had changed or remained unchanged since Italy entered the war. The churches were as open as they'd ever been. Much less traffic on the roads, many more military vehicles, a half or a third of the food that had been available, at three or four times the price. A dearth of young and middle-aged men on the sidewalks, more propaganda on the radio. At the station, he'd heard a woman saying that there were reports of uprisings on the streets of Naples, but here in the north, things were more or less quiet so far, under the steely German *ombrellone*. If there were a numerical measurement, he thought he might be able to say that 40 percent of things were as they had been in earlier years. And there was already so much suffering. What if that number went to 30 percent or even 20? How would they be able to endure it then? And what must the number be now, in Sicily, where the Allies had landed?

Inside the curia, he went past Bruno the guard—raised eyes, a nod, the shadow of a smile; God knew what secrets the man kept—and up the stairs to the archbishop's office. Though everything in this building seemed the same, the archbishop had told him there were spies among his staff; he was sure of it. The Germans offered food and other favors for bits of information, and sometimes even a devout church worker was desperate enough to succumb. Who saw the archbishop, how long he stayed, what were his habits—these were the kinds of things they reported on. Probably the appearance of the evil Austrian on the train had been the result of a spy's information: they were watching Don Claudio now, tracing his movements. He'd have to be even more careful, especially with Luca's visits.

The archbishop, a brilliant man, really, and the one who'd recruited Don Claudio, had now started playing the radio in his office during meetings. It served two purposes: made him seem like a loyal member of the Church hierarchy, anxious to hear news of the latest military triumph, eager for political encouragement and Fascist victory, and made it next to impossible for anyone to listen in on his conversations. But as Don Claudio knocked and then opened the door into the large office, he encountered nothing but silence. Unprecedented. Whenever he'd been summoned to Milan, the archbishop had been waiting there for him precisely at eleven. The hand of fear took hold of him again. The archbishop was never late.

He sat in a chair in front of the desk and began to pray. *Ave Maria, piena di grazia* . . . A quarter of an hour passed, half an hour. He was on the verge of getting up and going out to speak to Bruno when he heard the door open behind him. For a second, he dared not turn around, and then he heard his friend's greeting, a *click*, and the voice of a radio announcer spouting lies about victories in Greece.

The men embraced. Instead of sitting behind his desk, the archbishop lowered himself into a leather armchair beside a small table. Don Claudio swiveled his chair around to face him.

Federico's thin cheeks were paler than usual, as if he were in the grip of an illness, but his gaze was as strong as ever, his gray hair cut close to his scalp, his lips set in an expression of the deepest calm. "How is attendance at Mass, my Claudio?" he inquired. "How is the building? Repairs needed? Do you have any funds? How is your own spiritual life?"

With the possible exception of the last question, Don Claudio knew the archbishop's curiosity was merely *pro forma*, a feint for listening ears. Still, he answered in great detail. It had to seem that spiritual business had required this trip to Milan. In the old days on his visits, Don Claudio would sleep over in the rectory; he and Federico—friends since seminary days—would go out for a meal, sit up late into the night drinking wine and talking, making jokes, playing cards. But that would draw suspicion now, given the new dimension of their relationship, and so they kept it to one brief meeting every month, sometimes with the loud radio playing beside them, sometimes on a park bench with a view in all directions.

The radio—Don Claudio no longer had a working one in the rectory—cursed Roosevelt and Churchill but made no mention, none, of *il Duce*. If Don Claudio needed proof that Mussolini was actually gone, that was enough.

At one point in the conversation, though no one had knocked, Don Claudio heard the door open again and felt an icy chill scurry up the bones of his spine: The Austrian? A German soldier? An assassin?

He made himself look up and saw a mustachioed priest there, vaguely familiar. The priest placed a small statue on the sidebar, nodded to the archbishop, ignored Don Claudio completely, and closed the door quietly behind him as he withdrew.

When the church formalities were finished, when they'd exhausted all possible small talk, the archbishop leaned his body—still trim and lithe—across the low table between them and motioned for Don Claudio to do the same. He took a fountain pen from its holder, dipped it in ink, and wrote on a piece of paper. He turned the paper so Don Claudio could see it:

In the saint on the table, 1,000 lire in gold for Luca to pass on to Mentone

Three rifles and a pistol in your cloakroom when you return

Loaded!

Federico watched Don Claudio's eyes. Made sure he'd understood, then ripped the paper into small pieces and, as Don Claudio watched, put them into his mouth, wet them, worked his jaws and tongue, and swallowed. They stood, hugged each other warmly—*"Coraggio!"* Federico whispered in his ear—and Don Claudio nodded and turned toward the door.

He wanted a new mathematical formula then to describe what percentage of the sanity remained in each of his friends. He estimated his own number would be about 65 percent. The archbishop, swallowing paper now, perhaps somewhat lower.

But he had his marching orders. The sidebar—polished wood, waist height—was on his left as he made his way out of the office. On it, he now saw, stood a small porcelain statuette of Saint Jude. Patron saint of impossible cases. He picked it up—unusually heavy. A thin piece of green felt had been glued securely to the base of the statuette. He suspected that a cylindrical tunnel had been bored from the bottom of the porcelain up through the saint's torso. Stacked inside, he would find the gold coins. Into the pocket of his black trousers it went. If he were stopped and searched, it would be just another priestly relic for the Germans to mock. If by some chance they noticed the weight and peeled away the felt, they would see the circle where the tunnel had been bored. If they put a finger inside, they would find the money. If they didn't believe him when he told them it was his own personal stash, for food and emergency church repairs, then he would be arrested and tortured and killed.

He nodded at Bruno the guard as he went out into the day, stopped and smiled up at the sunshine as if his sanity index had fallen to 40 percent. And then he walked on in search of that impossible thing: an inexpensive lunch in the city of Milano. Food, the Italian sacrament.

Thirty-Four

Two days passed in the Rome office, days in which Skorzeny busied himself with preparations for he knew not exactly what. Parachutes, scuba gear, mountaineering equipment—it depended on where Mussolini turned out to have been taken, if, in fact, they ever figured that out. It bothered him to rely so heavily on Selenzen, so he made inquiries of his own, invited German-speaking Italian officers for expensive lunches and dinners, made friendly, probing conversation, circuitous inquiries. The whole game seemed rather foolish: they must know how badly Hitler was hoping to find Mussolini, but he was supposed to be discreet about it, hint, speak in circles, pretend the desperate search was secondary to other considerations. It was the same with the Jews: when dealing with the Italians, he and his comrades were supposed to suggest that the Jews were suitable citizens, that they might one day even have a place in the Reich, that the Italians' relative sympathy for them was sensible, kind, even useful, when in fact Skorzeny himself wanted nothing less than to eliminate them from the face of the earth, every one of them, to the last man, woman, and child.

He kept trying, kept pressing gently to find out where Mussolini had been taken, but his efforts yielded nothing in the way of hard information.

Still, there was work to do, if only in anticipation. He arranged for more of his best men to be called to Rome from duties in other parts of the Reich. He found a pilot he trusted, made a trip to the Pratica di Mare airfield to scout out conditions there, spent a little time in the headquarters' underground bomb shelter because the enemy was making the occasional air raid on Rome now, killing civilians mostly but damaging a few key roads and supply lines, as well.

After long hours of planning, thinking, and worrying, just when Skorzeny was beginning to feel an erosion of his customary optimism, *Obersturmführer* Selenzen knocked on his door. A *Heil Hitler!* An offer of a glass of white wine—accepted, of course—and Selenzen took his customary place in his customary posture, splayed out on the chair like a man about to fall asleep after having gorged himself on an elaborate lunch.

"News?"

Selenzen worked his fat lips, delaying for everything he was worth. It was all Skorzeny could do not to scream at him. The man was unfit, physically and psychologically, to be an officer of the Reich.

"Something, perhaps," Selenzen said in a coy manner.

Skorzeny waited, watched, thought: *I'm about to strangle you!*

"We have information that a 'special prisoner' was held in a local carabinieri barracks for a time and then driven away in darkness."

"Driven away where?"

"South."

"South?"

Selenzen nodded.

"That's it?"

"A beginning. For a time, we'd heard he was somewhere on the western shore of Lake Como, far to the north. But that information has proven to be inaccurate."

Skorzeny could no longer hold in his rage. *"Obersturmführer,"* he said, "you seem to be treating this as a game of chess when it is, in fact, direct orders from your führer. Get off your fat ass and bring me real information or you'll be reassigned to Kiev. You have one day. Go!"

Selenzen stood, glanced at his wineglass, and departed. Skorzeny was left to stand at the window and look out toward the crater of a long-inactive volcano where the pope's summer residence stood. Homes there, stone homes and a few plane trees, a scene too pleasant for wartime. He had Italian friends now, yes. And there were some excellent soldiers among them. But there were times—this was one of them—when the nation of Italy sickened him, when it seemed that the infamous Latin laziness and love of *la dolce vita* was contagious. At moments like this, he worried that the German army, the finest military force the world had ever known, would be mired in this hot swamp of wine and indolence until it met a terrible end.

Thirty-Five

When Maria went to the Rossos' house in late afternoon to begin preparations for dinner, she found that something—it must have been rumors of an Italian armistice: peace with the Allies at the Germans' expense—had tempered the mood of the five officers. There was no loud laughter, no hilarity from the rooms above, just a band of surly men in uniform sitting around the Rossos' family room listening to the radio and drinking their beer. She wondered what they did when they were gone all day—patrols in the mountains, no doubt, or along the shores of the lake—and if they were ever afraid of what might be awaiting them. Or if their notion of superiority conveyed, in their minds, an immunity to suffering and death, to any kind of punishment in the afterlife.

It was, of course, not a question she could ask.

As she was putting together a salad of fresh greens, with a lamb shank baking in Antonetta Rosso's oven and potatoes boiling in a pot of water on the stove, the redheaded officer—Rolf, he'd said his name was—came into the kitchen and stood not far from her.

"Any news for us?" he asked after watching her work for a moment.

Maria glanced at him and shook her head.

"You'll notice at dinner a change in treatment. You'll remember our agreement, I'm sure."

"I remember," she said.

"We're very generous to those who cooperate with us. We have plenty of food and can get more. For you. For your family and friends. What I asked of you in return was a simple favor. Not difficult."

"If I hear anything, I'll tell you."

"I hope so," he said, unsmiling. He put his hand on her shoulder, and she flinched. He let out a kind of laugh, one note, and left her to her work.

When she was serving the meal, the tall, bald officer didn't touch her. She set the plate in front of him, her own mouth watering, and without looking at her, he said, "You have children?"

At first Maria didn't realize he was speaking to her. He turned his face a few degrees in her direction and repeated the question out of the side of his mouth without looking at her. She wondered if he was already drunk.

"You have children?"

"One. One child. A son."

"And he is where?"

"Fighting," she lied. "In Russia I think, but I cannot know. He cannot write. My husband is there also, I believe. I haven't heard anything from them."

The man turned his face forward again, dismissing her. Maria made several trips into the kitchen for plates, served the men without speaking, and then stood off to the side for a few minutes, as she'd been instructed. The tall, bald officer—the others always seemed to defer to him—tasted the lamb and nodded. Drank from his glass of wine. Looked up at her. "How is the food there; did your boy say? In Russia."

"He cannot write."

"Ah, yes. I remember now. Well, in honor of him, why don't you cook us a Russian meal one night. Ha!"

"I don't know Russian food."

"Beef stroganoff," one of the other men suggested, and the tall officer nodded and laughed his airy chuckle. "Yes, we'll procure the ingredients. Stroganoff every Saturday! What else will you need, potatoes?"

She shook her head nervously and shrugged. Waited. Tried to but could not hold the word inside. "I have some mushrooms."

The other officer who'd spoken said, "Beef," as if she didn't know that, and they all laughed. When the laughter settled, he added, "My wife makes it. You need noodles, sour cream, mushrooms."

"The mushrooms, they seem to have," the tall officer said. "The other things we will procure." He turned his eyes to Maria. "Beef stroganoff every Saturday. In honor of your brave husband and son!" He raised his glass, and the others followed suit. Maria could feel the eyes of the redhead on her. She pressed her teeth together, waited until the men were involved in their dinners, and then went into the kitchen and tended to the pots. When they were cleaned and set aside in the strainer, she wiped her hands and paused a minute, looking out the window at a graying landscape. Maybe, she thought, despite their terrible suffering, despite having been beaten to death in old age, Antonetta and Rafaelo Rosso were to be envied: their torment was over.

She walked home in the dark, across the weedy field, through her small grove of olive trees, through the gate in her fence. The Germans would never let her stop cooking for them; she understood that now. Rebecca would have to be moved. But where? Maybe Luca knew someone who had a safe house. She'd ask him the next time he came, and she'd remind him never to let them see him with her or, if they did, to say he was a nephew not a son.

In her kitchen, she looked at the mesh bag of *lepiota*, sitting there on a shelf like a ticking bomb. So unlike her gentle boy to offer such a thing. So unlike his mother to accept.

Thirty-Six

From shortly after his first sexual experience—on his thirteenth birthday with a Palermo prostitute his uncle procured for him—Silvio Merino had come to the realization that the Church had been lying to him all along: there was absolutely nothing sinful about sex. In fact, it seemed to him as he grew older that the act of love should be considered sacred. It created life, after all (though he himself had not yet had the pleasure of fatherhood). What could be more sacred than that?

In the years since that first terrifying encounter (the woman, blonde, large breasted, probably thirty-five, had practically had to lock the door and wrestle him backward onto the bed), he'd made love with many women, some Italian, some not, some beautiful, some not. Never, not once, had there been any unpleasantries, except perhaps in those few cases where the woman had for some reason imagined him as a candidate for the corral of marriage. Thin, plump, dark haired, blonde, Catholic, Jewish, or unattached to any faith, calm as the mountains or as neurotic as the sea on a stormy day, he'd found something lovable in each of them and had tried, as best he could, to see that they took as much pleasure from the lovemaking as he did himself.

Of all these women, perhaps the one with whom the time in bed had been most enjoyable was Lisiella Aiello, a Milanese art collector, rebellious daughter of one of the city's wealthiest families, and someone who, like him, had decided early on that marriage was an arrangement for which she was ill suited.

After leaving the German checkpoint officer and supposed car lover to his underwear laundering, Silvio had paid a brief visit to the Duomo, Milan's magnificent cathedral. There, as instructed, he left the statuette of Saint Jude beside a bank of votive candles in a side chapel and watched until he saw a mustachioed priest carry it away. Everything, it seemed, had gone according to plan. The gold had been delivered—God knew where it would end up—and he was safe and unharmed. He offered up a prayer of thanks, lit a votive candle for his parents, dropped a fifty-lire note into the cup of an old blind woman begging on the front step, and drove to the Grand Hotel de Milan. There he enjoyed a celebratory drink with his friend, Bella, who managed the famous American Bar. They joked, very quietly, about when and if the bar might be renamed.

"Bar Roosevelt," Bella suggested, depending on how the war ended up.

"Or Bar Hitler," he said, "if it goes the other way."

"God forbid!"

Silvio's drink of choice was vodka with ice and lime. After he'd finished the first of what he expected would be several of them, and feeling another twinge of guilt at the wartime luxury, he walked over to a phone and dialed Lisiella's number. Never perfect to begin with, phone communication had been disrupted by the war, so he had to dial twice before getting through. The sound of her voice on the end of the line gave him a distinct sexual thrill. Yes, she was home. And yes, bored to tears by the suffocating war atmosphere. Yes, of course, she loved the Grand Hotel and had missed him badly and would be more than happy to find her way there for a meal and perhaps something more.

And so it was that, after a leisurely dinner of excellent sliced beef and fresh *broccoletti*, and a surprisingly good bottle of Friuli Valpolicella, he and Lisiella found themselves relieved of their clothing and tangled in the luxurious sheets of one of the Grand Hotel's corner rooms.

She was an energetic and inventive lover, fond of moving, mid-intercourse, from lying on the bed, to standing by the window, to sitting astride him on a chair. That night was no exception. What Silvio loved about her was that, in and out of bed, she was completely without self-consciousness. She laughed and joked and teased while they were linked to each other; she'd suddenly tell him to stop moving and she'd lie there—on top of him, often as not—gazing into his eyes and whispering things that would have turned the cheeks of the good priest at the Duomo shades of communist red. At the climactic moment, she called out, *"Dio aiutami!" God help me!* and then laughed at herself when the tremors had passed.

The early departure, the excitement of the day, the meal, the alcohol, the sexual gymnastics—when it was finished, just past midnight, Silvio lay beside Lisiella in a state close to total exhaustion. They were on their backs, holding hands like first-time lovers. He offered up a silent prayer of thanks, his second that day. His mother used to tell him that the last child in a large family was watched over with particular care by the angels. It had always seemed to be true. But along with the gratitude, he felt, yet again, the light tap of guilt: so much suffering everywhere, and he was so happy.

"Il nostro Duce è scappato," Lisiella said in a quiet voice. *Our* Duce *has skipped out.*

"Yes. No one knows where."

In the distance, they heard a faint thump, as if a single bomb had been dropped in Quarto Oggiaro on the far side of the city. They waited, listening, but there was no more of that.

"You knew that I was friends with Sarfatti, one of his lovers, yes?"

"Margherita, patron of the arts."

"She used to tell me he'd throw her to the floor and make love to her violently, quickly, like an animal. And then stand up and reach for his violin and serenade her in the kindest way."

"A madman."

"Agreed." Lisiella held on to his hand and turned so that her bare breasts, those wonderful works of the Creator, were pressed against his left shoulder.

A shame, he thought, that neither of them wanted to marry. "I've been asked," he said, quietly and in as modest a tone as he could manage, "to use my various contacts to help find our lost *Duce*."

"Really, Silvio?"

He nodded. He could sense that the assignment, the proximity to what might be called espionage, excited her, and he wondered if, in fact, his exhaustion was as complete as it seemed. "Any ideas?"

Lisiella pushed their clasped hands gently to her body, moved herself against them almost imperceptibly. Through the slight fog of new arousal, he believed he could hear the golden gears of her beautiful mind click into motion. "No idea," she said, also modestly. Her breathing had changed slightly. "Except that your father's a driver, isn't he?"

"For the Irish embassy, yes. You remembered."

"Well, wouldn't it make sense that, wherever our *Duce* was taken, he was taken there by a driver?" She paused, pressed closer. Now he could feel her chest rising and falling. "And drivers speak to drivers, do they not? They have a kind of . . . *linkage*, no?"

Silvio smiled up at the dark ceiling and turned to touch her lips with his. "You, my gorgeous friend," he said, "have, among other fine qualities, a magnificent mind."

Thirty-Seven

From the back of his mother's house, Luca slipped into the woods and went northward on mostly overgrown paths that traversed the hillside parallel to the lakeshore. Soon he was deep in the trees, so deep that the lake couldn't be seen. Even so, as was his habit, he went along without making a sound. His father had told him that in America, the native hunters had been exceptionally quiet, needing to kill at close range and able to move silently through the woods so as not to make the animals aware of their presence. In his case, it was German soldiers not animals, and he was the hunted not the hunter. Unlikely as it was, even this far from the town, they might have the occasional patrol, looking for people who'd left their homes—Jews, mainly, but anyone trying to sneak across the border into Switzerland. Or maybe there was a special team out searching for the man who'd stabbed the Fascist not far south of these hills. He had an excuse, yes: the mushroom sack, the missing eye. Still, it was wise not to have one's papers examined too often. And, if they searched him, the wire cutters and large knife would be difficult to explain.

It was impossible for him to use these overgrown trails without thinking of his father. And whenever he thought of his father—he imagined his body lying frozen on the Russian front, left there by retreating German troops—it was impossible to contain the frustration he felt at not being given more important assignments. Other men, he imagined, were blowing up bridges and shooting at German planes, freeing Italian prisoners, helping the Allies find their way through the Sicilian hills. All his life, people had underestimated him because he could see out of one eye not two, because he had a strong right arm and a weaker left. According to the word that reached him now from Mentone and his Bolshevik friends, German divisions and machinery were pouring over the Brenner Pass in greater and greater numbers. It made sense, of course. If the rumors of surrender were true, if Italy was, in fact, about to stop fighting the Allies, then Germany's situation would be perilous. Any fool could understand that if the Allies had bomber bases in Italy, the Fatherland would be easily within reach from two directions—the British in the north and the Americans here. There were other rumors claiming that the Allies were about to make another landing down south, Salerno or Battipaglia or Napoli or Sardinia—the stories varied—which meant that more Italian civilians would lose their lives, and more Americans, Canadians, British, and Australians would be fighting for *his* homeland. And what was he doing? Slowing down a column of German troops with a rockslide, closing a road for an hour with a felled tree, knocking out a phone line. Killing someone who wasn't even a German soldier.

Not enough.

Lost in thought as he was, it took him an extra second to realize he was hearing voices not far ahead. He cursed his carelessness under his breath. No wonder Mentone wasn't entrusting him with more complicated jobs.

He moved off the path, angling uphill. The voices grew louder, definitely German. He could hear branches snapping, words he took to be curses, boots on the path—the furthest thing from the silent Indian hunters. Luca had time to go only about twenty meters. He stopped there, crawled behind a large boulder, and flattened himself on the ground. If they caught him that way, he'd be finished, but this was better than having to explain what he was doing up there with wire cutters in his knapsack. He had to hope these particular Germans were too lazy to move uphill.

Here they came, though, talking, cursing. He could smell cigarette smoke, hear boots crunching in the stony soil, bodies crashing through the brush. It seemed to him they'd wandered off the path, closer now. The voices were clearer. He caught a few words he knew: *verloren—lost*—and then a phrase that made his spine go cold: *tötete ihn mit einem Messer—killed him with a knife*. It wasn't a random patrol: they were looking for him, or, at least, for the killer in the hills.

His eyes were closed, his cheek and right ear pressed into damp moss. He didn't dare look up or turn his head. He wondered if his feet showed at the side of the rock or if he'd left prints in a damp patch of earth. The men—three, he guessed—came even closer. He could hear them gasping now, winded from the climb. He squeezed his eyes tight and tried not to breathe. The Germans were resting just on the other side of the boulder. He smelled more cigarette smoke, could almost taste it in his own mouth. He heard someone pissing in the leaves, then a comment, the word *klein. Small.* Harsh laughter. The rock was the size of a delivery truck, but all they had to do was step around behind it and they'd find him, and that would be the end. Not only would he be killed, but there would be less food for his mother, less for Rebecca Zinsi. And what would become of Sarah and their child?

He kept his eyes squeezed tight, kept his breathing shallow, resisted a sudden urge to jump out from behind the rock and try to kill them all. He heard one of the men burp. The others laughed, made comments he didn't understand. He heard water gurgling in a canteen, the cap being clumsily screwed back on. He smelled the sulfur from a match and then more cigarette smoke. Then someone walking. Then all of them walking, the footsteps and talk and tobacco smoke fading away slowly to the south. He lay there for another quarter of an hour, making sure one of them hadn't been left behind, and then he stood, wiped the pine needles from his shirt and hair, and started off again. The daylight was disappearing; there would be guards at the border around the clock but, he hoped, no more patrols in these trees after the sun went down. Once night fell, he liked to think, Italy belonged to the Italians. He walked through the dusk and twilight, walked until the darkness grew so thick that he couldn't see the way, then sat and waited for the moon to rise. Hours it would be. As he waited, he thought of Sarah and Rebecca and his mother. How could the older women move through terrain like this? And if they somehow reached the border, how would he ever get them across?

Thirty-Eight

Mussolini had passed several days on La Maddalena—two or three or six; as one blended into the next, he lost count. Nicolina prepared his meals, Vittorio played games of *briscola* with him at the card table in the living room. Perhaps they actually respected him, or perhaps their polite deference was being paid for by the government he'd once controlled. Forbidden from all news, he was nevertheless allowed to walk around the island, exploring its hidden beaches, both sand and gravel, and nodding at the locals, who knew who he was now but still kept a distance, eyeing him with a mixture of fear and curiosity. Even on these walks, an armed soldier followed him, and the machine-gun emplacement in front of Casa Weber was manned night and day. No chance of escape, then. He didn't know how long he could bear it. That night, perhaps, or the next, he'd ask Vittorio if there was a chance of getting a pistol. He'd tell the man—not the brightest star in the sky—that he wanted to walk to the back of the island and practice shooting, keep his aim sharp in case the Allies landed on the beach early some morning. He'd hold on to the pistol and, if things became too bleak, if it seemed they were going to do something like turn him over to the Americans in exchange for Italian prisoners of war, then he'd take refuge in the noble deed and end his life.

In the midst of this musing, he heard a knock on the door. Nicolina, he supposed, asking what he wanted for supper. He sat up on the bed, called *"Entra!"*

A young man appeared on the threshold, little more than a boy, really. Fourteen or fifteen, he guessed. The boy seemed tremendously shy, looking up at *il Duce* from beneath dark eyebrows as if he were in the presence of a god. Glad for the company, Mussolini invited him to pull up the one chair and sit opposite. But something wasn't quite right. The boy was dressed in the rough gray shirt and heavy trousers of island fishermen, but his face was barely tanned, and his hands were soft looking. "Your Excellency," he said in a quiet voice, "m-may I speak with you for a moment?"

"Of course, of course. Are you unwell? Is there some problem on the island?"

"N-no, no problem," the boy said. He sat uneasily, hands clasping and unclasping between his knees, eyes somewhat dull, as if he were ill or medicated.

"What, then?"

"J-just," the boy said, "just that I-I'm a fisherman, or my father is. I help him sometimes. Like today. He comes over from the mainland with his boat." The boy floated one arm in the direction of the window and seemed to lose courage.

"And what happened?"

"N-nothing happened. It's my mother; she has dreams. She dreamed you ate a bad mushroom and died, and my father and I have been very upset about it, and he came here today to deliver some fish to this house. He's visiting now, with someone else, a woman, next door, and . . . and—"

"Don't be afraid, young man. I'd never harm you. I had a son like you. Bruno. A sensitive boy. Our third child. He died a hero, fighting for his country. When you're a little older, you will serve, yes?"

"Y-yes, *Duce*. Yes, of course. I . . . I just wanted to make sure you're careful what you eat. When we found out you were here, in this house . . . We weren't supposed to know, but the woman—h-his friend—said something to my father, that she had seen you, and he didn't believe it at first, so he wanted me to come here and tell you, warn you, and to see that it was really you."

"It is."

"And you're . . . safe? They're not taking you away again?"

"I don't know. Who knows? I'm bored, that's all."

"I-I'll bring you, next time, a f-fish," the boy said. "My father will, a tuna maybe . . . Would you like that?"

"Of course, yes," Mussolini said, though he'd eaten almost nothing but fish for the past week.

At that, the boy stood, too quickly, as if startled or terrified. His hands were twitching madly at his sides. "I have to go now," he said. "Be careful, *Duce*; so much depends on you still."

He reached out a hand and Mussolini, standing now, took it. The boy would never make a soldier, he thought; the handshake was weak. He put an arm around the boy's shoulders and squeezed in a fatherly way. The boy flinched. "Thank you for caring about my life," *il Duce* said in a grand tone. "Thanks to your mother and father, also. I'll be careful about the mushrooms."

"G-good," the boy said, and he slipped out the door, leaving it open as he went.

Mussolini stepped over to the window and, in a moment, heard the front door close below him and saw the boy hurrying down the stone walk, one shoulder lower than the other so that it seemed he might suddenly veer off sideways like a cart with one bad wheel. On he went, down the path, across the road, along a footpath that led toward the harbor. *Il Duce* studied him, thinking, This is what I've been reduced to, counseling troubled youth now, meeting with the sons of drunken fishermen instead of heads of state, generals, and popes. Listening to the dreams of women who are not even my wife.

He went and lay on his bed, clouds of depression closing in around him. These dark moods were becoming daily visitors. After a long time, he fell into a restless sleep disturbed by shards of dream. Claretta. Rachele. The members of the Fascist Grand Council sitting around a smoky table, arguing about him as if he wasn't even in the room, Grandi and Badoglio leading them into treachery.

Thirty-Nine

For the visit with his father—Lisiella's idea—Silvio decided he would take the yellow Fiat Cinquecento. The trip to the Irish embassy was risky enough—someone might think he was looking for asylum—so it was better to keep a low profile this time. Better to dress down a bit, too. His father was a plain, gruff man, overly concerned with money and resentful of those who were better off. Before he left the apartment, Silvio folded a hundred-lire note into his pants pocket, thinking he'd make a small gift, help the family, ease the conversation a bit.

On the drive to Via Giacomo Medici, he wondered why his father had never seemed to approve of him. Unfair, of course. Over the fifteen or so years that he'd lived in Rome, he'd brought three of his brothers, his father and mother, and two sisters to the capital; found work for all of them; found them decent places to live. True, in doing so, he'd enriched his network of contacts, but weren't his family members better off here than on the pitiful farm outside Troisi? Especially now, with all the fighting in Sicily?

He'd found his father a position as a driver for the Irish embassy, Villa Spada—not the ambassador's driver, more like the man they sent to market for supplies or to the airport to pick up low-level visitors. Because of Ireland's neutrality in the war, theirs was the only Western embassy that remained open after *il Duce's* alliance with Hitler. Once his father had established himself there, Silvio took to hanging around

Villa Spada, made friends, brought small gifts to the secretaries, even enjoyed a brief affair with one of them. Who knew how such acquaintances might come in handy if the fortunes of war shifted? His sisters—both of them nurses—worked at Bambin Gesù, the famous children's hospital, so he cultivated contacts there, too, and could sometimes be a source of certain medications for friends and associates who desired to use them without having to obtain a prescription. His brothers were working construction, at far higher wages than they'd been paid in Sicily, and were occasionally the source of extra building materials that were not really needed on the job. Was that wrong? Their lives were made easier, and he, the *facciatu*, was the source of their comfort.

But his father—a conservative man in every respect, a man who liked money as much as his son did but had much less of it—did not approve. With him, everything had to be official, sanctioned, legal. Every week he put his small embassy paycheck in the bank and guarded it as if it were a gorgeous mistress.

At the embassy, after a smile and a wave to the sentry at the gate, Silvio parked the Fiat and climbed the stairs to the main reception area. Assunta was on duty this day. He walked around the side of the desk and planted a kiss on each cheek, told her how lovely she looked, made her blush. The woman wasn't lovely at all; there was something crooked about her face, the eyes set at slightly different angles, the forehead too high, the mouth unflattering and thin. But so what? That was the face she'd been born with, it wasn't her fault, and the simple fact of its asymmetry no doubt made life much more difficult for her when it came to finding the pleasures of physical love. She was stranded here with bureaucrats twice her age. How many friendly kisses did she receive on any given day?

"My father around?"

Assunta was still blushing. She nodded, pointed. "In the cafeteria."

"May God help him, then," Silvio said, and Assunta laughed and shooed him away.

He found his father in the workers' dining room, a plain square hall that smelled of foreign foods Silvio had no intention of sampling. His father was continually complaining about the menu, but his wife— Silvio's mother—had passed away of poorly treated heart issues a year before, so there was no longer any hope of going home at midday for a delicious pasta puttanesca.

There his father sat, alone at a table, the ruins of lunch on a plate beside him and a newspaper tilted up before his face. He could read—a rarity for Sicilian farmers of his generation—but only with a painstaking slowness, forming each word with his lips, sounding it out, pondering. He had a great and abiding interest in current events, but it rarely led to conversation, not with his son, at least. Filippo Merino, Silvio often thought, was the person for whom the phrase *a man of few words* had been invented.

"Ciao, Babbo," Silvio said as he approached, putting some extra energy into the greeting, preparing himself for what was to come.

His father looked up from the paper and made a noise. "Unnh."

That, Silvio knew, was the best one could hope for.

"Lunch good?"

"Eh."

"Anything interesting in the news?"

"Nuh."

His father didn't ask him to sit, so Silvio decided to take a different approach. "Care for a game of bocce?"

A pause, a reluctant nod. His father folded the newspaper carefully under one arm and walked, more or less at Silvio's side, along an immaculate corridor. At the end of the corridor, a door opened onto a modest yard enclosed by a three-meter concrete wall, where the workers were allowed to smoke and take their ease. To the Irish bosses' great credit, they'd installed a bocce court there, little more than a dusty rectangle of earth bounded by low boards on all four sides. They'd invested in a set of ceramic balls, too, nine of them, four with a line around their equator and four unlined, plus a *pallino*, or *little ball*. One player tossed the little ball down the court, short or long, depending on strategy, and then they took turns trying to see who could get the larger balls closer. If all four of one player's balls were closest, that meant eight points. Three balls were six points. One or two balls closest and you were given one or two points, respectively. Most games were played to twenty-one, and victory had to be by a margin of at least two.

His father was a master player, though utterly conservative even here. Silvio, much more of a risk-taker, could enjoy stretches of greatness and then succumb to moments of epic failure. But he'd always loved the game. In his more optimistic hours, he liked to tell himself that bocce was what he and his father had instead of love.

They took turns, his father grunting, Silvio calling out to each ball as if it might obey him. In the first round, after all his father's balls had been rolled or thrown, the old man looked to have three closest to the *pallino* and was no doubt mentally giving himself six points. But Silvio had one more shot. He held the ball palm down, hefted it for a moment. Then, after swinging his arm like a pendulum three times and letting out three small grunts, he muttered, "Watch out now, *Babbo!*" and sent it out and up in a long, graceful arc. The ball crashed down between his father's closest ball and the *pallino*, sending the small ball careering sideways into the opposite corner, where Silvio's three other balls had been sulking in defeat.

"Six points for the son!" he said as they walked up the court for the next round, played in the opposite direction.

"Beh," his father said, almost an emotional outburst for a man like him. "Good."

Things, Silvio thought, were warming up. Soon there would be an armistice.

They played along, Silvio losing his brief lead steadily and happily, his father buried in concentration and playing with a cautious precision that marked everything else he did in life, from driving to eating.

As a teenager, in certain angry moments, Silvio had wondered about his father's lovemaking style. Precise, he guessed. Careful. Making sure the mattress was not overused so it would last longer. It was a miracle they'd had eleven children.

On that day, entertaining no such bitter thoughts, he told himself that, for strategic reasons, he'd allow his father to win, though the truth was the old man beat him eight of every ten games no matter what he did. The final score was 21–16, which his father announced with a certain muted satisfaction.

But Silvio made a big fuss of it. *"Babbo,"* he said, "you should see if there are any tournaments among the embassy employees and foreign service officers. You'd certainly win. You haven't lost your touch at all." And so on.

He'd brought along two cigars—another rare treat—and handed one over to his father in a posture of surrender. "Let's sit and smoke," he said, gesturing to a bench beneath a spreading fig tree.

A syllable of thank-you, of agreement. The slightest breath of warm air between them now. His father placed the folded newspaper beneath him before he sat.

"Everything all right here, *Babbo*?" Silvio asked when they were seated not too close beside each other and puffing out clouds of sweet smoke.

"Eh. Good enough."

"They're paying you."

"On time."

"My brothers and sisters? Well?"

His father turned to look at him and then moved his eyes forward again, as if to say: *Find out for yourself, why don't you?*

This mild version of torture went on for half an hour, Silvio pulling the answers out like a dentist pulling a series of deeply rooted teeth. He smiled, laughed, even once gently elbowed his father when the talk turned to the women at the embassy and the delicate question of possible romance.

At last, when he could sense that his father's patience for him had reached its end, and when the cigars had been put out and tossed aside, Silvio ventured the main question as casually as he could. By then they were walking back toward the building. *"Il Duce,"* Silvio said quietly. "You've heard the news, I take it."

"Unnh."

"A disaster, no?"

His father shrugged, looked away. It had always been hard to guess his politics. Some nights at dinner, he'd have two or three words of praise for *il Duce*. Other times, he'd frown when he said the man's name. In the end, Silvio believed he'd come to adore Benito Mussolini, like so many other gullible Italians.

"Where do you think they have him, *Babbo*?"

Silvio watched the smallest smile touch the corners of his father's lips. The old man liked to win at bocce, liked to drive, and he liked, most of all, to be the one who knew things others didn't know. Being around him in the old days, when his mother was alive and his father had been a bit more fond of speaking, meant listening to a constant litany of know-it-all complaint, delivered from on high. This driver made this mistake; that driver made that mistake. Look at the *stronzo*, making a turn like that. Look at the idiots who are running things. What do they care for the poor, the workingman? In time, the well of complaint had gone dry and, with it, his father's urge to speak.

Silvio kept trying. "You have your finger on the pulse of the city. What do you think happened to him? Did they turn him over to the Allies? Shoot him? Throw him in the ocean?"

"Maybe," his father said to the last possibility.

"Have you heard anything?"

His father looked away, swallowed.

Silvio studied the stubbled cheeks and small eyes.

"I heard," his father said after a long hesitation, "I heard they took him south. To the water. Put him on a boat."

Silvio thought: *A dozen words without stopping! A miracle!* He said, "Really?"

His father nodded, loosening up a bit. "A driver friend told me. To a port city. Latina, I think. Put him on a military boat, a ship."

"God help him, then, *Babbo.*"

"*Sì,*" his father said. Silvio waited, hoping in vain for more, then took the hundred-lire note from his pocket, palmed it, and reached out for one of his father's crushing handshakes. "What's this?" the old man asked, pretending he wasn't pleased. He was a proud man, yes, until it came to money.

"From your boy. For food, cigars, my brothers and sisters. Whatever you want. Some friends of mine are curious about *il Duce,* and they're paying me well for information, so if you hear anything else . . ."

Against all history and hope, Silvio waited for some signal of gratitude, a smile, an embrace, a quick *grazie,* even. Nothing. A glance. One half of a nod that might have meant anything from agreement to condemnation.

It didn't matter. Lisiella was a genius: drivers did, in fact, talk to each other. Mussolini had been taken to Latina and put on a small military boat! Giovanni, the half-American, would no doubt pay handsomely for that piece of news. And perhaps there would be ways of learning more.

Forty

That night, when the square of wood that covered the attic entrance was slipped aside, Maria saw the round metal bottom of the slop bucket, took hold of it, and brought it down into her arms. The smell was horrible. She couldn't keep herself from looking inside. Blood today, mixed with everything else. She was about to carry it off to the toilet when she heard Rebecca make a hissing sound, barely audible. She looked up—the once beautiful face, gaunt now, with protruding eyes. Gray hair hanging down like strings. "I must go, Maria," Rebecca whispered.

"Go where?"

"Into the woods. I can't stay here another day. I'm losing my mind; I'm dying. Let me go. I need to find my daughter. I need to breathe the air. Please!"

Maria watched her for a few seconds, then shook her head. "When my son comes again, he'll take you. Have courage. Another few days, a week at most. And then I'll let you go. Have courage. Have faith."

She could see that Rebecca didn't believe her, and she could see, too, the start of a thinly veiled insanity. It was asking too much of a person, living in a hot, windowless box. How long had it been? Seven weeks? Eight? She'd have to find a solution. When Luca came to visit her again, she'd ask him to do something, take Rebecca into the hills, procure false papers. Something. Anything.

She saw a flash of lightning outside the kitchen windows, then heard a long rumble of thunder. A stormy night, it would be; she hoped Luca and Sarah were safe. She said a prayer that the lightning would spare them.

Forty-One

Not long after first light, while the summer sun over Lake Como still had a soft, post-rainstorm quality to it—kind, not punishing—Luca stepped out of the trees behind Gennaro Masso's farmhouse and sounded three knocks on the old man's back door. After a moment, the farmer appeared. He'd just shaved—a bit of soap clung to the bottom of one ear—and, smooth cheeked and barefoot, he answered the door in a pale-blue T-shirt and black work pants held up by suspenders. The sight of him brought a rare smile to Luca's lips. There were various ways of protecting oneself from the Germans—hiding, collaborating, fleeing. Masso's way was to pretend, on occasion, to be stupid. For a few seconds, he made his fool's face for Luca, letting one side of his mouth hang down, dulling his eyes, wiping a palm upward across his high forehead as if it were the middle of the day and he was sweating, or as if he were trying to clear away the shield that stood between his brain and the world.

Luca reached out and wiped the soap from Masso's earlobe, playing along. "It's Thursday, Gennaro. *Hai dimenticato?* Did you forget?"

"Tursday when? Which Tursday, January?"

"August already. Market day in Dubino."

"Ah, Dubino!" Masso exclaimed, "a town in England!" and waved him inside.

For decades, Gennaro Masso had made a good living growing everything from apricots to zucchini on his large property. In the towns north of Menaggio—Dongo, Stazzona, Brenzio, San Benedetto, Dubino—people were used to seeing him carrying his fruits and vegetables along the roads in a wooden cart drawn by his famously stubborn donkeys, Culillo and then Culillo II. But Masso was seventy-five; it made sense that he'd hire a younger man to take over some of the trips to market. So now, every other week, Luca loaded up the cart, took hold of the reins, and led Masso's temperamental Culillo II along the *statale* with his load of tomatoes, or lettuce, or pickles, whatever was in season and could be sold. Often enough, the cart carried something else besides—a message, money, knives, tools.

They had their regular arrangement and a kind of friendship, but whenever he spent time with Masso, Luca heard a faint whispering in his inner ear, as if some message he could not quite understand was being relayed to him. The old farmer had somehow known about his secret work, and he, not Don Claudio, had been the one who introduced him to Mentone, Prinzano, and Scutarro—the men who had become Luca's three contacts in the northern mountains. Luca had never been completely comfortable with that trio of partisan fighters. They were communists, for one thing, and he had little sympathy for communism. But his discomfort went deeper than that.

Still, every other Thursday, he made this two-day trip, earned a little money, brought food to a few dozen hungry people, met his trio of secret contacts . . . and came back to the hills above Mezzegra listening to the nagging voice of doubt.

There was bread and cheese and good tomatoes, even a little salt—Masso had been expecting him—and Luca sat at a scarred kitchen table and, somewhat guiltily, ate a small meal. The farmer brewed two cups of espresso and joined him. "What do you hear?" Masso asked. "Word doesn't reach me. A radio is too expensive for an old man, the news too upsetting."

Luca shrugged. It was a chess game, a gambit, all part of Masso's disguise. The old man knew everything there was to know. "The Allies are in Sicily," Luca began, watching Masso's face.

Masso nodded, giving away nothing.

"And, since the last time I saw you, people are saying *il Duce* is gone, taken prisoner by the king, Badoglio, Grandi, and the other Council members, his old comrades. No one knows where they took him. Rumors are flying."

"As they always do."

"Is it true about *il Duce*? Is he gone?"

After a small hesitation, Masso nodded again, wrinkling his thick neck. So much for the lack of a radio, for the idea of word not reaching him. He twirled the small porcelain cup in front of him, met Luca's eyes, and at last spoke. "Think about where our little king finds himself, Luca. To the south, the English-speaking people of the world—Americans, Australians, Canadians, British—are conquering Sicily. To the north, Hitler is filling up the country with troops and weapons. Now the king has removed *il Duce* from power and hidden him away, and everybody is desperately trying to find him—the Allies to take him prisoner, Hitler to rescue him, our comrades to kill him. The intrigue, the rumors, the occupation, the invasion, the hunger, the suffering—a national nightmare. And our little royal sitting on top of all of it, riding a wild horse without a saddle."

Luca could find nothing to say. In his heart, there was no sympathy for Vittorio Emanuele. The king, after all, had practically handed Mussolini the reins of power and then cowered before him for decades, letting the *Duce* make decisions while he himself played the royal role . . . and did nothing. It had taken the Allied invasion to bring him out of his stupor.

Masso burped, brushed a sleeve across his mouth. "How are things for you, closer to home?"

"My mother suffers."

"Bring her here. It would be nice to have the company of a woman again."

Luca took a bite of the fresh bread. For a few seconds, that idea seemed plausible, attractive even—Masso had more food than most people, and the Germans had so far left him alone—until he remembered Rebecca. He decided not to mention her. Behind this semicomic, half-sincere veil, his farmer friend was a mysterious creature, a man he liked and almost completely trusted.

"The Germans are making her cook for them now," he said. "Dinner. Every night."

"She should poison them."

Luca looked up at Masso's tanned face and mostly bald head, the close-set, rheumy eyes and deeply cleft chin, a many-layered expression, impossible to read. Could it be that, among all the other things Masso somehow seemed to know, he was aware of the *lepiota* in Maria's kitchen? "I hadn't thought of that," he lied, and immediately felt a twinge. Here was the heart of the matter these days: you had to put your life in the hands of a few friends and not look back, not give in to doubt. *"A web of trust,"* Don Claudio had called it, the first time he'd spoken to Luca about the secret work. That conversation had led him to the mustachioed priest at the Duomo in Milan—who had never revealed his name—and eventually to Masso.

For some reason, though, with Masso, he found that kind of total vulnerability more difficult. Masso was watching him, perhaps not fully trusting him, either. "There would be reprisals," Luca said.

Masso pursed his lips, didn't move his eyes. "Tell your mother to kill them all," he said. "I'll help if she wants. If we have to die, we'll die, that's all."

A nod, a sip from the small cup, Luca's mind whirling and twisting, trying to understand how much of it was an odd joke and how much real.

"What else?" Masso demanded.

"Sarah's with child."

The jowls of the old man's face twitched, and a genuine smile blossomed, showing what remained of his teeth. "Congratulations!"

"Yes, ordinarily a great blessing."

"A great blessing even now. Your child will grow up without knowing war."

"You're so certain, Gennaro."

Masso kept smiling. "If *il Duce* is truly gone, then most Italians won't fight anymore. Not for Hitler, at least. The German *bastardo* can't conquer the entire world by himself."

"He's halfway there."

"Losing in Russia."

"You know that for a fact?"

Masso shrugged, adjusted the clasp on one of his suspenders. "I hear things."

"I thought you said news doesn't reach you."

Another shrug, another display of the bad teeth. "I have talkative friends, that's all. We play cards; we drink. There are rumors—the Germans losing in Russia, the Allies winning in Sicily. An armistice, maybe. The king making a deal with Roosevelt and Churchill now that our *Duce* is gone."

"Any word of my father?"

Masso shook his head. "I would tell you if I knew."

"Sarah wants to help. When I see Mentone tonight, I'm going to ask him to get her new papers." He tapped his shirt. "I have her passport with me."

"Ah . . ."

It seemed to Luca that Masso was about to say more but stopped himself.

"I don't want her to," Luca said. "Especially now."

Masso pondered a moment, salted another slice of tomato, and placed it on his tongue. He chewed and swallowed before speaking.

"Years ago, when my Amelia was alive, we used to have a beautiful bird that would come here in the summer." He paused, scratched his chin with one finger. "A bird like you've never seen. Dark purple here"—he rubbed his rough hands along the outsides of his arms—"but here"— he placed them flat on his chest—"a color like the inside of a peach. Incredible. It used to make her very happy to see this bird. Part of me wanted to set a trap for it and catch it and keep it in a cage in the house to give my wife pleasure. But if I had done that, the bird would have died, and Amelia would have been miserable. Me too." Masso took another sip from his small cup and raised his eyes.

Luca watched him for a few seconds, then nodded. "And the Germans think you're stupid, Masso."

"Let them."

The farmer took the last sip from his cup and set it aside, and Luca sensed it was a signal: the comic routine was over. "Anything for Mentone and the others?"

Something crossed Masso's face then, a flicker of trouble. "There was supposed to be," he said. "Don Claudio's delivery has been delayed, it seems. There were supposed to be . . . funds. Rome, to Milan, to me, to you, to them. But our good priest hasn't yet returned. Tell Mentone and his comrades they'll have it next trip."

"They won't like that."

Masso worked his lips, and the trouble appeared again. "And what are they going to do, Luca, shoot you? Fire you? You're the most valuable man they have."

They sat for a moment in silence, Luca nursing his surprise. *The most valuable man they have.* No one had ever said anything like that to him. Masso looked out the window, then back at his guest. "Someone was killed in the hills near Santa Eligia two days ago. A Fascist. Stabbed." He brought one hand up to the middle of his belly. "Here."

Luca nodded in a noncommittal way, watched.

"Know anything about it?"

The subject had caught him by surprise. In the space of two seconds, a silent argument took place within his thoughts, a voice making the case that he should hold back the true answer, protect himself, that there was something odd about this supposedly simple man. How did all this information reach him? His card-playing friends? Fascist contacts?

Masso was watching him closely now, the fake foolishness completely gone, a chill in the room. "Santa Eligia is on your route, that's all. I thought you might have seen or heard something."

"How did you know about it? How do you know for sure he was a Fascist?"

"A friend found the body. Dragged it off the path. Hid it as best he could. He said there was a Party ID in the man's pants. And nearby was a knife like the knives they carry."

At that, as if a curtain had been pulled to one side, revealing a complex mural that had been there all along, Luca suddenly understood. "You had someone following me. In Milan. There was someone else, behind me and behind the Fascist. I heard the dog bark, I . . ."

Masso was silent.

"The whole time I was at Loreto, two people were watching me, not one."

"*È vero,*" Masso admitted. *That's true.*

"Why?"

"Because if you were working for the other side, I needed to know. If you weren't, I wanted someone to watch out for you."

"That you'd think I would work for the Germans, that you'd think I needed watching out for . . . Two insults."

"I'm sorry," Masso said, but Luca detected no regret in his voice, no real apology at all. His anger was short lived: he'd been harboring the same doubts about Masso, after all. "I have my reasons," Masso said. And then, after hesitating one beat, "One of the three men you're going to see tonight is a spy, an informer. He won't live until your next trip north."

"Mentone?"

Masso shook his head. "Scutarro."

"That's a joke, isn't it?"

"Last thing from a joke. The very last thing."

"Then you want me to kill him?"

"That job is for someone else. Prinzano knows. You can give Scutarro Sarah's passport, play along. Prinzano will take care of him and get the papers changed for you, too."

"Does Mentone know?"

"Mentone's a minor player."

"Mentone's a minor player? But Mentone has been giving me jobs for months now. He acts like the boss, he—"

"Relaying orders, not giving them."

"Then who are the major players?" Luca couldn't keep himself from asking. But by the time the last word was out of his mouth, he had his answer. "You are, aren't you? You and the archbishop."

Masso didn't smile or change expression. "I'm an old farmer, Luca. You're my helper, an innocent mushroom gatherer who makes a little extra money driving my cart to market every two weeks because gas is so expensive and because I'm too old to wrestle with Culillo."

"And what then? What happens? What do I do? Who do I listen to?"

"You play your role. For now, listen to Mentone and say you'll follow his orders."

"And then?"

"And then we'll have other work for you, bigger things. *You* should be giving orders now, not Mentone. In fact, if something happens to me, I want you to take over."

"What?"

"That's to be discussed another time. For now, finish your coffee and go. It's a long way. Four bushel baskets. Peppers. Apricots already.

160

Apples. Fennel and zucchini, too. I doubt you'll get the new papers for Sarah on this trip, but if you do, keep them underneath the boards where you sit. In fact, put the passport there now, rather than keeping it on your person. You'll see how. I used to keep my money there when I slept at the inn. I made a secret place, a little wooden drawer. You'll see it. Go now. The trip will take longer with all the Germans on the road. Eat whatever you want of the food, and take some for Sarah, for your mother. I have all the money I need. God be with you."

Luca sat there, a dozen questions circling in his thoughts. But then Masso was standing, and so he stood, too; thanked him for the food; and shook his hand before he went out the door.

He walked across the dusty yard and toward the stubborn donkey. Masso's words—*"Most valuable man," "You should be giving orders now,"* and *"If something happens to me, I want you to take over"*—spun up swirls of dust in his thoughts. They were either tricks, horrible tricks, or the exact kinds of things he'd been hoping to hear for months. He wondered if killing the Fascist had been some kind of test. He'd passed, apparently, and now he'd be promoted . . . Unless Masso was the traitor and not Scutarro, in which case his meeting that night north of Dubino would be nothing more than an appointment with death.

Forty-Two

In his regular weekly meeting with General Kurt Student—the terrifying paratroop commander who had implemented Göring's order for the reprisal killings of hundreds of civilians after the invasion of Crete, and who kept an office next to the torture cells so he could listen in before going to bed—Skorzeny was obliged to give a report admitting that there was not yet any solid information on the whereabouts of *il Duce*. They had some of the best intelligence officers in the entire German armed forces on the job, he said, hundreds of sources in central Italy; Selenzen was raking his fingers through the mold, but so far, nothing beyond the fact that Mussolini had been put into a car late at night and taken south from the carabinieri barracks in Rome. "After that point," Skorzeny told his general, "the trail seems to have gone absolutely cold."

When he was finished, Skorzeny waited, uneasy in the general's company. Student was a good-looking man, but something about his middle-aged face—a slight downward slant at the outside of the eyes and edges of the lips, a bubbling pot of acid behind the pupils—hissed *torturer, torturer, torturer*—and Skorzeny found the echoes difficult to ignore. General Student had sat through the brief report with his lips pressed up beneath the bottom of his nose and an expression of the deepest dissatisfaction on his face. There was no noise from the room next door, but a terrible smell seeped into the office from that direction.

General Student seemed not to notice. He was staring at the wall, not blinking.

"Captain, listen to me," the general said at last, shifting his eyes to Skorzeny and moving them back and forth over his scar. "The Italians who are running this country now, Badoglio and the Little King, are—we strongly suspect—in secret discussions with the Allied high command. Surrender—or, as they are wont to call it, 'armistice'—is the likely outcome. Within weeks. Possibly within days. What do you think will happen then?"

"I'm a soldier, Herr General, not a politician, not a strategist."

"Then let me educate you. What will happen is that the Italians will side with the Allies. A few thousand soldiers, worthless though they might be, will remain loyal to us. All the others will turn. We'll find ourselves in the midst of a civil war, with the people who know the roads, towns, and mountains better than anyone, fighting for the enemy. The civilians will resist us even more than they already have. The only person who can keep this country together, and on our side, is this clown Mussolini. Their *duce* . . . What does the word mean anyway?"

"Leader."

"Their leader, their *duce*. If he's dead, fine, he's dead. A disaster. But if he's alive, and I suspect he is, then we have to find him as quickly as possible and bring him to the Führer."

"And then?" Skorzeny risked asking.

General Student fixed him with a merciless glare. "And then the Führer will decide what to do!"

The general pushed his chair back with a loud scraping noise, lifted his lanky body to a standing position in one lithe movement, and stormed out of the meeting room without another word, leaving the door open behind him. Skorzeny sat there for a time, staring at the map on the opposite wall, forcing himself not to flee the terrible smell. He ran his eyes over the Italian peninsula from bottom to top, trying to imagine where they would hide a man who'd become the most wanted figure in the war. His gaze moved to the island of Crete, and he wondered if the things that had been said about General Student's actions there could actually be true. Elderly men, pregnant women, small children—ordered killed without the slightest sign of unease, the slightest hesitation. The rattle of machine guns. The screams and fountains of blood. Slaughter in the street. The general, they said, had watched all of it, arms crossed over his chest, lips twisted into a thin smile.

After a time, Skorzeny stood and went out into the hall and up three flights of stairs. He was walking back toward his office, not in the best of moods, when he saw Selenzen coming the other way. Even before Selenzen looked up and saw him, Skorzeny could sense he had new information. It was written on his fat cheeks.

They saluted each other in the hallway, and Skorzeny immediately escorted the shorter man into his office. He did not even bother to sit down. "What do you have?"

Selenzen smiled; Skorzeny resisted the urge to slap him.

"Herr Captain," Selenzen said, "after a great deal of effort, after maximizing the use of my many sources, I have found him."

"You personally?"

Selenzen stifled an uppity little grin. "One of my . . . contacts. In fact, this contact—"

"Reliable?"

"I believe so. Absolutely. Yes. This contact, in fact, stood directly in front of Mussolini and spoke to him for several minutes."

"Where?"

"La Maddalena Island, close to the northern coast of Sardinia. A stone and concrete house called Casa Weber."

"You're sure?"

"Mostly sure, yes."

"Guarded?"

"Rather heavily."

"Thank you. Dismissed."

Skorzeny went over to the map table, seething, his eyes on Sardinia, his mind already formulating a plan. *"Mostly sure,"* the brilliant Selenzen had said. *"Mostly."*

And based on this *mostly*, he was supposed to put at risk the lives of a hundred of his best men.

Forty-Three

From the window of his sparsely furnished room, Mussolini looked out on the La Maddalena morning. Cloud cover, but he could see the first patches of blue sky, and he felt the day would be calm and warm. The promise of fine weather gave him little comfort. He couldn't remember the last time he'd felt lonely. He didn't like the feeling, didn't even like the word, which seemed to him to imply weakness.

Nicolina knocked on the door. When he called her in, she greeted him pleasantly, then set down a tray on the small table near the window. A bunch of green grapes, a glass of milk, half a loaf of bread. "It's a shame about your digestion, *Duce*. We could cook you something more suitable."

"It's nothing," he said bravely.

She nodded, offered a timid smile. He noticed the gold cross around her neck and stopped her as she was about to leave. "Sit and talk with me," he said.

"But I'll interrupt your breakfast."

"Sit." He almost used the word *please* but caught himself.

With the meager meal between them, Nicolina sat on the edge of the chair opposite, leaning slightly forward, anxious, as if she were ready to jump up and run.

"Tell me," *il Duce* said, watching her, "why do you wear that cross?"

The woman reached up and twirled the gold crucifix between her second and third fingers. "Why, Excellency, does it bother you?"

He shook his head. "I just ask why you wear it. What does it mean to you?"

"It means the sacrifice of Jesus Christ. For us. For our sins."

"Ah. And you really believe he existed, that what happened to him, what is said to have happened, is actually true."

"Of course, Excellency!" she said in a surprised voice. "It says so in the Bible!"

"But you never consider that someone may have tampered with the facts of the story, exaggerated. For the purposes of . . . propaganda?"

The woman peered at him, then made the sign of the cross. "*Duce!* How can you say such a thing?"

"I don't know," he said helplessly. He looked away, blood pressing up against the skin of his cheeks. "I don't know what I believe anymore."

She reached out a hand as if to touch him but didn't dare. "This is because of your suffering," she said. "Because you've been confined. You must get out and walk more. You must try, if you can, to have some pasta. Let me cook you some for dinner."

"Yes, thank you, of course," he said, but even in his own ears, his voice sounded weak, glum, grim, the voice of a captive.

Nicolina stood, keeping her eyes on him. She was worried now, he thought. Worried that he had become a prisoner, not just of Badoglio and the new government but of the Devil as well.

"You must keep the faith, Excellency," she said. "All shall be well in the end."

"Yes, thank you. I will. Yes."

"May I go now? I have duties—"

"Yes, go. Good. Good day to you."

"Thank you. Please call if there's anything we can bring you between now and lunch."

A revolver, Mussolini thought, but he pushed his lips together in a confident pretense and nodded to Nicolina as she left. Tomorrow he'd ask Vittorio for the revolver. Thinking about it, imagining the act, and going over the words he'd just spoken, he felt wrapped in a cloak of shame. He was becoming weak, physically and mentally. What would Hitler think of him?

When he finished his meal, he picked up the copy of the Bible in his room, paged through it absently for a time, then set it back down. At the window, looking out at the weather-carved stone formations, gray as depression, and the flat blue water, he said aloud, "He died for our sins." And then a second time, "He died for our sins."

Perhaps, one day soon, people would say that of him.

Moored just offshore, in the harbor below Casa Weber, he could see a Red Cross pontoon plane. It had been there for two days now, and he wondered what it might be used for—evacuation of the wounded? Here, where there was no fighting and probably never would be?

He went back and sat on his bed, feeling the bleak mood choking him. He shook his head violently, stood up, sat down again. He thought of doing his exercises—push-ups, sit-ups, deep knee bends; he should try to stay in shape—but the motivation was as feeble as a child's whisper. He passed the day in near paralysis, barely touching the pasta Nicolina prepared for him, barely moving. When the sun finally set, he took off his clothes and lay on his back beneath a sheet, eyes open, thoughts whirling in the gloom, until a shallow sleep finally took him.

He was awakened before dawn by a knock on the door—he ignored it. The knock sounded again; he ignored it a second time. Finally, a third knock, followed by a voice, a male voice. *"Duce?"*

Bleary-eyed, dreading the day, he mumbled, "Come in, Vittorio."

Into the room stepped a man in uniform, a colonel, unfamiliar. It was becoming a pattern—early-morning visits by military men. He was tired of it. The colonel gave the Roman salute and stood at attention. *"Duce,"* he said, "your whereabouts have been discovered. It's no longer safe here. We are required to move you again."

"I don't want to be moved. Let them find me, whoever they are."

"I'm sorry, *Duce.* I am Colonel Anzellini. I have my orders. We must move you today, now. Please cooperate."

No longer safe. What did that mean exactly? He wanted to ask the soldier. But he knew it would be useless. He was given fifteen minutes to get dressed, and he wondered, lacing up his shoes, if there was any chance the strange boy who claimed to be a fisherman's son had actually been some kind of spy, an Allied plant. Or someone recruited to report to Germans on the mainland, to confirm the fact that Mussolini was, in fact, on La Maddalena. Maybe that was the so-called "danger": Hitler had discovered where he was.

Forty-Four

Luca arrived in Dubino not long before the sun dropped behind the western hills. It wasn't exactly the typical market hour—in fact, most of the stalls were empty. All that remained of the day's activity were a few farmers packing up their boxes, a few stems and leaves in the gutter, and two smashed, rotten plums on the cobblestones. Nothing edible could be seen. The stubborn old donkey and the military traffic had made him late, very late in fact, but he was here now. He suspected there would still be people looking for food—hunger knew no clock—so he simply pulled the cart up in front of the row of stalls, tied the reins to a post there, and waited for customers. He didn't have to wait long.

Among those who came to peruse Masso's offerings were the usual array of kerchiefed women, their faces painted in various shades of pain. Luca recognized these expressions from seeing them on his own mother's face. A husband on the Russian front. A son or sons in Albania or Greece. Or buried not far away. There were those, of course, women and men both, who consoled themselves with the notion that Italy was fighting a great war of liberation, that Mussolini had been sent from God to bring order and prosperity to the *bel paese*. But his own mother had never been one of those. Luca didn't see a lot of triumphant patriotism on the faces of these women, either.

A few children stopped by as well, sent from home, clutching lire notes or ration cards in their small hands and staring up at his chalky eye with innocent faces. He charged them half price, always.

The rest of his clients included a young priest, a carabinieri officer, and one German soldier, bespectacled and quiet, who actually paid for his three apricots and actually said thank you—a miracle.

And then, at last, when Luca had sold the best of his produce, along came a very old woman walking with a cane and wearing a blue shawl on the warm evening. She paid with coins—one bunch of fennel was the purchase—and said not a word to him. It was the blue shawl that mattered. A signal: the barn meeting was still safe. He could tie up the donkey in the usual place; make his way into the hills in darkness, going by moonlight, taking a crooked route; do his business; and return in time to sleep at the inn, then steer the donkey and cart back to Mezzegra in the morning. Just the sight of her made an acrid sweat form in his armpits. One: he did not have the money the trio was expecting. Two: if Scutarro was, in fact, a spy, he might be bringing along SS friends or Fascist police who would arrest him. Three: if Scutarro wasn't a spy, if Masso was playing a trick, if the old man was actually working for the other side and bitter about the killed Fascist, then he would never see Sarah again.

Forty-Five

Before dawn, armed with a camera and accompanied by two of his best men, Skorzeny left the Pratica di Mare airfield southwest of Rome in a Heinkel He 111 medium-range bomber, headed for Sardinia. He doubted very much that Selenzen, so terrified of losing his position as acting assistant chief of Italian intelligence, so concerned about forfeiting the promotion it promised, had made up the story of *il Duce* on La Maddalena, but he didn't trust the man, not the way one needed to trust an intelligence officer. And so he was about to do a reconnaissance flight and see the area with his own eyes before he got too deep into detailed planning. Certainly before he committed any of his men to the rescue.

Because the skies west of central Italy were known of late to be busy with enemy aircraft, his pilot took a circuitous route, heading north toward Elba and then across to German-controlled Corsica and back south to Sardinia. En route, they saw only one plane—a Red Cross seaplane, trundling along slowly below them in the opposite direction, as if carrying the weight of the war.

His pilot refilled on Sardinia, at Pausania, and then took off again and made the short flight north to Palau, a stone's throw from the place Mussolini was supposedly being held. After conferring with some of the Luftwaffe officers stationed there—they'd heard nothing of note—Skorzeny boarded the He 111 a third time, crawled forward, and positioned himself on his belly in the bomber's glass nose, just behind the port gun. He had his camera and a marine chart, and he felt a familiar twinge of excitement. If Selenzen wasn't lying or misinformed, if he could get decent photos, if they had a little time to plan the operation, if they were able to include some of their troops stationed on Corsica for good measure, if they could retain the element of surprise, then he believed he had an excellent chance of success. And success would mean promotion, maybe even the Knight's Cross, Germany's highest battlefield honor. For a minute he allowed himself to savor an image of Otto Skorzeny, promoted to major, standing in front of the Führer in the camouflaged compound and basking in his approval, perhaps having a decoration pinned onto his chest. It wasn't so impossible to hope that the name Skorzeny would go down in the lore of the Waffen-SS.

For a little while, as they approached La Maddalena Island, he busied himself by snapping photos and admiring the pale greens and blues of the tropical waters. From an altitude of five thousand meters, Sardinia looked like an island paradise, Italian-style. He was no more a fan of sea bathing than of the too-warm Italian weather; still, he could imagine coming here for a month after the war with a beautiful woman, perhaps even his wife, eating and drinking, and then heading back north to work.

All was going according to plan . . . until his pleasant musings were interrupted by the words of the rear gunner coming over the plane's speaker. "Two British pursuit planes behind," the gunner said in the grim, calm voice that was called for in these situations. Another few seconds and Skorzeny could hear the *rat-a-tat-a-tat-a-tat* of the rear gun and see tracers flashing by. He took hold of the triggers in front of him, but there was no way to turn and fire backward, so he was forced to wait, imagining a bullet in the spine.

The pilot took evasive action, tilting the craft down and toward the starboard side in a sharp curl. Nothing but the screeching noise of air against glass and steel and the rough lifting of the entrails. Skorzeny thought that was the end of it—how could the British damage such a machine?—until he realized the downward motion wasn't changing. The descent had grown steeper; he was nearly standing on his head now, pressing one palm against the gun handle and one against the glass to keep himself from sliding forward. He glanced to the side. The port engine had been hit, the propeller twisting helplessly in the wind. Another two quick breaths and they were heading almost straight down, the green and blue surface racing toward them at a terrifying rate. Someone called out, "Brace for a hard—" and they struck.

Skorzeny was briefly knocked out. When he came to, he'd been thrown sideways and up into the cockpit, there was debris everywhere, and the plane was floating back toward the surface like a half-full beer bottle thrown hard into the sea from above. He was knee-deep in water, the ocean pouring in. He and the forward gunner managed to open the top hatch and pull themselves up and out. They fell over sideways into the sea. The pilot popped out next, clutching a signal flare and already inflating the rubber dinghy. Relieved of their weight, the plane lifted a meter or so higher in the water, enough to allow the two men in the rear bubble to get out. Non-swimmers apparently, those two clambered onto the wings and stood there, waiting for the pilot to maneuver the dinghy toward them. Skorzeny scrambled up past the ruined engine, climbed in through the cockpit hatch, hurried into the half-submerged fuselage for his camera, and squeezed out again seconds before the plane went into another nosedive, not in the air this time. Half a minute later, it had disappeared.

One man rowing and one of the better swimmers in the water, pushing the dinghy from behind, they managed, after twenty minutes of work, to reach the nearest shore. They ran the dinghy onto the pebbled beach and climbed a trail up the side of a low cliff, looking for high ground. Uniforms soaked, boots full of water, their brains recovering from the terror of the last few minutes, they stood silently in the sun, composing themselves like the soldiers they were, waiting to see what would happen. Skorzeny felt a pain burning along his left side—no blood, though—and stood apart from the others, wondering if the crash might be an omen. No, he decided, just the opposite: all his life, he'd been protected by a kind of miraculous luck. Nothing could kill him, not Russian bullets, not exploding tank shells that had taken the life of the soldier beside him near Minsk, not British fighter planes. He felt a strange certainty take hold of him then: he'd survive the war, rescue Mussolini, make a name for himself. In the end, the truth would win out. The master race would rule.

After an hour or so—almost long enough for the brutal Sardinian sun to dry their wet uniforms—they saw a military boat approaching along the strait that separated them from the main island. His pilot sent up the flare from the signal pistol. The boat slowed, turned toward them. They clambered back down, paddled out, were taken aboard.

Ironically enough, the ship was an Italian antiaircraft vessel. The men there gave them a lukewarm greeting, fed them, stood apart from them on the deck. *With allies like this,* Skorzeny thought . . .

Next day, after a night spent grinding his teeth against the pain and struggling to find a comfortable sleeping position, he learned from the company doctor that he'd broken three ribs.

Forty-Six

In the early-morning darkness, Colonel Anzellini and four armed men led Mussolini down the path to the water. The Red Cross seaplane had been moved up next to the dock, and *il Duce* was instructed to climb aboard. It was useless to ask where they were taking him; he knew that, but he asked anyway, in as stern a voice as he could manage.

"We can't say, *Duce*," the colonel answered. And not, it seemed to Mussolini, in a tone of apology.

"You can, but you won't," he said. The colonel wouldn't even look at him. The plane's engines were loud, the whole machine seeming to tremble, as if it were anxious to be airborne, as if it sensed how important it was to get him away from La Maddalena as quickly as possible. Unafraid though he was, Mussolini had long held to the superstition that he would die in an airplane crash. He was a skilled pilot, he'd flown many thousands of kilometers without incident, but the notion haunted him—at takeoff especially. He took his place grumpily in a window seat and, after two or three minutes of waiting, felt the plane leave its mooring. The pilot turned it toward open water. The seaplane gathered speed, bounced across the blue surface, and, as gradually as if it were carrying a battalion of soldiers, became airborne. Off they went in first light, the quiet bay dropping below them and then the broader expanse of the Tyrrhenian Sea showing itself and revealing the curve of the Earth. Through the glass, he could see the sun cresting the horizon. They were headed east, then, back to the Italian mainland.

He turned to the colonel beside him and over the noise of the propellers asked, "Who do you work for?"

The colonel pinched up his eyes. *"Che?"*

"Who do you take orders from? Who do you serve?"

"The Italian state."

"But I am the Italian state."

"No longer, *Duce*."

"The title has not been taken from me."

Colonel Anzellini shrugged, looked away. The engines droned on. The day spreading out around them seemed the very definition of peace, and for a moment, Mussolini let himself wonder if there was any possibility that some God presided over it all as Nicolina believed, a Jesus in the sky, watching them. If so, then how could such a God allow treachery and ingratitude? What kind of God would that be? No, his father had been correct: religion and belief in God were substitutes for action. Palliatives. Hopeful lies.

The colonel left his seat and went forward into the cockpit.

Staring out the window into the morning sunlight, Mussolini saw another plane above them, larger, moving in the other direction—back toward Sardinia. He squinted and tried to make out the insignia. A German bomber? It suddenly made sense to him why he was in a Red Cross plane and not one from the Italian air force: his captors worried that someone would shoot them down.

The larger plane moved on, west, a Heinkel it might have been; he couldn't be sure. Part of him worried it had been a lone British aircraft that had just dropped a load of explosives on the great city of Rome, an idea, a possibility, that made him sick to his stomach. The Vatican, the magnificent ruins of the empire, the civilians at risk—Churchill and Roosevelt, those two animals, would do anything, kill anyone, to win the war.

In less than an hour, the plane began to descend. Below, through wisps of cloud, Mussolini could make out his country's distinctive western shoreline, but he couldn't yet tell exactly where they were headed. North of Rome, he guessed. From beneath the thin clouds, he could see Italy's mountainous spine. There was the peak of Gran Sasso, standing tall over the Apennines like a father over his children. The fuselage began to rock and dip in moderate turbulence, and he heard one of the men behind him vomiting. Lower still and he could see the outlines of a large lake. Bracciano, it must be. North of Rome was correct, then. Not very far north, either. He sat up in his seat, wiped his forehead with the palm of one hand, brushed a few crumbs from his pants legs. They were returning him to power!

The pilot wasn't particularly skillful. After circling the lake once in gusting winds, he banged the plane down onto the water. It bounced high, hit the rough surface again, made another small bounce, and then they were skimming along the lake toward a dock set just downhill from a building that had once housed a famous hillside restaurant. It was closed now; Mussolini could see the shuttered windows. He himself had eaten there on several occasions, and now he tried to remember the name. After a moment, it came to him: *Il Re e la sua corte. The King and His Court.* The King and His Court was out of business now.

The seaplane taxied to the dock, where a small caravan awaited him. Three trucks, a police car, another squad of Italians in uniform. To a man, they saluted. He returned the salutes with dignity. He was escorted to the back seat of the car, a soldier to either side, two in front, and the caravan moved away from the lake like a dark serpent twisting along the curving country road. In the half hour of silence that followed, as they headed south on that road, his thoughts flipped this way and that like a fish on the dock. He was going to be returned to power. The king would flee or beg his forgiveness. Or perhaps, he thought after a moment, a surrender had been arranged.

But then, when they came to the ring road at Prima Porta, instead of heading straight on, into the heart of the city, the driver followed the truck ahead of him left, east, and then onto the Salaria, the ancient salt road that had been built by the Romans. *Il Duce's* thoughts flipped again. He could barely keep himself from crying out in joy, from laughing, from clapping his captors on their epauletted shoulders. They were heading into the Abruzzo, a part of Italy he loved, a people he admired more than any others. A meeting with the king there, perhaps, or with the traitorous Badoglio. A negotiation. A reinstatement under certain conditions he could soon ignore.

Through the windshield, he caught a glimpse of Italy's tallest peak, soon to be snow-covered, rising up like a father, a leader, a beautiful promise. "Gran Sasso," he said, almost in jubilation.

The driver glanced at him in the mirror. *"Si, Duce,"* he said, as if their destination had been obvious all along. *"Si."*

But something in the driver's tone of voice was off, and the idea of celebration suddenly seemed misplaced.

Forty-Seven

Culillo II was hungry and so, sensing the end of his day's work, a bit more cooperative. In the gathering darkness, Luca led the donkey north out of Dubino, away from the market, its hooves clacking on the cobblestone streets. Monte Disgrazia loomed close in front of him—*The Mountain of Disgrace*—almost purple in the last of the twilight. German searchlights flashed across it to the east where the road—one hairpin turn after the next—wound like a huge black snake across the pass from Innsbruck. The mountains and hills were living creatures to him, had always been. In the shadows now, they seemed to be whispering in his ear. Imagined instructions. *"A job worthy of your skills,"* they promised. *"The most valuable man they have . . ."* *"You should be giving the orders."*

But it was a kind of self-defense—he knew that. A distraction from worrying about Scutarro. He'd taken his father's knife from his knapsack and slid it into his belt, beneath the covering of his shirttail. He kept trying to parse Masso's words. For lies, for trickery.

The streets were quiet here, citizens in their homes, Germans asleep or going about their evil business. He passed the ancient church on the town's northern margin, the church where his mother had taken him once when he was very small. He remembered her kneeling before the thin wooden Jesus on a cross and that there were no pews. How many wars, how many treacheries had that stone building witnessed? He was tempted to stop and go inside for a few minutes of contemplation—a new idea for him—but it was already late.

In the tiny village of Nuovo Olonio, just outside Dubino, he stopped the cart in front of a two-story stucco building with a sign out front: LOCANDA ALPINA. Alpine Inn. How they stayed in business since the war started, he had no idea. No tourists now, no skiers in winter or hikers in summer. Maybe they, too, received funds from mysterious sources. Maybe there were Italian or American or British financiers funneling money to the resistance, through the archbishop, or Masso, or people he didn't know.

He unhitched the donkey and tied it to a metal fence rail. The innkeeper's teenage daughter—mind of a six-year-old, heart of an angel—brought Culillo a bit of damp hay and showed Luca upstairs to his room. He washed, was given an apple, dried beef, some bread and weak tea for his supper, and then, instead of lying down to sleep as a normal guest would have, he summoned the last of his energy, reached down to the bottom of his courage, went out the back door, and climbed a crooked kilometer along a grassy slope to the barn.

Just inside the door, he paused a moment to let his eye adjust to the darkness. The smell of hay, spiderwebs in the doorway, long-unused metal milk pails in the dirt at his feet. A bit of moonlight slanted in from a window in the loft. He checked the knife in the back of his belt, climbed a wooden ladder, and there, in the far left corner, found the three men who had been waiting for him, no doubt for over an hour now. Mentone, Scutarro, Prinzano. All of them wiry and dark haired. Intellectuals, politically active, self-serious. They nodded, gestured for him to sit. Without waiting, Luca took Sarah's passport from the pocket inside his shirt, handed it to Prinzano, and asked if it would be possible to have new papers made for her. Another last name, a different religion. Prinzano stared at the passport in the frail light, then looked up.

"She's Jewish."

Luca nodded.

"And you trust her?"

Luca stared back in answer until Prinzano looked away, nodded, set the passport aside. "She's pregnant," he said then.

Prinzano nodded again, unsurprised, and offered nothing in the way of congratulations. "We'll try to have it by your next visit," he said after a moment. "It isn't easy. A friend of a friend in Rome, some Sicilian, runs the printing operation. We have to be unbelievably careful trying to get things to him."

"I'll expect it," Luca said. "Next visit." Something in Prinzano's tone bothered him. These were his brothers-in-arms, yes, but hard-core Bolsheviks, too. There was only so far they'd go to help someone so indifferent to their miraculous party. For months, he'd been bringing them money and messages, following their orders, and they'd kept him outside the tight circle of confidence in which they operated, kept feeding him jobs large enough to get him captured or killed but too small to make him feel like a true member of the group. He could sense Scutarro staring at him. Suspicious, still, after all he'd done. A spy, a traitor, maybe a killer. Luca couldn't force himself to look in his direction. He cleared his throat and was about to make his case for a bigger assignment when Mentone said, "Do you have the money?"

Luca shook his head. "It wasn't delivered to Masso's by this morning, and I haven't had a chance to see the contact. I'm going there tomorrow . . . as soon as I get back. I'll bring it next time."

Scutarro was still staring. "I thought you always got the money at Masso's."

"If the contact brings it to Masso, yes."

"And he didn't bring it?"

Luca stared down at his hands, almost too angry to speak. "No, he didn't," he said after a moment. He lifted his eyes, felt a strange new thought sparking in his brain: What did these men do with the money anyway? Spend it on themselves? "I told you that already. Are you accusing me of taking it, Scutarro? And spending it on what? A new car—"

"*Basta,*" Mentone interrupted. *Enough.* And then, in a voice barely audible from two meters away, "All right. Next time, then. When you come to get the papers . . . Right now we have something else for you, though this something else won't happen for a while. A week, a few weeks, we can't say."

"My mother is cooking for the Germans now," Luca blurted out, as if that would convince them to make this "something else" happen sooner. "In the Rossos' house. They're forcing her to cook." He knew he shouldn't go on, but he couldn't stop himself. The nervousness had ahold of him. Beside it, he could feel the same demon that had inhabited his soul on the path west of Santa Eligia. He couldn't look a second time at Scutarro. "I brought her the *lepiota*. If you give the order, it will be easy enough for her to mix them in with—"

Prinzano shook his head impatiently. "Too much," he said. "They'll be killed, yes, and then their Nazi brothers will murder a hundred Italians."

"What are we supposed to do, then? Never kill them?"

"Your eagerness should be hammered into patience. Think of our comrades in the Soviet Union, what they're going through now."

Luca wanted to say, *Yes, and what my father's going through.* Instead he took a breath, said, "I've been patient a long time."

"And you've done us great services."

"Tiny things. I want something important. I want to be trusted!"

"You wouldn't be here if you weren't trusted," Scutarro said in a low, nasty voice. "You wouldn't walk out of this barn alive."

Luca turned then and looked him full in the face. He thought of the knife in his belt, the Fascist on the path. He tried to slow his breathing. The new idea sparked inside him a second time. Maybe there was another, better use for the money when Don Claudio passed it on to him. It was a risky game, but he'd come all this way again, done all these things, and he could feel, with a sickening certainty, that he wasn't yet one of them. He wasn't a party member, never wanted to be, but he was a partisan. A new breed of Italian fighter. Their goal was the same goal, at least for now: a free Italy. He could feel the new idea swelling up in his thoughts. *"You should be giving orders,"* Masso had said.

"Calm yourself," Mentone told him in a way that made Luca want to spit.

"There's a landing strip," Scutarro said, "in Varenna. On the other side of the lake from you. We have information that soon, within the month, there will be Luftwaffe there. Fighter planes. Focke-Wulf 190s. The Nazis are worried to the point of insanity about what will happen now that Mussolini's gone. And the Allied bombers are getting more aggressive. Doing more raids. On Rome now. They bombed Frascati the other day where the Germans have their headquarters."

"How do you know that?" Luca asked, and immediately regretted it.

Scutarro swallowed, glared at him, went on. "Everybody knows. Word is all over Rome. The Nazis feel the Americans creeping up the legs of their pants, about to cut off their balls. Our contact there tells us the landing strip is being readied."

Luca listened, watched Scutarro's eyes, waited. *Our contact,* he thought. *You and your Nazi-loving contact have maybe another day to live.* He pressed his lips tightly together.

"We have a boat docked in the flats not far from Lenno. You know the area?"

Luca nodded. He knew it well. Sarah had been born and raised there.

Mentone spoke up. "A friend's boat. A small rowboat. A fishing pole hidden there on one side. You'll know it because the gunwales are trimmed in blue. We want you to start using it to go out on the lake at dusk. Stay out in the darkness for a few hours. Pretend to be fishing."

Luca waited. "That's all? Pretend to be fishing? At night?"

"Patience, Luca," Prinzano said quietly. "We have to set things up. We're working on a tiny budget, with few weapons, a very small number of men. We have to put the pieces in place long before we do anything big."

"Later," Mentone said, "you'll use the boat to go to the other side of the lake, to Bellano. You'll leave the boat in front of a square white house just to the south of the main dock there, where the ferry departs from. You'll see the ferry because they keep it there at night. You're good with your hands, yes?"

Luca nodded.

"And you have some tools?"

"Every tool that exists," he said. And then, "From my father."

Scutarro smirked at him as if he were a little boy.

"Good," Mentone went on. "When the time comes, we want you to take the boat there, then go by foot from Bellano to Varenna, find the airstrip, do as much damage as you can to as many planes as you can, and then make your way back to the dock and bring the boat back to Lenno. If you can't get back to the boat for some reason, just leave it—leave nothing in it except the fishing pole—and go into the hills there and find your way home. Can you do it?"

"I can do anything!" Luca exclaimed, acting now, playing the role of the excited boy. If Scutarro were, in truth, a traitor, then the whole foolish plan—the boat, the nighttime fishing, the airplane sabotage—was probably his idea. A trap, a setup.

"You can take your Sarah along if it makes sense," Scutarro said. "Your decision. Or we can use her in other ways. Is this what you want, her working with us?"

Luca nodded with as much conviction as he could summon. A setup for her, too, he was thinking. Another Jew eliminated.

"Is that what she wants?"

"I think so."

"Take her with you, then. It looks better. A couple fishing in the moonlight. Romantic. For now, just take the boat out and pretend to fish. Can you row with . . . the arm?"

Luca stared at him, and eventually Scutarro nodded and broke eye contact, pretending to listen to the sound of a Klaxon beyond the barn walls.

"And do the other things you've been doing so well," Mentone said. "The crash on the curve above Cadenabbia claimed two lives and damaged a Nazi troop truck."

Luca tried not to show any expression. Finally, two actual German soldiers killed. Finally, something.

"That's it, then. When you get back, go see your contact and get the money to us as soon as you can."

Luca glared at him, waited for more. The men were silent. They wanted their money; the rest was talk and, in Scutarro's case, treachery. Luca stood and brushed a few pieces of straw from his pants. He could feel Scutarro's eyes on him. When he turned around, he felt a cold current run up along his spine, as if he were about to be shot.

Forty-Eight

Don Claudio lingered an extra day in Milano. He didn't know why he hadn't told the archbishop he was thinking of spending the night, why he hadn't gone back to the curia and asked to be put up there, why he hadn't suggested they have dinner together. He was exhausted; that was part of it—physically, emotionally, spiritually. Emptied of energy. Barely holding himself together. So, after his visit to the curia and after his inexpensive lunch, he'd found a cheap boarding house, rented a room (they still gave clergy a discount—that much hadn't changed), collapsed on the sagging mattress, and slept right through dinner and breakfast and until midmorning of the following day. Wrong of him not to hurry back to Masso with the money and wrong not to be back at Sant'Abbondio saying Mass, he knew that. But Masso would understand. And the four women, his only regulars, would forgive him: it was wartime; ordinary schedules, ordinary expectations, had to be set aside.

He left the rooming house and went and sat in the Duomo for a long while, burying himself in prayer, then found another inexpensive lunch and decided there was no option but to head home. With every step, the heavy statuette bumped against his leg, but it was the other part of the meeting he couldn't stop thinking about. Guns. There had been dangerous assignments before this, yes, increasingly so, but he'd never been involved with guns, and he worried he might see the sadistic

Austrian at the station, and the man, via some evil magic, might read the fear on his face.

He barely made the two o'clock train. On the ride north from Milan to Como, his second-class car was all but empty—one middle-aged woman with a crying baby sitting a few rows in front of him; that was all. Her grandchild, he was quite sure. Who knew what had happened to the mother and father? In the father's case, it was easy enough to guess. The great *Duce* had sent him off to Greece or Albania or Libya or to help the Germans in Russia, sacrificing Italian blood on the altar of Hitler's massive Nazi ego. The mother had been put to work in one of the armament factories in the Po Valley or lived in Milan and was sending her child out into the countryside because of the threat of air raids.

As if his thoughts had mingled with physical reality, off to his left, Don Claudio spotted a pillar of thick black smoke. A bombed factory, he guessed. It meant the Allies were gaining control of the air, even this far north. Which meant that, in spite of all their antiaircraft artillery and fighter planes, the Germans were unable to keep the bombers away. They were necessary, these raids; he understood that: the factories made the tanks and trains and artillery shells that would end up killing the enemies of the Reich. All the same, innocent people, innocent Italians, would die in the bombing, or be maimed, or burned in horrible ways. Babies like this one squalling up ahead would be orphaned. The sorrow caused by war would stretch into future generations and make for a genealogy of wound and loss. Hatred, anger, bitterness, mourning. Italy would never be the same, and it seemed to him that Benito Mussolini and his supporters bore the full weight of that sin.

As the train approached Lomazzo—the halfway mark—Don Claudio slipped his hands into the pockets of his robe and pretended to sleep. His left hand took hold of the statuette. He was doing what little he could, moving sums of money and now guns, keeping a few life-or-death secrets, relaying messages. He had to believe there were scores of Italians like him, men and women, old and young, priests and nuns and laity, all of them risking these small acts of resistance. It wasn't much against the hundreds of thousands of trained German soldiers with their tanks and machine guns, but the movement would surely grow, and maybe it would make a difference in the speed with which the Allies were able to fight their way up the peninsula. How long would it be? A month, a year, five years, ten? And what if Roosevelt and Churchill failed? What would happen to the resistance fighters then? What would happen to souls like Masso and Luca and Archbishop Maniscalco and the crying baby at the front of the train car? What would happen to Italy?

At the Como station, he had to wait more than an hour before catching the last bus north along the western side of the lake. In peacetime, this ride was an exhibition of stunning natural beauty, emerald hills folding down against sapphire water, sunlight playing on the lake and casting dark shadows in the valleys, small towns with their clusters of shops, quaint cobbled streets, church steeples. Now, although the physical circumstances were the same, all that beauty seemed to be painted in shades of gray. It made him think of how beautiful Rebecca Zinsi had been as a young woman with her long dark hair and vibrant eyes, and how age—not war—had gradually muted her good looks. Time wore all of them down, administered harsh lessons in humility to even the finest physical specimens. She was still such a fine woman, though; the years hadn't changed that. Still the same warm, brave soul she'd been during their brief affair and afterward. As the bus trundled along the *statale*, his mind traveled back to their childhood along this lake, their friendship, the skinny Jewish girl and the fat Catholic boy.

That early connection had persisted even after he'd taken his vows and been assigned, first to Verona and then, back in his own hometown, at the Church of Sant'Abbondio. They'd greet each other on the streets, sometimes stop to converse about simple things, the weather, mutual friends. For reasons he found puzzling—could it have been anti-Semitism even then?—Rebecca had never enjoyed a lasting love relationship, and he'd always been able to read the loneliness in her eyes without a word being spoken about it.

He had his own lonely hours. Seven years into his vow of celibacy, much to his surprise and shame, he'd found himself assailed by the voices of temptation, battered by waves of doubt. There had been a small slip in Verona—not lovemaking but physical affection. A slightly older woman. Two times.

And then, in his new assignment, as he walked Mezzegra's familiar streets, temptation reared its head again. He wrestled with it, tried to turn his thoughts away from desire and toward prayer, even spoke about it with Archbishop Maniscalco on one of his trips to Milan.

One autumn day, in a period of particularly intense loneliness, brought on, he supposed, by the passing of his mother, he was walking along the promenade and saw Rebecca coming the other way. It seemed to him that God had sent her—a female friend—to salve his pain. They talked a bit, agreed to meet for coffee. That was the beginning: first, morning coffees in the Bar Lake Como, then walks along the promenade, all of it so innocent, so helpful to him in his grief and spiritual confusion. Their deep conversations, circling as they did around their twin unhappinesses, their diverse faiths, the state of their nation, were like doses of medicine. One of those walks took them past her small ramshackle home in the flats, Quercia Street in Lenno, and, on a whim, she invited him in for lunch. Nothing could have been more innocent, nothing. Except that, alone with her in that tiny apartment, with the bedroom visible from the kitchen table where they sat and talked and ate, an idea took hold of him. A wisp of thought. Wasn't what he felt for Rebecca a genuine manifestation of love? And wasn't she suffering from loneliness? And wasn't it true that no one would be hurt, that the vow of celibacy was perhaps outdated, or that his vocation wasn't as sincere as he'd thought it had been? He reached his foot forward under the table and touched her ankle, tentatively, something that could almost have been interpreted as an accident. She looked up at him, surprise shining in her eyes. Surprise and a barely concealed joy. It was a short distance then, a very short distance, from that table to their secret life.

After that, for weeks after that, he'd find excuses to slip away from Sant'Abbondio and meet her. He supposed their love affair had begun like so many others, and that the thrill they felt, skin to skin in her small bedroom, kissing, touching each other in intimate ways, making love, was something billions of others knew well. But *he* didn't know it well. The feel of her naked body was a continual surprise to him, a gift from God. He remembered walking back uphill to the church, sticky with sweat, elated. He remembered feeling, despite the breaking of his vows, that he was blessed.

What had it been, five weeks? They'd stopped by mutual agreement because one night they'd come within seconds of being seen on a bench kissing in the dark. But perhaps there had been other, more powerful reasons: guilt, the limits of their affection for each other, a preference, in both of them, for the solitary life.

And then, a few weeks later, she came to the rectory bearing her news, with her beautiful face shadowed by dread. Immediately, he'd offered to leave the Church and be a real father to the child. Part of him wanted to do that, and part of him did not. But, terrified though he was of the shame that awaited him, he'd offered, multiple times. Rebecca had refused, absolutely, saying she couldn't bear any more guilt. But secretly he thought she realized, even then, that she wouldn't be happy with him as a husband. Something about him wasn't suited to the domestic life, and he'd be no equal companion for a beautiful, intelligent, vivacious woman like her. And part of him cherished his solitude, his hours alone with God. Perhaps she knew him better than he knew himself. Now she was living in an attic, hunted like an animal, and he was finding ways to keep her fed and alive until this madness passed.

Gazing out the bus window, studying the brush of afternoon light on the mountainsides on the far side of the lake, a new idea occurred to him. He pushed it aside.

But it returned and, just then, as the bus from the Como station passed through one of the road's many tunnels and emerged into a view of the pretty hillside town of Argegno, he made a decision. If he survived the war, if Rebecca survived it, he'd leave the priesthood and ask her to marry him. If she agreed, he'd be as much of a father to Sarah as he could in the time that was left to him.

The decision brought him a sudden sense of peace.

The bus let off passengers just beyond the River Telo, his next-to-the-last stop, and there a pair of SS officers climbed aboard and walked slowly down the aisle demanding papers. When they reached Don Claudio, one of them said, "You're fine, *Padre*," but the other stood there, shaking his head. "Papers," he demanded.

Don Claudio reached into the inside pocket of his robe and took out his identification papers. The SS man held them in one gloved hand and studied them carefully before looking up. "A real priest or a fake one?"

"Real."

"How do we know?"

At the unexpected question, Don Claudio felt a wave of fear rise up inside him, felt his feet, ankles, and calves start to tremble again. The statuette seemed to have grown five times as heavy in his pocket. The second SS man had come over now; they were both staring down at him. For some reason, just at that moment, Don Claudio remembered the decision he'd come to not ten minutes earlier: to leave the priesthood and marry the only woman he had ever loved, to give her a measure of respectability for the first time in her adulthood, to tell their daughter the truth and see if she would allow him to be a father to her after all these years. He looked into the eyes of the SS men, felt the fear, started to utter a stuttering response, but then he experienced what he could only describe as the hand of grace, the touch of an angel—it seemed to come directly from his new resolution. The fear remained, but now, in some inner world, he was no longer ashamed of being afraid. It seemed almost as if he were embracing his terror, then turning it to stand beside him as an ally, the way one might welcome a wayward brother with an arm around his shoulders. He looked directly into the eyes of the sterner of the two officers and said the first thing that occurred to him: "You will answer to God one day."

The officer stretched his lips in a flat imitation of a smile but, for a moment, couldn't seem to speak. Don Claudio didn't turn his eyes away. The kinder officer walked toward the front of the bus, tossing a word back to his partner. A very long quarter of a minute, during which Don Claudio imagined every horrible outcome. Still, he didn't waver, didn't surrender. The officer tossed the papers on the floor at his feet, turned, and walked to the door.

On the last ten minutes of the ride to Mezzegra, Don Claudio sat very still, gazing out the window at the lake, bathed in a sweet epiphany. It seemed to him then that, finally and at last, he'd broken free of a demon that had clung to him for most of his life. It wasn't fear so much as the shame he felt at being afraid, the way it caused him to despise himself, the last thing God wanted. He realized at the same time that Rebecca must have carried a similar shame around her neck from the moment she discovered she was with child. He could picture her, walking through the streets of the town with her eyes cast down, waiting for a real or imagined insult, reading the minds of the people she passed, the women and men who went to Mass every Sunday morning and felt superior because of it.

The bus stopped; he thanked the driver and stepped down. The late-afternoon sun had weakened. A mercy. He was hungry. The stores were closed, the restaurants not yet open for dinner, and he'd spent too much money in Milan in any case, so he stood there, fingering the

Saint Jude statue in the pocket of his robe and looking east, across the lake. There was nothing to do but stop at Masso's, make his belated delivery, and then endure the long, hard climb to his rectory with an empty belly.

He wasn't looking forward to what he would find there—loaded rifles and a pistol!—but it didn't matter so much now; one part of an enormous weight had been lifted from his spirit.

Forty-Nine

Luca slept deeply in the inn's sagging bed but was awakened, just as dawn broke, by a terrifying dream. He was in a small boat with a man he couldn't identify. Both of them were looking down into water. There, not far below the surface but unreachable, he could see Sarah's face. She was opening and closing her mouth as if speaking to him. No bubbles, no sound: the water might as well have been a thick sheet of glass. And then there was only blackness between them, and he opened his eyes.

He thought, before anything else, of Scutarro—the intellectual, the Bolshevik, the traitor . . . if he were, in fact, a traitor. He supposed that, if he had to trust one of the men he worked with now, it would be Masso, his father's friend, Don Claudio's friend. Still, the whispering doubts would not go silent.

The ceiling of the room sagged above him, the plaster stained and cracked. He could see a dozen ants crawling there in single file, and he wondered what they ate and what difference the war made to them. No difference, probably. Even so, he imagined they lived always in fear of their lives. It seemed to be a rule of this troubled, beautiful planet that nothing survived without killing something else. Don Claudio had said as much once in a sermon when Luca was young and still a churchgoer. He thought of the priest now, a man he'd come to know well, a brave man, yes, but someone utterly incapable of anger or violence. How would he ever survive in this shark-filled sea?

Luca washed his face in the sink and looked at himself in what was left of the broken mirror. He wanted, more than anything, to be a father his child could be proud of, a leader not a follower.

Trying to hold on to the optimistic thread, he went downstairs and paid for his room, accepted a cigarette from the owner, found the girl who took care of the donkey, and pressed a coin into her hand. He wrestled with Masso's stubborn beast for the better part of fifteen minutes before he had it hitched up to the cart and on the road again. Only then did it seem to understand its place in the world. And only then did its temporary master realize how strange it was that the three men in the barn loft had given him nothing to take back. No message at all—a first. Were they all traitors, then?

Luca lit the precious cigarette and tried to smoke it in a leisurely, confident way, listening to the music of the clopping hooves and squeaking axles, smelling the hay and the earthy scent carried back to him from Culillo II's hindquarters. One or two cars, another farmer's cart, and a short line of Italian military vehicles passed him, headed in the other direction, but all he could think about was what might be happening with Scutarro, if it had been a mistake to hand over Sarah's passport, to mention the *lepiota*, to have gone to Dubino at all.

Skin prickling every time someone swung even with him in the left lane to pass and every time he went through one of the lakeside tunnels, he brought the cart back through Dubino, picking up two empty wooden crates at the market as he went. He traveled south through the side streets and then rejoined the busier *statale* in the direction of Mezzegra. He had some money for Masso from the sales of his produce, a bit of news to share with Don Claudio. If anyone stopped him, he had papers to show and the empty baskets, some with remnants of tomato stems in them. An ironclad excuse. Even the Germans couldn't see into his brain.

Good with your hands, he thought. Yes, he always had been, in every way it was possible to be, even though one of those hands had half the strength of the other. As the donkey clopped along, Luca wrestled with the idea that had come to him during the meeting, an errant thought, different, surprising: instead of passing the money to Mentone on his next trip, he could use it to somehow buy Sarah and Rebecca and his mother and Don Claudio, and perhaps even himself, safe passage to Switzerland. No doubt there were people he could bribe, false documents he could purchase. Surely he could find a way to make it up to Masso, maybe even be of more use to the partisans from abroad, start a network of sympathetic Swiss and exiled Italians.

He tossed aside the last of the cigarette.

The day had turned hot and humid, and the road was suddenly much busier. As he guided the cart along one side of it, Luca heard grumbles of thunder ahead of him, to the south and west. He thought of his mother—it seemed as if the storm must be near Mezzegra—and wondered if she'd be frightened. She'd never liked lightning, always been afraid the house would be struck or that her husband, working in the yard or fishing out on the lake, would be killed. This far north, the sky was overcast, but there was no rain yet, no flashes to be seen.

Just in front of him at the side of the road, he saw a line of German military vehicles pulling artillery guns with their long, heavy barrels. Motorcycles with their sidecars. Trucks with officers in them. A single plane droning overhead. They were entering a new stage of the war; he could sense it.

A pregnant Jewish girlfriend, a brave, lonely mother risking her life. Were those reasons to leave or reasons to stay and fight? Where would the regrets lie later on?

A truck backfired just ahead of him; he flinched. The more he thought about Scutarro's plan, the more suspicious it seemed: sure, get him and Sarah out in a boat, alone, in the middle of the night. A freedom fighter and a Jew. What better way to make them disappear?

Fifty

After the stormy night—great booms of thunder in the hills—Sarah made herself a late breakfast and went out and sat on a fallen tree that was drying in the sun of what had once been a back field. She had her small notebook of poems with her and a sharpened pencil. In addition to Luca's visits, it seemed to her now that her writing and the promise of motherhood were the only forces keeping her sane.

For a while, she ran different ideas back and forth in her mind, and then she scratched out seven lines:

> *Da questo mondo*
> *È sfuggito il buonsenso*
> *E questo film*
> *Senza fine*
> *Fatto nella luce grigiastra*
> *Passa come una vita persa*
> *Una vita tristissima e persa*

From this world
All good sense has fled
And this film
Without end

Made in grayish light
Passes like a lost life
A life unbearably sad and lost

She read over the lines. *È sfuggito il buonsenso*—all good sense has fled. True enough. But she realized, looking at the page, that she wanted more for the world now than simply a return to sanity. The new life growing inside her had given her the sense that she had to do more than survive, more than simply wait for the end of the war.

It could be two or three days before Luca came back with the false papers, if, in fact, he could even do that. If, in fact, he *would* do it. When she'd mentioned the idea, she'd seen a shadow fall across his face. And something else, too. *Dismissal* was too strong a word, but it had been something like that. He simply wanted, she supposed, to be the heroic one. And he wanted the two of them—soon it would be three—to have a life like his own family had enjoyed. If the war hadn't come, they'd probably be married by now, renting a small flat in the center of Menaggio or Argegno, he making money with his stonemasonry, she buying, growing, and cooking food; writing her poems; translating articles; preparing the house for children. That would have been perfectly fine, each of them making a contribution. As it stood now, though, he was doing something essential, feeding people, fighting for freedom, and she was . . . waiting.

She was convinced beyond a doubt that the child growing inside her body was a girl, and she wanted two things for her daughter: first, that she'd be born in freedom and peace not war and fear, and second, that the girl would be able to choose the life she wanted, a life not bound by religious codes, political rules, or the unspoken social commandments that made certain kinds of behavior acceptable for a woman and other kinds not. Her own mother had lived beneath a blanket of continual embarrassment—pregnant, no lover in sight or even named.

She'd made a meager living for them working in the silk factories in Como at first and then, later, weaving scarves and blankets and sewing patches onto clothes—work even a disgraced single mother was allowed to perform. She'd lived in a constant state of shame in a simple house in the Lenno Flats. Rats in the walls, too cold in winter and too hot in summer, and the smell from the nearby fishing boats year-round.

But it wasn't the physical hardships that had bothered Sarah—she was a child, after all, and had been used to nothing better—it was the feeling she read in her beautiful mother's posture and eyes every time they went out into the world. Sarah herself had grown up in the shadow of that feeling, that disgrace. Illegitimate—what a word! Jewish, too, in a Roman Catholic nation, on top of everything else. Luca's friendship had legitimized her, at least in the eyes of the locals. And Luca's mother had never for a minute treated her with anything but respect. Now Maria was hiding her own mother. In the attic, Luca had said. Living on scraps. Shitting in a pail. Kept from sunlight and fresh air. Worrying about her daughter and wondering when the Germans would open the attic door, arrest and torture her or send her off to the camps they'd heard about, where Jews were worked until they were no longer able to work and then left to starve or freeze to death.

The day was clear and mild with breeze enough to keep the insects away, but Sarah felt as though a swarm of biting flies was circling her, dropping down to nip at her skin and eyes, clinging to her hair. She couldn't get the image of her mother out of her mind: the attic would be baking hot in the day, cold at night. She'd be sleeping on boards or rags, wearing the same clothes week after week. Hungry and thirsty. The whole day with nothing to do but worry.

She sat there for a long time, holding her pencil but unable to write another word, wrestling with a radical notion. She knew how Luca would feel about it. Two months had passed since she'd been seen in public. In that time, from everything she'd heard, the German occupiers had enforced the racial laws more rigidly than even the Blackshirts had enforced them. Luca, kind, uneducated Luca, had somehow foreseen that. He'd been right to take her away from the house and to warn her mother. It had been his idea for Rebecca to go to Maria's for help, his idea—the young atheist—to have her mother go see the priest, Don Claudio, who'd been so wonderful to her for all her life. Luca moved out of the house so there would be more food for their mothers and so he could spend more time with the young Jewess he loved. So it was out of kindness and care that he wanted her to stay here in the safety of the remote cabin, insisted on it, in fact.

Still, the urge to see her mother had grown and grown over these two months, and on this day, for some reason, it overwhelmed every other consideration.

Sarah fought it as long as she could, made a trip to the spring and washed there, ate another small meal, shook out the blankets and sheets, paced the cabin, sat, and, even though it wasn't the proper hour, recited the lyrical Shabbat prayer she loved, the *Ein Keloheinu*. At last, in midafternoon, she couldn't bear it any longer. She left Luca a note in case he returned unexpectedly early, wrapped her hair in a kerchief, put book and pencil in a basket, and hooked the basket over her left arm as if she were an ordinary housewife in ordinary times, going into town to buy something for dinner. And then she set out on the stony path in what she believed was the direction of Mezzegra.

Fifty-One

Much as he liked to see the young man—he considered him a friend
and might one day look upon him as a son-in-law—Don Claudio had
been advised to limit Luca's visits to his church. So instead of face-to-
face meetings, when the priest needed to pass on money or a message
from the archbishop, he went to Masso's house and left the object or the
note or the money in a large ceramic jar on Masso's back porch. This
worked well, because Masso's property extended from the main road
far back into the hills. It was easy to make it seem that, after stepping
off the bus from Como, the priest was simply enjoying a late-afternoon
social call with one of his older friends. And then easy enough for
Masso to take the package or note and bring it to the far back end of
his property, where another ceramic jar had been stationed in the trees,
and leave it there for Luca.

If Masso were at home, Don Claudio would stop for coffee and a
snack (the farmer had an abundance of food and was generous in shar-
ing it) and sometimes even get a sit-down meal and a ride up the hill in
Masso's truck or his donkey-drawn cart.

On this evening, however, the farmer was nowhere to be seen—
strange, considering the hour. No food, then, and nothing to do but
make the delivery and hike up the long hill on his two sore feet.

But for some reason, this time, the idea of depositing the Saint
Jude statuette there in the ceramic jar gave Don Claudio pause. Not

because of the amount of money it contained—Masso's integrity was beyond question, and the farmer's back porch was most likely safe from thieves—but because of a strange intuition, a feeling that straddled the border between mystical and superstitious. He'd been holding Saint Jude in his pocket for a full day by then, and it seemed to him that the gold-laden statue had become a kind of talisman, a source of courage. Look at the way he'd behaved with the German officers on the bus! Foolish, of course, to attribute anything supernatural to a piece of hardened, painted clay. Still, he felt reluctant to leave the Saint Jude there, unattended. He knocked a second time—no answer—then succumbed to the embrace of the odd mood. He'd hold on to the Saint Jude and hand it to Masso in person or to Luca the next time he saw him. The archbishop had said nothing about the delivery being urgent.

His decision made, Don Claudio sat for a while, hoping Masso might return, take the statuette from him, and offer a meal and a ride. But no. A string of Hail Marys, an hour's wait, and Don Claudio sighed and set off on the long, painful ascent to Sant'Abbondio.

Fifty-Two

The arrangement had worked for a while, Maria thought, but it couldn't be permanent. Especially with Germans coming to the house. Every few days, the redhead made an excuse to visit. At first, he'd knocked and waited; now he knocked and opened the door. Soon he wouldn't even knock. Rebecca was starting to make more noise now, too—another sign of her weak mental state—and one of these times, she was going to drop something, sneeze or cough when the redhead was here, and then both of them would be killed. No, she'd tell her son; it was time to move her. The risk of crossing to Switzerland was no greater than the risk of her being discovered here. She'd heard that the Swiss were no longer accepting Jews, but if she and Rebecca could somehow manage to seem like two Italian Catholic women, perhaps they'd be allowed to stay; perhaps they could find a place to work, a way to feed themselves.

As she was thinking that, she heard a rumble of thunder in the distance and then, like an answer, the familiar hard knock on her door. *Five p.m.,* she thought, almost two hours before she was supposed to start cooking, and they weren't even polite enough to let her have some rest. There was no limit to their rudeness, no limit to what they'd ask of her now.

She saw, as she went toward the door, that this time it wasn't the redhead, as she expected, but the tall one with the head as bald as a bocce ball, the one who seemed to be their superior, who'd been so rude to her from the beginning. The bald man had opened the door and stepped inside her house, uninvited, another invasion. He was drunk again and grinning.

Fifty-Three

Although he'd pasted a smile on his face at the end of their first meeting when "Giovanni" made the comment about looking in the mirror, the truth was that Silvio hadn't liked it very much. It wasn't the comment per se: he probably did spend more time in front of the mirror than many people (maybe, he mused, because it was a more pleasurable experience for him than for some others); it was the fact that the *bella figura* half-American had been so smugly confident about what amounted to an invasion of Silvio's apartment. True, the breach of privacy had been for an excellent cause: the delivery of the loaded Saint Jude statue along with a substantial amount of compensation. But it was an invasion all the same. Giovanni and his associates had obviously been spying on him.

And so, when he arrived home from the visit with his father and found a note under his door, written in a kind of strange code but apparently requesting another meeting, two days later, at the same café on Via Veneto, he decided to exact a bit of what might be considered revenge.

Given that he knew where Giovanni worked and that the man had such unusual facial characteristics—the badly bent nose—it wasn't difficult to find out his real name. Silvio had a number of friends in government, including a Sicilian pal in the transportation office who was engaged to a woman who worked at Palazzo Venezia, Mussolini's White

House—Giovanni's place of employment. It was easy enough to ask the friend to ask his fiancée to find out the name, and only a little more difficult to persuade the woman to tell him where this "Giovanni"—actual name: Italo Andreottla—lived. At an address just opposite the Pamphili Garden, it turned out, in Rome's Monteverde Nuovo section.

It proved easier still to call in another favor and ask another friend, who specialized in such things, had the proper tools, and enjoyed his work, to go over there with him for a few minutes and pick the lock on Andreottla's second-floor flat.

So on the eve of their scheduled meeting at the café, Italo Andreottla, perhaps tired from a long day at the office and the stresses of living his secret life, opened his own door only to find an uninvited visitor sitting at his kitchen table with his feet up on a chair and a half-empty bottle of expensive Ligurian wine in front of him. Silvio was sipping the wine and sampling a dish of sliced fresh figs garnished with a wedge of Gorgonzola. He'd brought the wine and figs, borrowed the Gorgonzola from the refrigerator. He allowed himself a moment to take in the look of astonishment on Andreottla's face, then lifted his glass and said, "Welcome home, my friend!"

Andreottla stood there, briefcase still in hand, and seemed to be deciding how angry he should be. But then—and this would endear him to Silvio for as long as they were both alive—he smiled, came to the table, poured himself a glass, and sat down.

"Nice place," Silvio said. "I'm assuming we can speak freely here?"

Andreottla nodded with his mouth full. Swallowed, ran his tongue inside his teeth. "The landlady let you in?"

Silvio shook his head. "Other methods. I have a bit of news, and I came to deliver it in person."

"You did well with the Saint Jude."

"Thank you. I enjoyed it, and the compensation was fair."

"There will be other assignments, if you're willing."

"Perfectly willing," Silvio said. He let his mind travel to Lisiella for a moment—another trip to Milan would be pleasant—then took his feet down from the chair and, since his mother had raised him to be a polite man, made a show of brushing off the seat. He leaned forward with his elbows on the table and the stem of the wineglass cradled between both hands and delivered his nugget of news. "On the night he was deposed, *il Duce* was taken from Rome to Latina by car."

"How do you know?"

Silvio shrugged, lifted his eyebrows, allowed himself a tiny grin.

Andreottla removed his eyeglasses and wiped them clean on his napkin, but Silvio could practically see the gears of his mind turning. "Latina's on the coast," the half-American said, as if speaking to himself.

"Exactly. No reason to go there unless you were heading out to sea. My sources tell me he was put on a small military ship."

Andreottla rested his fingertips against his temples, the classic pose of a thinking man. "Good source?" he asked, looking up.

"Impeccable."

"The trip to Latina could have been some kind of feint, a ruse."

"Almost no one knew he'd been deposed at that point. No one was looking for him. I doubt they'd waste time on a ruse. I've done some research—boats from there usually go to Ponza or La Maddalena."

"Ponza's had air-raid troubles," Andreottla said.

"La Maddalena, then. Or someplace else on the coast of Sardinia. Or Corsica, maybe."

Andreottla reached across, took a piece of fig between two fingers, and held it that way on the table in front of him. "The Germans are on Corsica. He's not in German hands, as far as we know."

"And we don't wish him to be, correct?"

Andreottla looked up and nodded absentmindedly. "I take it you've done this kind of work before," he said, putting his spectacles back in place and the fig into his mouth.

"I'm Sicilian. We're born doing this kind of work. Our mother is giving us the nipple, and we're reaching into the pocket of her dress to see what we might find."

Andreottla smiled, swallowed, nodded his approval. There were sounds of sirens in the street, voices, shouting; even in wartime, the symphony of the Italian night went on.

Silvio let his eyes wander around the apartment again. It was barely half a notch lower on the scale than his own, certainly not the kind of place one could afford on a bureaucrat's salary. Andreottla was being compensated for his secret work, then, and handsomely. Probably had been for a decade or more, since the Western intelligence operations— aware of a half-American in Palazzo Venezia—had decided Mussolini was something more dangerous than a simple-minded narcissist.

"And you're from where?" Silvio asked him. "Besides Chicago?"

"Napoli."

"Ah," Silvio said, already standing. "No accent left, but I had the sense it was Napoli. The way you carry yourself, the way you dress. Southern pride."

Andreottla stood, too, and escorted his visitor to the door. "We have resources on Sardinia; we'll start asking around. Thank you. Good work."

An honest man, Silvio decided as he went down the steps of Andreottla's building and out into the cool evening. A fellow southerner. Perhaps a future friend.

But all the way home—a twenty-minute drive through the heart of the city in his yellow Fiat—he kept one eye on the mirror to see if someone might be following him.

Fifty-Four

The bald German SS officer sauntered into Maria's house and strode along the hall directly toward her. He hadn't shaved that day; the dark stubble seemed to her like a shadow over his soul. "You have wine?" was the first thing he said.

Maria couldn't speak. She had an urge to put her arms straight out in front of her and push him away. She shook her head.

"Grappa?"

She hurried to a cabinet and took down what was left of the *limoncello*.

"Pour," the tall man said. "Two."

She filled two small mismatched glasses and brought one to him. He accepted it and took hold of her left wrist with his free hand. "Drink," he said.

She put the glass to her lips and sipped. She was shaking, and ashamed to be shaking. He watched her, waiting, she guessed, to see that she hadn't been poisoned, then he drank down his *limoncello* in one gulp.

"Finish," he said, pointing to her glass. She drank. He squeezed her wrist too tightly and tugged down hard. She fell to her knees and let out a small scream. There was a sound above the ceiling—Rebecca startled from sleep, perhaps, or driven so crazy by the isolation that she would now open the hatch above and behind the German and call down, "Maria, are you all right?"

Banging his empty glass down hard on the tabletop and then unlatching the strap of his holster, the German was too preoccupied to hear.

Fifty-Five

It was the thirst that bothered Sarah most. That and the need—the two seemed somehow to contradict each other—to empty her bladder. At one point, she left the path and went into the trees to squat. Her legs trembled, but she felt otherwise strong. Thirsty but strong. Prepared, as much as anyone could be, to give birth for the first time. She'd been walking every day, though Luca didn't know it, up into the hills as far as the spring and back again, five, six, seven times. To keep sane and to keep her muscles from atrophying. It was as if some angel, some spirit, had been telling her to do that, knowing she would make this downhill walk and perhaps a steeper one in the other direction.

As she expected it would, the trip from the cabin to Maria's house took two hours or more. She went horizontally across the hillside on the path Luca had used to bring her to the cabin, and then, at the tree that had been split in half by lightning, she stopped. She decided to leave the basket so she'd be sure not to miss this place on the way home. *Home,* she thought. A strange word for the cabin. She couldn't imagine sleeping there late into her pregnancy, but she'd face that challenge when the time came.

Just beyond the split tree, she turned right, went for a while along the wrong trail and then realized her mistake, doubled back, found another path, parallel, steeper, also downhill, and went on slowly and carefully, grateful that Luca had pointed out various landmarks the ordinary person might never notice: a cleft rock shaped like a pair of lungs, with a pool of rainwater in it (she drank but spat it out); a perfectly rectangular patch of moss that looked almost like a coverlet on a bed (she wondered if she and Luca would ever sleep again in a *matrimoniale*); a small tree with a few wrinkled apples hanging from its branches, still green (she picked one and put it in the pocket of her dress).

From time to time, she'd stop and run her hand in circles across her belly, calming the child there. Or she'd sit on one of the many large rocks along the path and rest. She could sense the light changing above her—late afternoon now—and she began to doubt she'd be able to get back before dark. If she could at least find her way as far as the mossy patch, she might sleep there and feel relatively safe. *"Once night falls,"* Luca had told her in an optimistic mood, *"Italy belongs to the Italians."* He wouldn't return to check on her until the following day. And if he brought the forged papers with him—how long would it take them to transfer her photo?—then she'd spend a last night in the cabin with him and go elsewhere—to Como or Menaggio, Gravedona or Milan, anywhere they needed her. Once she began to show—another two months, she guessed—the Germans would probably leave her alone. *Probably* being the operative word. Even the Devil, she thought, would be reluctant to harm a pregnant woman.

She heard a crack of thunder overhead and then a low, rolling rumble moving off up the lake. No rain yet, though. Another boom. A few hard drops. Then an eerie stillness.

She went on—no more raindrops but a few thunderous echoes from the direction of Argegno. At last, Maria's house came into view, brick chimney, tile roof, stone walls the color of the meat of a roasted chestnut. She liked to think of Luca sleeping there as a boy, lying in bed and feeling his first sexual stirrings, maybe imagining a girlfriend, a woman he'd someday sleep with. Maybe even thinking about his Jewish schoolmate with the long brown braids and nice eyes.

Beyond the house and far below, she could see a piece of the blue lake. She waited in the trees, hoping Maria might come out into the yard at the end of the afternoon or even that her mother might take a crazy risk and stand in the open doorway and drink in a few breaths of air. Unlikely, she knew, but she thought that, if she could at least catch a glimpse of her, see with her own eyes that she was alive and more or less healthy, that would be enough for now. That would justify the long walk and the risk.

When the day was beginning to lose its light—the first frail shadows crawling around the foundation of the house like animals looking for a place to sleep—she heard something through Maria's open kitchen window. One short *crack*. It sounded like someone banging a coffeepot on a table to loosen the grounds, or a hard, heavy object—a paperweight, a full tin can—falling on a wooden floor. Maria at work, she hoped.

Trying not to make even the tiniest sound, she crept up to one of the windows and peeked in through the side of the curtains. In the soft light she could see, at first, not Maria or her mother as she expected but a bald man in a German uniform sitting in one of the kitchen chairs, his head thrown back and his eyes closed. She drew in a quick breath, afraid he'd notice her, but something kept her at the window. Sarah stared, began to make sense of the scene, and then, horrified, stepped away from the house and vomited in the dirt. Driven by a gust of panic, trying to erase the moment from her mind, she turned and hurried back into the trees.

Fifty-Six

Don Claudio pulled open the heavy wooden door and stepped grate-fully across the threshold of his church. In the old days, the days before war, once he'd taken the train and then the bus back from Milan, he'd usually have offers of a ride from the center of Mezzegra up the hill to Sant'Abbondio. Sometimes total strangers, seeing his priest's robes or the black trousers and shirt he was wearing today, would go out of their way to bring him to the rectory. But civilian vehicles were scarce on the roads these days, and strangers kept to themselves. Once he'd left Masso's, he'd seen and been greeted by half a dozen neighbors, but none of them had a horse or even a donkey, never mind a car with gas in the tank. And there were storm clouds in the southwestern sky, the sound of thunder there, a few drops of cooling rain on his forehead and hands.

He glanced at his watch. It had taken him the better part of an hour to reach the door of the church, one foot after the next, up, up, and up. He'd lost count of how many times he'd stopped to catch his breath, how many times he'd promised himself to lose weight. But now daylight was fading behind an advancing army of thunderclouds, and he was hungry again—what a curse it was to have an appetite! Still, he was a thousand times more concerned about what he'd find in the closet where his robes were kept than what he'd eat for supper. Three rifles and a pistol! Loaded! What was he supposed to do with them? And who had managed to sneak into the church carrying such dangerous cargo? Not

Luca, certainly—he could never haul such an awkward burden through the woods. And why had he himself gotten into this work?

The last question was easy enough to answer. His calling was to minister to his flock. And that flock, shrunken now almost to nothing, was suffocating under the weight of evil. What was the devout Catholic to do, even the cowardly devout Catholic? Stand by and whisper prayers?

He sighed, lit a candle, and was on his way back to the changing room to make the unwelcome inspection when he caught sight of a man sitting at the end of one of the pews, near the confessional. The priest let out a small startled sound, a gulp of surprise. The man was bareheaded, bald, and Don Claudio could see the distinctive collar of his German army uniform. An SS officer, it seemed. Long neck, prominent ears. He felt his palms start to sweat.

"Buongiorno!" the man called in badly accented Italian. *"Buongiorno, Padre.* I came to get confessed!"

Badly as he wanted to, worried as he was about the guns, Don Claudio knew that, if his visitor had been baptized Catholic, his own vows didn't allow him the luxury of refusal. He walked down the side aisle until he was even with the pew. The German was sitting there with his knees apart, slouched down as if he'd been napping. He hadn't shaved—highly unusual for them—and was smiling with his teeth bared, his lips stretched sideways not upward. His hands were loosely clasped on one thigh, and for a moment, Don Claudio thought the man had actually been praying.

"My sins weight on me," he said in his bad Italian. "Confess me."

"You're Catholic?"

"I was baptized in the glorious Roman church!"

"I have to get my stole."

He could see that the SS officer didn't understand the word. He was squinting, still smiling, perhaps drunk. Don Claudio made a gesture as if wrapping something over the back of his neck. "I have to get my stole . . . purple . . . so it's a true confession."

"For me," the man said, "you don't need it." He was on his feet in one motion, a head taller, twenty years younger, turning the priest by his shoulder and pushing him toward the confessional. Certainly drunk. It seemed useless to resist, so Don Claudio went and sat there, behind the curtain, and waited for the soldier to arrange himself on his knees on the far side of the screen. Technically, without the stole, the confession and absolution wouldn't be sanctioned, but he had the sense that such a detail would matter little to the Lord. He found that his legs were trembling . . . from the climb, he told himself. The hunger gnawed at him. He wondered if the guns had been hidden or if they were sitting there in plain view. He reached down into his pocket and touched the statuette with two fingers.

"Father," the German began. "I am guilty of so many things."

Now, strangely, the man's Italian had improved. Was grammatically correct, at least, and with less of an accent. *Sono colpevole di tante cose.* So it had been an act, his bad speech. Don Claudio tried to get his breathing under control.

"Ma, devo incominciare con la più recente, si?" But I must begin with the most recent, yes?

"As you wish, my son. How long has it been since your last confession?"

The officer laughed cruelly. "One loses track," he said.

"Before . . . the war?"

"Long before."

"Before your military service."

"Yes, of course. I have another god now."

The force with which the officer spoke these words seemed to propel them through the screen like stone and dust from an explosion. Shrapnel from a bomb of heresy exploding there beside him. The percussion sent the priest into silence. He rubbed the outsides of his thighs with both hands.

"A very clear god. With very clear ideas. Easy to follow: no Jews, no weakness."

Don Claudio still couldn't speak. The German must have been leaning forward: alcohol on his breath. *Limoncello.*

"The Jews killed Christ," the man said forcefully. He was using the German word—*Juden*—not the Italian—*ebrei.*

"All killing is wrong," Don Claudio intoned, but the phrase sounded stilted, almost ridiculous, even in his own ears. He could feel his breathing change, sweat on his palms.

The German laughed. More dust and stone, this time of scorn not heresy. "And all sex is wrong, too, correct, Father?"

Could the man possibly know? Could his sinful thoughts have shown in his eyes, his voice? "Not all."

"You don't like sex?"

"We take a vow of celibacy."

"And you've always kept it?"

"Yes," Don Claudio lied—and then, to soften the sin, "to the best of my ability."

"Ha! Even with yourself? Celibate? All these years?"

"Let us talk of your sins, my son."

"Why? You have someplace to go?"

"I am hungry."

The officer shifted position, bumping his nose against the screen. He burped quietly and took a breath. "We have a woman who cooks for us; did you know that?"

"No." Another lie.

"We do. This Maria. You know her, I'm sure. She cooks. A woman. Middle aged. Not unattractive in a certain way."

"Married," Don Claudio hastened to say.

"But with a husband far off, like my own wife. It doesn't matter. He'll never come back; I'll never come back."

"We don't know what God has in store for us."

"So this Maria. I made her, you know . . ."

There was a long pause. "I don't understand," Don Claudio said, but he felt a horrible idea crawling through the screen now, a film, a scum.

"A kind of sex . . . You know. I forced her to, and that is my confession."

For an instant, there seemed an actual note of regret in the darkness on the other side of the screen. Don Claudio was suddenly nauseated, bile squirting up into his mouth. He listened hard, hoping it was some kind of ruse, the man's twisted fantasy, the dark play of his imagination, a horrible practical joke. But then the German began to go into great detail.

"Stop. Enough!" the priest told him too loudly.

"Good. Make it so I'm forgiven, then. Just in case."

"You must never, ever do this or anything like this again! She is a married woman, a good woman. This is a violation of all human decency, surely a great sin against God. You must ask forgiveness sincerely, do penance, and never bother her again!"

A vicious silence now. Don Claudio felt he could *hear* the man smiling. "Our beliefs are different," he said. "I have a stronger god now, and the strongest god rules, that's all. I came here just . . . I don't know why . . ."

"Christ is strongest of all. You'll face eternal punishment. Is that what you want?"

"I'll face it when I face it," the man said calmly. There was another long pause. The sound of breathing. The smell of alcohol.

Before he could say anything else, Don Claudio heard the word *sbaglio*—mistake—then the curtain being pushed aside. He listened to the sound of the man's boot heels on the marble floor and then, after a moment, the squeak of door hinges. The priest put his face in his hands and began to sob quietly, rocking back and forth in the dark cubicle with the crucifix beside him and the ancient wooden seat crying out beneath his shifting weight as if it were alive.

Fifty-Seven

At the well behind her house, in a miserable trance, Maria washed out her mouth again and again. It did no good. The shame could not be washed away. The feeling of abject humiliation. And now that the man was gone, taking the fear with him, her anger leaped into flames. It wasn't anger; it was fury—she was shaking with it. And they would want her to cook for them again in another two hours!

No doubt, she thought, if they found a young beauty like Luca's Sarah, it would be a thousand times worse than this. A dozen men upon her. Even if they let her live, she'd be ruined for life, a beautiful blouse that had been dragged through the manure and slop so many times that it would never be clean, never be worn. She'd never be able to marry Luca after that, never have children after that. She'd be seen walking the *statale* in ragged clothing, talking to herself, her hair hanging in dirty strands like the local woman they called "The Genovese." Who knew what had happened to her? Maria realized she'd never thought about it, always just assumed The Genovese had been born crazy, and too often turned her eyes away in disgust.

She washed out her mouth again. Went into the house and ate a piece of stale bread but immediately spat it into the sink. If he came home alive, her husband would kill the man. But what were the chances of him coming home alive? And of the bald Nazi still being here if he did?

Her thoughts spun and spun, replaying every moment. Again, again, again, buckets of gasoline thrown on the flames. She couldn't stop it. Time was passing; soon they'd want her to walk over there and prepare the meal. She leaned on the edge of the sink and lowered her face to the backs of her hands. Between sobs, between agonizing stabs of memory, she remembered the mesh bag Luca had brought her. *Lepiota.* Poison of poisons.

"A gift from God," she whispered to herself. *Un dono di Dio.*

Fifty-Eight

When Don Claudio was at last able to stand and leave the confessional, the notes of the German's words rang in his ears like an evil symphony. He kept seeing Maria, assaulted . . . in her own kitchen! He tried to banish the image. It would not be banished.

In the midst of this torment, he was overcome by a wave of hunger. Fists clenching his intestines. It had always been this way, even as a boy. In times of emotional stress especially. He'd be upset about something—his parents arguing, trouble at school—and he'd eat and eat to soften the bad feelings. There was no stopping it. His father cursed him for the expense and for the embarrassment of having an overweight son; his mother cooked and tried to make peace. His brother and sister were thin as stalks of corn, but it seemed the Lord had given him this cross to bear. He was fat. It had, he supposed, been part of what had led him to the priesthood, because women weren't attracted to a fat man. Most women, at least. When he'd been single and not yet ordained, at least. Then other things had happened. He'd discovered there were some women who didn't care so much about a man's appearance, who appreciated sensitivity, warmth, compassion. A good heart rather than the physique of an Olympian.

He wouldn't think about that now. He would eat.

On the way to his kitchen, he had to pass the cloakroom. He was tempted to go in. But the hunger pushed him past the door, past the thoughts of what he'd just heard in the confessional. He'd find a way to comfort Maria. God would give him the words.

But something else churned inside him, below that thought. *"We have a stronger god,"* the man had said, and in such a sure voice! It sounded again and again in his ears, the chant of Satan. *"We have a stronger god."*

On his shelves, he found a tomato and a half-rotten peach. Breadsticks, stale but edible. The barely drinkable wine. He sat alone at the kitchen table, once the scene of so much pleasure for him. When Elisabetta, the rectory cook, had been living here, she'd prepare the most sumptuous meals, and he'd often invite Masso or his friends from the card-playing group at the Bar Lake Como to join him. They'd sit here for two or three hours, beginning with a small antipasto—vinegar peppers, olives, a bit of cheese or some sardines, perhaps fresh tomatoes from the rectory garden with oil and salt and slices of soft bread. Elisabetta might bring out a soup, a small bowl of chicken soup with vegetables and a bit of egg white, and then, always, some kind of pasta—with anchovies and onion, with pesto and shrimp, with a rich tomato sauce spiced with goose or oxtail. Then meat—sausage, veal, rare beef—and finally a slice of Gorgonzola and a piece of fruit, coffee, grappa. Elisabetta would sit with them. He'd always suspected that she and Orlando—the owner of the bar— enjoyed a love relationship. There would be laughter, stories from the old times, once in a while a bit of political banter.

Political banter. In the early days of Mussolini, the situation in Italy had seemed . . . not quite innocent but *distant*, something far from their lives in these elegant hills near the lake. People who'd traveled around Italy, even around the world, said this was the most beautiful place in the whole picturesque country, perhaps one of the prettiest places on earth. He and his friends had been lulled by that beauty, deceived by it the way one might be deceived by a beautiful face. Even after the experience of the First World War, they'd convinced themselves that nothing awful could ever happen here again. True, once Mussolini came to power, there had been troubles, the killing of Matteotti foremost among them. But in the early years, there was the sense that *il Duce*'s ego was a comical thing. He pontificated about the sanctity of family life while openly keeping a young mistress, Claretta Petacci. He bared his chest on the stage while giving a speech at the Pontine Marshes. He stuck out his chin, shouted, boasted, waved his fists, made promises about bringing Italy back to the greatness of ancient Rome.

And as Don Claudio had admitted to the Austrian on the train, Mussolini had done some good for Italy—even those who despised him said as much. The sanatoriums for sick children, the aqueducts bringing water to places that hadn't seen clean water in a millennium, the agricultural communities and grand building projects, the trains running more efficiently, the insurance benefits for those who'd lost husbands and fathers in the first war. There had been that side to the man, and for a long while, many in the country were proud of him, despite the foolishness, the violence, the ego.

And then Hitler came into the picture. Mussolini mocked him at first, reportedly even referred to him as "that clown from the north." But Hitler courted him like a lover, invited him to Germany on countless occasions. Mussolini refused and refused, his pride wanting *il Duce* to be the strongman of Europe, not some vegetarian lunatic with a peculiar mustache. He refused multiple times, and then, finally, he relented, went to Munich wearing a uniform designed specially for the occasion, and there Hitler put on a show for him. A parade of military might and discipline.

Then everything turned to darkness. The military adventures—lives lost in Greece, of all places. What did Italy care about invading Greece? Horrendous things had been done there, just as horrendous things had been done to the Ethiopians five years earlier, in 1935—he'd heard it all in the confessional; he knew more than the newspapers reported, more than what people learned from the state radio broadcasts.

All this on top of the sinful foolishness of the racial laws of 1938. The idiocy of that. Rebecca, Sarah, another family in Mezzegra, the Manganellis—people who'd been neighbors for years and years, for generations, and now, suddenly, enemies not allowed to hold a job, earn a paycheck, have property? Why? Because of the Satan to their north! And because, instead of resisting him as most of the rest of the world had tried to do, Mussolini embraced him, signed the so-called Pact of Steel. What insanity had caused him to do that? Now look: Italy at war with the world, fighting for what? To keep Jews from owning property? So Hitler could invade and conquer Russia, along with Austria, Poland, and Czechoslovakia? So German soldiers could assault middle-aged Italian women simply to be dominant, to torment, to feed the evil beast within themselves?

Maria, Maria, Maria! His thoughts were overtaken by an image of her with the German, the man grinning, holding a pistol to her head. What kind of human being did that?

He swallowed a last sip of the wine and said a string of Hail Marys, asking that Maria's mind be purged of the horror. Asking that, impossible as it seemed, she'd be given a miracle, the blessing of forgetfulness.

In the morning, he would go see her.

And say what? he thought. *And say exactly what?*

And then, an honest man at heart, honest with his own failings, at least, Don Claudio realized he was putting off a visit to the cloakroom to see what had been left for him there. Now, especially, now after his torment in the confessional with the tall Nazi, he was afraid to embrace his assignment, his small rebellion against the satanic forces. As he stood up and brought his plate and glass to the sink and rinsed them, he realized, too, that he was clinging to a thin thread of belief that the German might have been lying.

But he knew in his heart that it wasn't so. As he left the kitchen, the images flooded his mind again like the overflow from a polluted river. Don Claudio shook his head violently. Maria, of all people. Almost fifty now, a mother, the wife of someone who'd spent the winter fighting for those same Germans in the ice and snow of Russia. It sickened him. He felt a fiery ball of fury growing in his big belly. The anger propelled him toward the cloakroom. He went along slowly, remembering his one brave moment on the bus. He touched the handle and pulled open the door, expecting to see a secret arsenal laid out there before him, and saying a prayer for courage.

Fifty-Nine

After hurrying away from the window of Maria's kitchen, Sarah climbed as far as the place where she'd left her basket—at the tree that had been split by lightning—and then almost immediately realized she was lost. The path, visible at first, had simply disappeared in a tangle of roots and dense underbrush. Her sense of direction evaporated in the quick mountain dusk. She tried going a little way right, then left, then straight forward, but saw only stones and roots and brambles. She stared up at the sky, but it offered no clue, and though she knew the stars would appear before too long, she'd never learned to read them and couldn't even imagine how people used them to navigate. There were two options then: sit and wait until morning, when she'd most likely be able to find the path again in the light of day, or go back down the hill to Maria's house, make her presence known—assuming the German was gone—hold Maria and then her mother close, and see what she could do to help. She had run away in a panic, that was clear enough . . . and she wanted to be a partisan fighter!

But what else could she have done? Go inside and attack the German soldier with her fists? Bang on the window? Throw rocks?

If Luca returned early, he'd read the note she'd left in the cabin and worry, but she decided her best option was to head back down the hill. She was thirsty and hungry, and in another hour, even this frail light would be gone.

It was almost worse than going up, with all the roots and rocks, the slippery stretches of loose gravel. She was on a path, yes, but was it the correct one? Her legs were shaking like the tops of trees in a storm.

By the time darkness fell, she had reached the bottom of the steepest part of the hill. She could no longer see the path, but a frail vaporous light shone above the town—starlight reflecting off the lake—so she was able to go along slowly and knew she was close. When she came to the edge of the trees and looked out, however, she saw not Maria's house, as she'd hoped, but the back side of the church. Sant'Abbondio. One outbuilding and a small empty lot lay between her and the church; the road was thirty meters away. As if sending her a warning signal—wait, be careful—the bells from a church closer to the lake rang the nine o'clock hour.

The problem was that, because of where she'd ended up, she'd have to walk a fair distance through the trees in order to reach Maria's house or step out onto the road in full view of any passing German patrols and simply hope they didn't stop her and ask for papers. It was true, as she'd told Luca in earlier arguments, that she didn't look any more Jewish than he did—whatever that actually meant: it wasn't as if all Jews looked alike. Even so, she had no papers on her person and, if stopped, wouldn't be able to say where she lived or what she did for work or who lived with her. For a long while, she stood behind twin tree trunks, staring out at the shadows, trying to focus her thoughts.

It occurred to her that she might be able to spend one night in the church—though it would cause Luca so much worry if he returned to an empty cabin. Surely Don Claudio would welcome her. No doubt he'd even hide her for a day or two if she asked—which she wouldn't. Too great a risk for him. And what should she say about what she'd seen? What could Don Claudio do about that? The priest had been unbelievably kind and generous to her and her mother, buying them food, giving them gifts, arranging for her to have transportation to Bologna for her college exams, paying for her to come home on vacations. She wondered sometimes if he felt a twinge of guilt at the way certain Catholics treated Jews in this land of Christian mercy or if he was just a particularly kind man and knew how difficult her mother's life had been.

Remembering his warmth and desperately needing some of that now, she kept in the trees but angled down toward the church. She drew close, stopped, waited. Just when she was about to step out into the open and move toward the back door, she saw a figure stand up from where he'd been sitting, on the ground beside the church's north wall. For a minute, the person leaned against the wall for balance, then started walking—stumbling, really—along the side of the building. As the dark figure came closer, she saw that it was a man. A man in uniform. A German uniform. Tall. Hatless. Bald. He was moving along slowly, still in shadow. She wondered if it could be the same man she'd seen in Maria's kitchen. She crouched on her haunches, slowly, silently, and watched the dark figure struggle with the door handle, curse, then swing it open so forcefully that it was nearly torn off its hinges.

Sixty

The church's cloakroom had no windows; only a little light trickled down the hallway from the kitchen. Faintly, through the open cloakroom door, Don Claudio heard the bells sounding one after the next from the larger church down by the lake. San Domenico. The sound had always given him comfort. Even in wartime, Don Giuseppe, the pastor there, had ordered the bells rung at seven in the morning and nine o'clock at night, moments to pause and say an Our Father in gratitude for the given day.

Just as the ninth bell sounded, Don Claudio opened the door and pulled the string that dangled from the bare ceiling bulb. With great trepidation, he approached the closet and took hold of the small round wooden handles of the accordion doors. The hinges squeaked their complaint. At first, he saw nothing more than six long vestments hanging from the pole, two of them white and gold for Mass, the rest black. *"Rifles and a pistol,"* the archbishop had told him, loaded guns. But Don Claudio saw nothing like that. He stood gazing at the robes, running his eyes from collar to hem, looking for anything unusual. If someone had, in fact, put guns in this closet, they'd done a clever job, because nothing could be seen, nothing. It occurred to him that maybe there was nothing to see, that the archbishop had gotten poor information or that the courier had been intercepted en route and killed. Or perhaps tortured until he revealed his destination. In which case, the Gestapo would be here momentarily.

But when the priest reached forward to examine the material more closely, he felt something hard beneath the fabric of the third robe from the left. He opened the robe at the chest and saw three automatic rifles hanging from a wooden coat hanger by their straps, neat as neckties. He couldn't bring himself to touch them. On closer inspection, he saw that one of the pockets of one of the black robes was sagging. The pocket faced the back of the closet, but even so, he could tell something was weighing it down. He reached out gingerly and tapped the cloth with two fingers. He hadn't held a gun since boyhood, when his uncle Patricio, a policeman, had sometimes let him shoot his service pistol in the back yard of the house in Benevento on Sunday afternoons. He'd enjoyed the feeling of power, and his uncle had taught him the safest way to handle and shoot the weapon. Cast back into the distant pleasures of his youth, curious beyond restraint, Don Claudio reached into the pocket, took the pistol in his hand, and turned it this way and that, admiring the way the metal stock gleamed in the artificial light. He was tempted, suddenly, to fire it. Foolish notions like that came into his head from time to time. On occasion, in the middle of Mass, he had an urge to simply lift the chalice and drink from it in big greedy gulps, or to burst into song, or to say he wanted a rest and walk off the altar in front of his astonished flock. Small temptations of the Devil, that's all they were. But this time, he held the handle of the pistol in his right hand and the barrel in the fingers of his left and slipped off the safety with his thumb, just the way his uncle had shown him so many years before.

At that moment, as if Uncle Patricio might be stepping out of the world of death and coming to pay him a visit, or as if the Gestapo had, in fact, come to arrest him, Don Claudio heard two loud footfalls. The door was pushed open wider. He looked up in terror and saw the tall German wobbling in the doorway, staring at the pistol in his confessor's hand.

Sixty-One

The confidence Skorzeny had enjoyed, standing soaking wet at the top of the rock formation in Sardinia, did not disappear, but at moments, it wavered. After the crash of his reconnaissance plane, exactly twenty hours before he was to give the order to land a commando unit on La Maddalena, he'd had a visit from Selenzen and received word—again, via the *obersturmführer*'s supposedly unimpeachable source—that Mussolini had been hastily moved. "Destination unknown at this time," Selenzen reported with one of his oily smiles. And then, after a pregnant pause, "However, we do know that he was flown away in a seaplane"—another pause—"which indicates a water landing."

"Helpful," Skorzeny told him, soaking the word in sarcasm.

Selenzen seemed tone deaf. He sat in his usual posture in the Frascati headquarters, breathing through his nose, slumped there like a lazy farmer who'd finished sowing his crops and believed he had nothing better to do now than wait for them to sprout and bear fruit. Skorzeny dismissed him, too weary of the man to shout or criticize or push any harder.

He had his own sources, and the minute Selenzen left his office, he began cultivating them with renewed urgency. Phone calls. Lunches. Meetings for coffee with Italian intelligence officers, political figures, and Fascist Party luminaries who seemed to have an endless appetite for sugary espresso and no useful information whatsoever. Included among the intelligence cadre was one Italo Andreottla, who worked at Palazzo Venezia and who, for some reason, spoke decent English. Skorzeny had high hopes for him. He thought, perhaps, that, given his position, Andreottla might have his finger on the pulse of the king and his inner circle, might have heard or read something that gave a hint of the Allies' intentions vis-à-vis *il Duce*. But no, nothing. A pinch of his crooked nose, a Neapolitan shrug, a genial profession of ignorance. The Palazzo Venezia crowd, Andreottla claimed, was as far in the dark as the rest of Italy.

Still, Skorzeny found it almost impossible to believe that anyone, even the devious Italians, could hide one of the most recognizable human beings on the planet for more than another few days. Somewhere a leak would appear in the system. Someone would boast about having been part of the operation—there had to have been dozens of men involved. His job was to be in position to hear those whispers when they were spoken. There was no need for discretion at this point: everyone he met with knew that the Führer was desperately looking for Mussolini.

Skorzeny had been trained to be methodical, a kind of scientist of the military world, so, over the next few days, on a pad of paper in his office, he wrote down every piece of gossip, every rumor, every tidbit of information that reached him. Little by little, with a crooked inconsistency that nearly drove him mad, these pebbles began to lead in a certain direction. A talkative Italian colonel let him know, as an aside, that the army was having trouble finding a new place for their trainees, who'd been moved from an isolated mountaintop hotel in the Abruzzo. Aerial reconnaissance reported a strengthening of Italian troops in the L'Aquila valley—near that same mountain. One of his men, known for spending too much time in the bars looking for women, had heard something about the same place—Campo Imperatore, it was called. An evacuation there, all the regulars moved out. Maybe it was being turned into a hospital, a nurse friend had told him.

Maybe, Skorzeny mused. *Or maybe not.*

At one of their daily meetings, General Student had told him about a German army doctor who was looking for a building where he could send wounded soldiers who might recover and rejoin the battle. It was clear by then that the conflict would be moving up the peninsula: Sicily was gone; a week earlier, there had been another Allied landing at Salerno on the southwestern coast; the bombing raids were becoming more troublesome. So, on a hunch, Skorzeny sent the doctor to Campo Imperatore on a fact-finding mission. To the Italians, it would seem innocent enough: Was the hotel a place where German soldiers might be rehabilitated when and if the front moved north?

True, the good doctor didn't realize it was a ruse. And true, there would be some danger to him if the Italians suspected the real motive. But Skorzeny felt no guilt in using him. This was war; everyone had to sacrifice.

Still, he was relieved when the man returned earlier than expected, alive and unhurt. And even more relieved when he heard what the doctor had to say. He came into the office, saluted, and made his report. "Herr Captain, I couldn't even get close to the hotel. There's no road, and the ski lift is heavily guarded from below. There are rumors it's a prisoner-of-war camp, high-level Allied officers there, taken in the battle for Sicily; you can't get anywhere near the place."

Before the doctor had even finished closing the door behind him, Skorzeny had his hand on the telephone. He told the Luftwaffe commander at Pratica di Mare that he wanted aerial reconnaissance of Campo Imperatore, and from an altitude that wouldn't bring suspicion. He hung up the phone, pondered a minute, then called back. "I want to go myself," he said. "Lieutenant Radl and I. Get us a recon plane for early tomorrow morning if the weather's clear. And tell no one about the destination. For now, not even the pilot. No one."

Sixty-Two

Don Claudio would never decide whether it was God or the Devil who took hold of him at that moment. Usually he was an indecisive man, prone to act only after long deliberation. But when he looked up and saw the German officer, and when he understood that the man must have returned for further counseling or to argue with him, and realized, in that same instant, that the officer could clearly see the pistol he held in his hand, Don Claudio simply aimed and pulled the trigger as if he'd been planning to do it all along. As if, after hearing what had been done to Maria, he'd laid a trap, the German had stumbled into it, and the trap was now sprung.

One shot was all he could manage. But one shot turned out to be enough. The bullet hit the German in his throat. He stumbled backward, a river of blood spouting from his neck. He had his hand there, blood between his fingers, blood streaming in two rivulets down the inside of his gray sleeve. He fell back against the wall beside the doorframe and slid straight down to the floor, his eyes fixed on the priest, his mouth producing the most hideous choking sounds. He took three short, horrible breaths, exhaling a fountain of bright-red sprays. He seemed to be trying to speak, to be repeating a German word, or a name. Don Claudio watched him in a state of shock. Without realizing he'd let it go, he heard the pistol drop from his hand and strike the marble tile floor. His eyes were locked on the German's eyes, going glassy now. The man's legs began to twitch violently, the backs of his heels tapping out a death rhythm. This went on for perhaps fifteen seconds—it seemed an eternity—and then the man went still, the bloody hand against the floor, the eyes open, the lips frozen in what might have been a grimace.

For perhaps a full minute, Don Claudio stood there, a wooden man. And then, as if he were accustomed to such things, as if he'd made a career of dealing with corpses instead of raising the sanctified host, his hands took on a life of their own. He grabbed one of the black robes in the closet and, moving like an automaton, went over and wiped up as much blood as he could. The floor was smeared with it. It had spurted onto the wall in odd spiral designs and onto the small oriental carpet that had been given to him upon his ordination by a rich aunt in Avellino. He took hold of the German's ankles and pulled him onto the carpet, then wrapped it and the blood-soaked robe around him. Grunting and breathing heavily, Don Claudio pulled the body out of the cloakroom and slowly along the hallway that led to his living quarters, looking to see if any trail of blood had been left. Yes, a thin trail. He kept going, walking backward, step by terrible step, dragging the rolled carpet with the dead body inside. At last, he reached the kitchen and stopped there, let go. It was dark outside the windows. But what was he going to do, dig a grave in the back garden and drop the officer down? Impossible. Soon enough, the man's colleagues would come looking for him and see the blood, or the fresh grave, and all would be ended. They'd torture him; he'd talk. The entire operation, his part of it at least, was in jeopardy. He decided he'd have to get messages to the archbishop and to Luca, yes, immediately, but how? Luca was in the hills, the archbishop's phone likely listened to by spies. His breath was coming in quick gulps, and his mind was a landscape ravaged by a hurricane of terror, thoughts whipping frantically back and forth like the branches of tormented trees.

He washed his hands, then grabbed the mop, wet it in the sink, and walked it along the route he'd just traversed, cleaning the trail of smeared evidence as he went. The marble tiles were black with irregular bands of white, and now there was a pinkish tint to the wet film covering them. It would never work. Too much blood. He stood staring at the floor for a moment, then set the mop handle against the end of a pew, went to the telephone in the kitchen, and dialed Masso's number. It rang and rang without being answered. Don Claudio set the phone quietly in place, walked like a hypnotized man to the altar rail, knelt, and began to pray.

Without a miracle, there was no hope now, none. He'd pray for as long as he could, then mop up the rest of the blood—more to sanctify the church than to protect himself—and wait for the Germans and his punishment.

Sixty-Three

Once the German officer had gone through the side door of Sant'Abbondio, Sarah waited a few minutes to make certain he didn't reappear and then, keeping inside the tree line, headed for Maria's house. A mountain wind had started to blow, producing eerie whistles in the higher branches and stirring the leaves around her. She heard a Klaxon, then another, rising up from the *statale*, and she wondered where Luca might be. Somewhere on that road, she hoped, on his way back to her, carrying the new papers. In their early months of dating, he'd taken her on a number of hikes in the beautiful hills on both sides of the lake, the "silent, perfect hills" he called them. They'd even borrowed a friend's car and driven up to St. Moritz one summer day, on a winding road that took them through territory so elevated they'd seen snow on their way back home—flakes in the air in July! They'd gotten out of the car and kissed in a chilly field. She'd written a poem about it.

She understood why he felt the way he did about the high territory and about the forest. There was a purity to those places, no one there to mock what he called his "deformities." But she'd never really been able to understand his godlessness. Jewish, Catholic, that didn't matter; it just seemed to her that some humility was called for in this life, some kind of bowing down before the majesty of creation. They'd talked about it a few times, never argued. He never criticized her for saying a Sabbath prayer or two. It seemed strange, though, that he was so close to Don Claudio and, from what he'd said, that his father and mother were devout, and yet he himself had no religious feeling. Was he angry with the Lord for not making him whole? Walking along, she wondered if it might be possible to bring up their child—children, she hoped—with some new idea of God, something both of them could agree on. God as a mountain spirit, a silent presence in the trees or over the surface of the lake. God as kindness, to compensate for the brutality they were living through now. She wondered if she would ever be skilled enough to express such a hope in stanzas on a page.

The closer she came to Maria's house—she guessed she was still at least five hundred meters away—the more difficult it became to imagine this God of Kindness. The scene she'd witnessed hours earlier through the window of that house had etched itself into her memory, and her own panic left her with the sour taste of guilt. She could imagine, easily, what had led up to that moment and what kind of raw wound it would leave. Somehow, combining sex with violence felt like an especially heinous crime. It meant taking the most tender and beautiful aspect of life, the warmest intimacy, and turning it inside out, drenching beauty with a putrid ugliness. She couldn't be sure, but she thought the man she'd seen entering Sant'Abbondio just now was the same one who'd been in Maria's kitchen, and, if so, she wondered if he might be going to the priest to ask forgiveness, the way Catholics did. How bizarre that would be! She couldn't imagine what Don Claudio would say to him.

A sudden tiredness swept over her. Not just physical tiredness from the pregnancy and the long day of walking, but a tiredness that came from being a good person surrounded by evil. The memory of what she'd seen through Maria's curtains had drained away part of her spiritual strength. She asked herself, suddenly, if it was better to try to run away than to fight. Fighting would only bring out the evil inside all of them, the anger, the hatred. Maybe, after all, it was better to flee.

She sat down to rest on a moss-covered rock and held her chin in her hands, wondering if she was going to spend the night sleeping in the woods, wondering if it would somehow harm the baby. She decided to lie back and rest for a while, gather her strength, gather her thoughts. Maria and her mother would be in the house when she arrived. Where else could they be?

Sixty-Four

Silvio Merino lay in his antique four-poster bed, eyes open, mostly awake, flexing and relaxing his toes. He'd stayed out too late the night before and drunk too much wine, but it had been a birthday celebration for one of his closest friends, and birthdays deserved to be marked, he believed, even in a time of war.

Otherwise enjoyable, the night had been tarnished early on by the presence of a table of German soldiers. Loud, obnoxious, spilling their supposed superiority over every surface. Having invaded Silvio's favorite restaurant on Via Sicilia as if they were conquering yet another European country, the Nazi bastards showed no appreciation whatsoever for the traditions of the place, for decent conduct, for the people who'd been there long before their arrival. But who was going to complain?

He and his friends did their best to ignore the interlopers. Silvio looked over once and saw a tall, terrifying-looking character with a deep, curving scar across his left cheek and a rather high, loud voice. The only saving grace was that this warrior and his German cohorts departed at an early hour, off to their beds and their murderous morning duties. All the same, they'd left a certain dirty mark on the festivities, a mark that required several bottles of wine to erase.

So, as a kind of revenge, he was lying in bed on this clear morning, relaxing. A beam of sunlight leaked in through the curtains, and there was the sound of a radio from the room below, where his deaf landlord lived. He could smell coffee; he drew in a long breath and savored the fragrance. Let the Germans get up before dawn and live out their evil fate; to the extent possible during wartime, Silvio Merino was going to keep a normal human schedule and enjoy the harmless pleasures of adult life.

There was something that resembled a knock at the door, two hard thumps. He sighed, swung his legs over the edge of the bed, pulled on a pair of pants he'd discarded in a drunken haste the night before, and answered it. To his utter astonishment, he saw his father standing there on the far side of the threshold. Short as a prepubescent teenager and wide as a small car, his father had not shaved the night before—unusual for him—and his cheeks made Silvio think of a forest of black tree trunks. Burned in a fire, chopped off near the ground. His father was wearing a neat green shirt and a pair of dark slacks—his work uniform—but the expression on his face suggested he'd slipped away from his embassy duties en route to the market or the airport. *Excitement* wasn't a word one could ever associate with the man, but something like a diluted thrill animated his black eyes on that morning. Silvio wondered what it was.

"Coffee, *Babbo*?" he said when he'd invited him in. "You've never come to visit me. I didn't think you knew where I lived."

His father was looking around, taking in the messy bedroom—seen through an open door—the expensive mahogany dining room table, the framed artwork on the walls. "Lucia knows," he said without meeting Silvio's eyes.

"Ah, the most beautiful sister," he said, spooning coffee grounds into the espresso maker. His father had taken a seat at the head of the kitchen table, moving his hands about on the wood in a way that was completely alien to him. He looked to be patting it, keeping it in place, smoothing the already perfectly smooth surface.

Silvio set the cup in front of him, slid the silver sugar container toward him, and sat down.

His father fixed him with an eager stare, as if his blood were pumping at twice the usual rate. He ignored the coffee at first. "I found out where he is," he said.

"Who, *Babbo*?"

His father waved one hand in the general direction of Palazzo Venezia.

"Mussolini?"

His father nodded and only then sweetened his coffee and took a sip. He smacked his lips. The look on his face was one of patriotic fervor. Unprecedented. In the first three minutes, he'd already spoken more words than in a typical lunch hour.

"He landed in a plane. On the water. Bracciano. Plane with the red cross on the side."

"When?"

"A few days ago. Before lunch. They took him to Campo Imperatore."

"Campo Imperatore? Gran Sasso? The hotel at the ski resort?"

A nod.

"That makes no sense, *Babbo*. What? They wanted to get him ready for ski season, give him the right size boots, a warm jacket?"

His father missed or ignored the humor completely. He was intent, focused. A runaway bull trotting down a narrow alley, one thing on his mind.

"No one else is there. They put him on the funicular. They sent him to the top. Three army men with him. All the other people, they made them leave the hotel before he came."

"Who told you this?"

"The man who drove him. Eugenio Sacrosancto. My friend."

I didn't know you had friends, Silvio wanted to say, but two thoughts occurred to him then. The first was that taking *il Duce* to Campo Imperatore, one of the most isolated spots in the whole country, might, in fact, make sense after all. If they were trying to keep him in a place where no one could reach him, then the top of a ski resort in summer was a good choice. Especially Campo Imperatore. He'd been there himself, years before, a second-rate hotel at the top of a mediocre ski mountain. You couldn't drive to the hotel because the access road went only as far as the base of the chairlift. It would be easy to guard him there, impossible for him to escape.

And then, the second thought: his father's excitement came not from patriotism but purely and simply from the idea that there might be money involved, that the information was valuable to the people who were employing his son. For a moment, Silvio was tempted to judge him: he looked like a little boy there at the head of the table; he'd left his post at the Irish embassy and driven across the city, not out of anything as high-minded as familial love or moral responsibility but because he thought he might earn a few hundred lire in doing so . . . even though he was well paid, even though Silvio had set him up in a perfectly adequate apartment, and even though there was no need for extra money.

The temptation to pass judgment evaporated: it occurred to him that he and his father were not so different after all.

But then, as he pondered the new information, sipped his coffee, and looked at the curtains to avoid his father's eyes, something else occurred to him. Two ways in which they were, in fact, very different. First, much as Silvio liked money, there was some other motivation acting within him these days—a hatred of the German bullies, a love of his beautiful *Italia*. And the second difference: he could keep a secret. His father, famously taciturn though he was, could not. He liked to be the one who knew.

"*Babbo,*" Silvio said carefully. "When you heard about this, did you tell anyone? Anyone besides me? Did you go into a bar after work or something and maybe mention it?"

His father looked down at his coffee cup. He didn't answer the question.

As far as Silvio was concerned, he didn't have to.

They sat there like that for another minute, old arguments clouding the air between them. His father, previously a grudging supporter of *il Duce*, was now, it seemed, willing to sell the man to his enemies for a few hundred lire. A few hundred it would be. Silvio went into the bedroom, found his wallet, and took out three hundred-lire notes. When he returned to the kitchen, his father was standing. He wanted to thank him, but for some reason, the words wouldn't leave his throat. His father took the money and crushed it into his pants pocket, then, halfway out the door, looked up and met Silvio's eyes. Something else there now. Still a boy, but a boy who'd accidentally broken a bedroom window with a rock, and wanted forgiveness. "I shouldn't a told anyone," he said.

"That's okay, *Babbo*. As long as the guy you told wasn't German, that's okay. Don't worry about it. Come see me anytime, and if you hear anything else, let me know."

A grunt, a nod. His father was in the hall, walking toward the top of the stairway. He turned his head and looked at Silvio with one eye. No expression there now. No love, not even affection. Then the back of his square head again. Silvio listened to his feet scuffing the marble stairs and then the sound of the front door closing.

As long as he wasn't a German, he thought, *or reporting to one.*

He went inside and dialed the secure number Andreottla had given him. Three rings and he heard a familiar voice say, *"Pronto!"*

"Italo," he said, "it's Silvio. I have something nice to give you. I need to wash and shave. I'll be at our café in thirty minutes."

Sixty-Five

Don Claudio couldn't stop shaking. His knees hurt, pressed as they were against the marble kneeler by the weight above them. His hands were clasped in front of him, elbows on the rail, mouth and nose resting on his knuckles. Again and again, he repeated his petition to Mary, the beautiful prayer that ended with those harrowing words, "and at the hour of our death." He had killed a man. It felt as if, in that one small movement of his second finger, he'd stepped through some kind of sacred barrier, a curtain of Christ's words, and away into another universe. He had killed a man. In his mind's eye, he could not stop seeing the bubbles of blood at the corners of the German's mouth, the wet scarlet spirals on the wall. In his inner ear, he could not stop hearing the horrid choking gurgles. Had the officer been trying to speak his wife's name?

He had taken a life.

And now he would pay. There was no possibility the Germans would fail to come looking for one of their own. Sant'Abbondio might not be the first place they'd check, but they'd be here eventually, and even in the unlikely event he was able to clean up all the blood himself, even in the extremely unlikely event he'd be able to hide the body, there was no way he'd be able to lie to them under interrogation. Even a simple question—"Have you seen Major So-and-so? A tall man, bald?"—would be enough, he knew, to set his face twitching. They were crude men, these Germans, but not stupid, and they seemed to have a sixth sense for secrets. All these months he'd been able to deceive them, protected by his robes and this building, by the improbability of a fat old priest working with the resistance. Now he would pay.

Mind whirling, he decided that he should at least try to make the dark, hours-long walk to Masso's farmhouse and warn him, but when he heard the squeak of the doors, he knew he was too late. They had come for him. Already. The shaking turned violent. His teeth ground against each other as he prayed, making a horrible scratching sound. *Mary, protect me,* he thought. *Protect me now. Give me strength now.* He heard footsteps, barely audible, followed by a terrible silence. There would be no running now. More footsteps. He tried but couldn't keep himself from turning to look. A man there, a dark figure. He heard one word.

"Padre?"

Sixty-Six

Maria did what she could to make the poisonous mushrooms resemble edible ones. Some shaping with a knife, a bit of color added by virtue of potato skins boiled in a pot for half an hour. When she was finished, she chopped them into pieces no larger than the top knuckle of a finger, then washed her hands carefully, placed the mushrooms back in the mesh bag, took her bottle of oil, and forced herself to walk across the empty lot to what she still thought of as the Rossos' home.

She kept her eyes down, fingers squeezing tight to the rough mesh and the top of the bottle. She didn't know what she'd do when she saw the tall one's face. She didn't know if she'd smash him on the head with the bottle or erupt in tears, but as she walked, she prayed to Saint Jude, patron of hopeless cases, to give her strength. There wasn't the slightest doubt in her mind now that God wanted this from her. She'd be acting, not only for herself but for all the other decent women in Italy, the girls, the female babies just being born. She stepped through the back door of the house as she always did, just another Italian woman serving the masters of the world.

In the kitchen, she set to work—lighting the gas stove from a box of matches she carried in her dress pocket, taking their fine beef from the refrigerator and chopping it, slicing an onion and setting it in a pan with the piss-oil, starting a pot of water boiling for the noodles, mixing flour and water and adding a spoonful of their sour cream to make the kind of brown gravy they liked on meat and which she herself would never in a thousand years put into her mouth. They had offered her some on other nights, and she'd refused, saying she didn't like the taste. *Perfect,* she thought. *A perfect excuse.* Her only concern was that, once set into a warm pan with oil, the *lepiota* would smell different, so she waited until the fragrance of the cooking onions had filled the kitchen before pouring oil into another pan and putting in the mushrooms. For good measure, she covered them: if someone came into the room, he'd have no reason to doubt that these were simply the same kind of delicious *funghi* they'd eaten in her chicken cacciatore.

One by one, the men thumped downstairs in their black boots—they were like animals; the smell of food drew them from their lairs. Maria's hands had started to sweat, and a drop ran down from her right armpit and into the side of her brassiere. She could feel her heart beating in her throat. She listened for the voice of the tall one and didn't hear it. Perhaps he'd gone off into the woods and hanged himself out of guilt, drunk as he always seemed to be.

Through the open window, she heard the bells of San Domenico sounding out the hour. Nine o'clock—traditional dinner hour for Italians, but the Germans liked to eat earlier, so there was a note of impatience in the dining room's loud voices. A woman had joined them. Well, that was a shame. She'd have to perish with her Nazi friends, that's all.

Maria took as long as she could over the preparations, wanting the men to be ravenous by the time the food was served. No one came into the kitchen. Everything seemed to go perfectly. When the noodles were almost ready, she put salt and pepper on the meat, added a few more spoonfuls of sour cream, a dash of their harsh red wine. Next, the mushrooms went into the mix. Her hands did not shake; her resolve did not waver, not for a second. She knew—everyone in those parts knew—what kind of death they'd face: agonizing stomach pain, vomiting, explosive diarrhea, paralysis, and then, with a terrible slowness that would last, in fact, only a minute or two, the loss of the ability to breathe. They'd remain conscious to the end. She wondered how long it would take—less than half an hour, her son had said—and if the alcohol would strengthen or weaken the poison.

With her preparations and slow work, the meal was unusually late. The officers were calling out for food. Even the woman called out once, a high voice, the men laughing at her imitation of their accented Italian.

Sixty-Seven

By the time Luca reached Mezzegra, darkness had enveloped the town. In anticipation of air raids, Mussolini had ordered the streetlights to be kept off and lights from homes and businesses to be hidden as well as possible by curtains and blinds. But there was still some light from the stars and from the shaded windows of the shops, and, in any case, he could have steered the donkey through the streets by memory. He heard the church bells sound the hour. San Domenico, the larger lakeside church that still had a bell ringer. He'd grown up with that sound—seven a.m. and nine p.m.; to this day, it comforted him.

At the bottom of Piazza Garibaldi, he thought of continuing straight along the lakeside road—it was only another three kilometers to Masso's house. Originally he'd planned to visit Don Claudio, return the cart with the proceeds from the market sales, and then slip up into the trees and come to his mother's house, like a shadow, from the forest. But the military traffic had put him well behind schedule. He paused for a moment, and then decided and turned the donkey right, uphill. The climb was steep and the beast exhausted, and there was a risk in visiting his mother this way, in plain sight. Still, he was working—anyone could see that. He was unfit for military service—anyone could see that, too. He had his papers in order. He had a few unsold apples and some leaves and stems in the back, plus the empty bags that had held his mushrooms. What could they do to a son visiting his own mother?

Two ambulances raced past him on the *statale*, their horns sounding and retreating, the pulse of someone's sorrow.

Up and up he went at the pace a man could walk. Exhausted as it was, the donkey seemed to have given up resisting. It placed one hoof in front of the other with a painful deliberateness, hoping for food and water at the end of its torment, hoping to be left alone then. *Not unlike the Italian people,* Luca thought bitterly.

He paused for a moment in front of the church but thought better of going in. Later, if there was time. He wanted to hold his mother, to bring her one of the apples, then carry the rest up to Sarah, later that night. The idea of taking her out in a boat on the lake had grown more absurd with every kilometer; he had another idea now about what to do for the cause . . . and what to do with Mentone's money.

He pulled the cart to a stop at the side of his mother's house and tied the reins to a tree. Without making a sound, he stepped quietly down the alley between the south wall and a steep drop-off. He turned the corner, every sense alert. There were no lights on behind the curtains, which was strange. It was too early for his mother to go to sleep. In the distance, he could see the Rossos' house. He wondered if they were eating at this hour—late for German soldiers—and pictured his mother at the stove, a slave for them. Mocked. Humiliated.

Nursing a flame of anger, he reached the door and turned the handle, torn between not wanting to make noise and not wanting to startle his mother, who, having finished her duties, might be sleeping in a chair just inside. He opened the door, stepped quietly across the threshold, and turned on a lamp. From there, he could see the living room and kitchen. No one. He turned off the light, felt his way down the hall, and peeked into both bedrooms. Empty. She wasn't asleep, so she must still be cooking or cleaning their dirty dishes.

For a little while, he stood in the darkness, seething, wondering if he should tap on the doorway above his head. But no—his mother probably had a signal, so his knocking would only terrify Rebecca. At last, time passing, he pulled the apple from his pocket and set it on the kitchen counter in a place he was sure his mother would see. He took out his knife, cut away a heart-shaped piece of the skin—an old signal of theirs from grade school days, a story that made Sarah smile—then went silently back outside, around the house, and turned the cart in the direction of Sant'Abbondio.

Sixty-Eight

It seemed to Maria that the meal had a somewhat strange smell, but, listening to the hilarity from the dining room, she decided the Nazi officers would be too drunk to notice. She carried in the bread and the butter they liked to smear all over it, a pot of noodles—overcooked on purpose—and more bottles of wine, as they'd requested. And then, with anger bubbling up inside her like water at the boil, she mouthed a prayer; lifted the large platter of beef, onions, and mushrooms; and carried it to their table. The tall one wasn't there. The rest of them raised a cheer for her when they saw the food, and said things, in their broken Italian, like "Our great chef!" "Maria the queen of the kitchen!" and "At last!" She nodded once and did what she could to keep any expression from her face. Not pride, not fear, not worry, not apology, not hatred. She could feel the redhead watching her, staring. When, after a suitable wait, she tried to retreat to the kitchen, he said, "Stay and eat with us tonight, Maria."

She shook her head, started to say, "Not hungry," but that would have been a too obvious lie. "I don't really want to tonight. This kind of food—"

"Ah, yes, but we want you to, don't we, men?"

A cheer went up. Mean. Sarcastic. Mocking. No one reached to pull out a chair for her. The redhead pointed to the place where the tall one usually sat and spooned a helping of the stroganoff onto a plate for her. "Wine?" he asked. "It's Manischewitz."

More brutal laughter. She pretended not to understand. Most of the men had started eating, shoveling food into their mouths and tearing at hunks of bread, sloshing the wine into their glasses and drinking down mouthfuls. But the redhead hadn't touched his fork. He was watching her, smiling with no teeth showing. She took the seat and looked at the huge Nazi flag on the wall behind him.

"Don't be shy with us," he said. "You are our cook now, our friend. We know you to be a good woman."

She picked at the food at first, just breaking off bits of onion and nibbling. The redhead still hadn't lifted his fork. "Lost your appetite?" he asked quietly. The others seemed not to be paying attention.

At that point, Maria realized the man must have detected something in her face or her movements. She decided it didn't matter anymore. If she was going to die without seeing her husband again, this was as good a way as any—painful, brutally painful, but fast. And she would take a houseful of German officers with her. She thought of her son. Of Rebecca. She swallowed several large forkfuls in succession, and only then did the redhead begin to eat. She waited for something to happen, but her stomach felt normal. She wished she'd asked Luca for a more exact timing, an antidote perhaps, but that was in the past now. Most likely Sabatino was gone, frozen to death months ago in an alien land. Most likely her soul would be joining his today in a more peaceful world. She asked for wine and was served half a glass. She asked for bread. She drank as much water as she could without attracting attention. Perhaps she could dilute the poison and survive.

The men ate quickly, emptied the wine bottles as if they were filled with water, mopped up the last of the gravy with pieces of bread. They sat back, sighed, complimented her, and made more bad jokes about Russia and Russian food. As soon as the first one stood up and went off with the woman to his other pleasures, Maria left her seat, left her meal half-eaten, and began clearing the plates. Poisonous though it was, the food had tasted fine, and the men—even the redhead with his late start—had eaten all of it. She felt something in her belly now, a bad tightening, as if a thin, venomous viper were winding itself around her intestines, preparing to bite. She was about to make herself throw up in the sink, but that would have drawn too much attention, so she left the plates unwashed and hurried out the back door.

She made it only about fifty meters before the first vicious cramp hit her, knocking her to her knees. She got to her feet, went on a few more steps, then another cramp hit, a knife in the lower belly, bad as the pains of childbirth. She fell to her knees again, went down on all fours, then rolled onto her side as the pain radiated through her abdomen, sharp fingers taking hold of her there and squeezing without mercy. She was lying in the dirt, looking back at the Rossos' house, as if it were part of a terrible dream. The men had eaten more than she'd eaten, but their bodies were larger, and they were in better condition. She retched, violently, and could think about nothing but her own pain and death. She began to pray and had gotten through the first line—*Ave Maria, piena di grazia*—when she heard the Rossos' door slam open and saw someone there, leaning sideways against the jamb, backlit by the kitchen lamp. The man had one hand on his belly and, in the other, what looked, from this distance, like a pistol.

Sixty-Nine

Luca tied the donkey to a tree beside the church and fed the tired beast three of the shriveled apples. He'd get water inside, water and a bucket. He'd visit with Don Claudio, perhaps share a glass of wine with him, ask his advice about what Masso had told him. He'd take the donkey back to Masso's, give him the report, get the money, then climb to the cabin so Sarah wouldn't worry. Though he doubted the front doors of the church would be unlocked at this hour, he approached them anyway. There was no sound from the nearby houses and very little light, but not many people lived in this part of Mezzegra anyway. To his surprise, the old wooden doors were unlocked. He tugged on one side quietly. The hinges squeaked.

Inside, a few votive candles flickered; it took his one working eye a moment to adjust to the meager light they cast. He walked slowly past them, toward the altar, scanning the empty pews and, as always, not feeling much inspiration from the marble statues along the walls. Something else hung in the air of the old building, though, some other spirit. He stopped and listened. From the front of the church, he thought he heard whispered prayers. Someone had come here at this late hour, praying for a husband or brother on the front or a son in the mountains. He went forward another few steps, and the praying ceased. He could see a figure at the altar rail now, kneeling. A man. A few more steps and he saw the man turn and look at him over his shoulder, a terrified gesture. It looked like Don Claudio himself, and across the pews of the dark nave, Luca called out one word: *"Padre?"*

Seventy

Sarah awoke with a start and found herself looking up, through tree branches, at a starry sky. She felt the damp moss beneath her back and heard an owl calling in the trees, and, for a moment, before she remembered where she was and what had brought her there, she enjoyed a bit of peace.

A strand of hair had fallen across her right eye. She tucked it back in place, stood up, and looked around. A few hundred meters ahead of her, Maria's house loomed in the shadows, moonlight like a dusting of flour on the stony southeastern wall. Sarah was overtaken by a sudden fit of terror, one of those vague premonitions, the same "bad air" she remembered from childhood. In the summer darkness, the house seemed to her like some kind of mausoleum, an oversize gravestone. What if, just after she hurried away from the window, the German had strangled Maria, then found out her mother was hiding there and raped and killed her, too? What if, by running away, she had failed to save them? She placed the palm of her right hand on her belly and walked closer, keeping in the first line of trees. No lamplight showed in the kitchen this time. She stood still, eyes fixed on the windows.

As the night deepened and the air cooled, as she waited in that spot longer and longer—ten minutes, fifteen—it began to seem strange to the point of impossibility that all was dark in Maria's house. She took the wild apple out of her pocket, had one sour bite, then threw it aside.

There was no sound from the house, no door closing, no water in the sink, no toilet flushing. Nothing. Luca called his mother *la regina dei nottambuli, the queen of night owls*: she never went to sleep this early— just after ten, she guessed. Never went out except to church and the market. It made no sense.

At last, she decided she had to take the risk. She stepped out of the trees and went quietly across the back yard, trying not to startle the sleeping hens, skirting the edge of Maria's garden, holding to the fence post there for a few last seconds. She didn't want to step into the house unannounced, and she didn't want to knock, either, for fear of waking the sleeping women—if they *were* sleeping—and frightening them to death. She hesitated another minute, considering her options. She decided to open the door as quietly as possible and step inside, and as she did so, she had a sudden sense that she'd find Maria sprawled on the kitchen floor in a pool of blood, having slit her own wrists.

But the house felt empty. All was silent. She went from room to room—first bedroom, second bedroom, bathroom, living room, kitchen—feeling her way like a blind woman. No one. At last, she turned on the smallest kitchen light she could find. One apple there, perched beside the sink. Maria's dinner or breakfast. Something had been carved into its skin. A heart. It would be so like her mother to come downstairs, find Maria gone, and leave her this message. So like her mother to starve herself to death so others could eat. So like her mother, with a determination that often crossed the line into pure stubbornness, to decide she'd had enough of hiding and convince Maria to climb into the hills and make a try for the border.

As she was about to turn away, she remembered something Luca had told her once—a little game he and his mother had played when he was young—and a spurt of tears blinded both eyes. He'd been here, maybe only minutes ago, stopped by on the way to the cabin, and left this apple. He'd find the cabin empty, see the note, come looking for her!

She took a broom into her hands, fixed her eyes on the hatchway that led to the attic, turned off the lamp, and walked forward until she guessed she was standing directly beneath it. She tapped the hatchway three times with the end of the handle. No response. She was about to give up—her mother and Maria were both gone—but decided to tap once more. There was a shuffling above her head; she heard the wooden square slide sideways. A person there, invisible in the darkness. A face, familiar. "Mother?" she said, barely above a whisper.

In answer, she heard one choked sob.

Seventy-One

Given what his father had said—or, more precisely, what he *hadn't* said—Silvio decided it was essential to get the new information to Italo Andreottla as quickly as possible. It wouldn't do to have *il Duce* fall into German hands.

A fast shower, a shave, and he was dressed and out the door twenty-two minutes after his father left him. He decided to take the coupe for this short trip, because there was a new feeling to the adventure now, a feeling worthy of celebration, and the convertible seemed to fit that. Not two weeks ago, his motivation for working with the mysterious "Giovanni" had been simple and straightforward: money. Lately, however, a different impulse had started to find its way into Silvio's thoughts. It felt strange and somehow uplifting: the money mattered, of course; Silvio Merino didn't work for nothing. But beyond that, and beyond the sense that his exploits would be exciting to Lisiella Aiello in bed, something else was moving him forward. To his surprise, he realized that he was actually feeling a surge of patriotism, a love of the true *Italia* . . . or his idea of it. He felt, as he left the apartment, almost noble.

It took him four minutes of fast walking to reach the warehouse. Another three to find the friend who worked there and who held on to his keys in case the cars had to be moved. Two more minutes to lower the canvas roof, and he was out on the streets of Rome in his white-walled American convertible, running late, going to a new meeting place Andreottla had just suggested on the phone—a restaurant inside Vatican City's walls—about to deliver a piece of information that would lead to the capture of the *Duce*, the evil clown. He felt bathed in a succulent satisfaction: he was playing a role in history, a good and important role.

Holding the wheel with one hand and listening absentmindedly to the whine of an air-raid siren in the distance—it seemed fairly far off—Silvio wondered if his name might eventually find its way into schoolbooks, in Italy and abroad. True, he himself had barely opened those books and certainly had never read them with any care. Still, it would be an honor.

He was imagining various outcomes—seeing his face in a chapter on WWII espionage, picturing himself telling the story to Lisiella in a room at the Grand Hotel—and at the same time working his way impatiently through Rome's notorious traffic (even in wartime, the streets of the city could be choked at certain hours). The sirens were still going off, a bit louder here as he turned onto Via Vittorio Emanuele, but he was lost in the new kind of excitement, enjoying what almost amounted to a nascent religious feeling. Maybe, after the war, he'd become a churchgoer again.

There was a thump, an explosion, the sound of tinkling glass. Only a few blocks over, it must have been, because it was strong enough to make the heavy car shimmy to the left. Another thump, this one very close. Cursing under his breath, Silvio turned away from the noise and concussion, down a side street. He was looking for an alley to pull into, someplace safer than the middle of an open road, when there was a deafening crash in his right ear and a tremendous rush of wind. The coupe flipped over as if it were made of balsa wood. His head hit the pavement, hard, and he was on his back on the concrete, a sharp pain in his face, his legs entangled in the steering wheel, blood running into one eye, the coupe upside down and covering him like the lid of a casket.

He took a couple of ragged breaths, tried to stay calm, to force a confident grin, but it hurt to move his lips, and there was blood on them besides. Probably his beautiful nose had been broken. He'd look like Andreottla now for the rest of his days. Another breath. A surge of pain but no panic. The coupe seemed to be slowly settling down on him, squeezing his legs against the wheel. The back of the driver's seat was just above his face now, so close he could spit on it. It was becoming difficult to breathe. He kept slipping in and out of consciousness, fading away, coming back. There were sirens, voices, someone screaming. Maybe, he thought, this is my time. So be it.

Seventy-Two

Sarah didn't want to turn on the kitchen light again. Stumbling about in the darkness, banging into the wall, a standing lamp, the edge of the same table where the German had been sitting, she managed to locate and carry over one of the kitchen chairs and help her mother down from the attic. She held Rebecca against her for a long time and let her sob there. She could feel her shoulder blades, feel the tears dripping down her own neck, and for a few minutes, nothing mattered but the fact that she was touching her mother again, that they were both alive. The quiet sobbing went on and on. At last, Sarah took hold of her mother's bony shoulders and held her at arm's length. In the darkness, her face looked like it belonged to a ghost. "Where's Maria?" she asked.

"I don't know!" Rebecca whispered. "She's here every night. Every night she feeds me, takes my . . . bucket. She's never missed a night!"

"It means the Germans have her, Mother."

"They can't; they can't!"

"We must leave."

"Leave where? How? There's no place to go!"

Sarah turned her mother toward the back door, leading her down the dark hallway and into the kitchen, one hand holding her by a skeletal arm, the other feeling for the wall and doorway, then the backs of the kitchen chairs.

"We should leave something, a note," her mother whispered frantically.

"Too dangerous."

"Sarah, something. She won't know. She'll worry."

"Not now. Stay here."

Sarah felt her way back along the hallway, stood on the chair, and lifted the attic hatchway back into place. From there, she could smell the slop bucket, and she knew that, if she left it there, the stink would only get worse. No time to worry about that now. Maria was dead or in German hands. She'd never come back to this house. If she were in the custody of the Gestapo, it would be only a matter of minutes before she'd be forced to admit she'd been hiding a Jew. Maybe Luca had told her about the cabin, and if so, she'd be made to tell them that, also, and soldiers would be sent up into the trees to find her and the man she loved. She brought the chair back to its place in the kitchen and, reaching around blindly, almost knocked over two canning jars. She filled them with water, gave her mother the apple with the heart on it. "Eat," she said. "You'll need your strength."

"My legs are like sticks. I'm unused to walking."

"Eat, Mother."

Feeling around in the darkness—dishes, cups, a small towel—Sarah found, at last, a canvas bag. She put the water jars into it, searched the refrigerator and shelves for anything edible, and, finding one piece of salami, size of a fist, hard as stone, and a few hard-boiled eggs, she put those in the bag, too.

"Let's go."

"Where?" her mother asked. "The church? Don Claudio could hide us."

Sarah shook her head. Just before they stepped out the back door, she tried to say "Switzerland," but the word caught in her throat. If Luca had found the cabin empty and left, looking for her, she'd either have to hope she'd meet him on the path, or go back to the cabin, wait there, praying that he'd return, praying the Nazis wouldn't come. Or she'd have to take her mother across the border and never see him again. If she made it to Switzerland, if they accepted her there, she'd raise their child without a father.

As she herself had been raised.

Seventy-Three

Three minutes before Skorzeny and his assembled men were to set off in their towplanes and gliders, the air-raid sirens sounded over the city of Rome, and the deafening whines sent them hustling for cover. "It's happening more and more now," he said to Lieutenant Radl as they trotted off the runway. "Three raids in just the past week."

They took shelter with the rest of the team, crouching in the airport's concrete bunker, a tight, cramped underground room that smelled of sweat and mold and was as damp, along the bottoms of the walls, as the inside of a wet boot. There was no conversation. They could sense but not hear the droning bomber engines above them, and, after a few minutes of nervous anticipation, they began to feel the concussions. Three-hundred-pound bombs, Skorzeny guessed. The Americans. From the force of the explosions, he could tell the difference between these and the five-hundred-pound British bombs—the American B-17s, the "Flying Fortresses," were so heavily armored that they had to carry a lighter load.

Still, three hundred pounds was enough. The concussions shook the thick walls and rocked the men in place, the earth vibrating beneath the soles of their boots. Skorzeny knew from his briefings that, though the Allies had been concentrating on the factories in the north and Naples and the cities of Sicily in the south, they were starting to focus more on central Italy now. The raids on Rome were quick and relatively light, aimed at railroad stations and key roadways, the massive bombers making one run, releasing their loads, and disappearing off to the south like flocks of angry geese fleeing winter. Very few Germans had been killed so far—more often than not, the casualties were Italian civilians—but the increased enemy activity was a bad omen for the forces of the Reich, and that, Skorzeny felt, gave his own mission even more urgency. Find *il Duce*, put him back in power, and they could hope to chase the Allies from the peninsula.

When the concussions ceased, the men had to wait another ten minutes before the all clear sounded, and then they were clambering out of the concrete box as fast as they could move. "Karl," Skorzeny said to Radl when the others couldn't hear, "General Student gave me the order that under no conditions should there be any crash landings with the gliders."

"Shouldn't be a problem, Captain. We photographed the grounds of the hotel ourselves. We both saw the open area."

"Right, but we saw it from five thousand meters. If it turns out we were wrong, if it's all rocks and steep slopes there, I'm going to give the order to land anyway. I wanted you to know."

Skorzeny couldn't read his friend's face. A crash landing could mean anything from broken bones, to paralysis, to death for the occupants of the gliders, and even if the pilots were particularly skillful and especially lucky and no one was injured, it would certainly mean the destruction of the expensive planes. Disobeying a direct order could mean court-martial, too—in some cases, execution. General Student wasn't known for leniency.

"Our Benito better be there, then," Radl said grimly. "He better not have been spirited off again."

"I think he's there. If I'm wrong, I'll bear the blame, no worries."

"None here," Radl said. "Those bombs were close. If they hit the gliders, none of this will matter."

But, though the runway was pocked with half a dozen craters, the planes themselves had been spared.

"Allied accuracy," Radl quipped.

Skorzeny detected the lining of concern behind the remark. Failure here, again, would be like the earth eroding under their boots. Gliders were notoriously dangerous tools of war, thin-skinned, difficult to steer, much more vulnerable to antiaircraft fire than the heavily armored bombers and fighter planes. And those could be shot down, too, as he well remembered. After the expensive, almost deadly debacle off Sardinia, if this didn't work, General Student wouldn't authorize a third mission, and he and Radl couldn't keep their men around indefinitely, waiting on information from Selenzen or a loose-lipped Italian. They'd be sent back to fight in Russia.

The sky had cleared beautifully, not only of American B-17s but of the earlier cloud cover. They checked their gear a final time and, silent to a man, climbed aboard. Shortly after one p.m., nine Hentschel tow-planes trundled one after the next down the damaged runway, dodging bomb craters and tugging nine featherlight DFS 230 gliders behind them.

Skorzeny commanded the mission, but the officer in the first glider—better trained for such things—was in charge of getting them there. So he was perched on the centerboard in the third glider, enjoying, as he always did, the lift and tilt, the rocking motion, the jostling excitement of flight. It made him wish, not for the first time, that the Luftwaffe hadn't rejected him. Then again, in the Luftwaffe, he might have passed the entire war without being given an assignment like this.

Once they'd reached altitude and turned east, he listened to the tow pilot give his coordinates and tried as best he could to trace their movement on a topographical map. As Radl had said, from the aerial photos, he knew there would be a triangular field just behind the hotel, perfect landing place for the gliders. If all went as planned, a second team of commandos would make an assault on the base of the funicular—the only other access route to the summit—at the same time the gliders were landing. The Italian guards would be stunned, paralyzed, he hoped, and would offer little resistance.

His only real concern was the accuracy of his own methodical calculations—educated guesswork, really: no one had reported actually seeing Mussolini at the ski hotel.

Fat cumulus clouds sailed in rows over the Apennines' forested slopes. When the gliders emerged into clear air again, at five thousand meters now, the pilot of the towplane told him the first two gliders had somehow disappeared. Fallen behind them, he hoped, or drifted off course. Their navigator was in one of them.

"No antiaircraft fire here, is there?"

"Not a whisper," the pilot said.

Skorzeny had no navigation instruments and not much training, but he volunteered to lead the rest of them in. Cutting a hole in the cellophane side window with his battle knife to get a clearer view, he peered down at a scene of folded slopes, winding roads, and small clusters of tile-roofed houses. It required a bit of back-and-forth maneuvering, instructions given to the tow pilot via the microphone system as he looked from the land below to his map, but at last he recognized the L'Aquila valley and saw the line of their own trucks moving toward the base of the funicular. Another minute, one last cloud slipping away beneath them, and the brown brick hulk of Campo Imperatore appeared almost directly below. He could see the small gray building at the top of the funicular and, beside it, the hotel's raised patio and curving front wall. He gave the order for the towropes to be slipped.

The flock of gliders swooped down in great silent circles, light-feathered birds of prey, Skorzeny balancing on the centerboard and staring through the hole he'd cut, looking for the triangular field. One half of the gradual downward spiral gave him a good view of the target; on the other half, he lost sight of it.

As his glider descended and the hotel came into focus, disappeared, came into focus again with each slow turn, he realized that, yes, there was a triangular field. But what he and Radl had been unable to see from an altitude of five thousand meters and what he could see so clearly now was that the field sloped steeply away from the hotel, so steeply it would be impossible to land there with anything but a parachute. "Trouble," he said to Radl between clenched teeth. "Not flat. Not flat at all."

"Land in front, then."

"All stones there. The planes will be torn to shreds. Student will—"

"The Führer, not Student, gave the order to find Mussolini. We've come this far, Captain. We're this close to getting him."

Skorzeny nodded once. He closed his eyes, counted to three, then gave the order into the microphone. "Crash landing."

The pilot didn't hesitate. He dipped the left wing, the glider descended much more sharply, circled, descended, flattened out, made a quarter turn, and smashed, belly-first, into the rocky ground barely twenty meters from the hotel's raised front patio.

Skorzeny heard the tearing of the thin canvas fabric, watched one wing fall away, and, an instant later, felt himself catapulted sideways out the door. He got to his feet and sprinted toward the building, shouting one of his favorite Italian phrases: *"Mani in alto!"* Hands up! He pointed his eight-shot Luger at the stunned Italian guards who stared, wide-eyed, from the front of the building. There would be more men inside, he was sure, but the Italians were watching one glider after the next crash-land in front of the hotel, dozens of German commandos pouring out and running straight toward them, guns raised, all of them screaming in two languages. Some of the Italians had rifles, but they weren't lifting them, just standing there, stunned. Exactly as he'd hoped.

He sprinted through the first door he saw and found himself in the telegraph room, one man with a headset there at the controls. Skorzeny kicked the chair out from under him, ripped the headset off, and stomped on it so hard that a piece went flying across the room and into the man's face. As the operator scrambled sideways toward the wall, staring up in terror, Skorzeny lifted the chair and smashed it against the telegraph machine, then sprinted out again.

Except for a handful of men who'd been badly injured, his cadre had gotten themselves free of the broken planes and were sprinting up the hill toward him, other gliders still landing, the small Storch—*il Duce's* means of escape—touching down behind them, roughly, bumping along the stony slope, then coming to a stop less than ten meters from a vertical drop-off.

Skorzeny grabbed Radl, bent him in two, leaped onto his back, and was able to climb from there onto the terrace of the patio. He heard a window open above him, second floor. A face appeared there. Haggard. Recognizable. A marvelous sight.

"Inside, inside!" Skorzeny shouted. "*Duce*, inside!" He ran through the main entrance and found a crowd of Italian soldiers and carabinieri there, all of them wearing the same astonished look on their faces, none raising so much as a fist. A head taller than the tallest man, Skorzeny pistol-whipped a path through them, knocking one sideways, shoving others, kicking, forcing his way through to the bottom of the stairs. He kept listening for gunshots behind him, but the Italians seemed unwilling to risk a drop of blood for their *Duce*, and no one on their side was giving orders. He took the stairs three at a time, turned left onto a hallway, guessed at a door, and shoved it open to find Benito Mussolini inside the room, wearing a white T-shirt, a two-day growth of beard, and staring at him as if he were a creature from a dream.

Skorzeny stood to attention and gave the Nazi salute. "*Duce*," he said, "the Führer has sent me. You are free!"

Seventy-Four

From her place in the dirt of the overgrown lot, her right shoulder, right ear, and right hip pressed into the weeds, her stomach and intestines on fire, Maria kept her eyes locked on the Rossos' house. She was almost sure now from his stocky build that the man in the doorway of the Rosso house was the redhead. Backlit by the kitchen lamp, he was on his feet but leaning in an odd way, at too sharp an angle, against the doorframe. He held something, the pistol, in his right hand. She watched him try to raise it, and then he stumbled backward and disappeared into the house. She closed her eyes, opened them halfway, saw him again, on his hands and knees now, the pistol pointed at her. A shot rang out. One explosive *pop* that echoed in the trees. A series of others, four, five—she lost count. She heard a small tree branch falling. She tried to move, to press herself into the dirt, but couldn't manage it.

The redhead was flat on his stomach, both elbows on the ground, his head raised and the gun held out in front of him. In the light from the doorway, she thought she could see his whole body twitching. She closed her eyes, focused on the pain, willed herself not to be taken into the next life. Not yet. Let them all die. Let the redhead die. Let his friends in the house suffer and die. Let the bald one come home to that sight, his men lying in their vomit and blood, poisoned dishes in the sink. Let him understand.

She tried again but could not make any part of her body move. The pain was like heavy chains wrapped around her middle, choking her. She was beginning to have difficulty breathing—the final symptom. *Not yet,* she thought. *I cannot die yet.* She watched the redhead try to bring the barrel to horizontal. With great difficulty, he pointed the pistol at her. His whole body was shaking violently. Before he collapsed, he managed to squeeze the trigger again one time. Maria heard the sound of the pistol firing and immediately felt a burning pain on top of her left thigh. She tried to turn and look. With an enormous effort, she managed to reach her hand down and feel the wound, the sticky blood and torn fabric of her dress. Superficial. She would live. She was determined to live. She'd get Rebecca and go to Don Claudio, and they'd escape together into the hills or find Luca and have him guide them to Switzerland, all of them.

She tasted blood. The pain in her belly was immense, horrific. The redhead had stood up again and fallen straight backward. She could see the bottoms of his boots in the doorway like two small, dark gravestones, monuments to defeat.

Seventy-Five

Don Claudio was so surprised to see Luca there in the darkened church that he was, at first, completely unable to speak, unable to get a single syllable to come out of his mouth. He stood up from the altar rail and embraced his young friend, led him to the cloakroom, and showed him the blood on the wall and then, in the kitchen, the dead German officer wrapped in a rug and priest's robe. His hands were trembling, his eyes pushed open wide, his throat so choked with fear that he couldn't swallow. "What?" he managed to pronounce in a hoarse whisper. *What should we do?* he'd wanted to say, but he was shaking so violently that he couldn't push the rest of the sentence into the air.

"Wet a towel," Luca told him, so calmly that it seemed to the priest the young man's mind had gone into a different zone. Cold. Clear. "Wipe the wall clean and the floor. I'm going to take another one of your robes and wrap him up better and drag him out to the wagon. When you're done, follow me to the door and make sure you wipe up every drop of blood. Every drop. Then take the towel and come with me."

"I have to stay. If I'm not here, they'll know. He may have told someone he was coming here—"

"No, *Padre*. Clean up every drop you can and come with me. You can't stay."

"He," Don Claudio blurted out, and then completely lost his nerve. He wanted to tell the truth but, looking into Luca's one working eye, he realized he wouldn't be able to speak the words to describe what he'd heard in the confessional. Not now. Probably never. But he had to tell him something. So he said, "He hit your mother, this man," and watched Luca's face change again. A new shadow across his features. "Assaulted her," Don Claudio stumbled on. "He came to confession. Bragging."

Luca watched him, waiting for more, and Don Claudio was almost physically pushed backward by the expression on his face, a face he'd been looking at since the day of Luca's baptism. High cheekbones; wide, expressive mouth; one foggy eye. There was a hardness there now, something he'd never seen; the expression belonged to a killer.

"Bragging?" Luca asked after a moment, very quietly.

The priest nodded, looked away, started to say something more, then stopped. He didn't want a lie to be the last thing he ever said to Sarah's lover. He still had the Saint Jude statuette in his pocket. He brought it out and thrust it at Luca, as if such a gesture expressed all the war's secrets, all the unspoken pain and battered hopes, all the mystery of suffering. "Money inside. Take it . . . From the archbishop."

Luca took the statue and jammed it carelessly into the deep pocket of his work pants. "Find me something heavy, Father," he said in a voice that was like wind on the coldest winter night. The voice of command now.

"What?"

"Anything. Anything heavy."

Don Claudio hurried into the nave and looked around frantically, his mind all static and rush. For one second, he thought of giving Luca the chalice, but he settled on the altar's tall brass candlesticks, so heavy he could only pull them across the floor behind him, one in each hand. By the time he returned, Luca was at the rear door, walking backward and dragging the wrapped body, leaving a trail of blood and carpet fibers. Don Claudio opened the door, helped Luca lift the body and heave it into the back of the wagon.

"Blankets," Luca said. "Or a tarpaulin. Something to cover."

Don Claudio went to his own bedroom, ripped the blanket off his bed, brought it out, and threw it over the body. It wasn't enough. Breathing as if he'd run uphill all the way from the Bar Lake Como, he went back into his church, hastily cleaned whatever blood he could find, and carried out an armful of firewood from the kitchen stove. He flung it on top of the blanket. Luca had brought some branches and twigs from the edge of the trees and was throwing them in, too. "Climb in, *Padre*."

With some effort, the priest hoisted himself up onto the wooden seat. Luca untied the donkey, turned the cart, and started down the hill toward the lake. At the bottom of the road, he turned right, then left, into a neighborhood of small, poor homes, set close together. Sitting beside him in a silent trance, Don Claudio realized after a moment that they were in Lenno, on Quercia Street, the street where Rebecca had lived. Another few seconds and the cart passed by the house that held the apartment where they'd slept together. For as long as he could, Don Claudio kept his mouth closed, and then, when the words, the confession, would no longer stay inside him, when the lie he'd lived had finally become too heavy to carry along with his other sins—*he had killed a man!*—he made himself say, "Do you know who Sarah's father is?"

"Even *she* doesn't know," Luca muttered between clamped teeth, staring straight ahead.

Don Claudio listened to the slow, steady *clop* of the exhausted donkey's hooves, waiting, every second, for a German officer to come out of an alley with a flashlight, shine it on them, ask what was in back. Luca pulled the cart past the ramshackle house. The priest turned his head to study it as they passed—the sagging roof, the untended yard, the windowpanes broken by the Gestapo raid, something illegible scrawled in paint beside the front door. It seemed to him that half his spirit still lived there, in the tiny bedroom where his daughter—*his daughter!*—had been conceived. Another fifty meters and they reached an inlet, the end of a small mountain river, really, that fed into the lake. A dock there. A boat with blue trim. As they came to a stop, Don Claudio was able to speak two more words: "I am."

Luca looked at him—it seemed that not even this could surprise him now; nothing could penetrate the hard shell of hatred that had formed when he'd heard about his mother. Frightening enough, that shell. What would happen if he heard what the German had *really* done?

Luca tilted his head slowly sideways, a gesture the priest couldn't read. "True?"

Don Claudio nodded, saw the hard expression soften for just a moment, saw Luca working backward across a series of clues. "I'm glad, *Padre*," the young man said, and then he climbed down from the seat and went to work.

Seventy-Six

"I can't make it; I can't walk," Rebecca told her daughter when they'd gone only a few steps across Maria's back yard. "My legs have no strength."

"You have to, Mother. Once we get into the trees, we'll go very slowly."

Sarah had hold of her mother's arm and was clasping it against her side. They moved forward at the pace of a toddler, stopping every few steps.

The third time they stopped, Sarah heard something, one syllable. An animal grunting, she thought, a boar that had come down this far to forage. They went forward again, stopped. The same sound. One syllable from the middle of the vacant lot.

"That's Maria!" her mother whispered. She tugged on Sarah's arm and turned her in the direction of the Rossos' house, through the gate in the fence. There was a handful of unpruned olive trees in front of them and then the empty square of land where, in better times, the Rossos had raised animals and grown food.

They'd gone only a dozen more steps when they saw a figure lying on the ground, touched by moonlight. They heard another strained syllable. Sarah let go of her mother's arm and ran. Maria lay on her side, one cheek pressed into the dirt, her hands trembling uncontrollably.

Vomit in a pool beside her, blood spreading across the fabric at her left hip.

Sarah put her face down close to Maria's and took hold of one shoulder. "Maria! What happened?"

"Burn!" Maria said, barely above a whisper. She was breathing with great effort, the muscles of her face squeezed tight in agony.

"Let us help you. Let us take you to the house."

Maria closed her eyes and shook her head in two tiny movements. "Burn!" she said again.

"Who, Maria? What?"

"The house. Germans."

"I don't understand! Let us—"

"Have to . . . Now! Rossos'. Go. Matches in . . . pocket. *Vai!* Go!

As if she were outside her own body and watching, Sarah hesitated, took one breath, and then pushed her fingers into the bloody pocket of Maria's dress and found a small box of stove matches. By then her mother had reached Maria's side. She knelt hard in the dirt and put both hands on her friend's arm. "She's bleeding," her mother said. "Maria, what happened?"

"Poison. Burn them!"

"They'll kill everyone," Rebecca told her.

"Make it," Maria grunted, closing her eyes. "Accident . . . Fire."

"The whole house?"

Maria breathed one last unintelligible syllable.

Confused, shaking with fear, clutching the matches in her blood-stained fingers, Sarah made herself go across the lot. Any second she expected a soldier to run out of the house and start shooting at her. In the weak light from the Rossos' kitchen, she could see that the door was open, a body lying there. A German soldier. When she reached him, she saw that he was holding one of their pistols, a thin-necked tool of the Devil, black as coal. She stopped, stared, and then, moving in a dream, pried the gun from his stiff fingers, pushed it down into the pocket of her dress, and dragged the body farther into the house. Inside, it was a scene from a painting of *The Inferno*, men and one woman lying in poses of agony. Some had fallen by the table, others in the kitchen, arms and legs splayed, faces contorted. The woman was sprawled at the bottom of the staircase, her left arm stuck between the balusters and broken at a horrible angle. All of them seemed to have been trying to make it to the door, as if eternal salvation lay beyond it. Sarah stood there for a few seconds and then, in a hypnosis of terror, lit one match with trembling hands and touched it to the tablecloth. She stood still, shaking, watching the fire catch and spread—the tablecloth, the clothing of a man who'd fallen facedown at the table, then a Nazi flag on the wall just beyond him. She backed away, holding one hand to her belly. There was a glass jar of grease on the stove. She poured it over the nearest body, lit it with another match, turned on the stove gas, and hurried outside.

By the time she reached Maria again, her mother was weeping, her head pressed down against Maria's shoulder. No movement at Maria's chest. No sign of life. Sarah hesitated only two seconds, then yanked her mother to her feet and dragged her toward the trees.

Seventy-Seven

Luca stood beside the cart for a full minute, making sure no one was about to step out of the darkness. He carried the heavy candlesticks over first, then pulled the branches, stove wood, and blanket to one side and, with Don Claudio's help, lifted the wrapped body and brought it over to the boat. It took some work—the corpse seemed impossibly heavy and, for the millionth time, Luca cursed his weak arm—but they managed to slide the booted feet under one wooden slat and the head under another, then they covered the corpse with the blanket, rinsed their hands in the lake, and settled themselves on the seats, facing each other. A three-quarter moon was rising over the mountains beyond the lake's far shore. In the boat, as Mentone had promised, was a fishing pole, a cheap model with a lure attached. Luca shoved off and began straining at the oars. In order to keep the boat moving out into the lake in a straight line, he had to make two strokes with the weak arm for every one with the strong. Hard as it was to row the extra weight, he decided not to turn on the small motor: the noise would attract attention.

"Pretend to fish," he told the priest, nodding down toward the pole. Don Claudio had to be told twice.

"*Padre*, take the rod, pretend you're fishing."

The priest lifted it awkwardly into his hands and, after struggling for a few minutes, managed to straighten out the line, toss the lure over the side, and offer a fair imitation of a man fishing. Once they were a hundred meters out into the lake, Luca asked him what had happened at the church.

Don Claudio couldn't meet his eyes. He held the fishing pole still and stared out over the black water. "A confession," he said. "The man came, confessed to . . . hitting . . . your mother. He was drunk, I think. His breath smelled. Drunk, rude. I tried to tell him to make a penance, and he stormed out. There were guns in the cloakroom."

"Guns?"

The priest nodded. "A pistol. Three rifles hanging in the closet. I was waiting for someone to come for them. You, Masso, someone . . ."

"Still there? Now?"

A nod.

"Who brought them?"

"I have no idea. The archbishop only—"

"You should've told me. We have to get them out of there before the Germans come and search."

Another nod. The priest seemed in a trance, a drugged man. "I was holding the pistol—as a boy I used to shoot them. I . . . was standing there, holding the pistol . . . I looked up and there he was again. He had come back for some reason. I—I shot. I didn't even think to do it; I just . . ."

Luca went silent then, pulling hard on the oars, feeling a coating of sweat form on his face and neck. He watched the shore fade slowly behind him. "They'll realize he's gone," he said in the same cold voice. "They'll give it a day, thinking he's out carousing somewhere. Then they'll come looking."

"I'm not sure I cleaned up well enough. There will be blood. They'll see it. They'll find the rifles . . . My God! I dropped the pistol!"

"We'll go back. We'll fix it. I can use the weapons."

Luca gave three strong pulls at the oars, two more with his weak arm to straighten their course, and then let the boat glide. Well to the north, he saw a light moving across the surface, a small craft silhouetted by the rising moon. The Germans weren't known to patrol these waters—no military activity here—but the Italian police would be out, checking for smugglers, looking for bribes. "I've decided not to give Mentone and the others the money in the Saint Jude," he said, looking across at the priest's tormented face.

"Ah."

"I don't know why . . . I stopped trusting them. I can use it to get Sarah and our mothers to safety somewhere."

"Once they find out, we'll both be hunted. The Nazis, the mountain fighters. Everybody will be after us."

Luca peered into the distance, trying to guess how long it would take for the small boat to reach them, how much the carabinieri would ask for. He could feel the statuette against the top of his thigh. He rowed another few strokes with both arms, several extra with the left, and let the boat glide again. "Masso says Scutarro is a spy. I don't know who to believe anymore."

"Five decades I've known Gennaro Masso. I would trust him with my life." The priest considered the remark for a moment. "I already trust him with my life. So do you."

Luca grunted, cupped a handful of lake water, and splashed it on his face. "What's the depth here, Father?"

"Fifty meters. Maybe more."

"Hand me the candlesticks."

Using all his remaining strength, Don Claudio slid one candlestick and then the next toward Luca's feet.

Luca handed over the oars, lifted the blanket off the man's body, then unwrapped the heavy bloodied rug and priest's robe enough so he could see the face. It was pale and stiff in the moonlight, half-hidden under the wooden plank on which Don Claudio sat. He looked at it for a moment, studying the bald head, the ragged wound in the throat, then he tugged on the legs to bring it closer, choked up a load of mucus, and spat it into the dead man's eyes. He ripped open the man's pants, jammed one candlestick upside down in the right leg, one in the left, tore two strips from the blanket, and tied the candlesticks in place, making certain they wouldn't fall out. He looked north. The light was closer.

"Father, move over to that side of the boat. To your right. Get over as far as you can. Hurry!"

The priest slid sideways. The boat tilted at a precarious angle. Luca lifted the German's legs—heavy now, with the brass—and positioned them so that they hung over the side, heels in the water, back of the knees resting on the gunwales. Every move made the boat wobble dangerously left and right. He slid to his left to compensate for the weight. "Press that oar down flat on the water so we don't flip." When the boat was more or less stable, he lifted the German's upper torso, balanced it, put his feet flat on the man's shoulder blades, pushed hard, and toppled him over the gunwale.

For a moment, it seemed the body wasn't going to sink. It floated there, upright, as if the man were standing on a hidden ledge, just the forehead and skull showing, and then there was a wet belch, bubbles beside him, and down he went. The top of the bald head, a shrinking circle of skin, rings of dark water.

Using his small flashlight, Luca checked the bottom of the boat for blood. A few drops. He tore off and wet another scrap of blanket, wiped the boards clean, then threw the cloth, the priest's robe, and the soaked rug over, too, hoping they'd eventually sink. He took the oars back from Don Claudio and pulled hard on them, turning the craft toward shore. Don Claudio pretended to be casting and reeling in. The light to the north moved closer, but now they were just two innocent fishermen, hoping for some unlikely late-night luck.

"We'll take the cart and go to the church," Luca said. "Make it look the way it looked before he came to see you. Hide the rifles under the altar; they should be safe there. I'll find out who's supposed to come for them. I'll bring the cart back to Masso tomorrow. Tell him I'll pay him later for the produce."

"He won't care."

Luca rowed in silence and then, "I ask you again, *Padre*. What you told me about Sarah and Rebecca and you. The truth?"

"Yes. My great sin."

Luca shook his head. "A sin produces evil, not good . . . You know my mother's hiding her, yes?"

"I've always known. From the first."

"They'll search every house. They'll find her there. I have to get them out now, take them someplace safe."

"No place will be safe now."

Luca was about to tell him that Sarah was pregnant, that he had to find a safe place for her as well, but at that moment, he saw the priest's face change. "Turn, look," Don Claudio said.

Luca turned to look over his shoulder and then used a single stroke with his right hand to swing the boat around parallel to shore. High up on the hill, he saw flames lighting the night sky.

"Sant'Abbondio," the priest said. "My church. They're already taking their revenge."

Seventy-Eight

Sarah and Rebecca had made it only a short distance into the trees when they heard the explosion. They turned in tandem and saw an eruption of flame leap through the roof of the house. "Ammunition," Rebecca said.

"Or the stove gas, Mother."

The roof was covered with ceramic tiles, but there was wood beneath them, and the rafters were wooden, and they were already ablaze. Flames poured through the open kitchen doorway and licked out of the windows. Sarah wanted to stand there and watch, to see how long it would take the fire department to arrive. A long while, she guessed; they knew who lived in the Rossos' house now, and most of the firemen—old men who hadn't been called into military service—wouldn't be anxious to race up the hill to save them. But her mother was struggling along at such a slow pace, she guessed it would take five or six hours to get to the Swiss border. She kept them moving.

Every ten steps or so, Rebecca had to stop and catch her breath. In her youth, she'd been an athlete, a superb swimmer, but she wasn't young any longer, and two months in the attic had taken a heavy toll. Sarah went along behind her and tried not to focus on the bony legs and thin hips, the heaving of her back and shoulders. She herself was exhausted from the long day and worried about the baby. They took it very slowly, one foot after the next, grateful for the three-quarters moon.

There wasn't enough energy for conversation, but they stopped every ten minutes and found a place to sit and catch their breath. The second time they stopped, her mother wondered aloud what would happen to Maria's body and if they should have carried it inside. "Such a brave woman," she said. "Such a friend. She must have found a way to poison the Germans."

"Luca gave her mushrooms."

"Did he tell you that?"

Sarah nodded. "He went someplace to try to get me false papers, too. I wanted to help, Mother. I wanted to be a courier, at least. And now all I want is to be away from this hell."

Even in the frail moonlight, Sarah could see that her mother's eyes were sunken in nests of wrinkles, her lips festering with sores, her hair filthy and hanging from her head in sticky strands. She wanted so badly at that moment to tell her about the pregnancy, but she held the news inside her like a secret treasure. Sitting there beside the woman who'd given birth to her, she realized she wasn't yet quite able to believe that she herself would soon bring a child onto this earth. Lately, the world had seemed like a prison of horrors—seeing Maria with the German, then finding her in her last moments before death, then—it still seemed unreal—the scene in the Rossos' house and the merciless act she had forced herself to commit there. The smell of smoke and death had found its way inside her skin.

"What will we do if we ever make it to the border?" her mother asked.

"Luca will be at the cabin, or he'll be out looking for me. He'll help us."

"And if we're caught?"

"Then we'll die. Or worse."

"It's the 'worse' that frightens me. Sometimes I thought I'd lost my mind up there, thinking about what that 'worse' might be."

They got to their feet and went on. After more than an hour of intermittent climbing, they came to a place Sarah didn't remember. She wondered if they'd taken a parallel path. In front of them stood a dark wall of foliage she thought not even an animal could penetrate. She stood and looked to see if there might be a path to either side, and after a minute of studying the terrain in the moonlight, she thought she did see a thin line of stones ahead and to the right. They had to crawl beneath a bush to reach it. They arrived on the other side scratched and bleeding, her mother breathing very hard, but now they could see a more or less walkable trail, little more than an erosion trough, leading upward and to the northwest. They followed that for a while, then found another stone and sat.

They had two small bottles of water, Sarah carrying both. "So many things I haven't ever told you," her mother said as they sat there.

Sarah waited. Her mother had always been a secretive woman, private in the extreme, constantly worried about what people thought of her, what they might say, what they *had* said. "Should I tell them to you now?"

"I think later, Mother. I have things to tell you also. I think we should save our energy, focus on getting to the cabin. Luca will be worried."

"Before I went into the attic, I heard that even the Swiss weren't taking any more Jews."

"The Swiss are human beings. What are they going to do, Mother, turn us back to the Nazis?"

"Exactly what I heard they would do. Assuming the Nazis don't catch us first."

"I have a pistol," Sarah said. She took the gun out of her dress and showed it to her mother. "I took it from the dead German in the doorway."

"Please shoot me if we're going to be captured," her mother said. "Please promise me you'll do that."

Seventy-Nine

As they were moving back toward the western shore, Don Claudio felt a tug on the line. He pulled the rod's tip back gently and then more firmly. The tip bent down almost to the surface. "I have one!" he said. "Luca, I caught something!"

"Perfect, *Padre*. Reel it in if you can. A good excuse in case someone stops to ask why we were out on the lake."

"A whitefish," Don Claudio said when, after a few minutes of pulling and reeling, he'd brought the fish aboard. *Un coregono.* "A big whitefish." He slipped it expertly from the hook, then smacked its head twice on the middle slat to kill it.

Luca watched the light to the north drift away, east, toward Bellano. After making doubly sure all the blood and evidence had been cleaned from the boat, he guided the small craft toward Lenno and up the inlet. Don Claudio helped him tie the boat securely, bow and stern, and then they stood looking into it for another full minute, searching every board, making absolutely sure there was nothing, not so much as a thread of gray uniform or a scrap of blanket or a dried drop of blood that could incriminate them.

When Luca was sure the boat was clean, he and Don Claudio walked over to the cart, climbed aboard, and sat there in silent exhaustion. The priest laid the fish on the seat between them and kept one hand on it as if it were a restless child who'd finally fallen asleep. Culillo

II refused to move. Luca lifted the reins and tapped them on the donkey's hindquarters, nudged the beast with his boot, tapped again with the reins, promised it food. Hopeless.

They were locked in that dilemma when they heard a vehicle come swerving around the corner. A German jeep, Luca thought, until he saw the blue and silver fenders. The car screeched to a stop, leaving its headlights on and pointing directly at the cart. Out stepped two burly carabinieri officers Luca didn't recognize.

"Out late?" one of them inquired sarcastically.

"Fishing," Luca said. "This is Don Claudio, the priest at Sant'Abbondio. He never gets a chance to fish, so I decided to take him out."

By the time he finished talking, the two officers had come up close, one on either side of the cart. In their eyes, no mercy.

"And you're not in the military, why?" the one nearest Luca asked.

Luca pointed to his eye, then held out his two arms, side by side. He saw a drop of blood on his left wrist. The man smirked, didn't notice.

"You always fish at night?" the other one asked.

Luca and Don Claudio both nodded at once.

"In this boat?"

Luca nodded again.

"Fish don't bite at night. Surely you know that."

Don Claudio grabbed the tail of the whitefish and lifted it up into the light like a trophy.

"You caught that?" the first officer said.

"Just now. A hundred meters from shore."

"On what?"

"A lure."

"Where's the fishing gear?"

"In the boat."

"You left it in the boat!"

"It's a cheap rod," Luca said. "I'm just going to drive Don Claudio back to the church. He's exhausted and has to say early Mass. Then I was going to come down and try my luck again."

"Did you get permission to go out on the lake at night?"

"I didn't know you needed permission. We never did before."

"This isn't *before*. Where's the permission slip?"

"I don't have one."

"Then we confiscate the fish."

"Please don't, Officer. We're hungry."

"Everyone's hungry."

"Please don't. This could feed Don Claudio for two days."

The carabinieri looked at each other across the seat of the cart. One of them unsheathed a knife at his belt and, holding the fish flat on the board to Don Claudio's right, sawed through it just behind the gills. "We'll leave you the head," he said. "And *viva il Duce*."

"*Viva il Duce*," they mumbled automatically. Mussolini is gone, Luca thought, biting down on his anger, and still we are required to salute him.

As the officers were walking back to the car, Luca called out, "Where do I go for permission to be on the lake?"

"Nowhere," the heavier of the two officers called over his shoulder. "You don't need permission."

The doors closing cut off the sound of their harsh laughter. The driver made a three-point turn and sped off into town.

Don Claudio picked up the fish head and held it loosely in front of him in the fingers of both hands. "And these are *our* people," he said bitterly.

As if by magic, the donkey began to move. Luca steered the cart along the empty shore road and then very slowly up toward Sant'Abbondio. Ahead of them, the road curved to the right, and from that angle, they could see the flames again. The smell of smoke reached them.

"It's not the church," Don Claudio said. "It's closer to your mother's house."

Eighty

After they'd been climbing for the better part of an hour, Sarah was caught and held by a terrible thought: if the Gestapo saw Maria's body, they'd search her house and find the slop bucket in the attic and her mother's clothes there. They'd send a party of men and dogs after them, track them into the hills and as far as the cabin. So, exhausted though she and her mother were, they wouldn't be able to stay very long, and if Luca wasn't there, they'd have to leave a note of warning and climb for the border on their own.

The idea haunted her: the cabin wouldn't be safe any longer. But there was no option—her mother had to rest. And so did she.

At last they came to the basket and the split tree. She knew to turn left there, and then, though the path was rocky and difficult to see—the moonlight dim now behind a bank of clouds—the walking was more or less level, and they were able to go along at a slightly better pace. At last, hours after they left Maria's house, Sarah saw the dark shadow of the cabin, dull moonlight on the broken tile roof. Inside, her note had not been moved, and there was no sign of Luca. It seemed to her that the child in her womb was wailing. Her mother collapsed on the makeshift bed and lay there with her eyes open and fixed on the ceiling. "You have no idea," she said, weariness in her voice, "what a joy it is to breathe the air, to be able to see trees and touch the ground." She took a deep, ragged breath and let it out. "Even these mosquitoes make me happy." She sighed and went silent. Sarah thought she was asleep until she asked, "Do you have any idea what happened to Maria, what made her do that?"

Sarah knew exactly what had happened. She opened and closed her mouth. What good would it do to tell her mother now? What good would that do? She shook her head and went over and took off her mother's shoes and filthy socks and began to massage her feet.

Sarah watched one tear dribble down the side of her mother's face. "You slept here?" she asked after a moment.

"Only the last few weeks. Luca moved me from one safe house to another at first, but they all became too dangerous, so he decided to bring me here."

"Where is he?"

"He'll come. Soon. I know he will."

They were quiet for a time. Sarah slapped at the mosquitoes and went on rubbing her mother's feet, trying not to look at the thin legs, listening for footsteps, for any sound at the door.

"What if they come here?" her mother asked at one point.

"We'll stay only tonight and tomorrow so you can get some strength back."

"Too long," her mother said. "Too risky. I'm too afraid, Sarah."

"We have the gun."

"One pistol against all of them. Let me rest for a few hours, and then we'll climb in the darkness. If there are no clouds, we can see by the moon."

"It feels like rain, Mother. And we have to wait for Luca."

"We'll slow him down. We should get a head start, leave him a note. I've been hiding in a house for eight weeks. I don't want to hide any longer. I can't carry the weight of my fear any longer." She lay there with her eyes closed, and Sarah thought, again, that she'd fallen asleep until she said, "It's Shabbat, isn't it? Friday?"

"Yes, Mother."

"Fine, then." She began, "Blessed are you, Lord our God—"

And Sarah finished the familiar line of prayer. "King of the universe."

Eighty-One

By the time Luca and Don Claudio reached the top of the road, they could tell it was the Rossos' house on fire. "My mother," Luca said. "My mother cooks for them there."

They tied the donkey to a tree, and Luca hurried on ahead of the priest up a dirt lane. A crowd of perhaps a dozen people, women and old men, had gathered at the end of the lane, firelight turning their faces into flickering masks and the leaves of the nearby trees into specters. The brigade had arrived, though it was obvious that, with their one truck and handful of elderly firefighters, there was little they could do. They faced an inferno, the dark skeleton of the house visible against an orange background, flames leaping out of every window and through what was left of the roof, rafters collapsing one after the next in great loud crashes and showers of sparks. Luca could feel the heat from sixty meters away. A German staff car was parked on the other side of the house, two Gestapo officers standing beside it, arms crossed over their chests, as if measuring the degree of effort made by the brigade or already calculating their revenge. One of the neighbors recognized Luca and, nodding at the Gestapo, said in a quiet voice, "They'll blame all of us."

"People inside?"

"SS officers, some women, too, I think."

Don Claudio arrived, heaving for breath, and he and Luca moved off to one side as a gust of wind sent sparks and burning air in their direction. Trying to push away a wave of panic, Luca searched the firelit perimeter of the Rossos' yard for his mother. He didn't see her. Another gust caught him then, a sudden premonition. He imagined her inside the house, lying dead in the embers. Maybe she'd accidentally started the fire by being careless in the kitchen. Or maybe not so accidentally. Maybe she'd escaped.

"We have to check my mother's house."

He and the priest started away from the blaze, across the uneven ground of the empty lot where Rosso had grown crops for as long as either of them could remember. Nothing but weeds and stones now, and for Don Claudio, the walking was difficult. Luca supported him with a hand under one elbow. His parents' olive trees ahead. He remembered picking the olives by hand—always on a sunny day in fall, before the weather turned—placing them carefully ("Gently, gently" his parents would say. "Treat them kindly and they'll treat you kindly.") into the *cesto di vimini*, the reed basket, so they could be brought to Giulianova for pressing. His parents would always give him the first taste of the newly pressed oil, on fresh bread. He'd harvested the olives as recently as two years ago, but the memories seemed a century old. He could hear Don Claudio breathing heavily beside him.

They'd gone only a short distance when he saw the figure lying there. Luca knew instantly that it was his mother. She was on her side in the flickering orange light, and even as he rushed over, he could see blood soaking her dress near her left hip and a small puddle of vomit next to her face. It took him two seconds to realize she was gone and two more seconds to put together the puzzle pieces. He knelt beside her, leaned his forehead down against her chest, and remained that way for a long time, speaking to her, promising the one thing he believed he could promise. He could feel Don Claudio's hand on his back; the priest was weeping. He sensed again the murderous fury he'd first felt when he'd killed the Blackshirt. And then, swelling up beneath it, a sadness the size of the surrounding hills. One memory after the next rolled across his thoughts, a parade of caring, sacrifice, love.

"We should have a burial Mass, a service," Don Claudio whispered.

Luca shook his head. What mattered now was survival. Survival and revenge, not services. "She poisoned them," he said quietly. "With my *lepiota*. Look at the bile. Look at her face. And then she ran, and they shot her. Look." He pointed to the blood and torn dress at her hip. "How she got the fire started, I don't know, but I'm sure they made her eat with them. They suspected something. We have to bury her before they find her here like this and figure out what I've just figured out."

"Those Gestapo with the jeep will see us."

"Too far away," Luca said. "Trees between us, the fence. And they're watching the fire, like everyone else. We'll dig in the garden on the other side of the house. My father kept shovels and a pickax in the shed. Help me lift her, *Padre*."

Struggling, breathing heavily, the two of them carried Maria's body into her back yard, around a corner of the house, and set her down gently there on a patch of grass. Before Luca took tools from the shed where his father and mother had kept them, Don Claudio put a hand on his arm. "What did you say to her? May I ask? I didn't hear."

Luca turned and met the priest's eyes. In the background, he heard a thunderous crash. The rest of the roof collapsing. "I promised her something," he said. "I made her a solemn promise."

"Yes, I thought so. What was it?"

"That I would live to see Mussolini dead."

Eighty-Two

Il Duce put on his black overcoat and black hat and allowed himself to be escorted down the stairs of the ski hotel and through the lobby by the German captain—Skorzeny, he said his name was. An unusual name, and a giant of a man with a most horrible scar on his face. To either side of the lobby, Italian soldiers, *Duce*'s guard supposedly, sat in a posture of surrender. Disarmed, backs against the walls, they stared at him as he went past. Cowards, all of them. He did not do them the honor of meeting their eyes. He and his rescuers marched out into the cool mountain air.

A wreckage of broken gliders and a squadron of German commandos greeted him there. The men saluted with their right arms held out straight. Mussolini returned the Roman salute. A small plane, a Storch, sat on a rocky patch of land beside the hotel. Next to it stood a man with aviator glasses pushed up onto his forehead. Skorzeny introduced him as Gerlach, the pilot, and Mussolini shook his hand.

"Let's go," Skorzeny said impatiently.

"Who? How many?" Gerlach asked.

"The three of us."

There followed a small argument in rapid German. Mussolini understood it perfectly. Gerlach was upset. Even though they'd moved the Storch as far back from the precipice as they could, he said, there was still not enough room to get up speed sufficient for takeoff. There were stones everywhere and, at the end of the more or less flat stretch, a drop-off so steep that, at a slow speed, the plane would go straight into a nosedive. The weight of two people was bad enough. With three, it would be impossible. "Suicide," he said in a firm, quiet voice. *Selbstmord.*

"Suicide for me," Skorzeny shot back, "is having to go to the Führer and tell him we had his good friend Benito Mussolini in our hands, but there was no room for me in the Storch, and there was a crash, and Mussolini is now dead. What will be left for me then is the revolver. If *il Duce* dies, I die with him. All three of us are getting onto that plane!"

Mussolini watched them talk and gesture for another minute, but Skorzeny was a larger and more powerful man, energetic to the point of controlled frenzy, the horrific scar on his face arguing for him. The pilot relented. They climbed into the Storch, Gerlach in front, Mussolini beside him, Skorzeny in back. With his face set in an expression of suppressed fury, Gerlach started the propeller and ran it up to its highest speed. Skorzeny's men held the wings.

On a hand signal from the pilot, the men let go, and the Storch bounced forward over the rocks and dirt. It went less than fifty meters, bumped hard against a rock, shot up and out into the thin air, and, exactly as Gerlach had predicted, immediately turned downward. From the moment the argument started, Mussolini had been haunted by the old superstition, by images of himself dead in a mangled fuselage. Now all he could hear was the wind screaming at the side windows. All he could see were the stones in the valley below, one large triangular boulder in particular. He glanced sideways at Gerlach's clenched hands on the controls, then turned and watched the boulder as it drew closer. Down and down they went at a terrible speed, his stomach in his throat, his hands squeezing the seat, the wind screaming past the fuselage. It seemed to him that the Storch was being sucked toward disaster by the twin forces of gravity and the turning propeller, and by some vengeful spirit besides. Some demon that wanted to end the reign of *il Duce* forever. The diagonal metal struts were vibrating, thin marsh reeds in a gale.

Less than a hundred meters from the bottom, he watched Gerlach pull back hard on the control stick and felt the plane start to respond. It seemed to be fighting against the vectors of nature, doing battle with the vengeful demon. Another three seconds and Mussolini could no longer see the boulder. The nose was turning up, slightly at first. Then up a little more. Then they were flying crazily across the valley, only twenty meters above the ground, and his stomach was settling more or less back into place, the superstitious vision retreating into the distance. Had there been any trees, the plane would certainly have crashed into them, but it was all slanted green meadow and stone here, and soon the remarkable Gerlach had his plane fully under control, and they were skimming along the valley at a fast clip, then turning back, lifting up and over a slope, over the crest of one of the park's lower hills. They rose into a brilliant blue sky, flew over the hotel, the wrecked gliders, the stunned soldiers, and then the pilot turned them west, toward Rome.

Mussolini offered two words, addressing them to both Skorzeny and the pilot. *"Ben fatto,"* he said nobly, with a *Duce*'s dignity, in a tone meant to indicate that he hadn't been afraid at all, had never doubted that he'd be rescued.

Well done.

Eighty-Three

The place Luca chose for his mother's burial was protected from view by the corner of her house. The earth there had been loosened by years of cultivation. He worked the pickax, lifting it over his head with both hands and driving it downward mostly with the right, his weaker left hand just keeping the handle in line. Even as tired and broken as he was, for the first meter or so, the work wasn't difficult. He and Don Claudio labored quietly, the priest shoveling out the softened dirt, heaving for breath, mumbling prayers. Only once did Luca stop to rest. Leaning on the handle of his pickax, he peered around the corner of his mother's house and stared across the dark vacant lot at what was left of the Rossos' home. He remembered that the house had always smelled of rosemary, because Antonetta Rosso grew that herb in the strip of soil beside their patio. Now it was a black shell, the roof caved in, two charred and burning rafters standing at angles in the moonlight like antiaircraft guns, the fire brigade spraying thin streams of water. Now, instead of rosemary, he could smell smoke—twisting gray columns were still rising into the sky along with a few spurts of flame—and the stink of burned human flesh. As he watched, a light rain began to fall.

No Gestapo officers there now, but he had very little doubt about what had killed their comrades, and he knew the deaths wouldn't go unanswered. The Nazis seemed actually to believe that human lives were valued on some kind of perverted scale, with German military men at the highest end and Jews just a notch below Italians at the bottom. It was as if a collective insanity had taken hold of them, all kindness, mercy, and compassion gone, replaced by hard, inhumane certainty and a violent belief in their own superiority. He thought of it as a disease, an infection Hitler was spreading—first in Germany, then Austria, Czechoslovakia, Poland, Russia. Mussolini had been suffering from a similar disease and had made the mistake of befriending the mustachioed madman and catching a more virulent strain.

Luca went back to his gruesome work, both eyes—sightless and sighted—lensed with tears. The ground was harder at this depth, the firm surface turning slick in the rain. As the night deepened, he and Don Claudio made progress at a slower and slower rate, at one point the two of them having to get down into the hole and wrestle out a stone the size of a soccer ball.

Don Claudio's black pants were muddy to the knees. "I can't go much longer, Luca," the priest said. "I'm sorry."

The hole was thigh deep. It would have to be enough.

Together they set their tools aside, lifted Maria's body, and carried it closer to the makeshift grave. While Don Claudio said another prayer over her, Luca went inside and took a sheet from his mother's bed. He wrapped her in it, tenderly, his tears making small gray stains on the blue material. He and Don Claudio lifted her again, both of them crying now, and carefully lowered her into the hole. For several minutes, Luca stood by the side of the grave, torn in half by an even mix of sorrow and fury, staring down at the wet blue sheet.

It began to rain harder. Luca took the shovel, used his foot to drive it into the pile of dirt, hesitated, then made himself toss the first shovelful into the hole and onto his mother's wrapped body. The wet earth made a sound like someone being slapped. With a little help from Don Claudio, he worked for another half hour, refilling the hole. When that was done, the priest fashioned a crude cross from two lines of stones and set them at the head of the grave. "Later," he said quietly, "we'll have a real burial, a real funeral Mass, as she deserved." He recited another prayer, but Luca only wiped a sleeve across his face and turned to the side and spat. Raindrops pattered on the roof. If they came here, the Nazis would see the fresh grave and wonder, but there was nothing to do about that now.

"Rebecca!" the priest said.

They hurried into the house, tracking more muddy footprints through the kitchen and up the hallway. Luca tapped the attic door with the handle of the broom. No answer. He tapped again. Pulled a chair into the hallway and climbed up and looked. A slop bucket, stinking in the close air. A small pile of Rebecca's clothes, a few books, a notebook and pencil. The old boxes he'd used for his childish war games. He climbed through the opening, hid things as well as he could, carried the bucket down and emptied it in the yard, then filled it with mud and left it there. The priest was sitting at the kitchen table with his head in his hands, too exhausted to move. Luca looked for the apple he'd left and didn't see it. Its absence, and Rebecca's, were the puzzle pieces he couldn't fit. He must have come here when his mother was still at the Rossos' house, cooking, and then she must have poisoned them, and then, perhaps, started the fire and escaped as far as the place where they'd found her. But how had Rebecca known? The sound of the shot? The fact that Maria hadn't returned? Was her body in the burned house?

"They're going to count the bodies," Don Claudio told him without looking up. "They're going to know one is missing. Even in the unlikely event they decide the fire was an accident—a houseful of soldiers asleep or too drunk to escape—they'll wonder about the other one. We should leave. Everyone in the town should leave now, before they kill us all."

"What does God do to them?" Luca asked. He'd almost said *your God* but had held the bitterness back. "What do you really believe happens to them . . . after?"

Don Claudio raised his face, a mask of pain and weariness. "Divine justice," he said. "We have to believe that, or else how could we go on?"

We make our own justice, Luca thought, but what he said was, "Sarah's pregnant," and he watched a ripple of something like joy cross the priest's round face. "I'm going to take her across the border. I'll take you, too."

The priest smiled tiredly and shook his head. "Too old, Luca. Too old and too fat to make a climb like that. Take me back to Sant'Abbondio. I'll pray there for your child"—he hesitated—"my grandchild. I'll pray there, and I'll wait to learn what fate the Lord has in store for me."

Eighty-Four

In midmorning, in a steady rain, having slept the sleep of the dead for a few hours and then shared with her mother one hard-boiled egg and a glass of water, having torn a sheet of paper from her notebook and left a coded message for Luca, and having stood in the open doorway and waited as long as she could bear to wait for her lover to appear, Sarah led the way out of the cabin. They were carrying extra sweaters and a bit of food and water. All she knew was that the Swiss border was directly to their west, and she remembered Luca saying it was a climb of a little over an hour. A little over an hour for him, she thought: for her and her mother, it could take the whole day.

"We can stay if you want," her mother offered.

Sarah shook her head. She guessed, she hoped, that Luca would come back to the cabin, probably that same day, and she knew he'd see and understand the message she'd left and set out immediately to find them. As they started slowly along the path, she began to leave fingertip-size scraps of cloth, torn from the tails of her blue blouse, to show him the route they were taking. Only the most attentive and suspicious German soldier would notice bits of cloth stuck to the bushes at waist height. She hoped the dogs wouldn't be able to track the scent on them, and she wondered what they'd find at the border. Guards, tall barbed-wire fences. And on the other side, Swiss military men protecting their country from desperate refugees. If Luca didn't come, they'd never make it.

But what were their options? Even if they weren't tracked and caught there, they'd go insane in the cabin and likely starve. What was she supposed to do—send her mother off to Switzerland on her own? Wait for Luca and then make him walk at their pace, with the Germans tracking them?

Her plan was to get as close to the border as she could without arousing the suspicion of the guards—though she wasn't sure exactly how she'd accomplish that or how, exactly, she'd know when they were near. Sneak ahead a little way and look for the tops of the fences? Once they were close, she and her mother would find a comfortable place and wait there for Luca. If he made it that far, he'd think of something. Barely a high school graduate, not fond of reading (though he seemed to appreciate her poetry), he was, she'd often thought, a certain kind of genius. He knew where to find edible plants and how to cook them. He could move through the forest like a deer and navigate by the constellations. He could take apart and repair any kind of motor or appliance, from an automobile engine to a simple household fan, and, with his hands and mouth, he could play her body like a musical instrument, bringing her with so much patience to moments of such physical ecstasy that her fingertips were left vibrating for minutes afterward.

What more could a woman ask for in a husband? As she walked, she thought of ways she might convince him to come with them. His mother was gone, but would he know that? Would she have to tell him? Shouldn't a wife and child mean more to a man than the hope of killing Germans?

Following her mother up the slick path, letting the older woman set the pace, Sarah battled an onslaught of worries: that Luca had already been killed or captured; that he'd arrive after dark, too late to follow the cloth trail; that he'd find them only to refuse to take the risk of sneaking across the border and insist that she and her mother go back to the cabin.

After only a few minutes of climbing, her mother had to stop and rest. They took shelter beneath a chestnut tree, drank from one of the water bottles, caught their breath, wiped the perspiration and rainwater from their foreheads and necks. The rain had stopped, but the day was still humid and overcast. What would happen to them if they had to sleep in the forest?

"I'm pregnant, Mother," she said suddenly.

Her mother turned to meet her eyes and then wrapped her bony arms around her neck and held on for a long time. When they finally separated, Sarah could see the tears.

"It's a happy thing, Mother."

Her mother was nodding, nodding, brushing at her eyes, unable to speak.

"It's a happy thing," Sarah repeated, convincing herself.

"I feel like I almost can't bear a happy thing now," Rebecca said at last. "I feel like I can't hope anymore for a normal life. I feel like I have to live one minute at a time and not let my mind move anywhere beyond the immediate present . . . Does Luca know?"

Sarah nodded, watching her.

"He's a good man. He'll make a good father."

Sarah tried to smile, but she was wondering if she would ever again see her child's father.

Eighty-Five

Luca accompanied Don Claudio as far as the back entrance to Sant'Abbondio and stopped there. By then, the overnight rain had strengthened a bit, but the sky in the east was touched with gray light, and he thought this might be the end of the storm. "Come in," Don Claudio said. "I have a little food and a little something to drink. Not much. But if you're going to climb, I want you to have it."

Luca hesitated, nodded. *"Va bene, Padre."*

The priest quietly opened the door. They paused at the threshold and listened, watched. The nave was empty. While Don Claudio set the fish head in his small refrigerator, then rummaged around in his kitchen trying to put together a meal, Luca wet a towel and went carefully over the walls of the cloakroom and the aisle that led to the altar rail where he'd seen Don Claudio praying. He found the pistol, cleaned it, put it into his pocket, and hid the rifles and a small cloth bag of ammunition beneath the altar. Three times he examined the marble tiles, going as far as the back door with his flashlight, making a slow inspection, and at last was confident that there were no traces left.

That done, Luca found the pew where his mother and father used to worship at Sunday Mass, and he sat there and rested. How many hundreds of hours had he spent looking at that gold crucifix, this marble altar, the colored glass in those windows? How many times, in cold and heat, had he endured the sermons that seemed so endless to a child? The God his parents worshipped had been unfair to him, bringing him into the world with no left eye and a weak left arm. He had never been able to believe in a God who would do that, never been able to love such a God.

Now he tried to make himself pray for his mother's soul, but the pain was too fresh for that, and prayer had long ago become alien to him. The resentment was boiling inside him, bubbling over, hissing as it splashed on a hot stove top. He fingered the statuette in his left front pocket, the pistol in his right. He wondered if there were any boundaries left for him now, anything he wouldn't do . . . And how would Sarah feel about having that kind of a man as a husband?

After a time, Don Claudio emerged from the kitchen carrying a cloth bag. "A little fruit and bread and cheese," the priest said. "Not much. Two wine bottles filled with water." He cleared his throat. "I've put some communion wafers in there, too. Unblessed, of course. Not much, but they're light, and they could help with hunger."

Luca nodded his thanks, tracing the thin lines of a sheepish new satisfaction on the priest's face. Amazing as it seemed, if they all survived, the kindly priest might someday be his father-in-law and would always be grandfather to his child. What other impossible secrets lived in the air around him? And what would Sarah think when she heard that her father was a priest, a man she'd known all her life?

"If you get across the border," Don Claudio said quietly, "go to the town of Bellinzona. It's not far into Switzerland. Five kilometers or less. There's a church there, Santa Teresa. The priest is a friend, Don Alessandro. If he's still there, I'm sure he'll help you."

"Good, thank you, *Padre*."

"Maybe they're together," Don Claudio said, and for a moment, Luca thought he was speaking of his own mother and father. Together in heaven. Another sweet myth. But then he said, "If you find them, give them my love, will you?" and Luca understood.

"I'll send your regards, yes, Father."

The priest pressed his lips together, seeming, for a moment, stronger than Luca remembered him, less afraid. "No," he said forcefully. "My *love*. Be sure to say I sent my love, not just my regards."

"*Capito,*" Luca said. *Understood.*

He embraced Don Claudio and went out into the breaking day.

Eighty-Six

An accomplished pilot himself, Mussolini watched Gerlach with deep admiration. No one else on earth could have managed a takeoff like that. Damaged but functional—Gerlach said the left landing gear had smashed into a rock just before going over the edge—the Storch carried them through the valleys and over the green hills of the Abruzzo. In places, to avoid detection by enemy aircraft, Gerlach kept them only thirty meters above the trees. Approaching the Pratica di Mare airfield—a place *il Duce* knew like he knew the grounds of Villa Torlonia—he wasn't surprised to hear Gerlach warn that the landing would be rough. But, as if he'd been practicing such landings all his life, the master took the plane down with a single bump and brought it to a twisting, skidding, sideways-leaning stop not far from the bland gray metal of the hangar.

Mussolini relieved himself in the washroom there, rinsed and scrubbed his face with both hands, looked in the mirror. Grateful to have been rescued, but ashamed, too, he supposed he'd be flown to see Hitler now. He looked sickly and thin; he was in pain. And he was being sent to see the greatest general on earth, the way a troublesome younger brother might be sent to see the successful older one.

It wasn't his fault. His own people had failed him, lost faith in him. His own friends had betrayed him.

In the hangar, he shook Gerlach's hand warmly, thanked him with another simple *ben fatto*, and then Captain Skorzeny waved him aboard a larger plane. This, he knew, was a Heinkel, a medium-size bomber, very difficult to shoot down. Soon they were airborne again, flying north up the peninsula at a normal altitude, observing radio silence. The weather was clear at first, but a storm was moving east from the Swiss Alps, and the pilot warned them of rougher weather ahead. Mussolini gazed out the window for a time, running his eyes over the landscape as if searching for a lost and forgotten Italy.

Once they were north of the Po Valley, they encountered the predicted cloud cover and then came the steady tick of raindrops on the windows. *Il Duce* turned to his rescuer, who was sitting beside him, perpetually at attention, it seemed. "Are we winning the war, Captain Skorzeny?"

"Absolutely, *Duce*. Without question."

But Skorzeny couldn't seem to make eye contact when he spoke those words.

They landed in Vienna under low skies and were taken by car from Asbern field into the city. A fine suite in the Hotel Imperial and a shot of morphine from Dr. Keilter greeted him there, along with word that another commando unit had evacuated Rachele; she would soon join him. He wasn't looking forward to his wife's "I told you not to go, Benito!" but it would be good to see her again, better if Claretta could somehow be rescued as well. The simple fact that he was thinking about his wife and mistress heartened him. He'd always had a powerful constitution, and, bathing and shaving in the luxurious suite, he could sense the beginning of the return of his faculties. The shot had temporarily taken care of his pain and given him some energy. He'd be flown to Munich the next day and was already working on a plan for reestablishing the Fascist Party. He and Hitler would sit together and talk strategy. Italy would be saved. Fascism—the only system that could ever work in a human society—would be resurrected. He could feel it in his bones.

Eighty-Seven

Luca hadn't slept in thirty hours. In that time, he'd buried a bloodied German corpse at sea and his mother in her own back yard. He'd also decided to hold back a thousand lire in gold from the men he was supposed to be working for, men whose honor, abilities, and commitment to Italy he'd long ago lost faith in. Who knew what they'd do with the money? Fund a communist cell, pass it along to a traitor, waste it on idiotic plans to disable a few aircraft that hadn't even been seen yet on Italian soil? Better to use it to save actual Italian lives. Better to use it the way his mother would have wanted it used—she'd risked more than they'd ever think of risking, hiding a Jewish friend. She'd probably killed more Germans in a single night than Mentone, Prinzano, and the traitorous Scutarro had in months of their so-called secret work. And she'd lost her own life doing so.

Climbing the familiar trail that led from the trees near the rear of Sant'Abbondio to the hidden cabin, he felt as though he were carrying a hundred kilos of guilt and sorrow in the small pack on his shoulders. What haunted him was the idea that, if he hadn't brought his mother the *lepiota*, she might still be alive. He was sure now that the deaths of the German SS men wouldn't go unanswered. New officers would appear in Mezzegra in the coming days. They'd arrest a group of villagers, line them up, torment them for a while, then shoot them one by one and leave their bodies in the street.

Still, his mother and Masso had been right. What else were you supposed to do? Wait like sheep for the slaughter, hoping the Allies would make it all the way up the peninsula before you were taken?

He put his hand over the pistol in his pocket. He moved quietly but, very tired, not as quietly as before. By the time he was within a few hundred meters of the cabin, the rain had started again in gentler fashion. It tapped on the tree leaves and trickled down onto his head and shoulders. He kept a sweater in the cabin, and Sarah had towels. He couldn't wait to see her, to touch her, to tell her everything that had happened.

But when he reached the door and gave the signal with his knocks, she didn't answer. He knocked again, not wanting to startle her if she was asleep, then pushed open the door and saw that the room was empty.

It was too much. His mother, his future wife, their child. All gone. Too much. In his exhaustion, he crumpled onto the floor and sat there, head in hands. His mind was filled with a thrumming wordless darkness, two parts sorrow, two parts anger, six parts hatred. He would kill them all now; it didn't matter. Reprisals or no reprisals, he would dedicate every ounce of strength and ability to killing as many Germans and Blackshirts as he could in the time left to him.

He opened the flap of his knapsack, and the first thing he saw was the cylinder of wafers Don Claudio had given him. God's body, the priest believed, when the proper prayers had been said over them. It didn't matter now; there was no one to save them for, no reason to leave food in the cabin. He put a handful of them into his mouth and chewed, but they were sticky and unsatisfying, and he washed them down with half the water he carried.

He set the pack aside and lay back on the blanket, exactly where he and Sarah had made love. He abandoned himself to sleep and dreamed an unforgettable dream, a dream so powerful and realistic that, when he awoke, he wondered if the communion wafers had planted in him a mystical vision. In the dream, he was a bit older and still without

Sarah—though he could sense her presence close by—and he was on one knee on a street in front of an elegant villa, the lake downhill behind him. There was an automatic rifle in his hands; he could feel the cool metal of the trigger against the tip of his second finger. Between him and the villa's tall iron gates stood Benito Mussolini and his young mistress, Claretta Petacci. *Il Duce* looked thin and sickly but strangely unafraid. At first, his eyes were fixed on the weapon, but then he raised them to Luca and opened his arms wide. "Shoot me in the chest," he said calmly, and in the dream, Luca did exactly that.

He woke hungry and filled with bitterness, hoping against hope that Sarah might have returned. But he was alone.

There was no chance now that he'd go back down the mountain and embark on the ridiculous fishing expedition. Even if it wasn't a trap, Scutarro's plan sounded foolish to him, an idea for amateurs. What if, after waiting for weeks, it turned out that the Luftwaffe didn't station any planes on the other side of the lake? And if they did have planes there, wouldn't they be guarded night and day?

Another idea came to him then: he could take the rifles from the church and organize a small band of men on his own. Perhaps Masso would help him. Maybe Sarah was wandering in the trees, lost, not captured, not dead, and she could join him as well.

He stood and went to the table where she'd eaten her meager meals and written her poetry. All that remained there, the only sign of her, was a sheet of white paper with a few words scribbled on it. The start of a poem, he supposed. He picked up the page and studied the words—written in haste, it looked like.

Siamo andate a prendere il cioccolato

We've gone for chocolate.

It took him five seconds to understand.

Eighty-Eight

With a broken nose, broken left leg, two broken ribs, and a face so scraped and bruised that he could hardly bear to look at it in the nurse's hand mirror, Silvio Merino lay in a large, open ward in Rome's Fatebenefratelli Hospital with eight other victims of the latest Allied bombing. He couldn't be sure, but it seemed to him that he'd been there several days, drifting in and out of consciousness and beset by all kinds of peculiar visions. At one point in the middle of the previous night, when the pain had been all but unbearable, a doctor had come to his bedside and injected him with something. Half-delusional at the time, Silvio wondered if the doctor—thick spectacles, one tuft of brown hair at the top middle of his forehead—might be a German operative in disguise, come to send him into the next world.

"*Sono il Dottor Grigiastro,*" he thought the doctor had said. *I am Doctor Grayish.* But no doubt he'd heard wrong.

Dr. Grayish administered the dose, patted Silvio's good leg, and disappeared. In ten minutes that seemed like ten hours, the pain started to ease, and Silvio drifted into a heavenly sleep. He dreamed of Lisiella. She was sitting directly in front of him, older but still beautiful, and she was bouncing a plump laughing child on her knee. Around her stood a bevy of other kids, boys and girls both, of various ages. A happy scene until, in the dream, Silvio turned sideways and caught sight of himself in a mirror. He was old and gray, his face lined, cheeks sagging, ears gone suddenly large. A nightmare vision.

Now the dawn had broken, and he seemed to be awake, trapped in a more youthful reality. Raindrops were tapping on the nearby window, and the pain had come to visit him again. How, exactly, he didn't know, but somehow, over the course of his luxurious adult life, he'd learned the secret of dealing with it. The trick was to welcome it as a friend, to pay close attention to it, yes, but without pushing it away. Strangely enough, it was the facial pain—from the least important wounds—that bothered him most. That, and the thought that his beautiful Oldsmobile coupe was gone forever.

A nursing nun came into the room. Prim, officious, her cheeks pinched tight in the white wimple. There was some activity with the bedpan—horribly embarrassing—but when that was finished, she wiped his face tenderly with a clean washcloth and asked if he wanted something to eat.

"Una piccola bistecca," he answered through bruised lips. "A small steak, medium-rare if possible, with grilled eggplant and perhaps some polenta on the side. Or, if that's not available today, a seafood risotto and a glass of cold white wine. Vermentino, if you have it. Or Vernaccia di San Gimignano."

The nun looked down at him with what amounted to pity. Silvio wondered: Could faith in God and a sense of humor coexist? "Well then, whatever you happen to have, Sister," he added in as respectful a tone as he could manage. The nun raised her thin eyebrows and went out of the room, the folds of her long white habit swishing behind her.

The rain slapped harder against the glass. Silvio looked out at blurred rooftops, a broken city, a gray occupied Italy at war. To his left, a half-conscious old man moaned in his bed, captive of nightmares. The room smelled of iodine and floor polish; there were crucifixes on the walls, bare light bulbs overhead, the sound of soft-soled shoes and lowered voices in the hallway. He winced at a sudden flash of pain and then, when it passed, wondered if one of his two nearby sisters—both nurses—would get the word and perhaps come visit him. He'd ask her for some extra morphine, ask quietly so the nuns couldn't hear, remind his sister of the favors he'd done.

The pain moved up a notch, harder to welcome now. He decided that, when the good nun returned with his tray of food—horsemeat, he guessed it would be, horsemeat and a single sliced tomato—he'd ask if the mysterious Doctor Grayish might visit again and allow him another dose of the magical medicine. She seemed to be taking a very long time—perhaps the kitchen was far away, or perhaps they fed their patients according to how compliant they were, how humorless, how devoted to the Lord.

He was watching the doorway anxiously when the bent nose, spectacles, and high forehead of Italo Andreottla appeared there. Another dream, Silvio thought for a moment. He blinked hard, three times, but no, there was the famous "Giovanni" in the flesh, approaching his bed. At the sight of his new friend, Silvio couldn't help letting out a laugh, but the laughter was cut short by pain in his left side. The ribs there. His mind flashed back to the feeling of lying under the upside-down coupe. He'd been ready to die then; there was a certain comfort to be taken from that. Despite his many sins, he'd been ready to be carried up into the next world.

Andreottla stood by the side of the bed with both hands on the railing and a look of what seemed to be sincere compassion on his face.

"Now my nose looks like yours" was the first thing Silvio said to him.

The man smiled in a rueful way but said nothing.

"I have some interesting information for you," Silvio went on quietly, uncomfortable with the silence. What if he'd been wrong about this "Giovanni" all along? What if the game had now played out to its final scene, and the half-American was going to poison him or reach down and tap a metal rod against the broken ribs until Silvio screamed in agony and revealed his secrets? What if the nuns in this hospital were actually sympathetic to Mussolini and his Nazi friends and had arranged for Andreottla to visit and squeeze information out of his suffering acquaintance?

Silvio waited, watched, blinked away the foolish thoughts, turned his head to be sure the man in the next bed wouldn't hear, and said very quietly, "*Il Duce* is at Campo Imperatore. The ski resort. In the mountains near Gran Sasso. My fa—"

"Gone," Andreottla said in a barely audible voice. "We just heard."

"Gone where?"

"He was there; you're right. But the Germans got him. Gone to Hitler now, no doubt."

"The bastards."

A nod, another rueful smile.

The pain spiked to a new level. Leg, face, ribs—at least the important parts of the machinery had been spared. Silvio wasn't sure whether to ask Andreottla to call the doctor or try to make another joke. On top of everything else, he was hungry.

Before he could get a word out, his guest said, again very quietly, "The Americans are in Sicily. And now in Salerno, too. The Russians have reached the Dnieper."

"It's over, then. The war is over."

"Not quite," Andreottla told him. "Not yet quite over. We'll need you again when you recover."

"Because I've performed so brilliantly."

"In fact, yes."

"And the money, the gold, went . . . where?"

A shrug, eyebrows and shoulders. The barest hint of a smile. "We trust you," Andreottla said, and at those words, strangely, Silvio felt a small obstruction form in his throat. Two seconds and it was gone, the sentimental mood chased off by pain. There was the nurse now, carrying on her tray an inedible lunch.

From an inside pocket of his sport coat, Andreottla took out a small bottle of grappa. He set it on the bedside table. The nun frowned. With the tap of two fingers on Silvio's shoulder, the half-American sauntered out of the room. He turned sideways at the door, glanced back for a moment, then disappeared.

Eighty-Nine

Sarah and Rebecca climbed on slowly in the light rain, stopping every five or ten minutes to sit and rest. They drank but did not eat, saving the food as long as they could, though it seemed her mother was growing weaker by the hour. At last, in late afternoon, Sarah told her they'd gone as far as they should go. They found a strange rock formation—a huge flat piece of granite with what almost looked like a stone roof over it. At first glance, it might have been taken for the mouth of a cave, but the cave was only a few meters deep. Mostly dry, though. She and her mother crawled in and sat with their backs against stone. Sarah opened their small package of food—a heel of bread, cheese, and apples from the cabin, the jars of water and piece of hard salami from Maria's house—and they ate for a time without speaking.

"Luca will find us now," she said, trying to convince herself. "He'll know what to do."

Her mother blinked and pressed her lips together.

"Don't lose hope, Mother."

Rebecca sat looking out over the tops of the trees, toward the mist-covered lake. A drop of rain slid down her cheek like a disoriented tear. "You'll raise the baby in Switzerland," she said.

"If I can, yes. Then we'll come back to Italy after the war."

"If there is an 'after the war.'"

"There will be. Luca says the Americans have landed on Sicily. The Germans will collapse in the sewage of their own hatred."

"I hope I live to see it."

Sarah waited a few minutes, gathering her strength, trying to decide on a plan. "I'm going to climb up a little farther and see if I can find the border. I think we're close. Stay here and wait for me. I'll get back as soon as I can."

Her mother was stubbornly shaking her head. "They'll find me here," she said. "They'll bring me down and torture me. I'll never see you again."

"Mother, don't."

More headshaking. "I want to go where you go. I've come this far."

"You can barely walk."

"I've come this far, Sarah. I can go a little farther."

"It's too dangerous, and we can't cut through the fence in any case without Luca."

"We could wait another day."

"We've eaten almost all our food, Mother. Let me go and see how close I can get, see what the fence looks like. We may have to dig under it tonight. I want to go up there while it's still light and scout out a place. If the rain has made the ground soft enough, we should be able to dig with our hands or branches. I'll leave you the pistol. Luca will find us. If the Germans come before he does, shoot them."

Her mother turned her head away, a gesture Sarah knew well—it meant that the plan was absurd, ridiculous; it was a way of expressing many things: anger, fear, frustration. She'd grown up with these wordless signals, her mother's way of trying to swallow her bitterness at the hand she'd been dealt. She had loved one good man, and her whole life had been a torment because of it. Sarah took the pistol out of her pocket and carefully handed it over. "You know how to use it?"

"I'm not a child, Sarah. It's simple, isn't it? The safety, the trigger. Anyone could do it. But I won't hesitate. I'll see them and I'll shoot."

"You won't need to shoot anyone, I'm sure." Sarah leaned over and held her mother for a long moment, then kissed her near the side of her cracked lips, crawled out of their resting place, and hurried away without looking back.

Ninety

Luca saw the first scrap of cloth almost immediately. It was raining again, but he climbed steadily on, his heart lifting each time he came upon another piece of wet cotton, a signal from the woman he loved. Up and up he went, rain dripping down inside the back of his collar, the soles of his boots slipping on wet stones and roots, a confusion bubbling inside him along with everything else. She was going to Switzerland, taking their baby and running toward a better life. It was a crazy scheme. She had no papers. There was a fence, two sets of guards to get past, and then what? Climbing down the Swiss side of the mountain, pregnant, in soaking wet clothes, hoping to find someone who would take her in? And then? Live somewhere until the war ended, give birth there, with no identification? And what was he supposed to do, abandon his battle against the people who'd killed his mother—and go with Sarah? And do what in Switzerland? Beg? He felt as though his insides were being shredded.

Ninety-One

Sarah tried to climb the steep hillside without making any sound. There was no path here, just slippery stones, stunted fir trees, and a stronger wind. The rain had quieted, at least. After every few steps, she stopped to listen, looking for landmarks that would guide her on the way back down, trying to make sure she didn't drift off to the right or left. She heard voices and flattened herself behind a stone. She heard footsteps fading. She waited another minute, then crawled around the side of the stone on her hands and knees and moved a few meters higher. There, in the distance, she thought she saw a pair of men walking, but it had been a quick glimpse, and she couldn't be sure. She angled away from them, crouching, climbing. The slope was flattening; she kept low to the ground and went along one step at a time. Suddenly she could see the top of a fence, such a surreal sight there in the middle of the dripping trees—barbed wire on top, chain-link below. The idea of crossing over suddenly took on a new level of reality. Save her child, her mother, and herself but abandon her lover?

She swung her eyes to either side. Ten meters to her right, she could see what seemed to her the perfect place to try to get through: there were two enormous boulders, pieces of the mountain, really, set less than five meters apart, the fence having been cut from the bottom so it sat tightly on top of them. Dirt between the stones. There were signs in three languages. STRICTLY FORBIDDEN. And fine print about *prosecution* and *imprisonment*. But if she and Luca could somehow manage to dig a hole beneath the fence, just at that point, with the large stone outcroppings to either side, hiding them . . . If they could find their way here unnoticed at twilight, start digging, and if the patrols were infrequent after darkness fell . . . then they might actually have a chance.

Just as she'd taken a last look and turned and started back down the mountain, crouching, stepping very carefully, she heard a single gunshot. It seemed to come from near the place where she'd left her mother. Suddenly she could barely breathe. She went along faster, slipping, grasping at the branches of small trees for balance, stopping every few steps to listen, wondering if she'd imagined the sound, if she was already losing her mind.

Ninety-Two

This stretch of hillside—no path now, no more scraps of cloth to guide him—was particularly steep, and Luca had to use his hands to help him get past the larger stones and outcroppings. He knew by the steepness and the stunted trees that he must be getting close to the summit of this range of hills, which would mean he was getting close to the border. From time to time, he stopped and raised his head, looking for the top of the fence and not seeing it.

He went forward again, stepped on a twig, and heard it snap. Atypically careless of him. He paused, came to a rock face, and, rather than walk all the way around it through thick wet foliage as Sarah must have done, he put one boot in a crack, found a handhold, and hoisted himself up. Another foothold. He pushed his weight down on his right foot and lifted himself above the top of the plateau and, at exactly the same moment, saw Sarah's mother sitting on an outcropping and heard the report of a pistol. The bullet nicked the top of his left ear with a horrible hissing sound. He ducked, heard a *click, click, click,* waited, lifted the top half of his face over the stone edge, and called as quietly as he could, "Rebecca! Stop! It's me!" He saw her drop the pistol, put a hand to her mouth, and burst into tears, and then he saw Sarah come out of the trees behind her.

Ninety-Three

After a rest of two days in Vienna and Munich, Mussolini and Skorzeny boarded a private aircraft, a Junker, and flew east toward the well-camouflaged FHQ, Hitler's headquarters. It was a bright day. They could see the landscape clearly, the gray tops of mountains at first, then brown and green foothills, and then the series of ponds dotting the East Prussian plain.

The two men engaged in a long conversation about Fascism and National Socialism, plans, war stories, life experiences. As they circled the runway and came in for a landing, Mussolini felt a mix of nervousness, excitement, and shame. It seemed to him that Skorzeny had looked upon him with a measure of pity, spoken to him with the tiniest note of falsehood in his voice, as if he were trying to prop up an old man who was still pretending to be young.

He worried about what Hitler might want from him now.

Once they landed and the doors opened, however, most of the shame and worry disappeared. From the top of the stairs, he saw that Hitler himself had come to greet him. They embraced on the tarmac, shook hands warmly, and stood that way for a long time, hands clasped. Hitler seemed moved to tears and was, at first, unable to speak. Finally, the Führer turned to Skorzeny, who was standing at attention off to one side, and said, "I will never forget what I owe you," and it was that remark more than anything, that confirmation of Hitler's esteem and love, that gave *il Duce* a warm thrill.

On this earth, he thought, on this vicious earth, what a fine gift it was to have a friend like Adolf Hitler.

Ninety-Four

The rain had started again. It took several minutes for Rebecca to stop crying. "I could have killed you! I could have killed you!" she kept muttering as Sarah held her with one hand and pressed a bit of cloth against Luca's bleeding ear with the other.

They told him about finding his mother and starting the fire, and he told them about Don Claudio killing the German officer and the two burials, and for a time after that, they sat watching rain drip from the edge of the overhang and said nothing. Still wrestling with Don Claudio's revelation, Luca couldn't keep himself from turning to Rebecca several times and imagining her with the priest. He couldn't say anything about that, of course, not at a time like this. If he had a moment alone with Sarah . . .

She moved so their bodies were touching from hip to shoulder. "Your ear has stopped bleeding."

He nodded without looking at her.

"I want the three of us to go to Switzerland," she said.

Luca stared straight ahead.

"Luca, look at me, please. I know you want to fight, but we can't stay here. If the Germans find us, and eventually they will, my mother and I are going to be sent to the work camps."

"I'm to blame," Rebecca put in.

"I'm not going to just push you across the border and leave you, Mother."

"You could. I can find my way. I've—"

"I'm not going to do that. You didn't abandon me all these years; I'm not abandoning you."

"I've arranged for papers for you," Luca said. "I can get them for you, too, Rebecca, but it will take time."

"We don't have time," Sarah said.

"It was you who said you wanted to fight with us."

"That was before this, before your mother was killed, before—"

Luca stared out into the wet trees. "There's something else," he said. "I've been thinking about it. There has to be something else. My mother wouldn't have just suddenly decided to poison a house full of German officers because one of them struck or insulted her."

He could feel Sarah go silent beside him. He turned and looked at her. Now *she* was staring straight ahead, not even blinking, the muscles of her beautiful face still, empty. "You know something," Luca said to her, and then she turned and looked, and there were tears in her eyes. Her lips were trembling. She made a very small nod.

"Tell me."

She waited, breathed, opened and closed her mouth, and then said, "I left the cabin and went down there. I wanted to see my mother so badly. I'm sorry. I know you didn't want me to, but I had to."

Luca watched her, reading her face.

"I got as far as the house, and I heard something in the kitchen. I went closer and stood beside the window and peeked in at the side of the curtain. I saw—" She stopped and looked away. "If I tell you what I saw, you'll never come with us, but I can't lie to you."

"Tell me, Sarah."

She swallowed, couldn't face him.

"Tell me."

She swallowed again, brushed at her eyes. "I saw a German soldier sitting in one of her kitchen chairs. He was leaning back with his eyes closed. Your mother . . ."

"Tell me."

"Your mother was on her knees . . . She . . . He . . ." She got that far and burst into tears. Rebecca let out a gasp and began to sob so loudly that Sarah had to reach out and put a hand over her mouth for a few seconds.

In a kind of trance, Luca moved his eyes from Sarah to Rebecca and back again.

One thought filled his mind: *No mercy.*

"Now you'll never come with us," Sarah said, squeezing his right forearm as hard as she could. "Now you never will."

Ninety-Five

The three of them climbed slowly in the rain, keeping as low as they could in the stunted trees and dripping bushes, stopping every few steps to listen. It was a bit flatter here but rugged terrain all the same, sharp outcroppings of rock, small ragged pine trees clinging to the stony soil, dozens of small caverns, ledges, low cliff faces. Sarah went along almost without seeing any of it, feeling her mother gasping for breath behind her, stopping when Luca stopped in front of her, giving one word of direction now and then to lead him back to the place she'd found. A heavy weight of dread lay across the backs of her wet shoulders, as if the strands of her hair were made of iron. She carried the sweaters in one hand and the pistol—empty of bullets now—in her dress pocket. She could feel it bump against her upper thigh every time she took a step.

After ten minutes, she could see the first of the two rocks that marked the ends of the protected stretch of fence. She tapped Luca between the shoulder blades, but he'd seen it, too, and he climbed on without turning or speaking. A few more steps and they were protected from view there. Still without saying anything, without turning to look at her, Luca took wire cutters out of his small pack and began to work, clipping away as quickly and quietly as he could. Her mother was holding on to her. Sarah watched Luca's right hand working, then lifted her eyes to the bright-yellow signs: VIETATO! VERBOTEN! INTERDIT! She was sure that somewhere on the other side, there would be Swiss guards, but the light was fading now, and perhaps she and her mother could cross over without being seen. They'd be given no better chance than this. Working methodically, Luca cut a neat doorway a meter high and half a meter wide, just three sides of it, top, right, bottom.

Then, at last, he turned to look at her.

"Please," she said. "Luca, please! I love you. Our child. Please!"

The stony face he'd worn since she told him about his mother finally broke open. She thought for a moment that he would cry, but he only reached out both arms, took hold of her shoulders, pulled her against his chest, and held her there. Sarah felt her mother let go, heard her weeping quietly beside her. Her own tears cascaded down both cheeks and onto Luca's soaked shoulder.

"I'll wait," he said very quietly into her left ear. "I'll never be with anyone else; I don't care how long the war lasts. I'll survive, and I'll wait. You wait, too."

She was nodding against his neck, great sobs filling her chest and leaking out against his skin.

"Go now. Don Claudio said there's a priest there who can help you. Father Alessandro in Bellinzona. The church is Santa Teresa. It's not far, he said. Don Claudio—your . . ." Luca squeezed her even more tightly against him. "Don Claudio said you'd be safe there. He said to be sure to give you both his love."

At those words, Rebecca turned away, toward the opening in the fence. She crouched, crawled through, and, with some difficulty, stood up again and looked right and left. Then Sarah. Once she'd made it to the other side, she pressed herself back against the fence, clinging to the chain-link with the fingers of both hands and pushing her face close. There was so much pain in Luca's one good eye that she could barely look at him. "I ask you one last time, Luca."

He shook his head. She watched him reach into his pocket and take something out, a small statue, porcelain, parts of it painted blue and parts red. A Christian saint, it looked like. He peeled away the felt at the bottom and banged the statue hard against his thigh. Coins fell out, hundred-lire gold coins, the king's face on one side and, on the other, a woman standing beside an old-fashioned plow. Eight, nine, ten of them. He bent and picked them out of the mud and handed them two by two through the opening.

Sarah took them and dropped them into the pocket of her dress, then pressed her lips against one of the diamond-shaped holes and kissed him that way, quickly.

"Go," he said. "Go now, Sarah. *Vai.*"

She held her eyes on him for another few seconds, as if to fix the memory of his face in her mind, then she turned, took hold of her mother's arm, and went downhill along a grassy slope toward a row of trees and a faint, misty glow of light below them in the distance.

Ninety-Six

Luca watched them until they were enveloped in gray mist, and then he stood there a while longer, staring at the point where they'd stepped into the trees, wondering if Sarah might reappear and wave a hand to him one last time. "Don Claudio is your father," he said quietly to no one. He pushed the statue—patron saint of hopeless cases—down into his pants pocket. Saint Jude in one, he thought, a pistol in the other. He tried to pray, got as far as saying, "Protect her. Protect them," then he turned and made his way with great care down the slope on the Italian side.

Ninety-Seven

It had rained hard for two straight days, and now a steady drizzle was falling on the cobblestones in front of Bar Lake Como. Don Claudio was wet and cold. Nineteen citizens of the town of Mezzegra were lined up on the sidewalk there beside him. They ranged in age from a girl of four, clasping a stuffed animal to her chest and weeping uncontrollably, to a woman in her late eighties—stooped, wearing a soaked wool sweater, and clinging to the arm of a middle-aged man who might have been her son. There were more women than men—the men of fighting age had been called away—all of them dripping rainwater, hair plastered against their faces. Orlando, the bar owner, was part of this group, chin held high, standing near the middle of the line.

A German motorcycle stood parked at each end of the ragged assembly. A short, plump Gestapo *standartenführer*, three green stripes on his sleeve, was stepping slowly back and forth in front of them in high leather boots and a dripping black-lidded gray hat.

"Più informazione?" he asked in bad Italian. *More information?*

For a moment, no one spoke—the only sound was the sobbing of the little girl—and then a young woman near the left end of the line called out, "We know nothing, Officer!" The German stepped over to her and, with a violent chopping motion of his right arm, struck her between the neck and shoulder and knocked her to the pavement like a felled tree. She lay there, half-conscious, bleeding from the mouth.

The little girl screamed, but no one reached down to comfort her or to help the fallen woman.

"Good, then," the officer went on. "*Molto bene.* Italian ignorance. Very good. Four of our best men, dead. And one missing. As I'm sure you know, we exact a payment of ten Italians for every German killed, so there should be more of you here. We're being generous today. And because there is the slightest chance, the very slightest chance that, as some of you claim, the fire could have been a strange accident, I am going to be even more generous. If one of you volunteers to go to the camps and work for us, for the cause, I'll issue a reprieve for the rest. Anyone?"

The seconds seemed to tick by like hours. Don Claudio watched. He'd been standing there so long that his back hurt. He was soaked to the skin, fear running up and down inside him like a herd of terrified animals. His cheeks were shaking, his mouth dry as paper. Any second, his bowels would go loose. The silence to either side of him seemed to be made of stone. He drew a breath, said, "Mary, help me," and took one trembling step forward.

The German looked him up and down and laughed. "You'll lose some of that fat, *Padre*," he said, and he gestured for one of his men to come and take the priest away. "To the camp," he said loudly. And then, after the officer had paced another few steps and Don Claudio was being turned and marched toward a waiting truck: "As for the others, shoot them."

The Nazi soldier was holding him by the back of the neck with one hand, pushing him forward, so Don Claudio couldn't turn around. When he heard the machine guns open fire and the screams, the priest cringed, nearly soiled his pants, but tried to twist his head and look back. The soldier kicked him hard behind the left knee, shoved him, headfirst, into the bed of a small pickup, and climbed in after him.

There was a sudden terrible silence in the square, broken only by a faint echo of gunshots rebounding across the lake. Don Claudio sat up and, holding on to the edge of the truck bed, forced himself to look back at the carnage. But it was too late. The truck was already moving. It bounced down an alley, a corner of the bar building blocking his view, then turned and sped away from the square. Caught in a trance, Don Claudio stared over the opposite side, past the German soldier. They were headed south—toward Como, he thought, and the train station there. He began to pray, very quietly, for the souls of the murdered ones.

One block south, not far from the place where he and Luca had left the rowboat on their fishing expedition and very close to the site of his glorious sin, he looked into the hills and thought he saw someone. A young man, standing half-hidden behind the trunk of a large oak tree, only his good arm visible, a rifle held along his body. For one second, the priest thought to raise his hand in greeting, or farewell, or to make a signal asking for help. But the guard was watching him.

"Ave Maria, piena di grazia," he said aloud, fixing his eyes defiantly on the German across from him. *Hail Mary, full of grace.*

Ninety-Eight

From his hiding place in the trees above the western side of the *statale*, Luca made his way, quickly and stealthily, to Masso's back door. He'd left the rifle against a tree at the edge of Masso's property, but in the right-side pocket of his light jacket, he carried the German pistol, loaded now; in his heart a fiery rage; and in his crazed thoughts one central question: Why hadn't Masso—one of the town's richest residents, a good friend of the priest—been arrested with the others and killed in front of Orlando's bar?

He hesitated a few seconds on the small wooden porch behind Masso's house, standing there beside the old farmer's muddy boots, with Culillo II braying in a small corral behind him. The rage at seeing his neighbors slaughtered, then seeing Sarah's father driven away with a Nazi guard, had brought him right to the brittle edge of sanity. Part of him wanted not even to give Masso a chance to speak but simply to step through the door, raise the pistol, fire one shot that would send the old man to hell, then retreat to the safety of the forest and embark on a murderous spree. *A hundred Germans for every Italian killed,* was the thought that gripped him. *A hundred Germans and a hundred Italian betrayers.*

But before he could open the door, he heard a sound behind him. He wheeled, already reaching for the pistol, and saw Masso himself there, bald head covered in a tattered cap, an apple in each hand. "Come inside," the farmer said, brushing past him and pushing the door open with one shoulder.

Luca waited a few seconds, then followed.

"Sit," Masso told him, setting the apples on a small table between two chairs, then going to the sink and pouring himself a glass of water. There was no comic act now, no pretend foolishness.

Masso was behind him, and Luca could feel the skin on the back of his neck, feel the handle of the pistol in the fingers of his right hand.

Masso came around the chair—touching the younger man once on his shoulder—and sat opposite. He placed the water glass on the table, removed his cap, and gestured at the fruit. "Hungry?"

Luca shook his head.

Masso met his eyes and spoke quietly. "I know why you're here," he said. "Listen to what I have to say, and then, if you still don't trust me, do what you've come to do. Most likely you'll be sparing me a much more hideous end."

Luca watched him and said nothing. He did not take his hand from the jacket pocket.

Masso bit into an apple, a large bite that sent juice flowing down one side of his mouth. He wiped a sleeve across his lips, chewed, swallowed, and said, "Just as the Germans were gathering people in the square, Orlando—another one of us—was able to call me from his bar." Masso looked at the apple as if he might take another bite, then set it aside. "He was able to make that call, and then he, too, was taken."

"Gone now," Luca said from between his teeth.

Masso nodded.

"All of them. Except for Don Claudio, who is gone in another way."

"I know."

"How? Your Nazi friends?"

Masso took a sip of water without moving his eyes from Luca's face. "I had someone watching from the upstairs room of one of the houses across the street. Someone hiding there. The telephones still work, at least. Some of the time."

"And you let it happen."

Masso blinked, waited. "I could hardly have stopped it, Luca. No one could have . . . I'm going to tell you several things now, and either you will believe me or you won't. Here, have the other apple."

Luca shook his head.

"First," Masso said, "I have learned from my contact in the government that Mussolini is most likely in Germany. After the king, Badoglio, and *il Duce*'s other former friends had him arrested, they took him away. I'm not sure exactly where at first. But he ended up at Campo Imperatore in the mountains. Somehow, God knows how, the Germans found out he was there. And somehow, God knows how again, they were able to free him and carry him off. To Hitler is my guess."

"Why?"

"Why? Because Hitler will want him back in power, here in Italy. In the north, probably, where the Germans still hold—"

"The Germans are everywhere. They're in Sicily. They're—"

Masso was shaking his head. "They've been chased out of Sicily already. And there was just now another landing in the south. At Salerno. Our soldiers have surrendered by the thousands—most of them don't want to fight. But the Germans are at their backs, forcing them. The real war has begun now, our war, and it will go on for a long time. Some Italian troops are loyal to the demon. If they think Mussolini has abandoned the country, they won't fight. Hitler knows as much. He'll force Mussolini to return, whether the *Duce* wants to or not. I'm sure of it."

Luca didn't remove his hand from the pocket. He had an urge to take out the pistol and point it at Masso, forcing the truth out of him, but it wouldn't do any good. The man was unafraid to die: that much, if nothing else, was true. "Go on," he said.

"When I heard Orlando's voice on the phone line—worried but not panicking—I thought the people would be taken to the camps, not shot. In order for them to be taken to the camps, they would have had to go in trucks, south along the *statale*, as far as the station in Como. The trains leave from there and head up on the other side of the mountains, through Lugano, eventually to Austria. It's the route along which they take the Jews. My people have seen the cattle cars. But they're taking Christian Italians now, too, to the work camps. They don't trust us to fight, so they're bringing us to their factories."

"How do you know all this?"

Masso watched him, both hands flat on his thighs now, almost in a posture of resignation. "I have contacts," he said. "I run a group of . . . fighters"—he waved an arm in a small circle above his head as if indicating his territory—"in this area." He looked away, looked back. "You among them."

"What else?"

"You know there are four tunnels along the *statale* between here and Como. I have men stationed near the end of the third tunnel. I called them as soon as Orlando called me, because I assumed our people would be taken by that route, not killed, as I said. By now my men have felled a large tree across the southern opening of the tunnel, as instructed. I chose that tunnel because they live close by, and because, just before the opening, as you're heading south, you come around a sharp turn—"

"I know the roads, Masso."

"You come around a sharp turn, and there's the opening right there, suddenly in front of you. A large tree will be across the road. The Germans won't have time to do anything but put on the brakes. My men will open fire, careful not to shoot Don Claudio, I hope. And then, if all goes well, they will take him into the hills."

"And if all doesn't go well?"

"How many Germans were in the jeep?"

"Three. The driver and the officer in front, one guard in back with Don Claudio."

"And I have eleven men there, with rifles. The only trouble will come if Don Claudio can't get out of the way fast enough. If he sees the blockade, the tree, and gets down immediately, he'll have a chance. The German soldiers will not."

"Why would I believe you?"

"Because late last night, I had a message from someone in contact with a certain priest in Switzerland. Sarah and her mother are safe. Exhausted, hungry, their skin and clothes torn by brambles but, as of yesterday morning, safe."

At the mention of Sarah, Luca released his grip on the pistol. "Who *are* you?" he said suddenly.

The tiniest of smiles caught the corners of Masso's lips, then instantly disappeared. He took another sip of water, blinked, ignored the question. "You told me once that you wanted bigger assignments. Is that still true?"

"Truer now than ever."

Masso picked up the half-eaten apple, raised it to his lips, then lowered it. "If *il Duce* is forced to come back, he will most likely come back here, to the north, because the Allies are in the south now, heavy fighting there, and that will be too great a risk. If he does come back to Italy, and if we can figure out where he is, we will, of course, want to assign someone to kill him."

As he watched the old farmer's face, Luca was picturing his mother lying in the dirt, covered with blood. He was remembering the promise he'd made to her, and he was remembering the sight of Sarah and Rebecca disappearing into the trees on the Swiss side of the border. He was thinking of his unborn child and of his father, too, and the people—including the little girl—who'd been slaughtered in front of Orlando's bar, the bodies of the partisans lying on the stones of Piazzale bombing raids became more and more frequent, damaging not only the German forces but cities that, for centuries, had survived war, earthquakes, and invasion.

Though many Jews were hidden by brave Italians, and a few escaped to other countries, once Mussolini was deposed, some seventy-five hundred were captured by the Nazi occupiers and sent to the death camps.

Eventually, in the spring of 1945, threatened by the relentless Allied advance, *il Duce* would flee the house on Lake Garda and try to escape to Switzerland, carrying millions in gold and cash, accompanied by Claretta Petacci, and embedded in a column of retreating German soldiers. He'd make it a hundred miles west, as far as the city of Como, and then halfway up Lake Como's western shore, before the column was stopped by a small band of partisans—tipped off, perhaps—who felled a tree across the shoreline road at the end of one of its many tunnels. The mountain fighters held Mussolini and Petacci for one night in a house in the hills above Mezzegra. On the next day, April 28, 1945, they brought their prisoners to a spot in front of the Villa Belmonte, where they were executed by a machine-gun-wielding partisan whose identity remains cloaked in the mists of history. Mussolini's last words were reported to have been, "Shoot me in the chest."

When the deed was done, the partisans loaded the bodies into a truck bed and brought them fifty miles south to Milan, where, in a symbolic gesture, they dumped them on the cobblestones of Piazzale Loreto. A mob of furious Milanese kicked, clubbed, shot, urinated on, and spat upon the corpses, then hung them by their ankles from a horizontal pole above a gas station.

There is a monument in that square now, *monumento ai martiri di Piazzale Loreto.* It bears the names of the fifteen murdered partisans whose bodies had been displayed there eight months before Mussolini was killed, but makes no mention at all of *il Duce.*

Begun: July 8, 2014, Campo Imperatore, Province of L'Aquila, Italy
Finished: April 14, 2019, Conway, Massachusetts, USA

ACKNOWLEDGMENTS

First thanks, as always, to Amanda for her love, unflagging optimism, and travel expertise. My gratitude also to our daughters, Alexandra and Juliana, who inspire me every hour with their grace, courage, loveliness, and excellent sense of adventure.

Special thanks to Robert Braile for his brilliant editing of an early draft of this novel, as well as for his friendship and encouragement.

My gratitude to Emma Sweeney and Margaret Sutherland Brown for their invaluable help in reading, editing, and placing this novel in good hands. To Peter Grudin, who read an early draft and who has been a friend and supporter of my writing for thirty-five years. To Simone Gugliotta for Italian language guidance (any mistakes are my own). And to Harold Lubberdinck for finding us the perfect place to live at Lake Como in the summer of 2007.

I'm indebted to Chris Werner and David Downing, both of whom went the extra mile in polishing and shepherding this story. My thanks also to the excellent copyeditor Stacy Abrams, and to Nicole Pomeroy and her fine production management team.

Writing is easy work compared to some of the things I've done in my life and many of the things others do to earn a living. But it is, for the most part, a solitary business, speckled with uncertainty, rejection, and disappointment. I am forever grateful to the many friends who have offered, over forty years, a word of encouragement or support in various forms. If I tried to mention all of you here, I'd surely forget someone and feel horrible for all my days. But your generosity is written on my heart. Thank you.

ABOUT THE AUTHOR

Photo © 2019 Amanda S. Merullo

Roland Merullo was born in Boston and raised in Revere, Massachusetts. He attended Brown University, where he obtained a bachelor of arts in Russian studies and a master of arts in Russian language and literature. The author of more than twenty works of fiction and nonfiction, including *Breakfast with Buddha* and *The Delight of Being Ordinary*, Roland is the recipient of the Massachusetts Book Award, an Editors' Choice Award from *Booklist*, an Alex Award from the American Library Association, a Best of the Year award from *Publishers Weekly*, and he was nominated for the International Dublin Literary Award. A former Peace Corps volunteer, he's also made his living as a carpenter, college professor, and cab driver. Roland, his wife, and their two lovely daughters live in the hills of western Massachusetts. For more information, visit www.rolandmerullo.com.